INTRIGUE

Seek thrills. Solve crimes. Justice served.

K-9 Sheild
Nichole Severn

The Red River Slayer
Katie Mettner

MILLS & BOON

K-9 SHIELD
© 2024 by Natascha Jaffa
Philippine Copyright 2024
Australian Copyright 2024
New Zealand Copyright 2024

First Published 2024
First Australian Paperback Edition 2024
ISBN 978 1 867 90554 3

THE RED RIVER SLAYER
© 2024 by Katie Mettner
Philippine Copyright 2024
Australian Copyright 2024
New Zealand Copyright 2024

First Published 2024
First Australian Paperback Edition 2024
ISBN 978 1 867 90554 3

MIX
Paper | Supporting
responsible forestry
FSC® C001695

Published by
Harlequin Mills & Boon
An imprint of Harlequin Enterprises (Australia) Pty Limited
(ABN 47 001 180 918), a subsidiary of HarperCollins
Publishers Australia Pty Limited
(ABN 36 009 913 517)
Level 19, 201 Elizabeth Street
SYDNEY NSW 2000 AUSTRALIA

Cover art used by arrangement with Harlequin Books S.A.. All rights reserved.

Printed and bound in Australia by McPherson's Printing Group

K-9 Sheild

Nichole Severn

MILLS & BOON

Nichole Severn writes explosive romantic suspense with strong heroines, heroes who dare challenge them and a hell of a lot of guns. She resides with her very supportive and patient husband, as well as her demon spawn, in Utah. When she's not writing, she's constantly injuring herself running, rock climbing, practicing yoga and snowboarding. She loves hearing from readers through her website, www.nicholesevern.com, and on Facebook at nicholesevern.

DEDICATION

To the men and women fighting for our freedom.

CAST OF CHARACTERS

Jones Driscoll—He just ended up in the middle of a war zone. Protecting a secretive journalist who fights him every step of the way pushes the combat controller to the limits, and danger is heating up—as is their mutual attraction.

Maggie Caddel—Being on the front line of the war on drugs isn't everything this war correspondent imagined. Abducted by the cartel, she's interrogated about her sources until a far-too-handsome stranger helps her escape. But soon she realizes the cartel will do whatever it takes to ensure she takes their secrets to the grave.

Socorro Security—The Pentagon's war on drugs has pulled the private military contractors of Socorro Security into the fray to dismantle the *Sangre por Sangre* cartel...forcing its operatives to risk their lives and their hearts in the process.

Sosimo Toledano—The prodigal son and heir to *Sangre por Sangre* won't stop until every last threat to the cartel is neutralized, including a war correspondent who could cost him everything he's worked for.

Scarlett Beam—The security consultant only wants one thing: for her skill set to do good in the world. She's signed on with Socorro for that exact mission, but this fight is far larger than she ever expected.

Chapter One

People were—or they became—what they pretended to be.

And Maggie Caddel had been pretending for a very long time.

Plastic cut into the sensitive skin of her wrists. She wasn't sure how long she'd been here. Getting dripped on from a leaky pipe overhead, told when she could eat, when she could stand, when to speak. Her tongue felt too big for her mouth now. Thirst did that. She'd pulled against the zip ties too many times to count. It was no use. Even if she managed to break through, there was nowhere to go. Nowhere she could run they wouldn't find her.

A thick steel door kept the animals out but kept her in. Maggie shifted away from the cinder block wall. She'd somehow managed to fall asleep, even with the echoes of shouted orders and footsteps outside her door. Another drip from above ripped her out of sleep. It splattered against the side of her face and tendrilled down her neck.

This place… It held an Aladdin's cave of secrets she'd worked the past year to uncover. But not like this.

Not at the expense of ten American soldiers dead. And not at the expense of her life. The war waging between the federal government and the New Mexico cartel *Sangre por Sangre* had already cost so much.

A metallic ping of keys twisted in the lock. Rusted hinges protested as the door swung inward. El Capitan framed himself in the doorframe. His eyes seemed to sink deeper in their sockets every time they went through their little routine. Darker than should be possible for a human. If that was what he was. Judging by his willingness to interrogate, torture and starve a random war correspondent, Maggie wasn't sure there was any humanity left.

She set her forehead back against the wall. It was starting again. The questions. The pain. She wasn't sure her legs would even carry her out of this room. "I'm guessing you didn't bring me the ice cream sandwich I asked for."

It'd been the only thing she could think of that she wanted more than anything else in the world. Other than being released.

El Capitan—she didn't know his real name—closed in. Strong hands pulled her to her feet and tucked her into his side. The toes of her boots dragged behind her, and it took another cartel soldier's aid to get her into the corridor.

The walls blurred in her peripheral vision. She'd spent the first few days memorizing everything she could. The rights and lefts they took to the interrogation room. The stains on the soldiers' boots, the rings they wore, the tattoos climbing up their necks. El Capitan, for instance, wore the same cologne day-to-day. It'd been overly spicy and would ward off demons in a pinch, but the ski mask usually hiding his face had taken some of the bite out. Given the chance, all she would've had to do was smell him to make a positive ID.

But he wasn't wearing the mask anymore.

Which meant he wasn't worried about her identifying him anymore.

Because they were going to kill her.

Both gunmen thrust her down into the chair she'd bled in for the past...she couldn't remember how many days had gone by. Three days? A week? They'd all started to stitch together without any windows in her cell to judge day or night. Like she'd been kept in a basement. But this room had a small crack in the ceiling. Enough for her to know they'd dragged her here in the middle of the night.

Maggie let the sharp back of the chair press into the knots in her shoulder blades. The wood felt as though it was swelling as it absorbed her sweat, her tears— her blood. Could crime labs pull DNA from wood? She hoped so. It would probably be all that was left of her given what she'd witnessed.

"I'm losing my patience with you." El Capitan rubbed one fist into the opposite palm. Like warming up his knuckles would make any difference against her face. "Where are the photos you took? Who did you give them to?"

Same old game. Same old results. That first day had been the hardest, when she had no choice but to be mentally present every second, to experience every ounce of pain inflicted. But now... Now she'd learned how to step out of her body. To watch from above while the Maggie below suffered at the hands of a bloodthirsty cartel lieutenant trying to clean up the mess he made. "What photos?"

The strike twisted her head over one shoulder. Lightning burst behind her eyelids. The throbbing started in her jaw and exploded up into her temple. And that was all it took. To detach. Disassociate. She wasn't in the chair anymore. Some other woman was. A part of her that was strong enough to get through whatever came next. She could stand there and observe without ever feeling that man's hands on her again.

"We've been through your home. We've been through your car. Next, we'll question everyone you care about." El Capitan was in a mood today. More hostile than usual. Desperate.

Maggie couldn't help but like that idea. That he was feeling the pressure of getting results out of her. That she'd held him off this long. The Maggie in the chair was having a hard time keeping her head up. She dropped her chin to her chest. "If you get ahold of my sister, tell her I want my green sweater back."

"You have no idea who you're dealing with, do you, little girl?" The cartel lieutenant stuck his face close to hers. Even separated from her body, she could smell the cigarettes on his breath. "What we can do to you, to your family, your life. All you have to do is give me the photos you took that night and this ends. You'll be able to go home."

Home? She didn't have a home. Didn't he realize that? All she'd done over the past two years was disappoint her friends, her family, her coworkers. Investigating *Sangre por Sangre*'s growing influence throughout the Southwest was all she had left. And she wasn't going to let them get away with what they'd done. No matter the cost.

Except no one knew she was here.

No one cared. Certainly not her ex-husband.

Not even her editor would know where to start.

No one was coming to save her.

And the photos she'd taken of that tragic night—when the cartel had slaughtered ten American soldiers and disposed of the bodies in an ambush meant to capture the cartel founder's son—would rot where she'd hidden them. Maggie licked her broken lips, not really feeling the sting anymore. Her head fell back, exposing her throat, as she tried to meet El Capitan's eyes. Sweat prickled at the back of her neck. "It's hot. Can I have that ice cream sandwich, please?"

The lieutenant fisted a handful of her hair, trying to force her to look at him, but Maggie wasn't in that body. All he was looking at was a shell. A beaten and bloodied ghost of the woman she used to be. "Take her out in the middle of the desert and leave her for the coyotes to chew on. She's worthless."

He shoved her body backward.

Gravity pitted in her stomach a split second before the Maggie in the chair hit the floor. The back of her head hit the cement, and suddenly she didn't have the strength to stay detached from that shell she'd created.

In an instant, she was right back in her body. Feeling
the pain crunch through her skull, realizing the warmth
spreading through her hair was blood. Her vision wavered as she tried to reach for that numbness that had
gotten her through the past few days, but it wasn't there
anymore. Shallow breathing filled her ears. "No. No.
Don't do this. You can't do this."

"Clean that up. I want this entire room and her cell
scrubbed down." El Capitan threw orders with a wave
of his hand as he headed for the corridor. "Make it so
no one will know she was ever here."

Two sets of hands dragged her upright. Every muscle in her body tensed in defense, but she'd lost her
will to fight back days ago. It wasn't supposed to be
like this. She was going to make something of herself.
This story…this was supposed to change everything.

Maggie tried to dig her heels into the cement, but
her added weight crumbled pieces of the floor away.
Her arms hurt. This was it. Everything she'd done to
rewrite her life had been for nothing. Tears burned in
her swollen eyes. "Please."

The men at her sides didn't respond, didn't lighten
their grip. Didn't alter their course. They pulled her
through a door she hadn't known existed in the shadows until right then. One leading directly outside.

She'd been so close to escaping without ever even
knowing.

A thud registered from behind her. Then another.
She tried to angle her head around, but it was pointless. Pointless to hope El Capitan had charged back into
the room with a change of mind. She was going to die.

A groan rumbled through her side a split second before the gunman at her left dropped to his knees. He fell forward. Unmoving. She didn't understand. The second soldier marching her to her death released his hold, and she hit the floor. Another groan infiltrated through the concentrated thud of her heart behind her ears.

Then…nothing.

For a moment, Maggie wondered if the head wound had caused damage to her hearing or her brain had short-circuited. Then she heard him.

"Don't try to move. You're badly injured, but I'm going to get you out of here." Something wet and rough licked along one of her ears. "Gotham, knock it off. Don't you think she's been through enough?"

A small whine—like a dog—replaced the sensory input at her ear. A dark outline shifted in front of her. Masked. Like El Capitan, but that wasn't… That wasn't his voice.

Maggie cataloged what she could see of his eyes through the cutouts in the fabric. She'd never met this one before. She would've remembered. Her vision wavered as a set of muscled arms threaded beneath her knees and at her lower back. He hauled her into his chest, and there wasn't a single thing she could do to stop him as darkness closed in. "You're not one of them."

SHE'D LOST CONSCIOUSNESS.

Jones Driscoll brought her against his chest, back against the wall, as he scouted for an ambush. *Sangre por Sangre*'s half-destroyed headquarters were settled at the bottom of a damn fishbowl in the middle of the freaking desert. Any number of opportunities for the cartel to take advantage. He'd managed to knock out a couple of the cartel lieutenant's direct reports back in the interrogation room, but the man of the hour had managed to escape down one of the corridors. Ivy Bardot—Socorro's founder—would give him hell for that. Months of research, of tracking Sosimo Toledano's movements, of trying to build a case for the federal government to make a move. And Jones had blown it the second he'd laid eyes on her.

He moved as fast as he dared straight out into the open. Cracked New Mexico earth threatened his balance as he headed for the incline that would take him back to his SUV. His legs burned with the woman's added weight, but Gotham wasn't helping either. The husky kept cuing his owner with every hint of human remains buried in this evil place.

Low voices echoed through the disintegrating parking garage. The structure was on the brink of collapse, yet satellite imagery and recon reported an uptick in activity over the past three days. Most recently utilized as a hideout for Sosimo Toledano, identified as *Sangre por Sangre*'s prodigal son. Heir to the entire organization, if and when the feds managed to capture the big dog. Seemed Sonny Boy was trying to make a name of his own. Ever since Ponderosa's chief of police had come back from the dead for revenge against the cartel, there'd been an increase in attacks on the small towns fighting to stay out of cartel business. Homes ransacked, residents running from public parks as gunfire broke out, businesses broken into and burned to the ground—all of it leading back to a single shot caller: Sosimo Toledano. Local police couldn't keep up with the onslaught and turned to Socorro.

But what was it about this place *Sangre por Sangre* couldn't seem to let go of? An explosion had weakened the supports months ago, the foundation was failing, water was penetrating the walls and eroding the floors. Yet the cartel lieutenant had abducted, questioned and tortured the woman in his arms. Caddel. He'd called her Ms. Caddel. No first name.

Jones backed them into the shadows at the sight of two gunmen taking a cigarette break under the overhang of the underground parking garage, staying invisible. That was his job. To get in and out of enemy territory without raising the alarm. To discern the cartel's next move and calculate their strategy before they had a chance to strike. He'd lived and thrived in combat zones for half his life, but this… He studied the outline of the woman's face highlighted by a single flare of a lighter a few feet away. This felt different. What the hell could *Sangre por Sangre* want with one woman?

Laughter ricocheted through the hollow cement darkness. One move. That was all it would take, and the soldiers would be on him. Wasn't normally a problem. He lived for the fight, to be on the front lines of defense. Just him and his opponent. Protecting a woman who'd been beaten to within an inch of her life was a whole other story. It would be hard to engage while worrying about whether or not she was still breathing.

Gotham pawed at Jones's cargo pants. A low groan signaled he'd found the scent of human remains close by.

"Shh." Pressing into Gotham's paw with one leg, Jones hoped to quiet the husky's need for attention. They were probably standing on an entire cemetery, given Toledano's recent crimes against humanity. But there wasn't anything he could do about it right now.

"You hear that?" One of the gunmen faced toward Jones's position. Though his lack of response said he hadn't spotted them yet. Too dark.

Gotham jogged to meet the nearest gunman. A low warning vibrated through Jones's throat, but the husky didn't pay him any mind. Jones adjusted his hold on the unconscious woman against his chest in case he had to make a jump for his dog.

The nearest gunman swung his rifle free from his shoulder, taking a step forward as Gotham waltzed right up to him, and a tension unlike anything Jones had experienced laced every muscle in his body. A smile broke out across both soldiers' faces, and the second took a knee, hand extended. "Where'd you come from?"

Hot damn. Gotham had provided a distraction, giving Jones the chance to get out without raising suspicions. Jones sidestepped his position, keeping to the wall as the gunmen searched for something to give the dog.

Joke was on them. Gotham only ate a certain brand of dog food and jerked pig ears.

He tightened his hold around Ms. Caddel as one of the spotlights swept across her face. Matted blond hair streaked with dirt and something like liquid rust caught in his watch. Not rust. Blood. His gut clenched as he got his first real good look at her swollen eyes, the cuts along her mouth, the bruising darkening the contours of her face. This woman had been through hell. But he was going to get her out.

Jones hiked the incline he'd descended to get into the structure. Sand dissolved beneath his weight, but he put everything he had into keeping upright with an added hundred and thirty pounds. Just a little farther. He could almost see his SUV on the other side of the barbed fence in the distance. He cleared the incline and stepped onto flat ground.

A yip pierced his senses.

The sound fried his nerves as he recognized Gotham's cry for help.

He turned back. The husky was hanging upside down by one foot in the soldier's extended hand, arcing up to bite at the man's wrist. Another series of laughs drew out a full bark from his dog. Setting Ms. Caddel down as gently as possible on flat ground, he tried to breathe through the rage mixing into his blood. He might not like being weighed down by a K9 sidekick who'd rather chase his own tail than pay attention to anything Jones had to say, but no one touched his partner.

He descended the incline, not bothering to keep to the shadows this time around. Two armed gunmen didn't stand a chance against a combat controller employed by the most-resourced security company in the world.

Surprise etched onto one gunman's face as he locked on Jones's approach. The guy unholstered a pistol at his hip and took aim.

Jones dodged the barrel of the weapon, sliding up the soldier's arm. He rocketed his fist into the gunman's throat. A bullet exploded mere inches from his ear and triggered a ringing through his skull. Grabbing onto the cartel member's neck, Jones hauled the attacker to the ground. They fell as one. He pinned the gunman's hand back by the thumb until a scream filled the night. The gun fell into Jones's hand as the second soldier lunged.

The second bullet found home just beneath the bastard's Kevlar, and the soldier dropped Gotham as his knees met the earth. The K9's yip and quick scramble to his feet let Jones know he hadn't been hurt.

Jones pressed one boot into the gunman's chest and rolled him onto his back.

"What did your boss want with her? The woman you were supposed to execute." He hiked the soldier's thumb back to increase the pressure on the tendon running up into the wrist and forearm. Once that tore, there'd be no squeezing saline solution into a contacts case or a trigger for the rest of his life. "Why take her?"

The resulting scream drowned out the ringing in his ears.

"She was there!" The cartel member shoved into his heels, trying to break away from Jones's hold, but there was no point. The harder he tried to escape, the more damage was done.

"Where?" he asked.

"I know who you are." A wheeze slid through crooked, poorly maintained stained teeth. That was the thing about cartels. Every member worked for the good of the whole, but that relationship didn't go both ways. No dental coverage. No health coverage. Just a binding promise to die for the greater good. "I know who you work for."

"Then you know I won't stop until every last one of you are behind bars." Clutching the gun's grip harder, Jones pounded his fist into the soldier's face. Bone met dirt in a loud snap that knocked the son of a bitch unconscious.

Gotham raced to Jones's feet as he shoved to stand, coming up onto his hind legs.

"This is why you're not supposed to leave my side. How many times do we have to talk about this? There are mean people in the world. Guys like that don't care how nice you are." Jones wiped down the handle of the pistol with the hem of his T-shirt and dropped the weapon onto the gunman's chest. Scratching behind the husky's ears, he headed for the incline to get the hell out of there. "Though I've gotta say, your distraction was on point."

Jones pressed his palm into his ringing ear. It wasn't so much the noise that bothered him. It was the percussion. He'd bounced back before when a gun had gone off next to his head. This time shouldn't be any different, but he'd check in with Dr. Piel when he got back to headquarters.

He hiked the incline to the spot he'd left the woman he'd pulled from the interrogation room. Only she wasn't there. Jones scanned the terrain, coming up empty. She couldn't have just walked out of there on her own. He'd known men overseas who wouldn't have been able to string together a sentence with the injuries she'd sustained. "I wasn't gone that long, right?"

Gotham yipped as though to answer.

A pair of headlights burst into life a hundred yards past the barbed fence. From his SUV. The beams cut across him a split second before they redirected around. Jones shaded his eyes with one hand and pulled his cell from his cargo pants pocket with the other. Seemed Ms. Caddel hadn't been unconscious, after all. Clever. Then again, it made sense. A woman in her position couldn't be sure of anything after going through what she had. Trusting the man who'd pulled her out of that torture chamber most assuredly didn't come easy.

Jones called into headquarters and lifted the phone to his good ear as the first ring trilled. Then started jogging to catch up with the SUV. "That's what I get for leaving the keys in the ignition."

Chapter Two

She wasn't even sure if she was headed in the right direction.

It was hard to see through the swelling in her right eye, and even then, driving at night had always been dicey. Maggie tightened her aching hands on the steering wheel. The split over her middle knuckle protested with the change in grip, but it felt as though the SUV would rock backward from the uneven landscape at this speed.

Maggie checked the rearview mirror. Dirt kicked up in the back window. She couldn't see anything. That didn't matter. She'd escaped. She'd survived against the odds. She didn't know how. Licking at dry lips, she directed her attention out the windshield. Served the cartel right for keeping the keys in the vehicle. She only hoped there wasn't some kind of locater device they could use to track her down. Because this wasn't over. El Capitan wouldn't stop until she took his secret to her grave.

"You can ditch the car when you get back to the city." Verbally guiding herself through overwhelming to-do lists had always helped. Though some pep talks didn't work as well as others, so she had to act logically. "Okay. A plan. You need a plan. You can't go back to the apartment. Can't use your cards or phone. Don't make this easy for them."

She had to get a hold of Bodhi. Her editor at *American Military News* would know what to do, who to contact. How to get the story out. She could tell him where she'd hidden the photos of the ambush. Once they went public, the cartel wouldn't have any reason to keep coming after her. They'd be trying to cover their own asses. "It's a start."

If the cartel had left the keys in the ignition, maybe they'd left a phone, too. She kept her attention on the minimal spread of landscape ahead and searched for the latch on the middle console. The lid popped back on its hinges, but from what she could feel with one hand, there was nothing but a pistol and a plastic baggie of something that smelled like death.

The gun would at least come in handy, though she'd never handled one in her life.

Maggie blinked through the burn of tears. Endless days of torture should've left her dehydrated, but it seemed she still had a bit left to give. Flashes of pain, of not being able to breathe, of the feeling her stomach was eating itself echoed through her. Swiping at her face, she straightened as dim lighting peppered through the lower corner of the windshield.

What was that? A town? For as much as fourth grade geography taught her about her home state, she didn't have a clue as to what was out here in the middle of the desert. "Pull it together, Caddel. You're not out of the woods yet."

Heading straight for the nearest town was a rookie

move. But the promise of food, water, a change of clothes and maybe a shower gutted her from the inside. Hotels would be the first place El Capitan and his merry band of assholes would look when they realized she wasn't dead.

Why wasn't she dead?

She let the question dissipate as she angled the SUV toward the lights. A road would appear sooner or later. Right? The town—she didn't know its name—seemed to sit between two large walls of cliffs. Protected from outsiders. Given the amount of lights, there couldn't be more than a few hundred residents. There was a chance one of them would take pity on her. "In and out. Get what you need and push through."

The interior of the SUV went dark.

Maggie pried her clammy grip from the steering wheel, pushing herself back into the driver's seat as the engine cut out. She was slowing down. The accelerator wasn't responding. "What? No. No, no, no. Don't do this to me. Please don't do this to me."

The SUV rolled to a stop then inched backward. She shoved her foot onto the brake. The headlights flickered before dying completely. Surrounded by darkness, she couldn't see anything other than the few lights of the town ahead. At least a mile away.

Maggie twisted the key in the ignition, but there was only a rhythmic click. She didn't understand. There'd been at least a half tank of gas according to the meter on the dashboard. Panic launched up her throat, hot as acid and just as suffocating. She couldn't stay here. She had to keep moving. Had to stay a step ahead of the cartel.

Fumbling for the door handle, she tried to shoulder out of the vehicle. But the lock wouldn't disengage. She pulled at the latch, immediately thwarted as the vehicle locked her back in.

Understanding hit. She hadn't run out of gas. The car had been killed remotely. Maggie climbed free from the driver's seat, launching herself to the passenger side. The door wouldn't open. She climbed over the console and into the second row of seats, but neither of the doors nor the cargo hatch would release. Slamming her hand against the glass, she felt as though the walls were closing in. "Let me out!"

She was trapped. A sitting duck. Waiting for the slaughter. El Capitan must've learned she'd escaped. Must've figured out she'd taken one of his vehicles and killed the engine before she had a chance to disappear. Desperate men did desperate things. "Okay. You can do this."

Maggie forced herself to take a deep breath. Pressing her palm into the warm glass, she closed her eyes. The door locks might serve whatever master command had been installed to keep her here, but the windows wouldn't. Interior carpeting caught on the healing skin of one knee as she felt for something—anything—she could use to break through the glass.

"There's nothing here." This didn't make sense. Not even a tire iron or emergency kit? Every car she'd ever bought had come with a spare and a jack. *Sangre por Sangre* was one of the most dangerous drug cartels in the entire country. They smuggled thousands of kilos of drugs across borders and avoided police detection.

It was their job to figure out every nook and cranny in a vehicle and use it to its best potential. Hiding spaces. There had to be… Her fingers fit into a crack between the vehicle's frame and the seemingly solid floor. There.

Climbing back into the second row of seats, she pulled up the cargo cover she'd knelt on. "Holy hell." An entire arsenal of weapons gleamed in the muted moonlight cutting through the back window. "That should work."

Maggie grabbed what looked like a shotgun and let the cargo cover fall back into place. Okay. It was already loaded. All she had to do was point it at the window and pull the trigger, right? Simple enough. She braced the butt of the gun against her shoulder and slipped her finger over the trigger.

A knock punctured the silence. "I believe you have something of mine."

Her finger squeezed the trigger, and the gun hit back into her shoulder. The pain knocked the air from her lungs, and Maggie collapsed onto the center console between the front seats. Something burnt and acidic charged deep into her lungs as it filled the SUV's interior. She tried to cough it up, but the fumes were too heavy. Her heart threatened to beat out of her chest as she gulped for oxygen. She cleared her head enough to see that the shotgun hadn't broken through the glass.

"Yeah. You should know that's reinforced bulletproof glass. It's going to take a lot more to get through it than a single shot." Movement registered from the driver's side of the vehicle. "I'm going to unlock the doors, all right? I'd appreciate it if you didn't shoot me."

"Come any closer and I will." That voice. She'd

heard it before. Maggie scrambled to match it with the catalog she'd made over the course of the past few days in hell, but it wasn't fitting. Her nervous system had reached its all-time panic mode. She couldn't go back. She couldn't take another round of interrogation. She had to get out of here. By any means necessary. Sweat beaded in her hairline and made her bloody, tattered clothes feel too tight. "Just stay back. Let me think."

There was nowhere for her to go. The SUV wouldn't start. The doors wouldn't let her out. She couldn't even count on the guns to get her out of this mess.

"Your name is Caddel, right? Maggie Caddel?" He seemed to be keeping his distance, though Maggie couldn't pinpoint his location with all the chaos fluttering through her head. No accent. Not like the others. American born. "You're a war correspondent for *American Military News*. You've been reporting on the *Sangre por Sangre* cartel for the past year."

"Knowing my name doesn't give you the right to execute me." She set aside the shotgun and righted herself. The second he unlocked the doors from his side, she would bolt out the other door. She might not be able to outrun him, but at least then she'd have a chance of dying on her own terms.

"Does this look like a face that wants to execute you?" The man's outline thickened through the window a split second before something else took its place.

Maggie stared at the face of a dog through the tinted window. A husky from the look of him. Full grown. His white hair stood out in the growing moonlight. He wriggled to get free of the strong hands holding him midair, nipping at exposed skin. That song, the one kids sang about buying a doggy in the window, came to mind. Okay. She was losing her mind. "Is that a dog?"

Her brain was playing tricks on her. That was the only explanation for a husky to be out here in the middle of the desert.

"His name's Gotham. You might not remember, but we're the ones who pulled you out of that interrogation room back at the cartel's headquarters." His voice wormed into the deepest recesses of her mind. *I'm going to get you out of here.* Not one of her captors. "You know, before you stole my vehicle and left me for dead."

Her skin felt too tight, her bones too big for her body. Maggie didn't know what to do, what to think. This was all…impossible.

"If you promise not to shoot me when I unlock the doors, I'll let you pet him. He's soft. I just gave him a bath this morning," he said.

What other choice did she have? She wasn't getting out of here without his help, and there was no way she could outrun anyone at this point. She couldn't deny the idea of petting a dog after what she'd been through wasn't everything she needed right then either. Exhaustion embedded deep into the fibers of her muscles, and her hand fell away from the shotgun. "Fine. If you unlock the doors, I promise not to shoot you."

JONES LET GOTHAM down and raised his cell back to his ear. He didn't know what waited on the other side of that fractured glass, but one thing was for certain: he wasn't going to let the cartel catch up to the woman he'd extracted. "Go ahead and unlock the doors, Scarlett."

The SUV's doors released with the touch of a button from Socorro's security consultant. Just as she'd killed the vehicle's engine. Scarlett Beam was a new addition to the team, but one that came in handy more often than not. "Need backup?"

"No." Undeserved confidence slid through him. "I've got it from here. Thanks."

Ending the call, he pocketed his phone, then reached for the back seat door on the driver's side.

The door flew open without him touching the handle, and Maggie Caddel lunged free. It took a lot of visible effort for her to stay on her feet, but Jones gave her room as her nervous system adapted. Her shoulders and chest worked to get as much oxygen as possible. Hell, she was in a bad state. It was a wonder she still had any life in her after what'd happened. She flicked her tongue over busted lips. "You said I could pet your dog."

"He likes it when you put your face next to his." He motioned to Gotham without invading her personal space. Suffering through what she had, she didn't need him imposing himself on her. She needed to feel safe.

Crouching, Maggie scratched bruised and cut fingers into the K9's fluffy coat as Jones had done hundreds of times in the short weeks they'd been together. Then she set her face against Gotham's. The husky pressed his face into hers, and they closed their eyes as one, enjoying the feel of one another. The sight was almost enough to ease Jones's defenses. How would he have convinced her to leave the SUV if he hadn't been dragging a husky through the desert?

"You're with Socorro, aren't you? That military contractor the Pentagon sent to dismantle *Sangre por Sangre*. I've read about you and your team. You're the combat controller from the air force. Driscoll, right?"

"At your service." Jones hiked his thumbs into his cargo pants pockets. The way she said his name... It wasn't anything special. She'd read it on a roster that belonged to his employer, but there'd been a bit of a catch on the last syllable that stuck with him. He dared a step closer as Maggie shifted—unbalanced—on her feet. She was running on fumes, and adrenaline could only take a person so far. Knowing the cartel, she'd been deprived of food, water, probably sleep. Any one of those came with disastrous effects, but all of them together? She was on the verge of collapse. "But considering you stole my vehicle, I think we're past the point of formalities. You can call me Jones."

"I didn't know it was yours." Maggie pried Gotham from her face, seemingly coming to terms with the events of the night. Her eyes, even in the dim light of the moon, were losing focus. "They were going to kill me. I just... I needed to get out of there."

"You don't ever have to apologize to me for trying to survive." Jones took that last step, grabbing for Maggie as her legs gave out. "It's okay. I've got you."

"I'm tired." She was slurring her words. Not a good sign.

"I know. We'll get you fixed up." Jones whistled for Gotham to follow as he worked to get Maggie into the vehicle. Hauling her into his side, he guided her across the back seat of the SUV. The shotgun she'd tried using to blast her way out through the back window lay across the floor. He had to hand it to her. She was mighty resourceful. Though, in her line of work, he imagined she had to be to stay out of trouble. Guess that resourcefulness hadn't been enough this time around. He let Gotham cuddle into Maggie's side. "Keep her company, would you?"

Because there was a chance she'd wake up panicked, not knowing where she was. Who she was. He'd seen it once before. The terror that came with imprisonment and torture. It wasn't anything he wished on his worst enemy. Jones slid behind the wheel and started the SUV. The engine growled to life. The headlights cut across the uneven landscape as he maneuvered toward home base.

Jones set Maggie in his sights through the rearview mirror. Hell. He should've gotten into the cartel headquarters sooner. He should've realized the reason Sosimo Toledano hadn't ventured out for the past three days. The son of a bitch had been in the middle of breaking Maggie down physically, mentally, emotionally. But why? What could a war correspondent for a failing military news magazine possibly have to do with *Sangre por Sangre*? "What did you get yourself into?"

He hadn't expected an answer.

"I saw them." Maggie turned onto her back, her voice distant, not entirely solid. "They killed…everyone."

Killed everyone? "Who did they kill, Maggie?"

She didn't respond this time. Her body would direct its energy to her major organs before it started shutting down. Heart, brain, lungs.

She needed help. Now.

Jones floored the accelerator as he fishtailed onto the single lane dirt road headed straight into the south side of the valley. As cartels battled over territory and attempted to upend law enforcement and government throughout New Mexico, organizations like Socorro Security were key in neutralizing the threat to the surrounding towns, but something had changed over the past few months. *Sangre por Sangre* wasn't just intensifying their assaults on the general public as they had in the past. They were strategizing. Hitting specific targets. Moving more product. Trafficking more innocent lives. Recruiting heavier than ever before.

And Maggie had somehow ended up in the middle of it.

Gotham's whine cut through the interior of the SUV.

"Hang on. We're almost there." A branch of dirt road split off from the main road, and Jones took it without hesitation. A spotlight lit up ahead. In the dead of night, it looked out of place surrounded by thousand-foot cliffs and bare desert, but once the sun came up, a gleaming modern structure of tinted glass and steel would peek out from the mountainside.

Jones followed the lesser-worn path as fast as he dared without dislodging Maggie from the back seat. The front of the SUV dipped as he lined up with the garage entrance. Scarlett had upgraded security to the point he didn't have to swipe his badge. The tracking node she'd implanted in his forearm was enough to get him through the gate as long as his heart was still beating.

He swung the SUV in front of the sleek elevator doors leading into the heart of headquarters and shoved the vehicle into Park. Shouldering out of the car, Jones raced for the keypad installed in the wall, and hit the emergency medical button. "Doc, I need you in the parking garage."

He didn't bother waiting for an answer as he rounded to the back passenger side door. Overhead lights reflected in Maggie's heavy eyes. Gotham refused to budge as Jones threaded his arms under hers and pulled her free from the SUV. Time seemed to freeze. Where the hell was the doc? "Help is coming, Maggie. Stay with me."

"Find them," she said. "You have to find them. Everyone deserves…to know the truth."

"Don't worry about that right now." Confusion wasn't enough to hold him back from getting her help, but Gotham didn't seem to want to let Maggie go. He planted his front paws on her legs as though he'd claimed her as his own. "Why do you have to make everything so much harder than it needs to be?"

The elevator pinged with its arrival. A flood of organized chaos exploded from within as two women breached the garage.

Dr. Nafessa Piel wasn't the type of on-call stitcher to wear one of those white lab coats unless she expected a lot of blood. Socorro's doc pulled her hair back in a tie and shoved her long sleeves over her elbows as she approached the back seat. "Tell me everything I need to know."

Socorro's security operative Scarlett Beam stood back, letting the doctor work.

"I found her." An unfamiliar loyalty urged Jones to keep his hands on Maggie as the doc tried to wedge him out of the way—to comfort, to console, he didn't know—but every second he kept Dr. Piel from doing her job was another second that could put the journalist in danger. "Cartel worked her up pretty good. I don't know how long. Couple days, maybe. She was conscious until a minute ago. Talking, even."

Dr. Piel pulled a flashlight and peeled Maggie's right eye open, shining the light in directly. "Her pupils aren't dilating. She's suffered some kind of head trauma. Possibly swelling. We can't move her without supporting her neck and head. Scarlett, get the dog out of here. Jones, get one of the guys down here. I'm going to need all the help I can get."

Scarlett dragged Gotham free of Maggie's lap and latched onto his collar. His whine punctured through the vehicle, as though the husky couldn't bear to be separated from his new friend. Jones didn't have the voice to tell his partner he knew exactly what that felt like. "Come on, rookie. Your dad's gotta work. Let's see what Hans and Gruber are doing upstairs," she said, referring to her two Dobermans.

Jones's head pounded in rhythm to his racing heart as he sent out the SOS. In less than a minute, Cash Meyers—Socorro's forward observer—hit the parking garage with portable backboard in hand. "What do you need?"

"I've got her head. Jones, you're in the middle. Cash, get her feet. We move as one. Understand?" The authority in the doc's voice would cut through rock. "There's no telling what kind of internal damage she's suffered. Any jostling could make her injuries worse."

Jones took his position, squeezing his too-large body between the back passenger door and Maggie's slim frame. He threaded his hands beneath her hips. And froze. Her underside was wet. Warm. Extracting his hand, he tried to breathe through the metallic-sweet odor hitting his senses. Blood. A lot of it. "Doc, I think we've made it worse."

"Move," Dr. Piel said. "Now!"

Chapter Three

She should've stayed in Albuquerque.

Maggie tried to crane her neck to one side, but something hard and itchy kept her in place. A groan escaped up her throat as a deep ache drilled through her. She was back in her cell. The one that leaked from the exposed pipe overhead. Coming around from another round of interrogation. El Capitan hadn't killed her yet. Which meant she hadn't given him what he wanted. Good. She'd hold out as long as she could.

A lightness took hold in her legs, in her back and hips. There wasn't really any pain there. She just felt... immobile. Maggie tried to curl her fingers into her palms. Pressure, not pinching. A tear burned in her left eye. She could still feel sensation. Not a spinal injury. Strapped to a chair? No. That wasn't it, either. Her hands were free. Though letting her captors know she was conscious hadn't worked out for her before, she cracked her eyelids.

Not darkness as she expected. Dim lighting—calming, warm, with a slight airy feeling—highlighted some kind of hospital room. Blackout curtains framed an entire wall of tinted glass to one side. It was dark on the other side.

Though middle of the night or engineered that way, she didn't know. Maggie memorized what she could of the room in the glass's reflection.

Including the man seated on the opposite side of her bed.

Familiarity seeped into the tension that came so automatically these days. That face. She knew that face. Worn, battle-hardened in a way she'd seen in so many soldiers, but at the same time handsome. Thick, groomed facial hair tried to hide the shape of his jaw. She'd felt it. When he'd held her against his chest. Her forehead had brushed against it. Soft. Softer than she'd expected. It'd been that single second of sensory input that'd kept her from spiraling through the fear. Which, now, seemed ridiculous. She'd been abducted, questioned and tortured for days that had now blurred together. And this man's facial hair was the only thing that kept her from falling apart at the very end. "Do you know how beautiful you are?"

The operative at her bedside leaned into her peripheral vision. The lines around his eyes had shallowed, and suddenly he seemed years younger. His mouth quirked to one side and accentuated the slight hood over his light eyes. "Doc said she gave you something for the pain. Though it seems she might've dosed you a bit too much."

Embarrassment heated through her. The lightness in her legs and hips. No wonder she couldn't make sense of her own thoughts. "Where am I?"

"Socorro. Try to take it easy. You've been through a lot, but you're safe here." A transformation took place in a matter of milliseconds. Where there'd been almost a kind of relief in his expression, there was a guardedness now. As though he'd already said too much. "You remember me?"

"You locked me in your SUV." Her throat burned with a dryness she'd become used to, but it felt so overwhelming now. Out of place.

His laugh rumbled deep through him. Not of its own accord but dampened. Controlled. The way he ducked his head down to avoid exposure for that break in composure said a lot, too. This was a man constantly on the defense. Always looking for the next threat and calculating how to neutralize it. "Yeah. I might be a little protective of my stuff."

Splinters of memory returned. Not all at once, but almost like an out-of-order slideshow she'd never want to sit through. Her being dragged from the interrogation room. Him catching her as she ran through every scenario of escape in the middle of the desert. And…a dog. Her neck itched. Maggie raised one hand to her throat, hitting something solid and plastic protecting her from collarbone to chin. Air evaporated from her chest. This…this was a neck brace. She clawed at it. Bandages around her hands kept her from getting a good grip on the edge. "What… What is this? What happened?"

Jones shot to his feet, closing the distance between them. "It's okay. Dr. Piel wanted to make sure you wouldn't aggravate any swelling in your neck or head while she was going through your bloodwork and scans. It's precautionary after what you've been through."

"Swelling?" She tried to sit up.

"You took quite a beating, Maggie. You're lucky to be alive." Calloused hands slid around hers to pry her fingernails from between the hard plastic and her jawline. The contact was warm and slow, but her nervous system wasn't convinced of his promise of safety.

"What did they do?" She couldn't hide the desperation sliding into her voice. This wasn't part of the plan. She'd started over. She'd made something of herself. On her own. Despite the lack of support from her family, friends and everyone else who'd turned their backs on her, she'd overcome it all. She couldn't take a step back. Not now. "What's wrong with me?"

A sadness that had no right to warp Jones's face cut through her. "You lost a lot of blood. Luckily the doc keeps a few bags of every blood type on hand in case one of us does something stupid. You needed a transfusion, and you sustained quite of bit of bruising and cuts over your whole body. There are a couple of minor rib fractures, but the worst is in your back. Dr. Piel called it a spinal cord hemorrhage."

"I don't... I don't understand." Maggie closed her eyes against the onslaught of memories coming now. Every strike. Every question. Every slice of pain.

Jones moved into her full line of sight. Slowly, strategic. Like he was approaching some kind of wounded animal he didn't want to frighten, but it was all done in vain. There wasn't anything that was going to make this okay. "You started bleeding on the way here. I didn't realize it until we were getting you out of the SUV. Dr. Piel found a puncture wound in your spinal column once we got you on the table. You've been los-ing small amounts of spinal fluid. Let me get her. She can explain it better than I can."

Maggie clutched his hand, digging her broken fin-gernails in deeper than necessary.

"Are you saying…" She was trying to wrap her head around each and every one of his words. Trying to make them make sense, but a thickness of pain medica-tion and sleeplessness and hunger and thirst seemed to be battling against her. There was only one that stood out among the others. One that would rip this new life she'd made for herself away. "Am I going to be para-lyzed? Can I walk?"

"Yeah, Maggie. You can walk, but it's going to take time. It's going to hurt, and you're going to need a lot of help with recovery over the next few weeks." His voice softened. The sound of pity. "Dr. Piel has already called in the best physician who has experience with this type of injury. You'll be back on your feet before you know it."

This type of injury. A downward pull started in her gut and pinned her to the bed. Time. Pain. Help. No. She'd already suffered through what she'd hoped had been the biggest hill in her life. She couldn't do this again. She couldn't let herself be that victim all over again. Maggie tried to kick at the too-soft sheets and heavy comforter to get free of the cage they'd created, but the prickling in her feet intensified to the point of hot coals. "No. I can't. I can't stay here."

"I know what you're going through." Jones backed up to give her space, but it wasn't enough. "I know you feel trapped, Maggie. I know this feels impossible, but if you try to leave, you're just going to hurt yourself more."

The walls were closing in, and Maggie didn't have the discipline not to let her brain's mind games get to her this time. Exhaustion broke barriers faster than anything else she'd gone through. If it hadn't been for Jones pulling her out of that interrogation room, she would've given in to El Capitan. She would've told that son of a bitch anything he'd wanted to know if he'd promised to just let her sleep. She clutched the bedrail to heft herself up. The neck brace cut into the underside of her jaw. The added sensation gave her mind something tangible to grab onto, and she wasn't letting go. She pulled her legs over the side of the bed with her free hand. Hell, she'd been turned into a mummy. So many bandages. So many injuries. How had she survived? "You don't know. You don't know...what I've been through, and I hope you never will."

He was suddenly there, right in her line of escape. Massive hands locked onto the bed on either side of her. A blockade of muscle and determination and authority, but Maggie's gut said he hadn't gone through the trouble of pulling her out of the cartel's lair to keep her captive. He'd move if pushed. Because that was the kind of man he was. Loyal but not dominating. "Yes, I do, and I give you my word it will get better, but you've got to put in the work, and you've got to let me help you."

Something hot stabbed through her. A sincerity in his words that made her want to believe he actually understood her mindset. That he understood her body wanted nothing but to die, but her spirit refused to give up and that she couldn't just sit here. No judgment in his voice. No room for excuses. This man—whoever he was and wherever he'd come from—believed she was safe. She could practically feel the heat coming off of him. Something she thought she'd never feel again, and Maggie wanted nothing more than to lean into that heat. To feel support from someone else so she could just take a couple minutes to breathe. "You don't understand. I can't stay here. They'll never stop. He'll never stop, and the longer I stay here, the more danger everyone is in."

Jones pried his hands from the mattress on either side of her, and she found herself missing the clarity of soap and man in an instant. "The men who took you." It was as though he could see right through her. That he knew her. "*Sangre por Sangre* doesn't take prisoners. Not unless you have something they want. So what do they want with you, Maggie Caddel?"

The pressure of holding back these past few days—or however long it'd been since that night in the desert—crushed her from the inside. "I wasn't supposed to be there, but I saw everything. The man who interrogated me. He killed them all. And I have the proof."

HER HANDS SHOOK, drawing Jones closer.

A simple flick of her tongue across those busted lips was enough to get his full attention. He should've gone after Sosimo Toledano. Given the bastard a taste of his own medicine for doing what he'd done to Maggie. But the choice to save her life or complete his mission hadn't been easy in the moment. Dredging those memories up wasn't going to do her a damn bit of good either. Her recovery. Her healing. That was all Jones could focus on right now. The cracks in his hands caught on the cuts and scrapes in hers against the mattress. "Tell me what happened, Maggie."

"It was stupid." Her voice lost the command he'd admired in the desert. Right after she'd pumped a round of shotgun shells into his back window and threatened to shoot him, and he couldn't help but hold her hand tighter. "I've been following *Sangre por Sangre* members for just under a year to try to get my first story. Low-level dealers to start with, but every once in a while, they'd break off from their routines and lead me to someone higher up the chain. I thought if I waited long enough, if I could uncover the man at the top, that would give me something to secure my future."

"You've been following drug cartel members, alone." The words almost didn't seem real. Socorro had people like him—trained in reconnaissance and combat, soldiers who knew what to look for and how to respond to a threat—to cover organizations like *Sangre por Sangre* and report back to the Pentagon. And she'd walked into the hornet's nest without so much as a second thought?

"You don't understand. I'm the newest war correspondent at the magazine. I don't have as much experience as the others." Maggie swiped at her face. The exhaustion wasn't hollowing her eyes as much now, but the bruising around her temples and cheeks had darkened significantly. "This job... I need it to work, and all the big stories were going to the veteran journalists. Bodhi—my editor—hasn't liked any of my submissions so far. He was going to let me go if I didn't produce a story worth printing. I needed something."

A suction of gravity triggered in his chest. Jones retracted his hand as that invisible force threatened to rip him into a million pieces. Shoving himself upright, he circled the room to try to walk it off, but there was no point. She'd risked this one precious life for the chance of landing a story. "And you really believe a job is more important than your life?"

"You don't know me." Her accusation didn't come with anger. Mere observation pulled him up short from raging around the hospital room, trying to make her see the absolute ridiculousness of her motives. "You pulled me out of that interrogation room, or whatever it was, and I appreciate it. You saved my life, but that doesn't give you the right to berate me for my choices."

Hell. She was right. They weren't friends. They were barely acquaintances. Jones scrubbed his hand down his face, hoping to take the heat burning in his veins with it. Didn't help. The best thing he could do was focus on the facts. On how she'd ended up in *Sangre por Sangre*'s grasp and why they hadn't killed her. "All right. So you started following low-level members. How does that get you under the fist of one of the most wanted lieutenants on our radar?"

"Two weeks ago, one of the soldiers I'd been following was pulled off his corner. Then I noticed others. *Sangre por Sangre*'s income depends on those corners in Albuquerque and other cities like it. I thought something had happened, but the longer I watched, the more I realized they were being recruited within the cartel. Under a single lieutenant."

"Sosimo Toledano," he said.

"I only knew him as El Capitan. That's what the others called him between…" She gestured to the length of her body. "I got the impression Toledano was organizing a coup against the old leadership. A story like that would blow my editor's mind and shoot me to the top of the roster for my next assignment. I couldn't pass up the opportunity, so I started watching him. The more I watched, the more I learned. Turns out your Sosimo Toledano is the son of the man at the top of *Sangre por Sangre*. The Pentagon has been looking for him for months in connection with a series of attacks throughout New Mexico. Executions, even raids going on in the smaller towns. One as recent as last week."

"Socorro is well versed in Toledano's profile." Because of him. Because Jones had been assigned to put the pieces together. Though he hadn't expected Maggie to be one of the missing pieces.

"A few days ago—I couldn't tell you how many— I followed him and the members he'd recruited. They drove out to the middle of the desert. I stayed back as far as I could with my headlights off. Then I heard the first gunshot. It was hard to see, so I got out and jogged to get a better view. I had my camera." She shook her head in some kind of attempt to undo the past. "And I walked… I walked right into an ambush."

Every cell in Jones's body hiked to attention. There hadn't been reports of an ambush against the cartel. It certainly hadn't come from Socorro. "What kind of ambush?"

"The kind where a cartel lieutenant kills ten American soldiers and buries the evidence without anybody knowing," she said.

Jones lost the air in his lungs. That…wasn't possible. There were any number of contingencies built into an operation like this. Backup teams, strategy, superiors who'd left the fieldwork to guys like him. If she was telling the truth, someone had to know what the hell had happened out there in the middle of that desert. The weight couldn't just fall to Maggie. "You got photos."

"I hid as soon as I realized what was happening, turned off the flash on my camera and just started shooting. They had no idea I was there." A shudder ran through her from neck to hips. "But once the bodies were buried, I knew I had to get out of there. I started running for my car, but it was so dark, I tripped over a rock. My camera broke, but I managed to save the SD card. I shoved it into a crack in the dirt where I fell. One of the cartel's soldiers must've heard me fall. He found me. I fought him off as long as I could."

The adrenaline rush of realizing she'd risked her life for the chance of writing the next military headline waned. "But the SD card with all the photos you took is still out there."

"That's what El Capitan wanted. My camera, but the SD card was gone. He knows I hid it." Tears glittered in her eyes. Knuckles tight around the hem of her sheets, Maggie refused to look at him. "He was going to kill me. The things he did…" She shut her eyes against the abhorrent images Jones had no doubt would haunt her for the rest of her life. "Nobody should be able to live through that."

"But you did." Pressure stuck behind his sternum. He'd been here before. At the side of a hospital bed just like this one, trying to come up with something significant and comforting to say. Holding another hand that'd been broken during the course of interrogation. Jones memorized the damage done to the smooth skin along the back of Maggie's hand. Just as he'd done all those years ago while he'd given consent to have his brother taken off life support. Only this time was different. This time, he could fix it. He could do something. "You survived. Despite the odds. That means something."

"That I'm too stubborn for my own good?" A scoff escaped her limited control. The break in her composure was only temporary, because behind the sarcasm was a wounded and badly beaten soul. "My parents always warned me my pigheadedness would get me into trouble. I thought they'd just meant what would happen if I left my ex. I didn't think it'd land me in the center of the cartel's cross hairs."

Jones didn't really know what that felt like. The whole parent thing. Not in any stable sense of the word, at least. That was what happened when you were moved from foster home to foster home. Some good, some bad. No attachment to any given place or the people in it. Attachment led to emotion. Emotion led to weakness. Weakness led to mistakes. And he wasn't about to make the same mistake as he had with his brother.

"All you have to worry about is getting better, Maggie. The photos, Sosimo Toledano, your job. None of that matters. Understand?"

"He won't stop. You know that, right? Toledano isn't going to stop hunting me. He'll come here." Maggie's eyes fluttered with exhaustion, casting dark eyelashes across the tops of her cheeks. They fanned out in a way that should only be possible through the gravity-defying technology of makeup, yet Jones couldn't find a trace of it on her face. Her chin deviated from its center position over her chest as she seemed to relax into the bed against her will. "And he'll hurt anyone who gets in his way."

"I'm not going to let that happen. I give you my word." He couldn't seem to let go of her hand, even as she drifted into unconsciousness. The painkillers were doing their job, but it would take a whole lot more than a combination of drugs to put Maggie back on her feet.

And he was going to be there. Whatever it took. Because she didn't deserve this. *Sangre por Sangre* had crossed a line, and Jones was going to be the one to make them pay for overstepping. Once and for all.

Convincing his nervous system he didn't have to hold on to her took longer than it should have. He could still feel her hand in his as he extracted himself from her hospital room and headed down the black corridor toward Ivy Bardot's office. Socorro Security had been contracted to dismantle the *Sangre por Sangre* cartel by any means necessary, but up until this point, everything he and the team had done had been reactionary.

Now was the time for them to make their move.

Chapter Four

The pain shot down the back of her thigh. Not as bad as the last time she'd pried herself out of bed. The need to get on her feet, to keep moving, tightened in her chest to the point she couldn't breathe beneath the soft, light sheets. Her stomach battled against the familiar taste of full-course breakfasts, lunches and dinners—with desserts—over the past three days.

She couldn't take it anymore.

Being taken care of. She couldn't sit here and wait for El Capitan and his men to finish what they'd started. Sosimo Toledano. That was his name, but knowing it didn't make any of this better. She'd given Socorro— given Jones—enough time and enough information to take what'd happened and construct their own narrative for action. She'd done her job. Now it was time to get back to her life. While she still could.

Maggie pressed her feet into the cold, black tile. This whole place looked as though it'd been taken directly out of a science fiction movie. Big windows stared out over the desert landscape—tinted, most likely bullet-proof—and when it got dark, there was nothing but stars and distant lights on the other side of the glass.

Alpine Valley. That was the little town she'd tried to run to the other night. Small, out of the way, isolated. It looked like any other town right now, but the people there had found themselves at the mercy of *Sangre por Sangre* and a bombing that led to a massive landslide that buried two hundred homes in the past two months. It'd been all over the news at the time. There was something to be said of that kind of strength. Of a community as underprotected and vulnerable as that one coming together against a threat.

She could hide there if she kept her head down. Not forever. Just long enough to secure a phone, maybe a car. The cartel would catch on if she stayed in one place too long, but it was a start. She was fairly certain she could locate the site of the ambush to collect the SD card she'd hidden. El Capitan had taken her wallet, phone, even her allergy meds. She'd lived with less. She could do it again.

Maggie stripped free of the gown that gave Dr. Piel access to her spine. The bleeding in her back had stopped two days ago, but there was still a bit of swelling around the puncture wound and an intense headache she couldn't get rid of. She'd told Jones the truth. She couldn't remember being injected with drugs or hallucinogens, but whatever Toledano had set out to do had failed. She wasn't going to give him a second chance.

Cold air constricted her skin as she grabbed for the packaged scrubs, a top and bottom set on the side table. She threaded her feet into the bottoms, forced to move slower than she wanted to go as the muscles around her

spine stretched and released. The top went on easier.
The socks took longer than both put together, but within
minutes, she was dressed. No sign of a pair of shoes.
Guess those weren't considered necessary for recovery.
Or the people here were trying to keep her from leaving.

Her left foot dragged slightly behind the right as
she headed for the door. The heavy metal took more
energy than she expected to wedge open. There were
no phones ringing off the hook, no PA announcements
overhead. No nurses and doctors rushing with crash
carts or responding to patients. Everything was quiet.
Empty. Only the slight pound of her pulse behind her
ears told her she hadn't suffered permanent hearing
damage from the high-frequency noise her abductors
had forced her to listen to for hours at a time.

She dared a step into the monochromatic hallways.
Black everywhere. The ceilings, the floors, the walls,
the artwork. There was nowhere to hide in a place like
this. Pressure grew in her chest, and she looked up to
see a single camera staring back at her from the space
where the wall met the ceiling. No light to indicate
whether it was recording or not, but this was a security company. Why else have it installed?

Maggie ducked under the device and pulled out the
single wire connecting it to the metal frame below the
lens. "You're going to have to work harder than that
to keep me here."

This place was a maze. Every turn led to another
corridor, another conference room, another door secured with a keypad. Disconnecting every camera as
she went along, she had the distinct impression that

somewhere in here the members of Socorro were just waiting to see how far she'd make it before she gave up and went back to her room. But she'd never quit anything in her life. She wasn't about to start now.

She had to get out of here. She had to get the SD card she'd buried and contact Bodhi. It was the only way to stop the cartel from coming after her for the rest of her life. Maggie turned into a dead end. "You've got to be kidding me."

A yip registered from behind.

She spun around, confronting the husky she'd met while trying to escape the cartel in a bulletproof SUV. The night she'd been brought here. He settled his furry butt on the floor, staring up at her with a whole wide world of innocence in his face.

"I remember you. Gotham, right?" Maggie dared a step toward him, hand extended to pet him, then froze. Did Socorro let their K9s roam the halls of their own free will? Or did this mean Jones was close by? She didn't have time to find out.

"Do you know how to get out of here?" Did she really expect a dog to understand her? Military K9s were intelligent, disciplined even. But that didn't make them capable of the English language. "Um, out?"

Gotham cocked his head to one side a split second before he padded dead ahead, nails clicking against the floors. She'd take that as a good sign. Maggie struggled to keep up with him. Even as steady as he was, he was much faster than her injuries allowed her. Another streak of pain shot down her left leg, bringing her to a stop as Gotham took a turn ahead. "Wait!"

She grabbed onto the back of her leg, willing it to move, but the pain was too much. Like a nerve had been pinched all along her left side. She'd never catch up to him like this. Which meant she wasn't going to be able to get out of here. Maggie sucked in a deep breath to counter the crushing effect weighing her down as she steadied one hand against the nearest wall. "Baby steps."

That was what her therapist had said. She wasn't supposed to look at the whole puzzle and try to solve it in one go. It hadn't worked in the middle of her divorce, and it wouldn't work now. She had to break it down into pieces. One step forward. Then another. That was all she could focus on. Not the pain. Not the hopelessness. Not anything but the next foot in front of her. Maggie took that first step. Then the second. Her leg threatened to collapse out from under her, but she held strong.

That success was enough to bolster her confidence. Maggie made it to the corner where she'd lost Gotham.

And faced off with the man whose voice she couldn't get out of her head.

"Figured if you wanted to leave this bad, I might as well show you the way." Jones scratched Gotham's ears, and the dog closed his eyes. Traitor.

"You were watching me on the cameras." She didn't have the strength for embarrassment or denial. Every second she wasted here was another second *Sangre por Sangre* got away with what they'd done. Evidence would be contaminated. The bodies would start decomposing, and while she fully believed in the science and technology used to solve murders, the first forty-eight hours of any investigation were crucial. And those were already gone. "I'm not going to apologize. I don't like feeling trapped. Did you at least get the show you expected?"

"All I saw was a woman bent on proving she's the one calling the shots. Well, before you started pulling the power on the cameras. Didn't see much after that, so I sent Gotham to find you. Scarlett isn't too happy, but I can't actually think of a time when she was."

Jones offered her his free hand. Like she had a choice in what she did next, but it was a ruse, wasn't it? Because there was no way he was going to let her walk out of here in her condition, let alone try to take on the cartel single-handedly. "Shall we?"

Maggie visually followed the cracked lines in his palm. Worn, rough, aged. Hands that'd seen a lifetime of violence and anger. And yet so contrary to the easiness in his gaze. It was almost enough to release the tension in her gut. Almost. "Fine, but I get to pet the dog."

Jones's deep laugh rumbled through the corridor as he stepped aside to give her room between him and Gotham. Dipping down to scratch the husky added to the strain on her back and leg, but within an instant, Jones was there. Holding her up. Letting her use him as a crutch without her uttering a word. As though he'd known exactly what she was feeling. How much she hurt. Not just physically. But emotionally. Mentally. He braced his arm at her back but let her lead at her own pace.

"How did Gotham know where to find me?" she asked.

"Don't take this the wrong way, but he's a human remains recovery K9." She could just see how hard it was for him to say that with a straight face.

"Do I really smell that bad?" Maggie tried not to stick her nose in her armpit to gauge how long she'd been without a shower. Any shift could disrupt the delicate balance they'd created these last couple of yards.

"You smell fine." Jones angled her to the left and down another corridor. How he knew where he was going in this maze, she could only guess. "He knows your scent now. Given the opportunity, he could track you down within a mile of your location."

"That's impressive." Maggie fisted her hands in Gotham's fur as she slowed. Despite the need to keep moving, to escape, she'd always been at the mercy of her curiosity. "But that doesn't explain why you sent him after me in the first place. Why you brought me here for medical attention. Why you even pulled me out of that interrogation room. I'm just some random stranger you happened to come across. Why bother?"

"That's easy." Jones kept his arm in place—in case she needed it—but there was some part of her just then that thought maybe he needed the connection, too. "Because I didn't want what happened to my brother to happen to you."

"WHAT DO YOU MEAN?" Maggie held her own as though out to prove she didn't need him. As though she didn't need anyone. It was a self-defense technique. Not one born out of training, but out of necessity. Though a part of him wondered why she was so desperate to convince everyone she could get through this life alone. "What does any of this have to do with your brother?"

Jones hadn't meant to expose that part of his life. Not to her. Not to anyone. Least of all someone he'd just met within the past seventy-two hours. And a journalist, for crying out loud. A burning sensation set up residence behind his sternum. It still hurt. Thinking about what his brother had gone through, how his strength—especially of a man of Kincaide's size and abilities—had dwindled in the end. It'd changed him. Inside and out. And there hadn't been anything Jones could do but watch as the only person who gave a damn about him struggled to survive. Then lost.

"It doesn't matter. My point is I can help you, Maggie. I'm good at what I do. I can protect you from the cartel. I can help you find out what happened the night you were taken and to recover those photos."

Not Socorro. Him. Because while he fully trusted Scarlett and the others to have his back in the field, this was something he had to do. For Kincaide. For the hole left behind in his chest after his brother's death. To give Maggie a reason to keep going. He needed this.

"I've studied *Sangre por Sangre* for close to a year. I've seen what they can do and how little they care for the people they do it to, Jones." The laceration in her lip split as she flinched at some pain he couldn't see. Her right leg was starting to shake under her weight, an indicator she was having problems with her left. "I don't even know you, and I know that I wouldn't wish what happened to me on my worst enemy." Maggie let Gotham slide back to Jones's side. "Thank you for pulling me out of that dark place. And for saving my life. I wouldn't be here without you or your team, and I owe you for that, but I can't let anyone else get trapped in this hell with me."

She used the wall for leverage as she turned her back on him and shuffled along the corridor.

Gotham's whine echoed off the walls.

That all-too-familiar sense of loss cut through him at the thought of her walking out those doors unprotected, injured. Jones barely acknowledged the consequences of his next question, willing to do whatever was required to keep Maggie from taking on an entire drug cartel alone. "Even a source?"

Three words. That was all it took to hook into her personal drive. He was good at that, seeing a person's— most especially a combatant's—deepest compulsion and dragging it out. It was those limited moments in the field that'd given him an advantage over so many others.

Stringy blond hair acted as an effective barrier to her expression as she pulled up short. "Is that an offer?"

"You told me how important your job is as a war correspondent, that you need it." Jones would pay hell for this. Socorro Security operatives signed NDAs once onboarded to the team. Any and all press went through one woman and one woman only: Ivy Bardot, Socorro's founder. He could lose his job for this. Worse, he could lose his team, but he hadn't known what else to do to keep Maggie from leaving.

"Think about it. You'll be the only journalist who has access to this team and our plans against *Sangre por Sangre*, after the fact, of course. That kind of information hasn't been available to any other news outlet before now. You'll be *American Military News*'s star reporter. All those other writers won't have anything on you."

Maggie angled toward him, and hell if it didn't look as though it took everything in her power not to collapse right there in the middle of the floor. The bruising around her face and down her neck shifted colors around the perimeter. More blue-green than black and purple. Her body was doing everything in its power to heal, but the second she left this building, she was putting herself at risk. "Why would you do that?"

"I told you. I can help." He realized the offer must've seemed ridiculous with him standing there with a husky at his side, but Jones had never been so sure of anything in his life than he was about this deal. "If you let me."

Maggie dropped her arm away from the wall. "Becoming a source isn't just about handing over information. It's about mutual trust. I need to know I can rely on you, that the information I'm getting isn't being filtered or rewritten in any way. That what I'm getting is raw and real. That's the only way this can work between us."

"You have my word." No matter what it took to keep it. "But I want the same deal. If we do this, we do this together. All I ask is that you trust me in return. No lies. No filtering. If you're in pain, I want to know you're going to take care of yourself. If you're going after those photos you hid before your abduction, I'm right by your side. Agreed?"

She attempted to cross her arms over her chest, but the effort looked harder than it should've been. "Does that mean you're going to tell me about what happened to your brother?"

Jones's mouth dried up, leaving nothing but a bad taste on the back of his tongue. Reliving that pain, remembering the way Kincaide had been before he'd died surged hot as acid in his gut.

"You said if this was going to work, we had to be honest with each other," she said. "If that's not something you're willing to do, it's better I know now. Before either of us gets in too deep."

"His name was Kincaide. He was my foster brother." Though Jones wasn't entirely sure if that'd actually been his brother's birth name or one he'd picked up along the way. "We were both in the system for a few years before we ended up in the same house. I was nine. Him, twelve. We hated each other at first. Looking back, I think we were both just trying to come to terms with how we ended up there and took it out on each other any chance we got."

Maggie seemed to soften, losing some of the bite she used against getting close to anyone she didn't have to. Either because of what she'd gone through or a characteristic she'd spent years building up, he didn't know.

"I'm sorry. I've known kids in the foster system. I can't imagine how hard that must've been."

"I didn't know anything different by the time I met Kincaide. My parents ditched me at a fire station when I was two. I don't remember them. I spent a good chunk of my life wasting time trying to figure out why they decided they couldn't take care of me, but I've since come to realize sometimes family isn't where you come from. It's who you trust."

Jones felt the assault coming. The grief he buried by throwing himself into the field day after day.

"The first few weeks, Kincaide and I did nothing but throw punches at each other. We were insecure, didn't know where we would end up next. Didn't know if the social workers would have us pack our garbage bags in a day, a week, a month. We were two angry kids who were caught in survival mode every hour of every day, and after a while, the only thing we could count on were those fights we picked with each other."

Maggie pressed her back into the wall, lowering herself onto the cold tile floor, and Jones wanted nothing but to scoop her up and put her back in that hospital bed. Only, he knew she wouldn't go. That she wouldn't admit defeat. "But you came to care about each other?"

He could see the moment his and Kincaide's relationship changed as though it'd happened mere minutes ago. "We were headed home after school. Our foster mom insisted we walk together, especially since I was younger, but I thought I was better than that. I'd always try to beat him home, then rub it in his face. I remember I'd gotten a new watch for my birthday. You know, the kind with the calculator built in. I was bragging to anyone who would listen all day about it because it was the best gift I'd ever received."

He still had that watch, tucked safely back in his room. "Well, these kids—I don't even remember their faces—jumped me a block from the house. They'd been waiting for me to pass by this dumpster to take it. I'd learned how to hold my own over the years, but it was three against one. I ended up curled in a ball while they beat the crap out of me."

Maggie's gaze glistened a split second before she swiped at her face with busted knuckles. "You must've been scared."

"I was. It was the first time in my life I remember thinking, I'm going to die. All for a stupid watch." Jones could almost feel every kick to his ribs, every fist that landed against his face. But there was something else. "Until my big brother came."

"Kincaide?" she asked.

"He wiped the floor with them. Got my watch back, though it'd been destroyed in the scuffle." Jones scratched at Gotham's neck with one thumb. "But I didn't care. Because I got something worth a lot more that day. I got a brother. Kincaide was pulled from that house because of that fight, but we didn't care. One of the kids' parents pressed charges, but it didn't matter where we were shipped off to. Nothing was going to stop us from having each other's backs. We wrote letters and called each other on our birthdays. Even after he went into the military, he made sure I knew I could count on him. I followed him, of course. Straight to the army as soon as I turned eighteen. Every few months I'd get word of where he was, but a couple years ago, the messages stopped. And I knew something had happened."

Maggie's expression fell. "In my room, you said you knew what I was going through. Is that because…"

"It took some digging. Me calling in every favor I

could over the course of two months, but I finally found my brother's last location." Jones tried ignoring the sick feeling in his gut, but there wasn't enough Pepto-Bismol in the world to touch that nausea. "Turned out Kincaide had been taken captive by a group of insurgents after an operation gone wrong. And the military couldn't do anything about it without starting a war." He notched his chin parallel to the floor. "So I did."

Chapter Five

He was going to be her source.

Maggie shuffled into a galley-style kitchen that'd been upgraded with chef-level appliances, beautiful countertops, sleek cabinets and expensive tile. It seemed everything about this place followed the same theme: the best of the best. Including the men and women operating out of this building.

"Our logistics coordinator takes her job very seriously." Jones ducked into the refrigerator ahead of her, pulling a stack of what looked like prepackaged food from one of the shelves. In her limited vision around his muscular frame, she caught at least four rows deep of those containers. "She tries to make sure we're not living off protein bars and shakes by putting together meals throughout the week. You want a Mediterranean bowl or peppercorn beef tenderloin?"

Her mouth watered at the possibility of having both. Right before her stomach knotted with hunger. Her body was working overtime, trying to repair the damage sustained over the past week. That took extra calories, but she wasn't exactly sure what her role here as guest entailed. Taking more than her share broke social conventions. At the same time, she could've probably eaten that entire refrigerator full of food. "I didn't think deciding what to eat would be such a tough choice."

"Then you can have both." Jones set the dinners— though was it dinner at four in the afternoon?—on the countertop and hunted for another meal. "I'll heat these up and bring them to the table."

"I can help." Her left leg thought otherwise, but she wasn't going to let Sosimo Toledano get the best of her. Not after she'd come this far. Maggie pried the lid of the Mediterranean bowl free, instantly craving the seasoned couscous beneath the fragrant chicken and tomato mixture. She made quick work of shoving the package into the microwave and hitting start as Jones withdrew from the refrigerator with his own serving in hand. She wasn't really sure what to do, what to say, as the countdown ticked off on the digital screen. She dug her fingernails into her palms—right where the pierced skin had started healing—and forced herself to release before she hurt herself all over again. "I'm sorry about your brother. About what happened to him. You said the military couldn't do anything to recover him without starting a war."

"Kincaide had been caught over enemy lines." Jones set his lower back against the counter, taking up so much space in the undersized kitchen, she felt small in comparison. Though not intimidated. Thick muscle banded beneath his T-shirt as he crossed his arms over his chest. He stood there, every ounce the operative she'd read up on when coming on board for *American Military News*.

"From what I'd been able to put together, he and his unit were assigned to pull a confidential informant out. It was all under the table. No official reports. Nothing on paper. The US wasn't supposed to be there, but this source was too valuable to let him get caught by his own people."

Maggie rested her weight against the opposite counter, facing him head on. His boots nearly touched her socked feet in the limited distance between them. And wasn't that the perfect comparison between them? He was solid, reliable, the kind of man who stayed on the defense while she'd rather curl up in bed and hide until the hard things went away. "But his unit was ambushed?"

"It was a setup. The informant turned on Kincaide and the others. Led them straight to their capture. In most cases, their deaths." Jones seemed to lose himself for a series of breaths. "Sending a unit to retrieve them would've been seen as an act of war. The US wasn't supposed to be there in the first place. Couldn't just ask for our hostages back without admitting we'd crossed the line."

The microwave shrieked, letting her know her first meal was hot and ready, but despite the invasive hunger carving through her, Maggie didn't move. "So you went after him?"

"Took some time." Two divots deepened between his eyebrows. Jones shifted his weight from one leg to the other. She could practically see his agitation at reliving those terrorizing memories, and Maggie wanted nothing but to close the distance between them. To offer some kind of comfort as he'd offered her the past four days. "I couldn't just up and leave my assignment when I heard. Nobody would tell me where he was. I had to call in a few favors to get the intel, and even then, I didn't have any support. No team. Superiors telling me it was all out of my purview."

"How did you manage to get him out of there?" The answer was already there, at the front of her mind. In the way he'd fought to get her out of *Sangre por Sangre*'s grasp. How he'd risked his life and Socorro's reputation protecting her. Jones Driscoll wasn't just doing a job. He was the kind of man willing to go down with the ship to save a relationship. The kind of man who put off his own needs in the face of his team's well-being. Who would disregard direct orders for the chance to save a life and didn't want anyone else making decisions for him and the people he cared about. The kind of man she only believed existed in fairy tales.

"I had a contact in the country. He got me over the border with an alias. Provided weapons, a satellite phone and an extraction." Jones seemed to come back to himself then, hiking himself away from the counter as he collected her heated food from the microwave. He somehow managed to make his movements look graceful despite his size. Something she'd never been good at, even though she was a hundred pounds lighter. "Took two days of surveillance to determine the hostiles were keeping Kincaide and another soldier from his unit in these underground tunnels. I had to go in hard. Take out as many combatants as I could in the first two minutes, but when I got to the end… I didn't even recognize him."

The bruising and cuts around Maggie's face seemed to come alive then, reminding her that thirty-six hours ago, she hadn't been recognizable either. The swelling had contorted her face into something alien. "But you got him home. You saved your brother. Him and his teammate, right?"

"I got them home, but I didn't realize until later I'd only saved a part of him." Jones pulled a drawer free and handed off a fork along with her meal.

She nearly dissolved into the warmth coming from the container. It was little things like this she'd missed the most while being Toledano's captive. Warmth. Light. Someone else to talk to rather than be talked at. "What do you mean?"

"The man I pulled out of there looked like my brother, talked like him even, but that was where the recognition ended." He didn't bother heating up his own meal, just stabbed a fork into the center, and her heart threatened to squeeze her to death. "He'd suffered several brain injuries in the weeks he'd been captive, to the point he'd forgotten big stretches of his life. He couldn't remember certain words. Sometimes he'd start talking, then lose track of what he was saying."

Maggie didn't have the stomach for couscous anymore. Her mouth dried up with the realization of why Jones had gone to such lengths to pull her out of *Sangre por Sangre*'s headquarters the way he did. Why he'd put so much time and energy into ensuring she recovered from her injuries. Why he paid attention to every word out of her mouth. "He didn't know you anymore?"

"No. He didn't." A reservoir of despair flooded into his expression. "Within a few months, the scar tissue building in his brain got so bad he lost fine motor control. He had to be put on a ventilator and a feeding tube. And I knew he didn't want to spend the rest of his life like that. I knew if he'd had the choice, he would've wanted to die in that ambush with his team rather than live the rest of his life in a hospital bed. He wouldn't have wanted me to sit by him hoping he'd snap out of it. So I did what I had to do."

She set her meal aside on the counter and, no longer able to keep her distance, reached out. Hesitant, careful. Her fingers skimmed along his arm, giving him the chance to pull away if he needed. Only he didn't. He didn't move, didn't even seem to breathe at her touch. She threaded her hand between his arm and rib cage, securing him in a hug. "I'm so sorry, Jones."

His hand found her shoulder blade, and within seconds the past few days diminished to a distant memory. Something she'd witnessed but hadn't lived through. Because of him. His resiliency, his concern, his drive to support the people in his life. And she needed that. More than she wanted to admit.

"How's the leg?" he asked.

"Stronger, I think." The lie left her mouth easier than she expected. In truth, her toes had gone numb since leaving her hospital bed, but she didn't want to give him another reason not to see this through. Without her to interrogate, Toledano would have started looking for that SD card, if he hadn't already. There were only so many places she could've hidden it in the short seconds between him and his men killing those soldiers and her racing to escape. He'd find it, sooner or later.

Unless she and Jones got to it first.

Jones unwound his arm from around her, and Maggie instantly missed the steady beat of his heart in her ear. Which was ridiculous. She wasn't in a position or in the right mindset to want anything more than a source at this point in her life. She'd spent years disconnecting herself from everyone around her. Her ex, her parents, her siblings—anyone who'd abandoned her in the divorce. She didn't need or want attachments that would get in the way of this new life she'd built for herself. But she couldn't ignore that deep loneliness either. Or that Jones seemed to ease that ache.

"You should eat up." Jones nodded toward her discarded food on the countertop. "We've got a lot of work ahead of us."

"Right." She grabbed the container and forked a heaping pile of couscous into her mouth. But Maggie had a feeling eating enough wasn't going to be the biggest hurdle they went up against.

JONES SCANNED THROUGH the satellite images for the tenth—or was it the eleventh?—time. Six nights ago. That was when Maggie had said she'd followed the cartel into the desert, that Sosimo Toledano had ambushed and murdered ten American soldiers to prevent his own capture.

Only that wasn't what the satellite had recorded.

As far as he could tell, there was nothing out there. How the hell was that possible? Or was there something Maggie wasn't telling him? Maybe she'd gotten the days mixed up. It was impossible to keep track of time in survival mode, when every second of every day threatened to pulverize you. But going back another couple days didn't produce anything either. Jones double-checked the dates as low voices registered from the news report on the TV across the room.

Maggie had turned it on and promptly fallen asleep on his bed after they'd finished dinner. Gotham curled up next to her, despite knowing the bed was off-limits to fur balls like him, and Jones couldn't help but feed into the jealousy as he watched the two of them asleep now. Seemed he wasn't the only one breaking the rules.

Jones took in the latest news report. No one was reporting on this. No one had noticed a war correspondent had even gone missing. Or knew that Maggie Caddel was alive. This didn't make sense. Someone would've noticed. While he knew the full effect of the military's need for confidentiality, Maggie's abduction would've at least made local news. So why hadn't it? Surely her boss would have reported it. Someone who knew her.

He unpocketed his phone from his cargo pants and scrolled through the contacts. Hitting the name and number for Alpine Valley's chief of police, he darted for the door and closed it softly behind him, watching to ensure Maggie didn't wake up in the process. The line rang once then connected. He kept his voice low. "Halsey, it's Jones. I need a favor."

"And here I thought you were checking in on me."
Baker Halsey had become one of the only outsiders
Jones trusted to get to the truth. Halsey headed the massive cleanup of the landslide that had buried a quarter
of Alpine Valley after a bombing meant to kill him and
Socorro's logistics coordinator. He would do anything
to protect his town. Something Jones wanted him to
do now. "What do you need?"

"Maggie Caddel. You know the name?" Jones checked
to make sure the door was still secure behind him. He
moved farther down the hall. As much as he believed
every word out of Maggie's mouth, trauma altered so
many facets of truth and perception. He had to cover
all his bases.

"Sounds familiar. I think she left me a message once.
You know, before my phone and the whole police sta-
tion got blown to hell a few weeks ago," Halsey said.
"She's a reporter or something like that, right?"

"Yeah. *American Military News.* Has there been a
missing person report filed on her? Anyone coming
to the police asking about her or her whereabouts?"
Because a woman didn't just up and disappear without anyone noticing. She had family, friends, coworkers, neighbors. Someone had to know something was
wrong when she didn't come home.

"Not that I know of, but I'm not really handling the
day-to-day while we try to clean up this mess. That
mostly goes to my deputies." There was a deafening
silence before Halsey's next question. "Why? Is this
Caddel lady in some kind of trouble?"

"Something like that." Jones was missing something.

He could feel it. "Listen. Can you get in touch with your guys? See if her name comes up? Check with Albuquerque PD, too. Nothing official. Try to keep it off the books."

"Sure." Halsey's voice lost the lightness the chief had taken on since partnering up with Jones's teammate, Jocelyn. "But do you want to tell me what's going on first?"

"I'm not sure yet." The muscles in his spine tightened disk by disk as his bedroom door cracked open, putting Maggie in his sights. Jones held up his index finger to buy him another minute. "Find out what you can."

He ended the call before Halsey could ask too many questions Jones didn't know how to answer. He trusted the chief to come through. The ambush Maggie described couldn't just be swept under the rug. Not without leaving some kind of evidence behind.

Maggie left the safety of his bedroom, her foot still slightly dragging behind her right. "Everything okay? I woke up and you were gone."

"Yeah. Everything's fine." He tucked his phone back into his pocket. "Just checking in with the local chief of police. How are you feeling?"

"Better. Thanks. It's amazing what a nap and a shower can do for the soul." She set the side of her head against the wall as she leaned into it for support. How the woman was still standing after everything she'd been through, Jones didn't know. He couldn't even imagine how much strength it took.

"I thought that was chicken soup," he said.

"I'll take that if you have it, too. Even after both of those meals you gave me, I still feel like I could eat." Her smile tugged at one side of her mouth and washed the heaviness from her expression in an instant, but Jones had the distinct impression it didn't come as easy as it looked. As though she'd reserved it just for him. "Did the police have anything to say about what happened?"

"No. Nothing yet." His phone vibrated from his pocket, but his smartwatch said he'd regret answering. Ivy Bardot wanted answers, and as one of her operatives, he was required to give them. And he couldn't hold her off anymore. "My boss is calling. I'll need to meet with her, give her a rundown of what's going on."

"I understand. Go. Gotham and I will be fine. Just bring me back something to eat if you can. I'm starving." Before he had a chance to comprehend his next move, Maggie reached out, brushing her hand along his forearm. "Good luck."

The feel of her skin against his triggered a subatomic reaction in his nervous system, putting him instantly at ease. History and training had convinced him he could only feel that kind of effect in the middle of the battlefield or an operation, but this was different. More intense. Warm, even. "Thanks."

Jones watched as she retreated into his bedroom and closed the door behind her before he navigated two floors up to Socorro's founder's office. He knocked on the solid wood door but didn't wait for an answer, shoving inside. "You rang."

Ivy Bardot shuffled through the stack of paperwork

in her hands. Low eyebrows matching fiery red hair refused to budge as she took in whatever information she was reviewing. "You've been busy over the past couple of days from what I can see. Made a friend, too. Tell me about her."

Always to the point. Though, while Jones had been careful about how much information to give Alpine Valley's chief of police, Ivy Bardot most likely already knew everything he was about to brief her on. Lying, even by omission, was pointless, but more than that, Jones had no reason to keep information from her. The former FBI investigator had been hailed as one of the best, racking up more closed cases than any other agent in history before she'd peeled off from the federal government and founded Socorro, a defense against the country's most vile and violent organizations. One he was happy to be part of. Trusted. "Maggie Caddel, war correspondent for *American Military News*. I found her half-dead at the cartel's hands three nights ago. I was going to come to you with this eventually. Just trying to sort out the details."

Ivy flipped one of the pages in her hand toward him. "You accessed the satellite footage of a stretch of desert from around the time you recovered her."

There was the investigator he'd always admired. The one who'd proven time and time again how to put the puzzle together long before anyone else. Jones dared a step forward, needing movement, something to distract his brain from the unease circling through him. "Maggie claims to have witnessed the slaughter of ten American soldiers the night she was abducted. She took photos. Hid the SD card out there in the desert right before the cartel found her."

"Claims." One word. That was all it took for Jones to reconsider everything he thought he knew about this investigation. Socorro's founder didn't believe in coincidence. She didn't trust investigations lacking evidence. And she didn't support assignments running off pure emotion. "These images you requested from our friends at the Pentagon don't show any activity in the area. Cartel or otherwise. That kind of operation would be hard to miss, especially with the loss of American lives."

"But not impossible." His theory didn't feel right, though. Like he'd missed something. That was the problem with satellite imagery—there were thousands of pixels invisible to the human eye. He needed more information. Something concrete. "She could be misremembering the time frame in which she was held. Or there's something more going on here. Something that might even be above our pay grade."

"Take a seat, Jones." Ivy leaned back in her expensive leather chair, not a single wrinkle daring to crease her navy pantsuit. "I understand why you pulled her out of there, got her medical attention. She needed help, and you provided it. I commend that in my operatives. I encourage it. Why else are we here if not to protect the innocent against *Sangre por Sangre*? I can even understand why you would want to see this through, despite the evidence contrary to her statement, but she is not your brother, Jones. If you take on this investigation, I need to know your regret isn't leading the way. That you will look at the facts."

Jones locked his grip around the ends of the chair arms. He forced himself not to let his ego respond. Because, yes, some part of him wished that he'd been able to save Kincaide, but the other... The other part suspected there was a lot more going on here than some journalist caught at the wrong place at the wrong time. "The cartel didn't detain, question and torture her for days on end for no reason, Ivy. They wanted something from her, and she didn't give it to them. You and I both know we can't just send her back out there without protection. They'll find her, and they'll finish the job. Maggie has been following *Sangre por Sangre* soldiers for a year. I believe her when she says there was an ambush that resulted in the murder of American troops, that *Sangre por Sangre* is trying to cover it up and that she has proof. I trust her."

"Then I suggest you and Ms. Caddel take a field trip back to the location she was abducted and find that proof." She motioned toward the door, and Jones shoved himself to his feet. Dismissed. Ivy called from behind. "But if you come back with nothing, I trust that you'll let this go. Before it's too late."

Chapter Six

The uneven landscape jarred her and the SUV to one side. The movement aggravated the ache along her spine. Maggie grabbed for the side door handle, but no amount of force was going to keep her from being thrown around like Gotham's favorite chew toy. Stars punctured the black velvet sky through the windshield. If they weren't headed to the same location where she'd been abducted, she might've even thought it was beautiful out here. Peaceful. The perfect place to escape the noise and violence and pressure of the world. And in her head.

Her throat constricted as she stared out into the endless black. There were no towns out here. No sign of Socorro's headquarters. Nowhere they could run if this went sideways. Before the cartel had dragged her kicking and screaming into an SUV just like this one, that wouldn't have bothered her. She'd relished being on location, lived for the excitement of breaking a new story that might catapult her further away from her old life. Even prided herself on the danger of that kind of solitude. But now... Now she was grateful she didn't have to come out here alone. That she didn't have to do this alone. It was an odd shift compared to the past two years.

Maggie studied Jones in her peripheral vision. It was hard not to. He took up so much space, armored in Kevlar and banded muscle. The prickling sensation in her foot had spread, burning up her left calf. She'd been instructed to inform Dr. Piel of any changes, no matter how insignificant, but the promise of proving to Jones and every *American Military News* reader she wasn't crazy had hooked in deep. Besides, directing her thoughts on memorizing everything she could about the man next to her seemed to take the sting out. For now. "Thank you. For doing this. For believing me. Doesn't seem like your team agrees."

Jones stared out the windshield. No change in expression. Nothing she could read to give her an idea of what was going on behind that mask of his. He was evasive on a cellular level. Preferred to keep to himself, to work alone, but when it came right down it, he was the one who was here. Willing to fight beside her for the truth. "What makes you think that?"

"The fact that you're the only one from Socorro here with me." She tried not to cross her arms over her chest. Not only because it hurt like hell but to show that the realization didn't affect her. That she didn't actually need anyone but herself. That she was enough.

"Hey. Gotham's part of the team, too, you know," he said.

"Right." How could she forget the husky asleep in the back seat? "I take it the meeting with Ivy Bardot didn't go as you'd hoped."

"Satellite imagery doesn't show any activity in this region going back three weeks." Jones cut his gaze to hers, but the dim light coming from the SUV's dashboard wasn't strong enough to highlight the gray of his eyes. "I have clearance to follow up—"

"But if we don't find anything, you have to cut me loose." The implication of that statement hit harder than she expected. She couldn't go back to Albuquerque. Not as long as Toledano wanted those photos. And local police had already proved time and time again they didn't have the manpower to handle the cartel. *Sangre por Sangre* had infiltrated and corrupted departments over the years. There was no telling how far the infection had spread. And without evidence or jurisdiction, Albuquerque PD had no reason to investigate what'd happened or to protect her. Maggie pressed her back into the seat to gain some kind of control, but she couldn't seem to even level her own breathing. "That's...not possible. You tracked the last location of my phone. I was out there. I saw what Sosimo Toledano and his men did to those soldiers. I didn't make this up."

"I know." Two words and a whole hell of a lot of confidence. "Ivy is using her contacts to try to get a read on any operations the military might've been running out here, but so far, she's been stonewalled. Which makes me think there's more to it than we thought. Is there anyone you could stay with until the heat dies down? A friend, family member? A neighbor even?"

"No." She shook her head as though that would do any good to fight the ice seeping into her veins. The pride she'd held on to—that barrier she'd created between herself and everyone she'd loved—didn't seem as strong anymore. Not since the abduction. "I don't have anyone."

"Everyone has someone," Jones said. "What about your editor, maybe one of the other journalists?"

The suggestion almost made her laugh if it wasn't so sad. "I'm not sure if you understand how cutthroat my line of work is. We're all waiting for someone's life to fall apart so we can swoop in and claim what we think we're owed. To get ahead. We live for the scandals and discrimination lawsuits and sexual harassment charges. And my editor is at the top, fending off anyone gunning for his job. It's the only way to survive in this line of work. I wouldn't trust any of them with details of my life. Not unless I want to give them the upper hand."

"That doesn't sound like any way to live." Jones leaned back in his seat. Not relaxed or disengaged from the conversation. No. Something along the lines of pity.

She didn't need his pity. "You were in the military, and now you're an operator for a security company hired to deal with a drug cartel that kills dozens of people every day. You're constantly on the alert for a threat. I see the way you check the mirrors and how you've been sure to stay off the main roads. You're trying to protect yourself and Gotham. Isn't what I do the same thing?"

"Sure. When you look at it that way, but I still have my team. People who will have my back in an instant if I need them." His voice remained steady despite the earthquake shuddering through the vehicle as they crossed the desert. "What about your family? Do any of them even know you've been missing?"

"I'm not sure." She hadn't thought about her family in a while. Didn't even consider whether or not they'd be worried about her if the story of her disappearance broke, but nothing had been reported yet. No one knew she'd nearly died at the hands of the very cartel she'd been investigating. "After my divorce, my parents, my brother and sister, my friends—everyone cut ties with me. I'm pretty sure they've been brainwashed into thinking I'm dangerous."

"You were married." Jones's voice didn't sound so steady anymore.

"For nine years." Though it seemed like a whole other life now. "I don't really know what happened. The divorce has been finalized for two years, and I'm still trying to make sense of it."

"I take it he's the one who filed," he said. "You had no idea he wanted out?"

"No. We hadn't been having any problems that I was aware of. We were just…going about our lives. Meeting in the middle a couple times a week for dinner. Weekends were always busy with projects around the house, but we managed to spend a couple hours together watching TV at night or streaming a movie." It was those rare moments she'd missed the most. Having someone to talk to, to just be there to listen to her. "I guess a lot of times it felt like we were living our separate lives. Him with his work and me with mine. Then one day, I was getting ready to go into the office, and my husband—ex-husband—told me I needed to make a stop on the way over. At his attorney's office. He'd filed for divorce. Wanted me to pick up the papers and sign them. No questions asked."

Jones didn't have anything to say to that.

"I was blindsided. I didn't know what to do. I drove to my parents' house. I was a mess, but I didn't even have the guts to tell them what'd happened. I missed work. I was a no-call, no-show, and I didn't realize it until I checked my voice mails later that they fired me for it." Maggie set her head in her palm, her elbow leveraged against the window. Her body temperature spiked with a rush of anger, but she wouldn't let it take control. She was better than that now. "When I got home, my ex and I got in this huge fight because I didn't pick up the divorce papers. He tried to leave, and I went to stop him by jumping on his back."

The steering wheel protested under Jones's grip. "Did he hurt you?"

"Not in the way you think. About five days later, he called the police, claiming he believed his life was in danger. He had me arrested. I went to jail." She traced a long laceration across the back of her hand. Some injuries were so clear. Others kept festering without her notice. "After that, I got to see what kind of man he really was. He drained our bank accounts, called everyone in my contacts list and told them what'd happened, that I needed help, that he didn't feel safe with me. He turned them against me. Convinced them I would hurt them, too."

The vehicle slowed to a stop, and Jones shoved the SUV into Park. Headlights cut through a group of scrub brush and cacti ahead, but Maggie suddenly didn't have the inclination to leave this protective bubble they'd created over the past few minutes. "Want me to hunt him down and break something important?"

She couldn't stop the smile tugging at the corners of her mouth. That was exactly what she wanted. "As much as I want to see that, I think the only way to destroy a man like that is to show him I'm better off without him. Though I have to say, getting kidnapped and interrogated wasn't exactly what I had in mind."

"Then let's get you that story. Show the bastard what he gave up." Jones shouldered free from the vehicle and rounded the hood. Waiting for her. And in that instant, she had the distinct impression he'd never give up something so valuable as a partner. That he would do whatever it took to keep his relationships going.

Maggie tried to take a deep breath, but the idea of being that partner—of being the one he focused all that intensity on—slid through her without permission. She forced herself out of the SUV. The area looked familiar despite the bland landscape, and a chill threatened to hold her back.

"This is the last location your phone pinged," he said.

She moved as though a gravitational pull was tugging her closer. Then froze. Here. Lowering to her knees, she fanned one hand over the dry earth as Jones handed her a flashlight. Claw marks in the dirt. She could still feel the tension in her hands as she tried to fight back. She drove the beam down into a medium-sized crack, desperate to bury the memories. This was it. This was where she'd hidden the SD card. Maggie wedged her fingers into the small cavern. Only…she came up empty. Panic infused the muscles down her spine as she searched again. "There's nothing here."

CHUNKS OF CRACKED earth dissolved under his weight as Jones knelt beside her with another flashlight. "Let me take a look."

"I don't understand. It was here. I'm sure of it." Maggie didn't wait for his assessment and shoved herself to her feet. Spinning in circles, she lunged for another divide in the dirt and dropped to her knees. Dust rained down behind her as she practically clawed the ground to find the SD card. "It was here."

The desperation in her voice cut through him, and in that moment, Jones wanted nothing more than to produce the small device she'd claimed she'd hidden from *Sangre por Sangre* that night. He cast his flashlight across the ground, picking up two lines of drag marks. His gut clenched as his mind automatically imagined Maggie as the source. Footprints too. Not left behind by boots as he expected. More like dress shoes. But something else caught in the beam, reflecting back at him. Something that didn't belong out here.

"I didn't make it up." Maggie's voice turned distant. Uneven. "I didn't make it up."

Every cell in his body focused on the glassy surface caught at the base of a weed a few feet away. Jones knelt and reached through the spiny, dead branches to retrieve whatever it was. The broken edge bit into his thumb as he dragged it free. A circular piece of glass.

Not just any glass. Like the lens from a camera. Maggie's camera.

He pushed to his feet, offering her the shard. "No. You didn't."

Maggie stared at the clear lens before stretching a shaking hand to take it. As though simply touching it would ignite a frenzy of memories she didn't want to relive, and hell, Jones didn't blame her. "My camera broke on the rock when I fell, but the SD card isn't here. Toledano or one of his men must've already found it."

"If that's true, I'd be seeing a lot more activity around here." Jones scanned the ground for something—anything—that would tip off the cartel's presence. But whoever'd recovered that card had clearly gone to lengths to clean up after themselves. He wasn't seeing any treads left by vehicles or a flurry of movement on the ground. His beam caught the footprints he'd clocked a minute ago. It'd always been easy to spot the cartel's movements around any given scene. Poorly trained soldiers moved in packs, and *Sangre por Sangre* didn't bother with trying to cover up their crimes. They displayed them as a warning to anyone brave enough to take a stand. So who the hell would come out into the middle of the desert in dress shoes?

Jones headed back to the SUV and pulled a shovel from the cargo area, leaving the hatch open for Gotham. He couldn't go back to Socorro empty-handed. Not with Maggie's life still in danger. "You said you watched Sosimo Toledano and his men bury the bodies of the American soldiers. If that's true, Gotham will find them."

The husky shot ahead into the dark.

Jones fell into line behind her as she cut through a grouping of dried, spindly bushes. Even in the limited light from the SUV's headlights and their flashlights, he noted the tightness along her neck and shoulders. All she'd wanted was a new life, one that she'd built on her own. Away from the man who'd taken her trust and ground it into dust with a trumped-up call for her arrest. A burn Jones had only experienced after the news his brother had been captured and the knowledge he'd lost the support of his government raged through him. There had to be something more out here. Something that would convince Ivy and the rest of the team Maggie was worth more than a cover-up they couldn't prove. Because she deserved it. Because she needed it. And Jones wanted to be a part of that. He wanted to make sure she got everything that would help her move on. To be her support when nobody else wanted to come near her.

She slowed to a stop just before what looked like a ridgeline that angled down into a bowl of dirt and weeds. Swiping her hair behind her ear, she stared down into a collection of dried, dead bushes. "This is where I hid."

He maneuvered to get a better look at the scuff marks in the loose dirt. Without rain, there were impressions. Perhaps where she'd planted her elbows for stability. A few branches of bush had broken clean off. Jones gauged the distance between here and the location where he'd recovered the broken lens. Nearly fifty yards. She'd never had a chance once the cartel had spotted her. "And the bodies?"

"There." She pointed down into the bottom of the undersized dust bowl.

A tinkling of Gotham's collar reached his ears. Jones took that first step, his ankle engaging to keep him from tumbling straight to the bottom. If they were going to find answers as to what happened the night of her abduction, he'd have to dig. But the thought of forcing Maggie to confront the faces of the men and women massacred right in front of her pulled him up short. "You don't have to do this. You can go back to the SUV."

Her gaze locked on a point past his arm. She notched her chin higher and washed the emotion from her face, every ounce the driven, competitive war correspondent he imagined she'd had to become. Only that wasn't all she was. He'd witnessed moments where that mask had cracked and let the woman beneath bleed through. Where she didn't put her feelings in a box and pretended they hadn't existed at all. Where she'd let him see the warmth that might've thrived before her world had come apart. Mere slices of time but ones that had stayed with him since he recovered her. "I'm a journalist. This is part of the job."

Right. Jones offered her his free hand to help her down the incline. They moved as one toward the bottom, and the pressure behind his sternum intensified with every step. His gut knotted in warning as he scanned the rim of the bowl. It was impossible to see any kind of oncoming threat from down here, but his instincts said the proof they needed wouldn't wait for them to come back in daylight. Unrooted weeds—

dug up and discarded every few feet—caught on his bootlaces. Someone had been out here. The floor of the bowl was churned with loose dirt. Jones kept to the perimeter and swept the flashlight over the dried-up soil. A pair of bright eyes shined back in the beam. Gotham barked loudly enough to alert anyone within a mile radius. Jones handed off his flashlight. "He's got something."

Stabbing the tip of the shovel dead center, he was surprised by how easily the metal cut through the earth. Jones tossed shovelfuls of dirt over his shoulder as Maggie took up position in his peripheral vision. This was it. All they needed was a single body to start a government-wide investigation. Maggie would get her story, and Jones could get rid of the sick feeling in his stomach every time he thought of Kincaide. He could fix this.

Only the deeper he dug, the more that hollow feeling spread. The wood of the shovel was slick with sweat from his hands. His knuckles threatened to break through the thin skin as his grip tightened. Harder and harder with every discarded weight of dirt.

Visibly agitated, Maggie fisted her hands at her side. "Anything?"

"Not yet." His lungs worked overtime to keep in rhythm with his attempts. Jones sidestepped the four-foot hole he'd dug and launched the tip of the shovel back into the ground in another location. Two times. Then a third. Lactic acid burned in his arms and down his sides as he struggled to catch his breath. "I'm not finding any bodies, Maggie."

"No… They have to be here." Her voice cracked on the last word as she tore the shovel from his grip. Maggie pressed her heel into the lip of the metal and kicked down, but her left leg wasn't strong enough to support her. She lost her balance and tipped sideways.

Jones launched to catch her before she fell, securing her against his chest. "They're not here."

"Yes, they are. Gotham said they are. We just have to dig deeper." She fought against his hold as he tried to pry the shovel from her grip, and he let her go. Stepping back, Maggie clung onto the shovel as though her life depended on it. And right then, it did. "They have to be here. Because if they aren't, then I have nothing. I'll be nothing, and I can't go back to being nothing, Jones."

She swiped at the tears escaping down her cheeks and speared the shovel back into the ground. Once. Twice. Each time, he read pain in her arms, in her legs, in her back. But she didn't stop. Not even when she'd dug her own spread of holes and came up empty. In her mind, she had to do this. To prove she could. To earn that feeling of control over her own life.

Blisters stung in an arc on his palms, but they wouldn't stop him from giving Maggie everything he couldn't give Kincaide. Jones closed the distance between them and set his hand on the end of the shovel. She tried to wrench away, but this time, he wouldn't let her. "I'll dig through the night if you need me to, Maggie."

The hardness in her expression collapsed the longer they stood there. Time didn't mean a damn thing right then, but this did. This connection they shared. This partnership.

"Thank you." She released her hold on the shovel and stepped back. Surrendering her personal mission to him. And he would take it. For as long as she needed. No matter how heavy it was. Because he could. Because she needed something to believe in again.

Jones ignored the flare of discomfort in his arms and hands as he worked in a grid pattern through every inch of dirt within the bowl. Minutes distorted into an hour. Into two. There was nothing out here. Gotham wouldn't have signaled unless he'd recovered a human scent, but whoever'd retrieved the SD card must've taken the bodies. And with them, everything Maggie needed to get her life back.

"Stop, Jones." Maggie stared at the mess they'd made from the edge of the dig site. Her strength had failed her sometime during the past few minutes, leaving her paler than before. "You were right. There's nothing out here. No matter how much I want there to be."

His heart threatened to beat straight out of his chest as he let the shovel fall to the earth. Truth was, he didn't know how to do this. Be a partner. Wasn't sure what he was supposed to say or do in moments of despair, but he'd try. For her. "Maggie, I—"

A red light registered from the rim of the bowl.

Jones launched himself between Maggie and the potential threat.

Just as a gunshot exploded through the night.

Chapter Seven

Maggie wasn't prepared for the crushing weight of Kevlar slamming into her.

Her lungs collapsed under the attack. Her heart rate rocketed into her throat. A crack of thunder distorted Jones's voice as he ripped her off the ground and shoved her up the incline. No. Not thunder. A gunshot. Someone had taken a shot at them. "They found me."

Jones was still yelling orders at her, but she couldn't hear through the high-pitched ringing in her ears. He seemed to use his body as a shield between her and the shooter as he pushed his hand into her lower back. Her leg threatened to collapse straight out from under her, but he somehow made up for the difference.

Maggie slapped her hand on flat ground as they reached the rim of the oversize crater and dug her fingernails in to get a good grip. Only she didn't have to drag herself over the lip. Jones was already pushing her upward.

"Run for the SUV, Maggie. Don't stop. Not even for me." His mouth was close to her ear, and a pool of dread liquefied at the base of her spine. His voice remained even as he unholstered his weapon and took aim at the invisible threat. "I'll cover you. Go!"

Two shots. Three. The gun kicked back in his hand, but the force didn't even seem to faze him. Not like the shotgun rocking against her shoulder the night of her escape. This was the soldier in action. Socorro's combat controller. The one she'd been too traumatized and injured to appreciate when he'd pulled her out of *Sangre por Sangre*'s hands. This was the man who'd risked treason and death to save his brother—and paid dearly for it.

"I'm not leaving you here!" Maggie scrambled to her feet. The SUV's headlights cut through the night, but they suddenly seemed much farther than she'd originally estimated. Pressure intensified in her ears as bits and pieces of the night she tried to run for her life took control. Fear snaked into her brain and spiked her senses. The numbness in her left leg pricked at the back of her knee and held her hostage. Dryness scratched along her throat. She couldn't move, couldn't breathe. In an instant, her body betrayed her.

"Maggie, you've got to go!" Jones latched onto the back of her scrub top and pushed her forward.

She wanted to. More than anything, but her body suddenly had lost the ability to obey her commands. Gravity sucked her feet against the earth, trying to drag her into the sandy depths. Holding her back. And she wanted to let it. She wanted to disappear and pretend that none of this was happening. That she could do something for the lives lost here that night. Her lungs hurt. She couldn't get enough air. No matter how many steps Jones forced her to take.

A red dot zipped ahead of her. Then steadied.

"Get down!" Strong hands dragged her off her feet. Jones tucked her into his side and rolled, and all she could do was hold on to him for dear life. They landed in a sticker bush that bit through her clothes and pulled at her hair, but it was nothing compared to the pain that would've come with a gunshot.

The stars overhead streaked into her vision as another bullet kicked up dirt after impact. Mere inches from her head. Her protector returned the assault, but even with her limited knowledge of weapons, she knew his ammunition was running out. What felt like minutes sped up into distorted seconds until she couldn't distinguish one moment to the next. It was all a jumble that threatened to shut her down for good. There was only one way out, as she'd taught herself in the days in Toledano's hands. One way to make the pain go away. Maggie tightened her fist around the shoulder of his vest, desperate for something real to hold on to as her mind went to that numb place and started to detach from her body. "I can't go back."

Putting himself between her and the gunman, Jones dragged her to face him. "I'm going to get you out of this, but I need you to do everything I say. Understand?"

Another red beam cut through the night and crept up the side of Jones's neck. The gunman had him in his sights. She'd done this. In an instant, she'd put them in a position to lose. And they were out of time.

"Stay with me, Maggie." His jolt shuddered through her, and the numbness she wanted so badly drained away. Jones's hold on her was too strong. Too real and impossible to ignore. "I need you to trust me."

Trust. She didn't trust anyone. Not even her own family and friends—people who'd known her all her life. Who'd let themselves be manipulated and gaslighted by a handsome liar who'd built her up to be some kind of unstable attention seeker. But Jones... Jones wasn't like that. No. This was the kind of man who defended others far more and with more determination than himself. Who would give up anything for his team. And her. Even his own life. He'd already proven that, hadn't he? Her fingers rushed with blood as she released her grip on his vest. "I trust you."

"Then take Gotham and run. Now," he said.

The crack of another bullet screamed through the night.

Gotham raced ahead of her.

Maggie launched forward as a patch of dirt exploded at her feet. Right where Jones should've been. She couldn't look back. Couldn't assure herself he hadn't gotten caught in the cross fire. She pumped her legs as hard as she could take, and a cramp knotted at the back of her thigh. She made out the SUV's frame through the headlights ahead. Maybe fifty feet. She was going to make it. Her left toes caught on a protruding rock, but she wouldn't let it trip her up. She had to keep going. No matter what. Because as much as she trusted Jones to protect her, he trusted her to follow through with his commands. To get help.

She'd spent so long trying to prove she was worth something—to someone, anyone—that she'd forgotten what that felt like. To be valued. Feeling flooded into her legs and reinforced the last of her strength as she closed in on the SUV. Her hand slammed onto the hood as she ripped the driver's side door wide open.

Gotham launched into the back seat. His short claws scratched against the glass as she secured the hatch. He tried to get free of the vehicle when he realized Jones hadn't followed, but there was no way she was going to send him back out there.

"He's going to be okay." She had to believe that. Maggie hit the push-to-start, locking her and the husky inside. The engine vibrated at her feet, and she didn't waste any time launching the SUV into Drive. Momentum hauled her into the back of the seat as she flipped the vehicle back the way they'd come. "We're going to get help. Okay? We're coming back for him."

A second set of headlights cut through the night and beamed through the passenger's side window. No. Too strong to be manufacturer headlights. They had to be spotlights. Blinded by the onslaught, Maggie raised one hand to shield her vision. She couldn't make out the vehicle, but her gut said if she took her foot off the accelerator, she'd end up right back in that dank hole Sosimo Toledano had put her in. Maneuvering away from the source, she floored the pedal.

Another set of lights brightened ahead.

She turned the wheel so fast to avoid the collision, Gotham slid across the back seat with a stressed yip. Maggie shook her head as though that would somehow free her of the fear clogging her throat. Just as a third vehicle lit up its spotlights. She slammed on the brakes, and the SUV slid a dozen feet across the water-starved ground.

Surrounded.

It was an ambush. Toledano and his men had been waiting for her to come back for the SD card. Just as Jones had warned. There were too many of them to outrun on her own. Damn it. The photos, the bodies, her eyewitness account—anything that would prove the atrocities *Sangre por Sangre* had committed—would be extinguished if she didn't find some way out of this. Tremors shook through her hands as she slid her palms against the steering wheel. She was out of options, her best one being facing off with a shooter at least a hundred yards behind them.

Silhouettes of men filtered out of the vehicles, with one taking the lead. Her heart kicked in her chest as she automatically filled in the dark hole where a face should've been with Toledano's features. Other things came into focus then, too. The outline of guns registered through the spotlights. This SUV's windows were bulletproof. She'd already tested their strength, but that'd been with one weapon. Not an entire army ready to tear apart anything that got in their way.

The head figure started walking toward her.

The same survival instinct that'd gotten her onto her feet after Jones and Gotham had rescued her from the cartel slid in to take control. That blind fear threatened to steal logic as Maggie twisted around in her seat. The curve of the man-made cemetery took shape out the back window. One second. Two. No movement. Nothing to suggest Jones was alive, that he'd taken out the gunman or that he was on his way to her right now.

She'd left him to fight this battle alone. Like the coward she'd become during the divorce. Never wanting to have to sacrifice anything more than she had to. Waiting for someone to come and intervene, for a hero to knock down the door and fix the problem. That hope had died when her mom had stopped returning her calls, when the invites for nights out with girlfriends got fewer and farther between and coworkers avoided interacting with her in the office. When she'd somehow survived another day of interrogation. Jones had been that for her. Her knight in shining Kevlar armor.

But no one was coming this time. Her breath eased out of her chest as Maggie rammed the gearshift into Reverse. She didn't know what would happen, but she couldn't let Jones fight this battle himself. Not when she was the reason it'd started in the first place. "Hang on to something, Gotham. I think it's about to get really bumpy."

She slammed her foot onto the pedal.

HE WAS PINNED DOWN.

Jones assessed the amount of ammunition left in his weapon. Not enough. The boulder at his back worked as cover for now, but any move on his part and that sniper would finish him off. He studied the blacked-out terrain spreading out in front of him. Maggie had gotten to the SUV. He could just make out the headlights swinging around.

Then another set.

And a third.

His pulse thudded harder as he took in the vehicles closing in around her. Oh, hell.

A bullet ricocheted off the rock mere inches to his left. Dust flicked up into his eyes, and Jones automatically raised his arm to protect his face. The sniper had the advantage here. Hold Jones hostage while the rest of the cartel got what they'd come for. Maggie. What he wouldn't give to get his hands on a rifle of his own.

The SUV skidded to a halt. Surrounded.

He wouldn't make it in time. *Sangre por Sangre* was going to take her.

And there was nothing Jones could do about it.

A section of the boulder jutted into his spine, and he pressed into the shard deeper to keep him in the moment. To stop the onslaught of failure from creeping in. He wasn't overseas. He didn't have to do this alone. And Maggie was going to make it through this. No matter what it took.

Jones tried to gauge the sniper's location without putting his head in the cross hairs. A bullet ripped through the ledge of rock and broke a chunk away. He would lose his cover in a matter of minutes.

Except the SUV was coming right at him. Backward. And it wasn't slowing down. Confusion barely had the chance to take hold before Jones was forced to evacuate his hiding spot. The vehicle slammed into the boulder standing between him and a sniper's bullet. The cargo tailgate snapped free. "Get in!"

He didn't have time to question Maggie's tactics as two more heavy rounds cut through the SUV's side panel. The back driver's side tire deflated beneath the vehicle's weight. Jones shoved to his feet and launched himself into the cargo area. He managed to grab onto one of the back seats as Maggie floored the accelerator. Gotham centered his head between the seats to get a look at Jones in the back. Throwing back the removable floor, he catalogued the weapons every Socorro operator was required to carry and pulled his rifle free. "What the hell are you doing? I told you to get out of here."

The back window caught a single bullet. Aimed directly at Jones's head.

"I tried!" Maggie wrenched the wheel to the left to avoid a head-on collision with another vehicle coming at them too fast. The SUV fishtailed and grazed along the truck's fender. Two more sets of headlights were headed straight for them as the third kept on their tail. "I'm not sure if you know this, but I'm not a very good driver. They took away my license. I didn't have any other choice."

"You don't have a valid driver's license?" Jones loaded a round into his rifle.

The truck on their tail surged forward. Metal screeched against metal as the two vehicles locked in a spar for control, but the windows held.

"Is that what you really want to be focusing on right now?" Maggie jerked the wheel into the other vehicle, to keep them from flipping. The truck was trying to guide them straight into the two up ahead.

Gotham slid across the back seat with a yip, his oversize paws attempting to grab on to anything solid. He fell behind the driver's seat but popped his head up a moment later. Probably loving the ride.

"I'm just saying that information would've been good to know before I got in." Jones braced his shoulders against the back seats and kicked at the compromised back window. The sniper bullet fell free before the window dislodged in one piece. Air rushed into the SUV as he wedged the butt of the rifle against his shoulder and took aim. Then pulled the trigger.

The bullet found its mark, taking out the back tire of the truck. The tail end swerved to one side, then caught against something on the desert floor. Shouts cut through the grind of engines as the driver of the truck failed to keep all four wheels on the ground. The truck flipped, landing with a gut-wrenching crunch. Jones unpocketed another round and loaded it into the rifle. "Anything else you think I need to know while we're trying to stay alive?"

"I'm allergic to dairy. Is that helpful?" She whipped her head around, then grabbed for Gotham with one hand, guiding the husky into the front seat.

"Only if the cartel tries to torture you with cheese." He leveraged the barrel of the rifle against the window frame and set his eye against the scope. "Slam on the brakes on my signal and turn right as hard as you can. Let off the accelerator at the curve, then get us up to speed when we've straightened out. The wheel will want to follow, but I need you to keep us steady. Understand?"

Maggie held strong, and he couldn't do anything but admire her sense of humor in a situation like this.

She wasn't trained for evasive driving, let alone combat, but she was meeting him in the field regardless. Most civilians would've given up by now. But she was a fighter. "Did you miss the part where I said I'm not a good driver?"

"You're doing just fine. Remember what I asked. I need you to trust me. This will even the odds." Jones settled into that familiar space. The one created over years of missions and violence and death. He'd relied on it so many times to get him through whatever lay ahead. Only this time felt different. It felt more personal than ever before. The rocky landscape threatened to loosen his grip on the rifle, but he wasn't going to let Maggie get captured again. He wasn't going to be too late this time. He was going to get her out of this mess. "Now!"

She hit the brakes. Momentum tried to rip him free of his position as Maggie wrenched the steering wheel to the right, and the SUV swung around, putting one of the approaching vehicles dead in his sights. The engine vibrated through the entire frame as the SUV launched forward.

Jones found his mark.

And compressed the trigger.

The bullet embedded in the front fender of the truck but didn't have any overall effect. He backed away from the scope. Damn it. He'd hit the target. It should've put the engine out of commission. Unless… "That truck's armored."

"What?" The question left Maggie's mouth a split second before the impact.

Time seemed to speed up and slow down all at once.

Maggie's head rammed toward the steering wheel just as the airbag engulfed her. Glass and metal protested from the passenger side where Gotham had been sitting a moment before. The world barrel-rolled once. Twice. Three times. Gravity lost its hold on his body, and Jones was flung between the two back seats. Upholstery failed to cushion each blow as the SUV battled against the earth's physics. He tried reaching for the front seat, but blood clouded his vision. He couldn't see her. Couldn't touch her.

In an instant, Maggie was gone.

The ground rushed up to meet the driver's side of the SUV. The back seats pinned him in place, his feet grazing against the shattered side window and collection of artillery that'd come loose in the collision. Dust drove into his lungs as the vehicle came to a rest. Hell, his head hurt. He couldn't think, couldn't take a full breath. "Maggie, can you hear me?"

No answer.

The silence pressed in from every angle and shot his nerves into overdrive. He should've picked a bigger gun to get through the truck's armor. Now Maggie was in danger. Because of him. Because he hadn't been enough to protect her. Just as he hadn't been enough to get to Kincaide before it'd been too late. That echo of grief and loss cut through him. His eyes burned. He'd given Maggie his word he wouldn't let *Sangre por Sangre* get their hands on her again. How much was his word worth now?

"Gotham?" He couldn't hear the husky through the ringing in his ears. Jones reached toward the front center console, trying to claw free of the grip the back seats had on his middle. Pain radiated through his insides, but it wasn't enough to stop him from getting to his partner. Either of them. "You both better be alive."

A low rumble of an engine vibrated through what was left of the SUV's frame. Crushing realization hit him harder than the initial impact. The cartel was going to take Maggie. They were going to kill her. Because they no longer had reason to keep her alive. The SD card she'd buried had been recovered, the bodies they'd tried to hide removed from the site. He was going to lose her.

"Jones…" A section of blond hair fell from around the driver's seat headrest. A shaking, bloodied hand pawed at the airbag, and white powder kicked up in a fresh beam of headlights. She was alive. Against all the odds, she'd survived the accident, and something he didn't realize had been squeezing the life out of him released.

"I'm here, Maggie. I'm coming for you. Just hang on. Okay?" he said.

Voices registered from outside the vehicle. A burst of footfalls rocketed Jones's instincts higher. Three, maybe four sources. Moving fast and coming right for them. They had mere seconds. He latched onto the two front seats and hauled the rest of his body free of the back. Black-and-white fur demanded his attention from under the passenger airbag on the floorboards. Gotham. Jones brought his oversize frame into the front and scooped the dog into his chest. Gotham's pulse kicked against his palm. Alive.

Rock and glass peppered Maggie's scrubs, but the only blood seemed to be coming from a laceration down her arm. Jones swept her hair out of her face to get a better view with his free hand. "Stay with me. I'm going to get you out of here."

"It's too late." She lifted her injured arm and pointed out the windshield. Silhouettes paired off, growing bigger as they approached. "They're already coming."

The driver's side window exploded.

Chapter Eight

Her shoulders were pulled tight.

They protested as though they were about to disconnect from their sockets. She was moving. Though Maggie didn't understand how that was possible. The crash. The airbag. Gotham diving for the floorboards. Jones. Fractures of memory jumbled until she wasn't sure of the order, but they were all there.

Her bare heels dragged against the ground. She tried lifting her head to gauge where she was, but something scratchy and tight dulled her vision. Her exhales collected just in front of her mouth and nose. A bag. Toledano had used a bag. He'd enjoyed keeping her guessing as to where the next strike would come from.

Maggie dug her fingernails into her palms and pulled at her hands, trying to gain some semblance of control. "No. No, please. Don't take me back."

Whoever had a hold of her hands didn't slow, didn't stop. Didn't even seem to hear her. Or care. Her jaw and cheekbones ached with every word, but she wasn't going to go back into that hellhole without a fight. Not again. Rocks cut through the thin scrub top, scratching along her skin. She dropped her head back between her arms as a sob built in her chest. "I don't have what you want. I'm telling the truth. Please."

"Quiet." The voice grated against her nerves. Too rough. No accent. Not one of the soldiers who'd questioned and tortured her before. There were outsiders within the organization she'd learned about over the past year of investigating. Contractors hired to carry out a variety of jobs. Executions, frame jobs, undercover work within other cartels or within police departments. At least, according to the rumors. She hadn't been able to make heads or tails of any of it. Not without exposing herself. *Sangre por Sangre*'s management was careful. Neither local law enforcement nor the feds had any luck either. And now, she was going to be one of those cases that got lost in some file room. Just waiting for someone to come along and make the connection.

Fear pricked at the back of her neck as the man dragging her suddenly let go. Blistering heat singed her arm hairs, and Maggie tried to roll away from the soft glow through the fabric of the bag over her head. In vain. Strong hands wrenched her to her feet and pinned her against a wall of muscle twice her size. The bag was torn from her head, taking a few strands of hair with it. She winced against the brightness of the roaring fire.

"Maggie Caddel. I've been looking for you." Masculine features darkened from the onslaught of the flames as a man approached. The bonfire was on the verge of reaching at least fifteen feet in the air, but not one fueled by wood alone. No. A distinctive sour odor lodged at the back of her throat as she took in the masked faces of the men and women circling the fire. Six. All heavily armed. None of them Jones. "I've got to say, you've given me and my unit a lot of grief lately."

Unit? *Sangre por Sangre* didn't work in units.

"Am I supposed to take that as a compliment?" Her voice broke on the last word, giving away the terror and confusion clawing through her. She'd survived interrogations, starvation, dehydration and physical torture from a cartel lieutenant, not to mention a night in jail on a faulty assault charge, yet there was still a part of her that hated her weakness showing through under intimidation. Maggie jerked against the hands holding her in place, but it was no use. Every single one of these soldiers was so much…bigger than she was. Stronger. Faster. She didn't have a chance against any of them. A bone-deep ache resonated through her shoulders at the pressure. "The man who was with me. Where is he?"

"He ain't coming for you, sweetheart." A hint of a Southern drawl filtered into the man's voice as he crossed his arms over a vest similar to Jones's. Though, not the same in color. Other distinctive features bled into focus as he stepped into her personal space. The watch on his left wrist. It wasn't one of those complicated gadgets that read data and synced with other devices. Simply an analog with a brown leather strap that'd seen a thousand lifetimes. Inherited, if she had to guess. Important. "Turns out, your new friend is former military. Emphasis on the former. Something about disobeying direct orders and crossing into enemy territory. Lieutenant Driscoll almost started a war with his little stunt to pull those soldiers out of that cave. Me and my guys? We don't cross the line. We know that compromising an assignment gets people killed."

"Jones. His name is Jones." The haze fogging her brain after the accident was cracking. Maggie tried to step free of her captor, but that only made him dig his fingers deeper into her arms. "But you called him lieutenant. Like you think you're supposed to. You're... you're military. All of you."

Hope lit up behind her sternum at the thought of the army responding to the ambush that led to her abduction by a drug cartel. Then faded. "Wait. You said you and your unit don't disobey orders. What part of your orders were to shoot at and endanger two US citizens tonight?"

"You really don't know when to stop asking questions, do you, Maggie?" The dark ski mask failed to hide a thin five-o'clock shadow around the soldier's mouth. "You think uncovering the truth will make everything better, but I can tell you from experience, that's almost never the case."

The use of her name—so intimate, as though they were old friends—hit her nerves wrong. Nothing compared to when Jones said her name. Her stomach threatened to revolt. Her skull bounced against her captor's chest in rhythm to his heart rate. Which had just jumped a few beats. Pressure tightened in her gut at the change. Something was wrong. These men and women—military or not—weren't who she wanted them to be. "I don't understand."

"Then let me put it in terms you will understand." He got close enough she could smell a hint of deodorant as he threaded her hair out of her face. But not from under his arms. From his palms. To control any sweat that might leave his DNA behind. "That night you followed one of our units into the desert and took photos of an off-the-books operation, you became a liability. The people of this country rely on us being able to do our jobs, Maggie. That comes with a certain confidentiality we have to maintain. We can't have you risking their lives with your lies or recruiting others into your fantasy of what you think you saw that night. One life compared to thousands? It's not a hard choice."

The finality of that statement cut through her. Sharp and fast. Fantasy? No. She wrenched one arm free from the man at her back and lunged. Only to be brought back to heel. "Confidentiality. You mean cover-up, don't you? I didn't follow one of your units out there that night. I was investigating *Sangre por Sangre*. I know what I saw. I know the cartel ambushed and murdered ten American soldiers that night. I have proof. What I don't know is why you're okay with that. Why any of you are okay with that."

Jones had risked his life and his entire career for the soldiers who'd been captured behind enemy lines. But these men and women… They weren't the same. They weren't fighting for their country. They were fighting for themselves.

"Is this the proof you're talking about?" He unpocketed something from his cargo pants and held up an SD card. A perfect match in brand and size to the one she'd buried in the ground the night of her abduction. Then tossed it in the fire. "What proof?"

"No!" Maggie ripped free of her captor and went after the card. Heat painfully flared up her neck and burned across her face. It landed at the perimeter of the fire, its edges sizzling and smoking instantly. She collapsed to her knees—adding insult to injury in her left leg—and grabbed for a stick that hadn't caught fire. She tried to drag the card out, but within seconds, the blue plastic had melted in on itself, taking her future with it. Her throat burned. She turned on the leader. Struggling to her feet, she shoved his chest. Not even throwing him off balance. "Why would you do that? Those soldiers deserve justice. They deserve peace."

Anger she'd felt only once in her life exploded through her. Maggie shoved him again.

He caught her wrists in both hands. "Peace comes at a price, Maggie. A price me and my unit and every other enlisted soldier are willing to pay. Those men and women you claim you saw die that night? They knew that. They knew what they were getting into when they joined up, and they died heroes. You don't get to take that away from them or their families."

He returned her shove.

Maggie fell back. The impact jarred old injuries and aggravated new ones. The circle of soldiers seemed to close in, cutting off her escape. None of this made sense. "So what now?"

"I told you. We never break orders," he said.

Movement registered from behind the man standing over her. Flames highlighted two more men hauling something heavy between them. A body. Dressed in uniform. Maggie could do nothing but watch as they swung the load—back and forth—before releasing it into the flames. Sparks flew overhead and cooled against the black night sky. That smell, the one she'd noted a few minutes ago... It hadn't been accelerant as she'd believed.

It'd been human remains.

First, the SD card. Then the bodies *Sangre por Sangre* had buried in the pit that night. These soldiers—whoever the hell they were—were getting rid of evidence of the ambush. Only none of this made sense. Why would the US military clean up after a cartel slaughter? What good came of sacrificing ten American lives and letting an organization like this get away with it?

"It's done," a familiar voice said. Accented. Deep. It triggered a nuclear response in her nervous system and seized any thoughts of escape.

Her throat threatened to close in on itself as Maggie forced her attention to the newcomer maneuvering into the circle of light cast off by the bonfire. El Capitan wiped his hands on a stained bandanna as she'd watched him do so many times before, and her blood ran cold.

The masked soldier took a final step toward her and crouched, leveling that dark gaze with hers. "Good. Then that just leaves the last piece of the puzzle."

BROKEN GLASS CUT into the blisters in his palms as Jones pressed upright.

His head hit the dashboard and ignited the pain ripping through his skull. He wasn't supposed to be here. Maggie. He had to get to Maggie. The team that'd flipped the SUV had moved fast and gone straight for her. He hadn't even gotten the chance to fight back before one of them clocked him over the head from behind. Organized. Trained. Almost militaristic in strategy. *Sangre por Sangre* didn't move like that. Not in the dozen encounters Jones had survived. No. This... This was something else. Someone else.

Twisted metal and darkness stretched out in front of him. The windshield had somehow survived the accident, but the driver's side window was gone. Dry midnight air carried a hint of something unrecognizable into the cabin of the SUV. Hell. How long had he been unconscious?

A soft whimper drilled through the haze dimming his senses and spiked his blood pressure. "Gotham? Is that you, buddy?"

It came again, but he couldn't get eyes on the source with the passenger side airbag in the way. Pulling the blade from his ankle holster, Jones deflated the airbag in a rush of white powder and stale air. The dog's outline took shape along the floorboards. He tossed the blade onto the front seat and reached for his partner. Matted fur caught between his fingers as Jones carefully pulled Gotham into his arms. "It's okay. I've got you."

The husky tucked his dry nose into Jones's neck and licked the skin there. Jones checked him for injuries but found no blood or broken bones. The K9 had taken a beating though.

"Let's get you back to HQ." Compressing the emergency call button on Gotham's collar, Jones tucked his undersized sidekick beneath one arm. He reached for the driver's side door with his free hand, but his strength gave out. He dropped his shoulder first against the steering wheel. Pain ricocheted down his arm and into his chest. "That's going to leave a mark."

Time pressurized the air in his lungs. He wasn't sure how long ago the team that'd ambushed them had taken Maggie. Didn't know if she was injured. If she was alive. One thing was for certain: he wasn't going to leave her to fight this battle alone. He wasn't going to fail her as he'd failed Kincaide. His own life be damned.

Jones kicked at the driver's side door. Corrupted hinges protested as the door snapped back. He and the dog fell through the opening as one as he twisted to avoid landing on Gotham. The dog's paws braced against his chest as Jones surveyed what might be broken throughout his body. "I don't suppose you're carrying some ibuprofen."

Gotham cocked his head to one side.

"I'll take that as a no." He hauled the K9 off of him and forced himself to his knees. "All right. Help is on the way. You're going to stay here while I try to hunt down the bastards that took Maggie."

The husky's whine speared through Jones's resolve. Gotham didn't like being alone.

"I know." Jones stretched back inside the busted frame of the SUV and pulled his sidearm from the wreck. Dropping the magazine free, he counted the rounds left after dueling with a sniper back at the pit. Two. He was going to need more than that to take on a small army. "But you were damn lucky you didn't get hurt in the accident. I can't risk worrying about you while I'm trying to pull her out of…wherever she is."

Gotham didn't give an answer this time. Simply ducked his head and pressed his forehead to Jones's shin.

"You're not going to take no for an answer, are you?" Just as well. Leaving Gotham here ensured Socorro operatives would discover the K9 and the wreck through his emergency signal, but they wouldn't even know where to start to find Jones or Maggie by the time they arrived on the scene. "Fine. Come on."

The husky followed as instructed.

Jones rounded to the back of the SUV and collected all the ammunition and weaponry he could sustainably carry. He extracted his discarded flashlight and tested the power. Worked. Casting the beam over the desert floor, he picked up on four sets of footprints. One direction leading straight to the SUV. The other heading back where they'd originated. Boots. Heavy tread. He followed the line, realizing the number of prints didn't change, but the depth of one set got deeper. One of them had carried Maggie out. Which meant she'd either been bound or unconscious. Either way, she'd never had a chance to fight back. "Keep a nose out, dog."

The flashlight picked up two lines of ruts. Vehicle treads. Though there wasn't any sign they were within a mile of his location. The team that'd taken Maggie could be anywhere by now, but that wasn't going to stop him from getting to her.

Jones jogged to follow the treads, Gotham bouncing

in rhythm with every step. He wasn't sure how much time had passed or when his knee had started screaming for rest. Twenty minutes. Maybe thirty. But the warm glow up ahead told him he was headed in the right direction. The fire lit up a natural arch and unique rock formations, providing protection for the group camping at the base. The reddish color and eroded towering rocks took the formations straight out of some science fiction book set on Mars, but would allow Jones to approach from behind. As long as he kept his distance.

He slowed as a hint of something sour collected at the back of his throat. The odor threw him back to a mission set during his last official tour overseas. Where an entire village had been burned to the ground mere minutes before his unit arrived to help. That smell had stayed with him all this time. Not fueled by wood alone. But by human bones. "Maggie."

He couldn't see her from this distance. Jones circled the rock formations, cutting off his access to the group and hiking his nerves into overdrive. He didn't like not knowing what he was getting himself into, but his need to get Maggie out dominated his doubts. She was there. She had to be. Because if she wasn't... If she was already gone... No. He couldn't think about that. Jones hiked the incline leading to the arch—honed over hundreds of years—and slipped his hand through the middle to keep his leverage. Grains of coarse dirt dislodged in his hold, threatening his balance. But he gained a perfect view of the camp and the masked men and women circling the fire.

And of Maggie.

"Please, let me do the honors." Sosimo Toledano closed the distance between him and Maggie, setting all of Jones's defenses on high alert. He was outnumbered. Outgunned. Any move on his part could put her at risk, but doing nothing guaranteed it. "After all, Ms. Caddel and I are friends."

"Friends don't torture each other for photos." She shoved her hands into the ground to back away, but another of the gunmen ensured she couldn't escape. The man she knew as El Capitan reached for her arm. Maggie landed a solid kick to his shin, but it was no use. He latched onto her, hauling her into his chest. "No!"

Her scream bounced off the rock formations and etched deep into Jones's brain.

Jones unholstered his weapon and slid down the front of the arch on one hip to avoid colliding with Gotham. Then took aim. "Didn't your mama teach you no means no, Sosimo?"

Seven soldiers reached for their weapons. Jones only had attention for one.

He pulled the trigger. The bullet ripped through Sosimo Toledano's side and catapulted him away from Maggie. The man's screams cut through the night as the fire caught on the lieutenant's clothing. She covered her ears with both hands and ducked as Jones launched for her. He fisted one hand into her scrub top and swung her behind one of the smaller formations as cover.

The human torch formerly known as Sosimo Toledano ran straight for a handful of soldiers, but they had no compassion to help.

"You're making a mistake, Driscoll." One of the

masked soldiers took center stage, his unit at his back. Ah, this was the man in charge. Seemed Toledano had merely been serving a purpose, but with the cartel lieutenant running for his life, that left room for the real monster to show his face. American military, Jones guessed. At least, based off their formation and tactics. But did that make them former or current? He didn't know. "There's no way out. Maggie's gotten herself in too deep. There's no scenario that we let you walk away from here with her alive."

His heart pounded hard behind his ears as Jones calculated their chances. Okay. The guy behind the mask had a point, but if Jones had let himself accept defeat against the odds, his brother would've died in that cave and not with the people who'd loved him.

Taking a defensive stance, Gotham growled at the men putting Jones in their crosshairs with a flash of fangs.

A rolling laugh reverberated through the small circle of armed soldiers.

It was the distraction he needed.

Jones backed up, using his body as a shield for Maggie. "Then you haven't considered all of the scenarios."

One squeeze of the trigger. Then another. Each bullet found its mark, knocking two gunmen out of the lineup. The rest dove for cover and started to return fire. A round missed Jones's ear by mere millimeters as he took another step back. He whistled low to call Gotham then turned to Maggie. "One of their trucks is parked about a hundred yards west. Keys are in the ignition. We can make it if we run now."

Maggie's hand found his arm. A bolt of heat that had nothing to do with the growing bonfire burned through him, spurring adrenaline through his veins. "Just say when."

Jones took down another of the gunmen. "When."

They moved as one. Him as the shield, her navigating over the terrain. Four hostiles left their cover to follow, but he had one last trick up his sleeve to make sure that didn't happen. Jones pulled a flash grenade from his cargo pants. He detached the tab and tossed it straight into the bonfire. "Go, go, go!"

Maggie ran straight into the darkness with Gotham close on her heels.

The device exploded in a burst of light. The resulting blast wave knocked the last gunmen off their feet and sent bolts of fire in every direction. A guttural scream bounced off the rock formations, which threatened to tip at any second, but Jones wasn't going to wait to watch the aftermath.

"This isn't over, Driscoll!" The warning broke through the pop of flames. "We'll never stop coming for her. You can run, but you can't hide!"

Chapter Nine

A hiss ignited the sensitivity in her teeth as Socorro's physician added another stitch in Maggie's forearm. Could've been worse. She could've ended up burned at the stake with the rest of the bodies. Would have if Jones hadn't showed up.

"About three more. Keep breathing." Dr. Piel—a woman Maggie judged to be around late thirties, maybe early forties—worked quickly as blood seeped from the four-inch gash. "I'm sorry the topical anesthetic isn't doing anything for you."

"I'd rather feel it." Because it meant she was still alive. That Toledano hadn't gotten his way. Though she could use a few more days before her next abduction. *You can run, but you can't hide.* The masked soldier, the one who seemed to outrank *Sangre por Sangre*'s own beloved heir, was on a mission. He and his unit never broke orders. Never gave up. He'd destroyed the SD card, burned the bodies of the American soldiers she'd witnessed slaughtered. They were ready to kill her and cover up the whole operation. And for what?

Orders. The word seemed to bury deep in her brain, waiting there between every thought. Soldiers like

that—like Jones and the rest of Socorro's operatives—
went to extreme lengths to complete their assignments.
But soldiers thrived in the field. They liked getting their
hands dirty. They weren't resigned to shuffle paperwork
from behind a desk. The plan had to be handed down.
But from whom? *Sangre por Sangre*? Or someone else?

Pain kicked her back into a bright white room so out
of place in Socorro's headquarters. The lights were getting to her. The aches were getting to her. The lack of
sleep and food and pure confusion were getting to her.
Adrenaline only carried a person so far, and Maggie
had run out of that a long time ago.

"All done." Dr. Piel tossed the curved needle and
surgical thread into a stainless steel bowl on the move-
able cart beside her. The physician seemed meticulous,
moving with confidence and efficiency. It was easy
to imagine how she spent her nights when she wasn't
on call here. Most likely with her nose in a nonfiction
book and a glass of wine in one hand. Surrounded by
expensive upholstery, good art and an entire library at
her disposal. Definitely not the kind of woman Maggie
would've been friends with in her past life, or even the
type who scrolled through Pinterest. "I'm going to wrap
a bandage around this to keep you from snagging the
stitches on anything. Try to keep it from getting wet
and let me know if the pain gets worse. I cleaned it out
the best I could, but there's still a chance of infection."

"Thank you." Maggie stared down at the angry red
pricks along her opposite arm where glass, rocks and
embers from the fire had made their marks. It was noth-

ing compared to the welts and internal damage several days of interrogation had left behind.

"How's the back?" Dr. Piel disposed of her latex gloves in a hazardous materials bin on the other side of the medical suite before she collected her tablet from the counter. "Any changes I should be made aware of?"

Maggie scrunched her toes around the dust that collected inside her shoe from her left leg dragging behind her as she, Gotham and Jones had made a run for the truck mere hours ago. The numbness had spread from her toes, into her ankle, up her calf and now around her knee. She didn't know what that meant. Didn't know how long she had before she lost use of the leg entirely, but it didn't really matter. She'd walked straight into a cover-up that had the potential to change her life if she dug deep enough. And she had to move fast. Things like this came with a deadline. If she was going to be the one to break the news, she couldn't waste another second. And she couldn't let anyone try to stop her. "A little soreness in my lower back, but it's getting better."

"Good. Be sure to keep me updated if that changes." The good doctor made a few notes on her tablet, too distracted to read Maggie's lie straight from her face. "I don't see any other injuries that need immediate attention. Feel free to take ibuprofen as needed, get into a nice hot shower for the muscle aches and sleep as much as you can."

"I will. Thank you." Maggie slid off the examination table, careful to hold her weight in her arms and not her left leg. She'd gotten good at pretending over the years. That her marriage was perfect, that her family and friends hadn't hurt her when they'd taken her ex's side, that she deserved this new life she'd created. Keeping her leg steady as she walked out of Socorro's medical suite was just another version of that.

She headed back into the black corridor, the awareness of being watched instantly pressurizing between her shoulder blades. Not out of fear. Familiarity. Trust. Relief. The knot in her stomach almost released, but Maggie wasn't sure she wanted it to. Because the second she gave up her guard, she put herself at risk. And she'd come too far to take a step back now. "You don't have to follow me around, you know. I'm not sure I could even find the front door if I wanted to leave. This place is a maze."

"What did the doc say?" It took nothing for Jones to catch up to her as she shuffled down the hall.

"Apart from the gash in my arm, everything looks fine." Lie. Her toes caught on a grout line in the black tile, and Maggie forced herself to slow down. To take a breath as her chest tightened. Jones had done nothing but fight for her, to the point of risking his own life and the lives of his team. She owed him the truth about the side effects from whatever Toledano had injected into her spine, but telling him only guaranteed her sitting on the sidelines. Or letting Socorro take control of her life. She wasn't going to let that happen. Not again. "I've been ordered to take a long hot shower and sleep myself into a coma."

"I think I can help with that." Such a simple statement, but one that held so much meaning if she let herself read into it.

Maggie pulled up short of the kitchen. "Are you of-fering to help me shower?"

"What? No." Pure panic contorted his handsome fea-tures as Jones raised both hands in surrender. His palms had been cut up—like hers. A scratch cut through his hairline and came dangerously close to his eye. Scabs would start building in the next day or so, but right now, everything was fresh. There were still streaks of dirt around the wound. He hadn't been to see the doc-tor. He'd waited outside that room for her. "That's not what I meant. Unless you need my help. Then, yeah. I can do that."

"At ease, soldier. I think I can manage on my own." Her upper lip stung as she found herself smiling. She'd never seen him flustered before. It made him human. Maggie leveraged one hand against the wall as she rounded into the kitchen. As much as she wanted to follow straight through with Dr. Piel's orders, she couldn't do any of it until she had something to eat. Training for her first marathon last year had taught her the body physically couldn't repair itself without the proper macronutrients. She'd feel better faster after a substantial amount of calories. "I needed the laugh, though. Thanks for that."

She could almost feel his hand at her lower back. Just waiting for her to need his help. But the part of her that'd picked herself up off the floor after her divorce wouldn't let her rely on anyone but herself. It was that part that'd given her the courage to leave everything she'd known behind and gotten her the job with *Ameri-can Military News*. This was who she had to be now.

Morning sun peeked out from behind the canyon walls protecting the small town less than a mile east. What would it be like to live in a place like that? Outside the city, away from the mania and rush. Where neighbors knew each other's names and checked in with homemade goods and smiles. To live slow and without the pressures of trying to keep up with everyone else. Her heart craved that. Or maybe she was just tired. And beat up. And bleeding. Maggie used the galley-style kitchen counters to take her weight as she passed through to the oversize dining table on the other side. "What's for breakfast?"

"I make a mean omelet, if you're interested." Jones moved about the kitchen with a grace she'd never be able to pull off even if she wasn't injured. He grabbed a pan from one cupboard and a cutting board from another before verbally greeting each of his items as he collected them from the refrigerator. "Peppers, onions, eggs, cheese, salt, pepper and my secret ingredient. Our logistics coordinator is something of a chef in her downtime. She's been teaching us to cook in case we have to fend for ourselves."

"Great. I'll take three." She eased herself down onto the nearest chair, giving up her need to put her back to the wall so she could see the entire room. "And I'm not kidding."

"You got it." He dumped his haul on the counter with a little too much force, splitting the bell pepper along the top. "You don't have any allergies, do you?"

The question shouldn't have meant much, but she wasn't sure anyone had ever asked her that before. If they'd ever put her well-being first. Her ex certainly hadn't, and her parents had turned over that responsibility to herself long before she'd left the house at seventeen. "No. I'm good. Don't all of you soldier types know how to fend for yourselves in the field?"

"MREs are not the same as a home-cooked meal." He cracked an entire dozen eggs, one after the other, against the countertop before dropping them into a mixing bowl.

"So there's no one cooking you meals at home? Girlfriend, wife?" She shouldn't have asked. It wasn't any of her business and the answer wouldn't change anything between them. They'd been thrust together for the sake of survival. That was it. There wasn't any version of her story that included getting involved with another man capable of breaking her. And Jones Driscoll had the ability to break her. "Boyfriend?"

"I live here." His smile cracked at one side of his face as he whisked the eggs together and combined them all in a pan to cook along with the cheese before he started dicing vegetables. A gravitational pull suddenly held her pinned to her seat. This wasn't the soldier who'd pulled her out of danger. This was the man beneath the armor. The one who might've existed before his brother's death. And he was giving her, of all people, the gift of seeing it firsthand. "And, no. I don't have a significant other, if that's what you're asking."

Gratitude and raw desire propelled her to her feet. Maggie put everything she had into getting to her feet. Her leg tried to keep up, but she was losing her own determination to hide from him. Stopping mere inches away, she reached for his face, framing his jaw between both hands. "That's too bad."

She dragged his mouth to hers.

A BURST OF adrenaline twisted his stomach tight.

Jones knew this kind of excitement. It was the same feeling he lost himself in when heading into the field for an assignment. There was nothing like throwing himself into a dangerous, chaotic situation, and knowing his life would never be the same when he came back out.

The laceration on Maggie's lip caught against the oversensitive skin of his mouth and rocketed his heart rate into overdrive. It elicited a growl from somewhere deep inside his chest and seemed to urge her on. She parted her lips and gave him access to everything he'd denied himself over the past two years.

Jones let the whisk fall from his hand and speared his fingers into her hair. Bits of dust lodged against her scalp, but that only added to the explosion of sensitivity coiling through his system. Her palms pressed against his chest as though trying to convince herself this was a bad idea, but at the same time giving her the stability she needed to stay upright. And, damn, she tasted perfect. Though he hadn't expected any different over the days they'd been together. He'd known long before this moment she would be an indulgence he'd never be able to get over.

She dug her fingers into his shirt, and it took every ounce of discipline he had not to push her limits. Because no matter how much either of them wanted this, he couldn't give her anything beyond this moment. Despite his desperation for contact that had nothing to do with his work, they were on two separate paths. Him facing down a bloodthirsty cartel with Socorro, and her clawing free of a man who hadn't taken her at her worth. This… This was all there was.

And he'd take it. Every second. Every hour. Every day she'd lend him. He'd soak it all up until he couldn't take any more. He was selfish in that way. He knew that now. Because crossing the lines—breaking orders and risking his entire military career—into enemy territory hadn't been about saving Kincaide from his captors or keeping his brother from suffering more than he had to. That'd been part of it, but Jones realized deep down it'd been about holding to that single connection for himself. Of not having to lose one more person in his life. Of having someone who gave a damn about him as much as he cared about them. And he cared about Maggie. More than he wanted to admit.

Jones broke away from the kiss, curling his arms around her middle to pull her closer. His mouth found the highjacked pulse at the base of her neck as she tipped her head back.

"Something smells." Her words were breathy. Not entirely coherent. And he couldn't help but love the fact he'd done that to her. That he'd cost her an ounce of that legendary control.

"Sorry about that." Though he wasn't sorry enough to stop. "I haven't showered."

"No. Not that." She set her hands on his shoulders and pushed. "I think your omelet is burning."

The smoke detector's alarm pierced through the pleasant haze and ripped Jones from the edge. He set Maggie back a couple of feet as smoke filled the kitchen. Covering his mouth with the crook of his elbow, he shut off the stove and tossed the mess into the sink as fast as possible. Water scorched the pan and most likely warped the metal, but he'd just have to buy Jocelyn a new one. He grabbed the dish towel hanging from the front of the oven and flapped it in front of the detector to clear a bit of the smoke. The alarm ceased its deafening beeping, and Jones's blood pressure started coming down. "Look what you did."

"Me? You're the one who forgot you were cooking. I'm innocent in all of this." Maggie waved one hand in front of her face. A smile that had no business visiting a moment like this brightened her face and gutted him faster than any blade. She reached for the dining table behind her and took a seat. "But if it makes you feel better, I'll keep my distance. Because I still want eggs."

Jones whipped the dish towel over his shoulder and set about pulling another carton of eggs from the fridge. "Save me from the cartel. Make sure I don't get shot. Help me escape from being burned alive. Cook me eggs. Is there anything else I can do for you, Ms. Caddel?"

"You could do it without a shirt." She leaned back in the chair, completely at ease, and damn, he'd never seen anything so beautiful in his life.

And it was right then he knew. Maggie's life hadn't always revolved around the idea she could change everything by meeting some goal she'd convinced herself would finally make her happy. She'd been in survival mode. Not just running for her life from the cartel over the past few days, but from being the person her ex branded her as to her family and friends. He could see why breaking a story that had the potential to shoot her to the top of her profession would look so tempting. To prove her worth, that she was someone, that she meant something. And Jones wanted to give her that.

"I wouldn't mind," she said.

He set to work cracking another dozen eggs, then whisked them together with the cheese to start a second batch of omelets. That kiss had brought him down to his baser instincts. Going much longer without a full stomach would finish the job. Jones layered a base of eggs in a new pan and let it sit while he started chopping the vegetables. "Why don't you tell me what happened after the accident instead?"

The playfulness drained from her expression, and he hated himself for being the root cause of her anxiety, but if they were going to live up to the deal they'd made at the start of all this, they needed to be honest with each other. That was the agreement. No secrets. No holding back. Maggie cut her gaze to some invisible speck on the table, scratching at it with one finger. "All right. I think the men who took me from the SUV were US military. Active. From what I could gather from the short—and terrifying—conversation I had with the leader of their little party, they were ordered to cover up what happened the night of the ambush."

He'd assumed as much in the mere minute and a half he'd engaged with the unit. Though her theory was new. Jones tossed the vegetables in with the eggs and let everything cook together. Straight up accusing the military of a cover-up wouldn't get them anywhere but a dark hole in which neither of them would escape. They needed proof. "Cover up how?"

"They recovered the SD card with the photos I'd taken. It was right there in front of me. Within reach. I don't know how they found it, but I guess that doesn't matter now. I tried to grab for it, but…" Her voice turned almost wispy, as though she were trying to bury some kind of emotion she didn't want him to see. "The soldier in charge made quick work of destroying it. That and the bodies Toledano burned before you got there. I'm not sure they had any part in that, but from what I could tell they were working together."

"Sosimo Toledano is heir to *Sangre por Sangre*'s entire organization. As soon as his old man kicks the bucket, it's rumored he'll take control. Why the hell would the military or any part of the federal government partner with him?" And why would they cover up the lieutenant's dirty work? Jones was on the verge of letting the eggs burn again. He forced himself to take a minute, to wrap his head around what this all meant.

"That's what I want to find out." She let her hand fall away from whatever she'd tried digging off of the table. "He told me I was the last piece of the puzzle. They were going to kill me, too."

Jones flipped the first omelet, ensuring it was cooked all the way through before slipping it onto a plate with a sprinkle of green onion and his special ingredient: sour cream. He handed it off, his thumb brushing into her palm. "I'm not going to let that happen, Maggie."

And he meant it. No matter what deal they'd struck when they'd gotten into this mess together, he wasn't going to put it ahead of her life. *Sangre por Sangre* wouldn't have to just go through him to get to her. Jones would bring the entire US government down on its head if he had to, and if that didn't work, he'd get her out of the country. Someplace safe. Where she could live the life she deserved.

"I'm not so sure you get a say anymore." Her skin warmed against his for a series of breaths before she pulled the plate to the table. That contact stayed with him as he went back to the stove to start another, tunneling deep into bone. "This is delicious. Who knew someone who communicates in differing levels of growls could cook this well?"

"I think that was a compliment." Jones finished up another omelet and brought it straight to her plate.

"Don't get a swollen head." She stabbed another mouthful of egg and took a bite. Most people might have been grossed out by her ability to talk and eat at the same time, but there was something real and raw about the way she'd opened up to him. About her marriage, her family, her career. His gut said that didn't happen often, if at all. But that maybe she was keeping something else to herself. "It's been over a day since I've had anything—I almost forgot what good food tastes like. For all I know, you're the worst cook in America, and I can't tell the difference."

"I'll take it." A laugh he failed to strangle vibrated

up his throat as he took a seat opposite her. It felt uncomfortable and out of place, foreign, but right at the same time. He'd spent so much of his life trying to be as small as possible—in foster homes, at school, in the military—so as not to gain attention, but with her, he felt…himself. As though he could say or do anything without earning criticism or judgment. Jones reached to grab a bite of omelet from her plate.

She poised her fork above his hand, ready to strike. "I said you're a good cook. Not that I would share. One more move, and you'll never use that hand again."

"Is that a threat?" he asked.

"There's a reason I'm still here." The small muscles in her jaw flexed and released in an attempt to keep her smile under control, but he could see right through her. Had from the beginning. "I won't go down without a fight."

Pure desire tightened his insides. Jones dropped his fork against the table and hauled her against his chest in less time than it took for her to suck in her next breath. "I think I'll take my chances."

Chapter Ten

She was in his bed.

Dark high-end sheets worked to soothe the scrapes, bruises and aches from her body. A hint of his citrus shampoo and conditioner combo filled her lungs as she took in the sunset dipping behind the west mountains through the floor-to-ceiling windows. Maggie let herself lie there, recalling how Jones had carried her back to his room. How he'd started the shower for her—hot as it would go—and left her with fresh towels, toiletries and a pair of sweats and an oversize T-shirt to change into.

She'd taken her time. Not wanting to give up that small amount of peace too quickly. Washed the dirt from her hair, scrubbed her skin raw until the first few layers swirled down the drain. Then conditioned and lotioned while trying to keep the bandage on her arm dry. It was amazing how much a shower could bring back a bit of humanity.

When she'd come back into the main room, she found him changing the sheets. The automatic blackout shades had been drawn, the lights dimmed. He'd looked at her as though she was his whole life right then, and she'd liked it. Felt as though she mattered. That she didn't have to take care of herself. For once, she could let someone else do the job so many others had failed to accomplish. Warmth had started in her belly for the first time in…years. A need that'd triggered when she'd kissed him and hadn't let go. She'd been ready. For him. Ready to move past the loneliness and betrayal she'd gone through with her ex and to start something new.

But Jones had simply wished her good night and left her to sleep the day away.

And in that moment, a shift rocked through her. No. Not a shift. A damn earthquake. She was falling for him. Undeniably, irrevocably falling for a man she intended to use as a source in exchange for providing a layer of protection during this investigation. Jones Driscoll had fought his way into her life and somehow managed to take up space where there shouldn't have been any room left. His loyalty to the people he cared about, how he treated Gotham and fought for his beliefs, had the power to erase the pain she'd insisted on carrying to protect herself. To the point it'd become too heavy around him. And she wanted to leave it behind. Once and for all.

She had that chance. To start over again. Question was, would she take it?

Maggie sat up in the king-size bed and scanned the room she'd been too tired and unfocused to take in this morning. It wasn't as dark as she'd originally estimated. If anything, everything seemed to be in perfect balance between camel-colored leather, dark green paint and highlights of white in the artwork. Complete with a few indoor plants. Very boho. A built-in against one wall took up a good majority of space. Most likely his closet, given there weren't any other doors other than the bathroom. She slid from the bed, landing on a faux fur rug perfectly positioned beneath the frame. Every inch of this room testified to Jones's attention to detail. Yet somehow it felt…empty. Almost cold despite the warmth of colors.

Walking the room, she took in everything she could. No family photos. Not even of his foster brother. Nothing to suggest any hobbies. It was like this place was merely a way station. A place he intended to pass through after enough time. Though, Maggie imagined that'd been intentional. The kind of work he did had to come with a hazard warning. He wouldn't want to leave a mess of possessions for someone else to have to go through. Or maybe it was the result of being moved from one foster home to the other growing up. At the same time, he'd painted, hung the artwork and picked out the furniture. A bundle of opposites.

She skimmed her fingers along the sleek, modern built-in and pressed one of the doors inward. Magnets. The door swung open, revealing a clean line of T-shirts and a shelf stacked with folded pants. Everything in its place.

She couldn't help but reach out. Soft fabric warmed in her hand as she let herself enjoy the sensory input that couldn't bruise, cut or hurt her. It'd been a long time since she'd let herself slow down, to just…feel. There'd been some part of her that was terrified by the idea. Slowing down meant not moving forward, of being stuck. Of not proving she was better off after the divorce. But the past week, working beside Jones, had shown her she couldn't physically live her life going from one goal to the next without taking a breath in between. And the truth was, she was tired of pushing so hard. Of trying to prove to everyone but herself she was worthy of their love and support. She'd lived these past two years in spite of her ex, unconsciously giving him a power over her he didn't deserve. She'd just wanted to get away, but she'd ended up bringing him along with her.

Maggie brought a T-shirt to her nose and inhaled, long and deep. Making Jones's earthy, clean scent part of her. As though it were enough to keep her safe from what waited outside these bulletproof walls.

"That's not creepy at all," a deep voice said.

Her nervous system spiked in defense. She threw the T-shirt at the source with a pathetic yip as she backed away about a foot. Her heart lodged in her throat as recognition flared. "You scared the crap out of me. How long have you been standing there?"

Jones pulled his T-shirt free of his face and balled it into his hand. "Long enough to thank heavens you haven't gotten to my underwear drawer yet."

Embarrassment heated up her neck and into her face. She didn't know what to say. "For your information, I was… Okay. I was smelling your shirt. I liked the feel of it, and one thing led to another."

"Hey, whatever gets your engine going, I'm all for it." Jones tossed the T-shirt she'd considered smuggling

out of the building on to the end of the bed, humor playing at the edges of his eyes. "Thought you might still
be asleep. I didn't want to wake you. Doc wanted me
to check on you, make sure you were still breathing."

"I'm still breathing." Her arms automatically made
an attempt to cross over her midline, as if that would
protect her from any further embarrassment on her
part. Didn't do any good. Realistically, she didn't have
anything to be embarrassed about. At least, that was
what she was going to tell herself.

"Searching for anything in particular?" The mattress dipped under Jones's weight as he took position
off to her left.

Her throat convulsed. "Not really. Hoping maybe
you had a phone or a laptop stashed somewhere in
here. It's been a few days since I've touched base with
my editor. The last time I talked to him, I came clean
about following those *Sangre por Sangre* members.
Told him I was going to see this through to the end. I
was captured that night. I can't imagine what he's going
through not being able to reach me, how many people
are looking for me."

"Reaching out could tip *Sangre por Sangre* and
whoever the hell else they're working with to your
whereabouts." No hint of emotion or surprise. Just
statement of fact.

"You and I both know Socorro has ways of mask-
ing GPS signals. Otherwise, you wouldn't be able to do
your job." Her gut said there was more to his detach-
ment. Maggie stepped closer to him, almost between
his knees. "What aren't you telling me?"

His jaw flexed under the pressure of his back teeth. "Your editor isn't looking for you, Maggie. I've been monitoring the police bandwidths and cross-referencing missing person reports. Even had Alpine Valley's chief of police reach out to Albuquerque PD. No one knows you were abducted."

He didn't have to finish the rest of that thought. The last two words were already at the front of her mind. *Or cares.*

"That's…not true." Blood rushed from her upper body and pooled in her thighs. A knot pinched behind her shoulder blade, cutting her next breath short. She had coworkers. Neighbors. Even her ex must've noticed he hadn't been able to torture her for a week. Someone must've realized what'd happened. Someone had to care. A low ringing started in her ears. She wasn't alone. Because if she was, that meant everything she'd done over the past two years had been worthless. That she was worthless. No friends. No family. No one to miss her. That wasn't a life. That was living as a ghost. She stretched out her hand. "Give me a phone."

"I've been monitoring the news for days. Your name hasn't been brought up." His voice leveled, which somehow cut deeper than his initial accusation. "This is a good thing, Maggie. Staying off the radar gives *Sangre por Sangre* a chance to forget about you over time. You can move on. Start fresh, maybe somewhere else. You can leave all of this behind."

"I already started over. I already gave up everything and everyone I loved. I can't just walk away from that." Because the unknown was far more terrifying than the threat she knew. Her hand shook as she waited for him to budge. "Give me a phone."

"This is a mistake." Jones unpocketed his cell, tapped in the passcode and handed it off.

"I don't care." She latched onto the device as though it would solve the problems closing in. She knew better than to trust her emotions. They hadn't done her any good before, but she had to know for herself. Dialing her editor's direct line, she pressed the phone to her ear. The line rang once before connecting. "Bodhi?"

"You got him. Who's this?" he asked.

Her heart squeezed at the fact he hadn't recognized her voice. Which was currently shaking. "It's Maggie."

"Maggie, where the hell are you? You missed your deadline. I had to give your piece to Don. You were already on a short leash, and now you think you can just skip out on me?" The tap of a keyboard cut through his end of the line. "You know what? I don't care. I've got to have something from you by the end of the day or you're gone. Got it?"

The nerves in her temple lit up as she pressed the phone harder to her ear. "Bodhi, you remember what I told you about those *Sangre por Sangre* soldiers? The ones peeling off from their corners?"

"What about it?" A palpable energy shifted as the *tap tap tap* of the keyboard died on the other end of the line. Bodhi lowered his voice. "You got something for me, Mags?"

"I followed them out into the desert." Her skin felt too tight as Jones leveled that gaze on her. Like he could see right through her. "I saw them kill ten American soldiers during an operation to capture Sosimo Tole-dano. The cartel buried the bodies, then a military unit came along and burned them, but I had proof. I took photos. They abducted and tortured me for them. People need to know, Bodhi. This is big."

There was so much more she needed to tell him, but the excitement of the story was getting to her. Her editor's heavy exhale filled the silence, but he hadn't given her an answer. "So do you think we have something?"

"Where are the photos?" he asked.

Her stomach clenched. It always had to come back to proof. *American Military News* wasn't some tabloid that ran pieces on the promise of getting subscriptions. Journalists had to work through classified intel, establish contacts within the military and walk a thin line between exposing government secrets and doing their jobs. "I don't have them anymore. They were destroyed."

"I didn't want to do this, but now I don't have any choice. You're fired, Maggie." Bodhi's voice sounded sad. And afraid. "Don't contact me or any of the other writers here again. I won't answer."

The line disconnected.

MAGGIE HANDED BACK the phone, her face white, jaw slack. "I need a computer."

Hell. She wasn't going to take the truth at face value. No one had filed a missing person report. No one had gone to the landlord when they couldn't get her to answer the door. No one had attempted to contact her since her abduction. Not a scammer or the bank to ask about the inactivity on her cards, according to her phone records. That feeling—the one trying to convince her she was utterly forgotten and alone—was a lie. She had him. She had Gotham and the rest of the team at Socorro. "Maggie, I know what you're—"

"He fired me." Her eyes glittered with unshed tears. "I told him what I'd uncovered, and he fired me. Said I shouldn't contact him or any of the other writers. Then he hung up."

His instincts prickled as Jones got to his feet. He took back the phone he'd lent her, on high alert. "Why would he fire you?"

"I have no idea." Maggie threaded her hands through her hair, turning away from him. The armor she'd donned against the world was starting to shed. She was coming apart at the seams. "This job...was everything, Jones. It was providing the income I needed to finally live on my own. I'm going to lose my apartment, but worse, I'm going to have to use the money my ex pays in alimony every month to survive and prove him right. That I can't live on my own, that I'll always need him. That I'm nothing without him."

"He told you all those things?" Deep-seated anger filtered through his muscles until his arms and legs ached under the pressure.

"Amongst other things." She swiped the back of one hand against her face. "But I was finally figuring this out for myself. I was...happy. I felt like I belonged there. It was cutthroat, but the pressure to perform was making me better. I wasn't stuck. I had a plan. And now... It's gone." She collapsed onto the bed, her head in her hands. "What am I going to do? No news outlet is going to touch me after this, and you were right. My editor didn't even know I'd been abducted. No one knows, or they don't give a damn, and isn't that just pathetic?"

Jones wanted nothing more than to hunt the bastard down who'd dared step on her confidence and self-worth and show the man the error of his ways— and maybe what a few cracked ribs felt like. But Maggie needed him more at this moment. He dropped to his knees in front of her, setting both hands along her thighs. Lean muscle contracted at his touch, an automatic response honed over the course of permanently living in fight-or-flight mode. "Maggie, look at me."

She didn't move, didn't even seem to breathe.

"Maggie." Something in his voice brought her head up. "The people who believed a narcissistic, manipulative jackass like your ex and turned their backs on you are dicks."

Her laugh jolted her upper body. "That's one way of looking at it."

"You want to know why your friends and family chose his side? Because they were afraid. They thought letting you slip out of their lives would be easier than disproving the lies he told them about you, and they were right." Jones squeezed her leg as an unfamiliar tightness constricted around his rib cage. He wasn't good at this stuff. Empathizing. Showing how much he cared. His entire life had been forged from abandonment and searching for support that might not even exist in his line of work. Of being the first through the door and getting the job done in hopes someone would be proud of him. He was the wrong person to sit here and try to convince Maggie she didn't need to earn her happiness.

"I can't tell you that you're better off without them because we all need those connections. We all need to know that if we fall, someone will be there to catch us. But look at you. You took a stand. You made a life for yourself all on your own. You survived multiple days of interrogation and pain and came out the other side stronger. I know at least one man who wasn't capable of that."

Grief tugged hard at his insides at the thought of Kincaide's last moments, where the effects of brain damage had gotten so bad Kincaide had no longer recognized his own brother. "You're a fighter, Maggie. You see something and you go after it, and I admire the hell out of that. You stood up to an entire unit of soldiers ready to kill you, not to mention put up with me the past few days. That doesn't come close to pathetic in my book."

"I can definitely say putting up with you is a feat in and of itself." Her smile deepened the dimple at the right side of her mouth. Just before it slipped from her face. "But the past week has shown me something. I don't want to be a fighter anymore, Jones. I don't want to be strong or resilient. I don't want to inspire people with my struggles or have my entire self-worth dependent on my job. I'm so tired of fighting." She took his hands in hers. "I want to be soft. And loved. I want to feel safe enough to make mistakes and be normal instead of going from one life trauma to the next. I want to be able to sit on the couch and watch a TV show without feeling guilty for slowing down. I want to be happy."

His throat dried up on his next inhale. She deserved it. She deserved all of it. And, hell, Jones wanted to be the one to give it to her. To make her feel safe and loved and soft. Because maybe he wanted a little bit of that, too. And why couldn't they give that to each other? Her soft skin caught on the callouses along his knuckles.

"But I'm not giving up on this story." Determination bled through the exhaustion playing at the corners of her eyes. "Bodhi might've fired me, but I know there's something big going on here. Somebody ordered that unit to cover up the *Sangre por Sangre* ambush the night I was taken hostage, and I want to know who. I'm owed that much, and I need your help."

"I gave you my word when we got into this mess I would see this through," he said. "And I keep my promises. What do you need?"

"Access to a laptop or computer or a notepad and pen." Maggie shoved herself to standing and started pacing the room. A frenzy of energy burned behind her eyes. Though her left leg seemed to drag slightly behind the right. He hadn't noticed that before. "I need to write down everything that's happened so far so I don't forget any details. About that night, about the military unit destroying evidence and Toledano's involvement. That soldier, the one in charge, he burned my SD card, but we might still be able to recover the photos I took that night if we can get our hands on my camera. Maybe not all of them, considering the limited memory, but there's a chance."

"Slow down. You're talking about the camera *Sangre por Sangre* confiscated when they took you captive?" Jones got to his feet and approached the built-in. Pressing one cabinet corner down, he revealed a safe. The fingerprint reader glowed green, giving him access to the contents inside, and he extracted his laptop. If he didn't give Maggie something to do in the next few seconds, he feared she might explode. "I thought you said it broke when you fell."

"The gunman who found me hiding in the bushes took it from me and handed it over to Toledano. After that, I'm not entirely sure what happened to it." She hadn't stopped pacing, the excitement of a lead clear in her voice. "But even if we have the photos, that doesn't prove who ordered Toledano's capture or who is trying to cover up the deaths of those soldiers. We'll need more. My editor... He sounded scared after I told him what happened. Like he needed to wash his hands of anything having to do with the story. I think he might know something."

"I'll have Alpine Valley PD run a background check on him, review his financials and phone records. He told you not to contact him or anyone at the paper, but if your editor is connected to the cartel in any way, we'll at least have leverage we can approach him with."

Though explaining his continued involvement in all this to Ivy Bardot—despite not finding evidence at the ambush site—had the potential to end his access to

Socorro's internal systems and their partnership with local law enforcement—and end his career.

Hesitation had his thumb gripped over the contact information for Alpine Valley's chief of police. Socorro had given him a second chance after he'd directly disobeyed orders not to go after Kincaide overseas. Ivy and the rest of the team trusted him to do what was best for the company and the people they protected. Going off script—following Maggie to the end of the line and disobeying another set of orders—would put all that at risk. Could cost him everything.

He watched as Maggie took the laptop to the edge of the bed and navigated to a notes app. Within seconds, he'd lost her to a frantic pace of typing. Her mouth silently followed the words she put on the page, and it was easy to see, despite not working for *American Military News* anymore, she had a passion for investigating. For getting to the truth and ensuring the public got the answers they deserved. That she was good at this. Happy, even.

"There's another option." Jones tucked his phone back into his cargo pants pocket without reaching out to the police again. He would. In time. The editor was a good start, but they had the means to cut out the middleman and end this sooner rather than later. Without putting his second chance in danger. "Another source we haven't considered."

"What source?" Maggie pulled herself away from the soft white glow of the screen, setting that newly brightened gaze on him. Understanding sank in the longer she studied him, and a tenseness that'd taken days for her to lose infiltrated her upper body. She dragged herself off the bed. "You've got to be joking. No. No way in hell."

"You and I both know he's the fastest way to get to the truth, Maggie." Though Jones would give anything not to put her in this position. Because he wouldn't have asked it of his brother. He wouldn't have asked it of anyone on his team. But this story was something that could destroy her from the inside if she let it, and they had a chance to finish this once and for all.

"You mean if he's even still alive, which for the record, I hope he is and that he's suffering from the bullet you gave him and being slowly eaten by that fire." She pointed a strong index finger at him. "Toledano kidnapped and tortured me for three days, and now you just want me to walk right up to him and ask, 'Hey, want to tell me about who's trying to cover up your massacre that killed ten American soldiers? Oh, and can I have my camera back? Pretty please?'"

"I'll let you throw a couple punches if it'll make you feel better," he said.

She cut her attention to the laptop and the beginnings of the story she had there. "If you want me to do this, it's going to be more than a couple."

Chapter Eleven

She could do this.

She had to do this.

Maggie held her breath as the compound came into sight up ahead. In truth, she didn't remember a whole lot about the outside. The *Sangre por Sangre* soldiers who'd taken her the night of the operation to capture Toledano had dragged her inside unconscious. The first thing she'd remembered was waking up in the dark, dank hole she'd come to treasure between interrogations.

She would've done anything to escape this place. Now she was going back into it willingly. But Jones had been right. The fastest way to get answers was by questioning the source. Though she couldn't imagine why Bodhi had opted to fire her instead of chasing a story of this caliber. The answer to that question would have to wait, but the betrayal refused to let up.

She'd had no illusions *American Military News* would be a career home forever. It'd been meant as a stepping stone, one that'd helped her land on her feet after the divorce. Support her long enough to get a place of her own and build a reputation in the media world.

Before her marriage had imploded, she'd cut her

teeth on articles here and there in tandem with her day job as a freelance copywriter for a variety of different companies. Her husband hadn't wanted her to work at all, hoping to convince her to start a family before she lost all her eggs to age. But it'd been her own little private investigation into a case of a missing naval officer she'd read about in the papers that ended in him being found. She spent her nights watching true crime and gobbling up every book she could get her hands on. It was the investigations—of one clue leading to the next, of reliving the journalist's setbacks and triumphs, that propelled her to give it a try. The naval officer's aunt had been calling for any information, offering a reward, but something had seemed off. The aunt's insistence he would be okay—that he was strong and resourceful and a fighter—had Maggie watching the aunt's home for a couple days. There hadn't been any sign of the officer between news outlet campouts, but she'd noticed an uptick in groceries. More than a woman of his aunt's size would need. She'd marched straight up to the door during one of the "please find him" interviews and exposed him as a coward hiding in his bedroom. The resulting attention had given her a base to apply for the war correspondent position.

But while she'd ultimately taken the job to help dig her out of what was left of that old life, there was a mass of emptiness in her chest at its loss. She'd thought she was doing something she was good at for once. Subscriptions had been up, with spikes every time Bodhi had published one of her pieces. The people of New Mexico found it more important than ever to keep an eye on the war between the federal government and *Sangre por Sangre* after what'd happened in Alpine Valley about a month ago. Because any one of their towns could be next. She'd been a part of that. Made a difference. And now...

Now she didn't know what she was supposed to do.

"You two sure know how to make a girl's day." Scarlett Beam turned her gaze out the driver's side back window as they shot across the desert, one hand set on a Doberman she'd called Hans. The other one, Gruber, prodded Gotham in the face with his nose. "It's been weeks since I've taken on a good assignment. You can only run diagnostics on security equipment so many times before you start imagining threats. Except for the part where one of my teammates brings home a journalist who starts unplugging my cameras."

Heat flared into Maggie's face. Bits and pieces of memory broke into the moment. She'd done that. Right after she'd woken up in the medical suite that first time. She hadn't thought much about it at the time. Especially that someone would've had to go back and fix what she'd done. "Sorry about that. I hope I didn't damage your equipment."

"I would've done the same thing in your position." Scarlett scratched the nearest Doberman, but there was something in that statement that hinted at a similar experience. One where the woman in the back seat might've had to face her own survival.

"Unofficial assignment." Jones cut his gaze into the rearview mirror. "We clear?"

"We're clear. I honor my deals, Driscoll." The security consultant nodded. "I won't tell Ivy about today's little field trip and that you have nothing to support your cover-up theory, and you won't rat me out for... my little indiscretion you walked in on."

Silence bubbled between the three of them. Maggie forced herself to stare out the windshield. The chain-link fence surrounding the compound glinted under the hot desert sun ahead. The curiosity embedded deep in her soul and that'd urged her to apply as a journalist in the first place built to the point Maggie couldn't help but turn in her seat. Finding out why people did what they did. That was the basis of a good investigative reporter and war correspondent. If she bothered to slow down and let herself think about it, that was why she'd applied to the magazine in the first place. To understand what type of person, who'd claimed he was willing to stick with her until the end, suddenly felt the need to destroy her from the inside. "What did you—"

"She smuggled in a guy she was sleeping with without clearing it through Ivy first." Jones fought the slight rise at one corner of his mouth. "Which doesn't sound as bad as it should. Except we have security protocols every operative swears to live by when they sign on to work for Socorro. We can't risk outsiders coming across our data or accessing our systems and files."

"The best people to get around security protocols are the ones who built them in the first place." Vibrant red hair alluded to the fiery personality armored beneath her own Kevlar vest and protected by more weapons than Maggie could count. But Maggie had never counted on stereotypes. Data. Behavior. Connections.

Those were the categories that defined a person. Not their hair color. But from what Maggie could see, Scarlett Beam wasn't the type of person to roll with the punches. She was ready for any possibility and planned every detail accordingly. Probably liked to stick to a routine, stubborn about change. No, not stubborn. Terrified. Maggie imagined a security consultant like her didn't care for surprises in her work or personal life. And she most certainly hadn't planned on Jones.

Funny. Neither had Maggie.

"Let's just say I did my own background check on him." Scarlet winked. "It was very thorough."

"We're here." Jones let the SUV roll to a stop before shoving the transmission into Park, and suddenly, the lightness they'd created in such a small amount of time evaporated, leaving Maggie heavier than when they'd decided on this plan. "Satellite footage isn't giving us any activity here in the past twenty-four hours. That's the only reason I agreed to this, but you know the deal. Scarlett and I will surveil the perimeter before heading inside. I'll give you the all clear if we deem it safe enough. If we come into contact with Sosimo Toledano, we'll secure him and his men before we question him."

He studied her for a beat, and Maggie knew exactly what he was going to say before the words left his mouth. That was what happened when relationships were honed from a biological need to survive. A connection—stronger and deeper than anything she'd experienced—had forged between them since that terrible night. As though he felt every twinge, every nodule of doubt in her body, and she in his. Jones didn't want to do this. He didn't want her to have to come back here. He didn't want to risk her well-being to prove there was something to their theory. But it was the only way. They both knew that. "You don't have to face him."

"I suddenly feel the need to not be here. Hans, Gruber." Scarlett clicked her tongue to call the Dobermans, and Gotham's whine at losing his friends filled the SUV's cabin. The security consultant slammed the door behind her.

Spearing his fingers around her ear and into her hair, Jones brought Maggie's forehead to his over the center console. "We can come at this another way. Take a shot at your editor. See what he knows and why he killed the story."

She wanted that. More than anything. To get away from here. To forget what she'd been through and wipe it clean from every angle of her life. It was the shame that hurt the most. The fact that she'd failed to protect herself, that she hadn't seen the threat coming at all. That she'd let another man beat her at her own game.

Maggie set her hand over his, borrowing his strength. Just a little bit. That was all she needed. Him. She closed her eyes, memorizing this moment, feeling him against her skin. She'd never done that with another man, even while she'd been with her ex. Because on a cellular level, some part of her hadn't trusted him, feared what he'd do if she took her eyes off him. But she trusted Jones. From the very beginning, he'd fought for her. Sacrificed for her. Defended her to the very end. Data. Behavior. Connections. His told a story of loyalty and support and love, and that there didn't seem to be anything that could break him. Least of all her. He was everything she'd wanted for herself. He was everything she deserved. "No. You were right before. Questioning Sosimo Toledano is the smart move. And I need to do this, Jones. Otherwise, that fear is going to control me for the rest of my life, and I've already lost too much time to men like him."

"Okay." He extracted his hand from her hair and reached for the door handle. A gust of hot wind intensified the heat he'd curated along her neck and head as his boots hit the ground. "I'm coming back for you, Maggie Caddel."

"I know." Not a lie. The SUV shook as he secured her inside. Visually following him through the windshield, Maggie admired the grace both operatives somehow managed with over thirty pounds of gear and weaponry. The Dobermans fanned out ahead of their handler but soon vanished beneath the rim of the man-made crater protecting *Sangre por Sangre*'s abandoned headquarters below.

She reached for the radio pinned to the dashboard, the plastic frame protesting under her grip. One minute. Then five. No word yet. The sun cut through the windshield and spiked her internal body temperature. Sweat built up at her temples as her heart rate climbed higher. No signs of gunshots or an alarm. Not even a bark from the Dobermans. Was this supposed to be a no-news-is-good-news operation?

Gotham threaded his front paws over the center console and wormed his way into the driver's seat. Lengthening his neck, he studied the landscape through the window, then turned those iridescent blue eyes on her for answers.

"I know how you feel." Maggie scruffed the fur along his back, which obviously meant she wanted him in her lap because suddenly the husky's butt landed on top of her thigh. She couldn't fault him for needing a bit of assurance. She needed it, too. "It'll all be okay. Jones and Scarlett know what they're doing."

Static crackled through the radio, and Maggie brought it to her ear. She needed something—anything—to feed that panicked part of herself ready to bolt from the SUV and follow after them.

"We found him. Toledano and his men." Jones's voice tensed every muscle down her spine as seconds distorted into agonizing silence. "But we're not going to get answers here. They're all dead."

THEY'D BEEN TOO LATE.

The bodies were cold. Dead for more than a day based off the smell.

"Ambush." Scarlett Beam wove between the corpses, her mouth buried in the crook of her elbow. She bent down to collect a container of some sort as Maggie stood at the peripheral of the scene. Gotham was going nuts, signaling each time he encountered another set of remains. "Food wrappers, empty water bottles, burn ointment. I'd say Sosimo Toledano and his men were hiding out after what went down at the arch two nights ago. I doubt they cut their own power though.

I'm guessing the team who surprised them yesterday did that."

She was right. Jones grazed his flashlight beam over the walls. Blood mixed in with cinderblock, water and bullet holes. Setting the end of the flashlight between his teeth, he pulled the blade from his ankle holster and dug at one of the holes. The projectile popped free as the rotting cinderblock crumpled to the floor, and he dropped the flashlight into his hand. "Three different calibers. Five targets, most likely three separate shooters. Wouldn't have taken them more than a couple minutes to finish the job once they penetrated the perimeter."

His gut clenched as the picture became clear. Jones followed the trajectory of the bullets to the source, the end of the corridor they'd come down. "My guess is they used the garage as an access point. Same as we did. If you had a layout of the place before we blew it to hell the last time, they would've seen that was the best entry point." He tossed the bullet to Scarlett, which she caught against her vest. "Maggie and I met a team capable of this. Seven-man team, all highly trained and determined to tie up loose ends."

The military unit ordered to kill her.

Gotham went from one body to the next, turning in circles. The smell had to be driving him crazy.

"But why? Why leave them here? Why kill them at all?" Maggie's voice… It gripped him until he swore his heart stopped pumping blood. There was something hurried in the tone that worked to counteract the calmness in his. As though she were an emotional regulator for him, and when he thought back, he could see where that was true. How she seemed to bring him down on a logical level when none of this had made sense. Maggie kept her distance from the mass of bodies left to rot away with the rest of the structure. "Toledano was there that night. He helped those gunmen get rid of the bodies from the ambush. They were clearly working together. Why would they kill him?"

"Whoever did this wanted to make sure Sosimo Toledano didn't walk away with their secrets. Or maybe his usefulness just ran out." Scarlett crouched beside the leader's bloated corpse but didn't move to touch anything that might upset the scene. "You said those soldiers were US military, most likely army. As much as it pains me to consider the country I put my life on the line for would step into a deal with people like this, I can't deny your story makes sense now that I've seen evidence for myself." The security consultant watched as her twin Dobermans circled the other side of the room. "I've still got an enlisted contact. Let me reach out, see what I can put together."

"I don't want your name on any requisition forms." That was the only way this was going to work. Scarlett had worked too damn hard for too damn long to put distance between her and the people she'd once trusted to get wrapped up in anything army-related now, and he sure as hell wasn't going to be the one to upset the slice of peace she'd found with Socorro. "Everything stays off the books. You got me?"

"Understood." Scarlett whistled low for her companions, and the Dobermans obeyed without hesitation.

"I'm going to get the lay of the rest of the building. See if I can pick up anything that gives us an idea of who's behind this. Meet you back at the car."

"I'll call this in. Make sure these bodies end up in the right hands." Jones pulled his cell and sent a ping to Chief of Police Baker Halsey. The deaths hadn't occurred within Alpine Valley boundaries, but he was the only man in the department Jones trusted. Halsey would know what to do and who to reach out to. Most likely with Socorro's logistics coordinator—Jocelyn Carville—running point. "Whoever did this wanted to make sure Sosimo Toledano and his men weren't found, and I'm pretty much up for anything to disrupt their plans."

Maggie didn't respond, her gaze locked on the face of her torturer. "It doesn't even look like him."

"Decomposition eliminates a lot of features." Jones didn't really want to get into the specifics. No one should have to witness the slaughter of a human being. No matter how much hatred existed for the deceased. "The medical examiner will have to compare DNA, fingerprints and dental records to get a positive ID."

"No. I know that." Her tongue shot across her lips as she dared a step closer to the body. "I mean, I memorized every centimeter of this man's face while he was interrogating me. I've seen it so many times when I close my eyes, I was sure I'd never forget the small details. But this... This doesn't feel like him."

"It's going to take some time for you to adjust to the idea you don't have to be scared of him anymore," he said.

"You're probably right." She backed away from the body, seemingly realizing how close she'd gotten in the first place. There weren't many civilians willing to confront their greatest fears—especially those in the form of a torturer or person who'd hurt them—but Maggie continued to keep him off balance. She was stronger than she gave herself credit for, but that strength had only come from surviving what most people didn't. His brother included. And, hell, he didn't blame her for wanting a break from it all. To be soft, as she'd put it. Happy. "So the one source we had any chance of getting answers out of is dead. Our only other option is going to my editor. Hoping he knows something."

"I don't make moves based on hope." Jones surveyed the bodies a second time, studying each one after the other. He moved in order of closest to farthest, ending with Sosimo Toledano. "Bullets don't come with serial numbers. The only way we'll be able to trace these are if their striations matched something already registered in the state or federal database, and I doubt these guys would risk using anything to connect back to them or the army. Problem is, we still don't know if they're the ones who made this mess. If they are, it means they would've had to supplement their arsenal. But just like switching from one instrument to another, getting used to a weapon takes time. A couple days at least."

Jones crouched beside Toledano. He targeted a spread of blood in the lieutenant's side. A parting gift of that night at the bonfire. Wrinkled, angry skin contorted the bastard's face and along his left arm. On top of that, a bullet had gone straight through the lower section of his left lung, drowning him from the inside. And hell, Jones wasn't the least bit remorseful of the bastard's final minutes after everything he'd done to Maggie. "They didn't plan on us coming here. Could work in our favor."

"You think the soldiers might not have cleaned up as well as they would have if these bodies were meant to be found. Like they might've left behind prints or maybe some of this blood belongs to one of them if Sosimo Toledano got a shot off." Damn, he loved the way her brain worked. How she almost seemed to read his thoughts and put the puzzle together ahead of him. Maggie shifted her weight between both feet. "How long until your contact in Alpine Valley PD can sort this out?"

No. That wasn't the question she was asking. She wanted to know how much time she had left. How long it would take for the group sent to kill her to finish what they'd started out there at the arch. He shoved himself to his feet. The smell was getting to him. The heat, combined with the lack of air conditioning in an underground basement, only made matters worse. "Processing the scene? Couple hours as soon as they arrive. Getting any kind of result on DNA or prints? Weeks. Every piece of evidence they collect goes through a specialized lab out of Albuquerque. The chief can order a rush, but no one is going to care much about a bunch of dead cartel members."

Silence spread between them.

"I know some people who would care." Her voice barely reached through the darkness.

"What do you mean?" he asked.

"The articles I wrote about *Sangre por Sangre* and what the DEA, the military, even towns across the state were doing in response increased the magazine's subscriptions. Every time." That frenzy, the one he'd noted back in his room, started burning in her eyes in the glow of his flashlight. Her excitement was almost contagious, rocketing his pulse into higher territory. "Once all that business about Alpine Valley hit the news, the public grew obsessed. They couldn't get enough. It was in every paper, on every news site. You couldn't look anywhere without seeing some anchor covering the story. It's a classic universal fantasy. A small town stands up to a drug cartel and comes out on top. Who wouldn't read that?"

"You think this is about media ratings?" He didn't understand. "I wouldn't count a quarter of a town being buried during a landslide set off by an explosive meant to kill the chief of police and one of my teammates as a fantasy."

"No. I'm saying this is about perception." Maggie closed the distance between them. "What if the operation to apprehend Toledano was supposed to end with casualties? He's a high-level target whose capture would make a big impact on *Sangre por Sangre* operations if successful. Given the right kind of intel, it wouldn't be hard to get a mission like that approved. But something goes wrong. Soldiers end up dead."

His gut said she was onto something.

"All right. Let's play this out. *Sangre por Sangre* is accused of killing American soldiers. The media gets ahold of the story. The public is in a rage, most likely calling for action." His brain couldn't help but jump to his employer. Socorro's contract with the Pentagon was binding until the next review in a week, but there hadn't been a shortage of outrage from towns in the vicinity at having a private military contractor setting up shop close by. Outrage from local government officials, too. There was one in particular… Jones couldn't think of his name. A senator who'd been calling for the Pentagon to revoke contracts with private military outfits like Socorro's. Jones tried to force the pieces to fit into the puzzle they'd stumbled into. He pointed to the cartel members at his feet. "But good news. The US military has taken down the bad guys responsible."

"Except units like the one we came across don't issue their own orders." Maggie slipped her hand up his forearm as the truth gutted him from the inside.

"They follow them." Jones tried to breathe through the acid burning up his throat. "Someone higher up sent those soldiers to die."

"Only I wasn't supposed to be there." She scanned the bodies. "And they're trying to kill me to cover it up."

Chapter Twelve

They still didn't have any proof.

Jones and Scarlett had searched the entire compound. There hadn't been any sign of her camera. Their theory was just that. A story that fit, but no one was going to buy it unless they pinpointed the source of the kill order at the top.

And she was beginning to think there was only one way to identify them.

Maggie scrolled through the photos loaded to Jones's laptop they'd taken at the scene before calling in Alpine Valley's police department, once again caught off guard by the swollen face of her torturer. She didn't feel anything. Wasn't she supposed to be relieved? Knowing the man who'd interrogated her—hurt her—wouldn't appear over her shoulder had to come with some kind of pressure release, right? She deserved that much after everything that'd happened. Yet all she felt was emptiness. This feeling that no matter what she did, she couldn't make a damn bit of difference.

It'd been the same after her divorce. Trying to convince her family they'd been gaslighted and manipulated while on the receiving end of accusations of being at fault had led nowhere. And this... This was just like that.

She'd lost her job, her credibility, her support system. She'd suffered trauma and been left with a numbness climbing up into her lower back she didn't know how to stop. No one was going to believe her. Not without the photos she'd taken or eyewitness accounts of the five dead cartel members rotting away in that basement. Any evidence police recovered from now on would support the story ready to be fed to the public. Only she knew the truth.

And she was going to make sure it got out.

Maggie switched back to the document she'd created cataloging the events of the past week. From the moment she'd identified a low-level *Sangre por Sangre* member on a street corner in Albuquerque a year ago to finding Sosimo Toledano and his men dead inside their own compound. So much had happened in between, things she wanted to make sure she didn't forget. Because it was all she would have left once this was over. Cartels like this didn't die when one head was severed from the body. Two replaced the loss until something came along and went for the heart.

Jones slid a steaming mug of coffee across the built-in desk, and the fumes instantly urged her brain into all-nighter mode. "You've been writing for the past four hours without taking a break. Figured you'd need a pick-me-up."

"There are still a few details to work out. Motive, for one. Identifying who marched those soldiers to their deaths, too. I just don't want to mess it up." She cradled the mug between both hands and inhaled the sharp scent of robust beans, cream and sugar. "I can't tell you how much I needed this. Thank you."

She liked this. Him bringing her coffee. Her taking breaks to chat with someone who wasn't trying to steal her job. She even enjoyed the fur ball groaning in his sleep from the dog bed in the corner. It was almost as though they'd slipped into a relationship without ever having really talked about it. Like they fit in a way she hadn't fit with anyone since her divorce. "How much trouble are you in?"

His meeting with Ivy Bardot clung to the tenseness in his shoulders. Jones lowered himself down onto the edge of the bed, his knee brushing against hers. Only he didn't move to avoid her, which she appreciated. Warmth, stability, strength—he was all of that and more. Right when she'd needed it. "I've been ordered to back down from this investigation."

"What does that mean?" The muscles along her spine tightened one by one as she leaned forward to meet him. The answer was already in his expression. He'd warned her about this. About getting in too deep and putting Socorro and what they did here at risk. It was a chance he hadn't been willing to take. With good reason. Understanding settled into her grip around the mug, and Maggie forced herself to set it down on the desk. "You've been ordered to take me back to Albuquerque."

Voicing the words sucker punched her harder than she expected. This past week—the meals together, the kiss they'd shared, the way he'd made her laugh—

they'd meant something. They'd given her hope she didn't have to suffer through the rest of this life unwanted and blamed. That she could mean something to someone again. And now he was going to leave her to fight this battle alone? "I don't understand. You and Scarlett saw the bodies in the compound. We have photos of the scene. You saved me from the unit that was about to kill me. You told the police where to find the victims and the SD card that were burned. It's not like we don't have anything to show. This is all evidence."

"You're right, Maggie, and I wish there was something I could do to change management's mind." His voice leveled as though he was talking to a complete stranger. Not a woman he'd partnered with, kissed, made dinner for and given his bedroom to so she could recover from a brutal attack. "But Scarlett reached out to her contact in the army. The second she asked about the classified operation to apprehend Sosimo Toledano, the army arrested her and threatened Socorro's contract with the Pentagon."

She couldn't sit still anymore, shoving herself to her feet. Her head was spinning. All the dominos they'd stood on end were starting to fall out of their control. "No. They can't do that. Private military contractors are separate from active military. They have no jurisdiction when it comes to—"

"Unfortunately, they can. Scarlett is not even a year out of discharge, which puts her well within military reach, and Socorro works for the federal government, Maggie. We follow a set of rules and we don't deviate from them, and interfering with a military operation—

warranted or not—is a felony no one comes back from. We're working to get Scarlett out of custody while Ivy runs interference. With any luck, we'll still have jobs at the end of this." He cradled his mug between both hands, leveraging his elbows against his knees. "I knew what I was doing when I made the choice to see this through, but it was my career I was willing to put on the line. Not that of my team. I'm supposed to take you back to your place in Albuquerque. Within the hour."

Her blood iced in her veins. He intended to follow through. She could hear it in his voice, the way he refused to meet her gaze. Maggie shifted her weight onto her good leg, trying to take some of the pressure off, but there was nowhere else for it to go. "And do you think taking me back to a place where that unit can find me is the best option?"

"You're not staying." Jones got to his feet, his coffee forgotten. "I can get you a new identity with a passport, a sizeable chunk of cash and a new phone. It won't be much, but it will get you out of the country. What you do after that is up to you, but I recommend finding a new career. You'll have to avoid anything that can hint at the life you had here."

"You want me to drop all of this and run?" She motioned to the laptop. "After everything we've uncovered, you're okay walking away and letting whoever did this get away with the deaths of those soldiers?"

"I don't have a choice," he said. "Not if I want to keep the life I've built here."

"Yes, you do. You're just afraid to make it. I understand disobeying orders is what lost you your military career in the first place, but if you hadn't gone after your brother, he would've died in that cave, Jones. You never would've gotten the time with him that you did." Couldn't he see that? Couldn't he see there were some things worth breaking the rules for? "You asked me to trust you, and I have. You made the decision once before. Why can't you do it this time? For me?"

He didn't even flinch under her accusation. Didn't answer. And in that moment, Maggie realized what a colossal mistake she'd made. That she'd fallen for a man she'd thought had seen something worthwhile in her. But the truth was, he only valued the people who had something to give him in return. Who had a use. All she'd offered him was a hail of bullets, five dead bodies and a theory they couldn't prove. She wasn't family or someone he relied on to have his back in the field. She wasn't anything.

Maggie swallowed to counter the tears burning in her eyes. He'd systematically destroyed the armor she'd built to save her from breaking for Toledano, and a rush of heat flared over her neck and face. Damn it. She needed to get out of here. She turned back to the laptop and emailed a copy of the article to everyone in her contacts list. She didn't have anything else. "Don't bother with the cash or the phone or the new identity. I've built a new life before on my own. I can do it again."

"Maggie, don't do this." Jones dared a step toward her but stopped as she turned on him. "The moment you step foot back in Albuquerque, they'll know. They've been watching your apartment, monitoring your financials and phone. Most likely watching your friends and family in case you reach out, too. They will kill you, and everything you've survived will have been for nothing. Please. Let me help you."

Doubt crept in through the heartbreak. All she had to do was slow down and think this through, but her heart didn't want to see logic. It only felt betrayal. And now that betrayal had a new face. "Aren't you worried you'll lose your job?"

Maggie wrenched the door open without looking back. She'd taken careful mental notes on navigating the maze of black corridors over the past few days and found the elevator. Stabbing the descend button as many times as she could without breaking her thumb, she dropped out onto the main floor and walked straight out the front door.

Her heart constricted tight in her chest with every foot she added between her and Socorro's headquarters. But she wasn't going back.

A line of dirt kicked up ahead as a dark SUV raced along the desert floor. It pulled to a stop a few feet away, and the driver's side window lowered to reveal Scarlett Beam, free from military custody. "I take it you're not lost. Need a ride?"

Maggie fought the urge to look back as she rounded the hood of the SUV and climbed into the passenger side seat.

"Where to?" Scarlett asked.

She stared out at the bare landscape capable of eroding even the strongest of mountains. She had to be stronger for what came next. "I'm going home."

He'd screwed this up without even trying.

Jones watched from his bedroom window as the SUV flipped around and sped off toward civilization with Maggie inside. She was stubborn enough to walk the entire way back to Albuquerque, but he was grateful she didn't have to. His phone pinged with an incoming message. One tap revealed Chief Baker Halsey's attachment. A police report from a nearby department. He read through the document. "Damn it all to hell."

Maggie didn't have a chance out there on her own. The military unit ordered to clean up after the *Sangre por Sangre* massacre would catch up to her. They'd ensure she never said a word about any of this, and the truth would die with her.

His hands were tied. He'd had a choice. Pursue this investigation to the end of the line with Maggie and risk everything he and the rest of the operatives here at Socorro had built. Or finish the job the Pentagon had contracted them to do: dismantle *Sangre por Sangre* and protect the people of this region. Ivy Bardot had made the stakes clear to him at the beginning.

"Nah. This isn't finished." Jones whistled low to wake Gotham. The husky shot to his feet and followed close on Jones's heels as they navigated through the building and up to the fourth floor. He didn't bother knocking this time, shoving the door to Ivy Bardot's office open. "We need to talk."

Socorro's founder cut her sharp gaze to him. Though there wasn't a single ounce of annoyance as she excused herself from her current phone call and hung up. "I wasn't aware we had another meeting scheduled."

"We don't." His heart refused to drop out of his throat. He'd disobeyed orders before, and it'd cost him his career. Loyalty was what kept him and the rest of his team alive. They had to trust each other in every regard, each a vital cog in the machine that ensured cartels like *Sangre por Sangre* were kept in check. Because the second they lost sight of Socorro's goal, every one of them would fail. But Maggie had been right. If he hadn't disobeyed his orders while at the tail end of his service, he would've lost those precious months he'd gained with his brother. Kincaide would've died at the hands of his captors, buried in an unmarked grave in the middle of the desert. Never to be found. He couldn't stomach the thought of something like that happening to Maggie. "I'm here to tell you that you made the wrong choice about Maggie Caddel."

Hesitation slowed Ivy from restacking a set of documents on her oversize desk. Amusement scratched at the surface of her expression but nothing more. Socorro's founder was out of touch. Safe up here in her ivory tower, where she didn't have to get her hands dirty anymore and operatives did her bidding. Where she didn't have to see the violence and hurt they exacted on her behalf every day. He'd told himself over and over that wasn't the case, but when it came to Maggie, he wasn't so sure anymore. Ivy leaned back in her seat, interlacing her fingers in front of her. "Okay. Enlighten me."

This was his chance. To do what he should've done a long time ago. Save the person he loved. Jones took a step forward and offered her his phone. "Alpine Valley PD ran the ballistics on the bullets found in our friend Sosimo Toledano and his men from that basement. Apart from my bullet, one set came from an XM7 rifle, another from an XM250 automatic rifle and the third from a pistol. All part of the military's move forward with the Next Generation Squad Program proposed by Sig Sauer."

"Military hardware. We don't see a lot of that. At least not new weaponry." Ivy reviewed the report. "You believe this was done by the same team you claim destroyed proof of the operation to capture Toledano the night of Ms. Caddel's abduction and burned the bodies of the soldiers caught in that ambush?"

"I have a hard time believing they're not part of this. Or that they're working rogue, but the order would've had to come down from on high. Someone who has a close relationship with the army, possibly even served and has a couple friends to call in a favor from." Jones was starting to feel that same frenzy, the one Maggie lost herself in when on the cusp of another piece of the puzzle falling into place. It started in his fingers until he grasped the back of one chair positioned in front of Ivy's desk. "Who in the state senate had been calling for us to stand down since we got here?"

A tightness Jones had never witnessed in Ivy flexed the muscles at her jaw as she handed back his phone. "Senator Hawkes. Former army captain. Served his twenty before stepping into the political arena. The man considers *Sangre por Sangre* and organizations like it one of the biggest threats to the state with the amount of drugs they pump into our cities and schools."

"Why the hell would he have anything against Socorro?" he asked.

"Regulations." Ivy sat forward, her elbows on the edge of the desk. "He's managed to get himself on the contract review committee for the Pentagon. He's tried to have our contract terminated every year, insists that despite our military origins, the regulations and laws that apply to the army, navy, marines and air force don't apply to private military contractors as it's spelled out in the agreement. That we're in the business of making money, not protecting this country, and that's why we've let *Sangre por Sangre* spread like a virus through the state."

"He blames us for the cartel's growth," he said.

"Accused Socorro and me of working for our own interests last time I was called in front of the committee. Got quite the support, too. Only not enough to terminate our contract. He's still working on it though. One of these days he just might get what he needs." She dropped her hands open as though that was nothing more than a bridge to cross in the future. "And he's right, in a way. As long as there is a threat from the cartels, we have jobs."

"Whereas the army wouldn't be under the same expectation." He tried to loosen his grip on the back of the chair, but the adrenaline had already taken hold. "That's our motive. What better way to undercut Socorro than to have the army step in and save the day after the cartel is connected to the deaths of ten American soldiers. Show we're not doing enough. That we're not needed, and the army would be much better suited for this job. When is the Pentagon review committee meeting next?"

"In a week." Ivy seemed to consider his words for a series of breaths. "It's clever. I'll give you that, but you have nothing more than an eyewitness who's been through an abduction she didn't report to police, and a ballistics report that Sosimo Toledano and his men were shot with military-grade bullets that could've come from anywhere with enough effort. Even if you had the photos Ms. Caddel claimed she took that night, you don't have the evidence to accuse a state senator of misuse of power, let alone corruption."

"What if I could get it?" Jones had already made his decision. No matter what Ivy said, he wasn't going to sit here and wait for Chief Halsey to forward him the news of Maggie's body showing up in the middle of the desert. "Maggie's on her way back to Albuquerque. The unit sent to cover up all these loose ends is going to come for her. They can't afford to leave her alive. I want to be there when they make their move."

"You want to apprehend and flip one of their soldiers to prove a connection to the senator," Ivy said. "What makes you think they'll talk? Based on what I've seen of their handiwork, these aren't the type of men to negotiate. Their entire lives revolve around orders, and you're not exactly on their Christmas card list."

"I don't know," Jones said. "All I know is I can't leave Maggie to face this alone. She deserves better than that. She deserves to have someone finally keep their word."

"You like her." Socorro's founder stood, rounding her

desk. Ivy cracked her pinkie finger knuckle with one thumb. A tell he hadn't noticed until now. She knew she couldn't stop him, and the lack of control was getting to her. Crossing her arms over her frame, she leaned back against the solid wood. "I can tell you to keep your emotions out of this, but I doubt you're going to listen. Even after what I've seen, some part of me still thinks our emotions are what make us the team we are. I'm not willing to put that to the test, but take it from me, Jones. The only way any of us get out of this is if we trust ourselves. Can you tell me, without hesitation, that you truly believe this is the right course of action?"

Jones evened out his weight between both legs. Surer of himself than ever before. "It's the only course of action, ma'am."

"All right, then. Take your K9 and a partner. Preferably Scarlett as she's been through all this with you up until now," she said. "And, please, for the love of all that is holy, keep this out of the news. We don't need to give Senator Hawkes more ammunition to shoot us with if you fail."

"Understood." Jones was on the move. Excitement for the upcoming fight burned in his veins, drove him harder. He unpocketed his phone and hit Scarlett Beam's contact information as he rounded into his room. The line rang once. Twice. Three times. Nervous energy skittered down his spine as he checked the screen for a good connection. Full bars and Wi-Fi. Pressing the pad of his thumb to the safe's keypad, he listened for the familiar click from the other end of the line.

Only it never came.

The line disconnected, and he tried again.

Gotham groaned as he hiked himself up the floor-to-ceiling window with his front paws. As though he wanted to go after Maggie himself. Jones knew the feeling. It'd been Scarlett's SUV he'd watched Maggie climb into. He was sure of it. The security consultant wouldn't give him the silent treatment in the middle of an assignment like this, even if he was at fault for her arrest.

The call connected.

"Jones…" Scarlett's voice scratched through from the other end of the line, out of breath, wheezy. "It happened so fast. I couldn't stop them. She's gone. Maggie is gone."

Chapter Thirteen

"Do you know who I am?" an unfamiliar voice asked.

Maggie tried to drag her chin away from her chest, but it hurt. Everything hurt. Her head slipped back, hitting something solid. Pain lightninged across her skull and into her face. Like she'd been hit straight on by a train. She knew this feeling—hated it—and suddenly she was right back in that room. Waiting for El Capitan's next round of questioning. Her throat worked to come up with the answer her brain automatically relied on to get her through the next few minutes. "Maggie Caddel. War correspondent. *American Military News.*"

Name. Rank. Serial number. It'd become a mantra of sorts. Something to help her disconnect from her body when she needed it the most. But she hadn't needed it since… Since Jones pulled her out of *Sangre por Sangre*'s headquarters. Maggie forced her eyes—too heavy—to split. And was immediately assaulted by a circle of electric lanterns and flashlights.

"I know who you are, Ms. Caddel." A calloused hand framed her chin, directing her gaze to a face on the brink of sliding right off. It felt too low, as though gravity was winning. Age defined small eyes and creased lines horizontally across the man's chin. Some sections were deeper than others. She'd never seen that before. A tall forehead tried holding onto a receding gray hairline. Though the man keeping her head upright hadn't lost much elsewhere. An open collar hinted at a spread of chest hair. Perfectly manicured. It went with his expensive-looking suit. This was someone who saw himself as important. "Damn it, lieutenant. You hit her too hard. She can barely get herself going. How is she supposed to tell me what I want to know like this?"

"Sorry, sir. We had to move fast. One of Socorro's operatives—Beam—caught us off guard. She wasn't as easy to take down as we estimated." Movement registered off to the left, and a second outline came into view.

That voice. She recognized it between bouts of dread and panic. The bonfire. He'd been there. He'd burned her SD card in front of her along with the bodies of his military brothers and sisters. Maggie tried to take in the gunmen poised with weapons clutched close to their vests. Six of them. All at the ready for their next order. "Scarlett."

"Ah, there we go. She's coming around." Sir… Whatever-His-Name dropped his hold on her face, and her neck dipped forward. He was getting his suit dirty crouched in front of her like this. Probably have to throw it away, but something told her keeping himself clean had been the plan from the beginning. Dirty work wasn't his forte. "I asked you a question a minute ago. Do you recognize me?"

How could she not? It was her job to recognize him.

His face had been smeared across news cycles for weeks leading up to the Pentagon's annual contractor review. Senator Collin Hawkes had branded himself New Mexico's savior against the drug cartels. Zero tolerance. Bigger sentences. More aggressive policies. He was a husband, a father, a grandfather even. Not only campaigning for companies like Socorro Security to operate under stricter guidelines and laws—under his control, funny enough—but proposing the military step in against the cartels slowly strangling this state one town at a time.

And he was a liar.

Because now she knew the truth. Everything that'd happened in the past week—the murder of those soldiers, her abduction and torture by Sosimo Toledano, the cover-up—it'd all come from him. He didn't give a damn about the people affected by the drug cartels. He just wanted the glory of taking them down. And she wasn't going to give him anything. "Maggie Caddel. War correspondent. *American Military News.*"

A burst of laughter popped from the senator's mouth as he struggled to turn and face the men and women at his back. "Somebody get this woman to answer me."

The soldier—the one on her left—stepped forward. Pain ripped across her scalp as he jerked her head back by a fistful of hair, but it was nothing compared to the blade pressing against her throat. "You're going to want to lose the attitude, Maggie. This isn't the kind of guy you want to mess with right now."

"You think killing me will do any good?" She couldn't stop her own laugh from rocking through her chest. More features clarified and bled into her awareness as her vision adjusted to the brightness of the lights. No masks this time. Seemed the soldiers who'd destroyed the evidence of the ambush weren't too worried about her identifying them now. Most likely because they were going to kill her. No one was coming. Scarlett might've had the chance to call in the cavalry after they were attacked at Maggie's apartment, but Socorro and Jones had made their position clear. They weren't in this fight. This was something she had to do herself.

It was then she realized where she was, and her confidence shook loose. She was in that same room. Zip-tied, at the control of others. Only this time she understood why she was here. And that her captors were afraid of her. Maggie forced a deep breath to counter the alarm signaling through her defenses. "You might've gotten rid of the photos and the bodies, but you couldn't get to me in time. I wrote the story."

She directed that to the senator. "How you sent ten American soldiers to their deaths during an operation they thought would hurt *Sangre por Sangre*. How you ordered a highly trained military unit to get rid of the bodies and kill the journalist who could expose you, then slaughtered cartel members to cover it all up. It doesn't matter that I don't have proof or that you'll probably get rid of my body the same way you got rid of those soldiers. All it takes is a nudge."

A slight shift in his jowl told her how uncomfortable this conversation was getting. That he'd underestimated how much she knew of what he'd done, and a small victory charged through her at the idea of destabilizing the man responsible for so much pain and suffering.

"You partnered with a known fugitive. I don't know the details of your deal with Sosimo Toledano, but he must've outlived his usefulness after you got your henchmen to get rid of all that evidence. So you had him killed, too. What do you think will happen once that story breaks, and his daddy learns the truth, Senator Hawkes?" Maggie gave into the needles of pain stinging at her neck from the blade. Because it was something to focus on. Something she could feel when her heart wanted nothing more than to numb itself as her left leg had done.

Heartbreak did that.

Whitewashed the mind, body and spirit of color. She'd wanted Jones to be the one to pull her back from the brink. To make her believe her past didn't have a hold on her future. And they'd gotten so close. She'd fallen in love with him. Only to once again find herself at the mercy of a man she thought she could trust. The hurt inside overwhelmed anything Senator Hawkes and his gunmen could possibly do to her physically. She'd already survived one torturer. That was the easy part. Believing in love again? That was another beast altogether.

She slipped her fingers along the structural crease at her lower back where leaking water had eroded a section of the cement floor. "How long do you think you'll last before the cartel comes for you?"

"You want to know what I think will happen, Ms. Caddel?" Senator Hawkes got to his feet, revealing an overweight frame brought on by years of serving behind a desk. Pulling a white handkerchief from his suit pocket, he wiped his hands. "I think my constituents will see I get things done. I think they'll see that I'm willing to put my own career—even my life—on the line to ensure organizations like *Sangre por Sangre* stop getting away with murder, stop pumping drugs into our schools and stop abducting our women and young girls for trade. I think they'll want action. Action that only I can give them. Because once the people of this state see how Socorro and Ivy Bardot have let the cartel grow like a cancer to bolster their bottom line, there will only be one solution—me and my willingness to do whatever it takes to win."

"It won't work." Her argument was nothing. Pathetic and weak.

"Why? Because you've written some piece that points the finger at me in the end? You're nothing but a blogger whose reputation as a bipolar schizophrenic is archived in your divorce proceedings, Ms. Caddel." The senator handed off his handkerchief to one of the gunmen as though he owned every person in the room. Maybe he did. He reached back for something from another soldier and brought it forward. Her camera. He turned it over in his hand. The lanterns glinted off what was left of the shattered lens. He thumbed the power button and a miniscule amount of light cast back onto his suit jacket. It worked. "You're right in that Toledano and I had a deal. I guess there's no point in keeping it a secret, seeing as how you're not leaving this room alive. I got word through the grapevine there was a civil war simmering inside *Sangre por Sangre*. You see, the guy at the top has let too many of Socorro's interferences slide without repercussions. Toledano kept pushing his daddy to make things right, but it turns out, the old man is more interested in profits than in remembering how he got them in the first place. So I approached Toledano with a deal that could benefit us both. All he had to do was be at the time and place I gave him and make sure nobody left alive."

"It was a setup," she said. "You got the approval for the operation by showing the military you knew exactly where Sosimo Toledano would be and at what time."

"Yeah. Well, Toledano didn't know the entire mission was proposed as an effort to guarantee his capture. He learned about that later. The second he slaughtered those soldiers, he'd signed his death warrant. There was nothing he could do or say to get out of us coming for him. And it worked out, too. Two birds with one stone. Toledano and his men were brought to justice, and now I've proven Socorro doesn't have the resources or the motive to get the job they were hired to do done. I win on both sides. Took some doing to make sure that nobody figured out what I was up to. Altering satellite footage is harder than it looks. Not to mention making sure no one got wind of the fact that Toledano left you alive, but it all worked out in the end." The senator fanned his hands out as though he'd just golfed a perfect round without having to cheat. "I was hoping you were smart enough to back off once I asked your editor to cut you loose, but I see I'm going to have to get nasty. You thought three days with Sosimo Toledano were rough? It's nothing compared to what these guys will do to you once I give the order."

"All this for me? I'm flattered." Maggie dug one finger into the hole in the floor growing bigger at her insistence. A shard broke away, and she gripped on to it with everything she had. He was right about one thing. There was no way she was getting out of this room alive, but she sure as hell was going to fight until her last breath. She'd make it hurt, too. Make sure her remains held on to a bit of their DNA.

"I think we're done here." Senator Hawkes handed off the camera and nodded to the man with the knife at her throat. He backed off, sheathing it before he stepped back. "The photos you took are gone, Ms. Caddel. The bodies of those soldiers will never be identified, let alone recovered. It'll be hard for the families, sure, but I'll be there for them. Make sure they're taken care of. After all, it's the least I can do for their sacrifice in this war."

"You're a monster. You're provoking the cartel, and they'll retaliate. Only the next set of American lives taken might not be under your control." He had to be stopped. Before this went any further. She pressed the shard through the zip ties. The plastic broke free. Maggie launched herself off the floor with the cement blade in hand and arced it directly toward the senator's neck.

Only the makeshift weapon didn't make it that far.

The soldier to the left caught her wrist.

"Heroes are overrated, Ms. Caddel." The senator stared at her from behind the tip of the shard. "They don't have the guts to do what needs to be done."

THE SUV'S TIRES skidded across graveled asphalt with a scream.

Jones threw the transmission into Park and shoved himself free of the vehicle with Gotham launching from the cabin behind him. Two Albuquerque PD patrol cars angled inward on either side of the front door. Two hours. Every second she was out there was another second she might not make it home. And he couldn't live with that.

He rounded the hood of the SUV, taking in the four-story apartment building planted just west of Albuquerque's Old Town. Gray stucco and clean lines nodded to the state's heritage, while electric neon paint brought the structure into the modern century and attracted millennials who preferred to work from home. Over-size windows stared out over the park across the street and the botanical gardens on the other side. The place came with a hell of a view, and, for a split second, Jones couldn't do anything but imagine Maggie building her new life here. Searching each balcony, he tried identifying Maggie's apartment, but they all looked the same. Her commitment and desperation to make journalism her life wouldn't have left time or energy for her to decorate, yet he couldn't help but want to believe her place was the one with the planter holding on to the remains of an underwatered houseplant.

Something new to signify the life she wanted to build.

Scarlett rushed through the glass front door leading into what Jones assumed was the building's lobby, and the rest of the world caught up in a rush. Blood dried in a crusted line down her face at the left side. But it was her freshly busted knuckles that told Jones his teammate had fought like hell to protect Maggie. "Any word?"

"No. You?" He anticipated the security consultant's answer before she shook her head. Scanning the property, he mapped out where he would've set up shop and waited for a target to walk into the cross hairs. The building itself wasn't large. At least not compared to a few others going up in the area. The park didn't provide any cover. The sons of bitches would've had to have seen Maggie and Scarlett coming to get the jump on them so quickly. He headed for the lobby. "Tell me what happened."

Scarlett brought both hands to her hips as though she was trying to catch her breath after sprinting long distance. "I did everything I was supposed to, Jones. I swear to you. I walked her upstairs and cleared the entire apartment. I checked all the windows and the back door and clocked any surveillance cameras. There weren't signs the place had been broken into. But I figured this wasn't over, that even though we were ordered to stand down, she was still in danger. So I followed protocol. Only it wasn't enough. Once I cleared the apartment, I left her there. Alone. I got back to the car, and I noticed the parking garage arm stuck open."

They pushed into the stairwell and climbed the three floors before entering Maggie's apartment. A small round dining table greeted them just inside the entryway with a terrace straight out the back door. With a single hanging planter holding onto a dying fern. The

rest of the place was neat, bright and bare. They turned
into the main living space, bypassing a massive kitchen
island. Square cubby bookshelves lined the wall floor-
to-ceiling and held stacks of books, magazines and
notebooks. A desk—too large for the room—held as
many, if not more, articles and notebooks. And photos.

"They stayed out of sight until they got eyes on her.
Most likely through the building's camera network.
Once they saw you leave, they came from the garage."
Pressure accumulated in Jones's gut as he shuffled
through surveillance photos. Shots of men on corners,
each dated over the past year with bright sticky notes.
Not professional in the least. Scribbled handwriting
crossed out and rewrote theories as to the identities
and movements of one subject in particular. *Sangre por
Sangre* soldiers. Maggie had spent months following
and identifying low-level members of the cartel before
winding up in their hands. This was where her obsession had started.

"I got off a couple rounds before they put her in one
of their vehicles." Scarlett's voice shook, spiking his
blood pressure higher. There wasn't much that could
rattle one of the best security consultants in the country.
But losing a client didn't sit well with any of them. This
wasn't about cushioning their bottom lines, Pentagon
contracts or employment security as Senator Hawkes
was determined to gut them for. This was about protecting those who couldn't protect themselves. Of pen-
ance for the sins of their pasts. "I was so focused on
getting to her, I didn't see they'd left a man behind.
He clocked me when I came around the corner. I held

my own for a few minutes. I imagine that's what they wanted so they could get away."

"It wasn't your fault, Scarlett. These guys knew exactly what they were doing and when to strike." He forced himself to focus on the rest of the apartment and not how being in this personal space unsettled him in ways he didn't want to think about. This place was a step into Maggie's world, where he didn't have control of any of the variables. Her abduction happened because of him. Because he'd crumbled at the idea she could be taken from him as Kincaide had, that he wouldn't be enough to protect her. And he'd proven himself right by not choosing her over Socorro's and Ivy Bardot's agendas sooner. He'd let her slip from his fingers, and now she was going to pay the price.

He'd been so careful not to get close to anyone over the years that he'd honestly never saw Maggie coming. Her competitiveness to prove herself, her warmth despite having a cartel try to break her in every way. She was easily distracted by new leads, overthought everything and put all of her self-worth into goals she had no control over, but those were the things that made her unique. That set her apart from the other women in his life. She wasn't perfect, but Jones didn't want perfect. He wanted Maggie. He wanted her stressed-out workaholic approach, her inability to stick to a routine and her need for approval from others. He wanted everything she disliked about herself and more. Because he loved her.

"Security footage is no good. I already tried. Bastards destroyed the system on their way out," Scarlett said. "I found the guard unconscious in a maintenance closet. Cops are getting his statement now, but so far, he hasn't been able to identify a single member of the team that took her."

And they wouldn't. Scarlett had already proven that any nosing into military business would put them in a set of cuffs with a court date set in the far distant future. They didn't have that kind of time. They had to come at this from another angle.

"We don't need to identify them." Jones tapped the edge of Maggie's desk. He had experience with deconstructing operations, reworking them and putting the pieces back together. Iteration was key across enemy lines, improving one thing at a time over the course of a mission until you got the result you wanted. A journalist with no prior professional experience had managed to start at the bottom and work her way up. "We just need to locate them. Put in a call to Senator Hawkes's office. I want to know where he is today."

"The guy trying to get our Pentagon contract terminated? You think he's involved?" Scarlett pulled her phone from her pants pockets. The shiner in her left eye was swelling by the minute, but Jones knew her well enough, she wouldn't let something as minimal as a scalp laceration and a black eye slow her down. Putting the phone to her ear, she cut her attention to him and flashed a wide smile. "Yes, Senator Hawkes's office, please. My name? Uh... Ivy Bardot. He's been expecting my call."

One second. Two.

"Oh, he's not in the office today. Out on personal

business. Oh, that would be great. Thank you." Scarlett shook her head, dragging the phone from her ear. She punched in a series of commands on the screen. A loud ringing filled the apartment as she set the call to speaker. "She's forwarding me to his personal cell. I can run a trace on his GPS from here."

"Don't you need a court order for that?" Jones asked.

The ringing cut short, sending the call straight to voice mail.

"Haven't you heard? Socorro doesn't live up to the same standards as the rest of the country. We can do whatever we want. It's in our contract." Scarlett tried to keep her smile to herself. The line clicked. "Bingo. Voice mail."

You've reached—

The security consultant thumbed a few more taps against the screen, drawing Jones in. She worked fast, then turned the phone toward him. "And, I'm into his phone. Easy peasy. I can do anything from in here. Want to send a bunch of dirty messages to his contacts list and see how they respond?"

"I want his location, Scarlett. Now." Nervous energy tightened the muscles down the backs of his legs. Maggie was in the hands of a man desperate to destroy every shred of evidence of how he'd overstepped his authority. How long would he leave her alive? "We can send the messages after Maggie's back in our protection."

"Got it. I guess he's not smart enough to put his phone in airplane mode when he's in the middle of an abduction." Scarlett's smile fell as she handed off the phone. The blue dot signaling the current location of the senator's phone swelled and relaxed. Right in the middle of the one place Jones never wanted to step foot in again. "You think she's there?"

"There's only one way to find out. Get your gear and call in the rest of the team." Jones took one last look at the apartment, envisioning Maggie back at her desk, working on her next story when all of this was over. They were about to officially declare war on the US military. But the realization didn't come with the sense of dread he expected. He was going after Maggie. He was going to bring her home. And he'd take down anyone who got in his way. "We're going to need them."

Chapter Fourteen

"The only reason you're still alive is because I need to make sure you didn't share your little theory with anyone else." Senator Hawkes added some distance between them as his military henchman twisted Maggie's arm behind her back. Wouldn't want to get any blood on that suit, after all. "As much as I believe what I've done here is perfectly within justification for the greater good, I can't have anyone else coming out of the woodwork, you see."

A groan escaped up her throat, but she kept it from leaving past her lips. She wasn't going to give them the satisfaction. Any of them. She tried to wrench her arm out of his hold, but bone-deep pain warned of dislocating her own arm. "Well, let's see. There's my editor, who you bullied into firing me. There's the founder and operatives of Socorro Security. You know, the people who have been making sure I stay alive the past few days. Alpine Valley police, who've offered to clean up the mess you left behind on the other side of this complex. Oh, and that little circle of friends I curated at every news outlet in the country."

The senator lost a bit of that smugness etched into

the corners of his eyes. He turned to face her fully, waiting for the punch line to drop. Only she didn't have one. "You're bluffing."

"I'm not." Maggie savored the victory despite the oncoming suffering. Every cell in her body wanted relief. To be out of this room, to go home, to see Jones walk through that door as he had that first time and take her away from all of this. She tried to breathe through the pain igniting in her shoulder socket. "I'm sure you've been monitoring my email accounts. Check my outgoing folder. You'll see I'm telling the truth."

"Give me my phone." Senator Hawkes reached back without taking his eyes off her, and one of the soldiers behind him produced the device. Thumbs touched with a bit of swelling at the knuckles thumped too hard against the delicate screen. Shock swept the arrogance from the senator's expression. If he hadn't already been washed in light from the surrounding lanterns, she would've sworn he'd lost all the blood in his face. "You bitch."

"After you had my editor fire me, I started collecting a long list of news outlets I want to pitch stories to in the coming months. Bodhi was scared. I could hear it in his voice, and I didn't think that was ever possible." Her chest ached at the intersection of her pinned arm and torso. So much so, her nerve endings started tingling. Just as they had in her leg. Maggie tried to force as much oxygen into the strangled limb as she could, but it was no use. "I figured someone with a lot of authority had threatened him to drop me as one of the magazine's writers, but the evidence I'd gathered didn't pose any threat. All I had were pieces of a bigger puzzle that didn't make sense. No big picture. But whoever was behind this wanted me taken out of that picture so much they sent a highly trained military unit who doesn't question orders. Just follows them. Turns out, I was onto something. So you can tell me that your constituents and the Pentagon will support you after this all gets out, Senator. But I know the truth. You're scared of losing everything you've worked for. And now you know how it feels."

The strike came so fast, she didn't have time to brace herself.

Pain ricocheted through her face and twisted her head to one side. Her vision battled to catch up as lightning struck behind her eyes. Maggie recovered quickly with the telltale salty taste of blood. A small cut stung as she probed her tongue through her mouth, and she spat a mouthful at the senator's shoes. He wasn't just going to have to get rid of that suit. "And you hit like a five-year-old."

Senator Hawkes closed the distance between them. "You think you have any leverage here? I've been telling the media what it can and can't do since I took office. None of this is going to make a difference, Ms. Caddel. People might be upset over the next few days, but they'll change their minds once they see my results. They'll beg for me to oversee further action against the cartels. I'm going to be their poster boy. And you... You'll be nothing but a has-been who never really was. A one-hit wonder. Everyone you love, everyone you care about is going to forget you even existed by the time I'm finished."

A twinge of fear cut through her as the past week with Jones infiltrated the moment. Was that true? Would he forget her? Would she be the assignment that went wrong but had little effect on Socorro's overall mission? All she'd ever wanted was to be important to someone. To matter. She hadn't always gotten the attention she'd wanted from her parents or siblings growing up, but that'd been life. Three kids split by four years each demanded different levels of interest from two working parents trying to cover the monthly bills. She'd had friends, sure, but nothing concrete that lasted past high school. Marrying her high school sweetheart after she graduated college started to fill that hole constantly begging for her attention, but within a year, she'd noticed the signs of isolation. Of snide comments on her appearance or how she talked to his friends. Of his expectations of her growing more disciplined and intense. Of never being good enough for the man she'd married. Even during her tenure for *American Military News*, she'd been shoved to the back of the queue compared to the more veteran reporters.

But with Jones… Everything had been about her. Which sounded so selfish, even in her own mind, that it physically made her cringe. For once, she hadn't been the one trying to hold everything together. She'd been allowed to eat what, when and however often she pleased without waiting for a nasty comment about her figure. She'd rested without feeling lazy or guilty and put herself and her recovery first for the first time… ever. And he'd let her. Encouraged her. Showed her what real kindness looked like, and that asking for what she needed was the bravest and best thing she'd ever done for herself.

No. He couldn't forget all that. She wouldn't let him. Because she was getting out of here. She was going back to Socorro to show Jones how he'd changed her from the inside out. He was going to know how she felt.

A steady pulse pounded through the right side of her face, but Maggie could still make out a bead of sweat at the senator's temple. Along with the slight deepening of his voice. He was trying to stay in control. And losing the fight. "If you're so sure my article isn't going to ruin you, then why are you sweating?"

Senator Hawkes pulled at the lapels of his suit jacket to straighten some invisible wrinkle. "Get her out of my sight. I don't want to know the details but make it quick. I've got a review committee meeting to prepare for and a press release to write."

"Yes, sir." The soldier at her back hauled her against his chest.

A rumble rolled through the room and dislodged dust from the crevices along the ceiling.

She felt the vibration from the front of her foot to the back charge up both legs. Silence pressed in through the room as the dust settled against the broken-up floor.

The senator raised both hands out in front of him as though he'd found himself on some kind of balance beam. Or the ground under his feet was about to swallow him whole. "What the hell was that?"

An uneasy feeling swept from one soldier to the next. They widened their stances in preparation, but nobody knew what was coming.

She did. Socorro was coming. Jones was coming. For her. "You're going to want to start running now, Senator. I'd hate for you to meet my partner face-to-face when he's in a bad mood."

The senator didn't waste a single second. He motioned to the soldiers in his immediate vicinity. "You five, get me the hell out of here. And you—" He nodded to the gunman holding Maggie captive as Hawkes dashed for the door. "Finish this. That's an order."

"Yes, sir." The soldier's grip tightened on her arm, cutting off blood flow. "Move."

Her left toes caught on a raised section of floor, and she stumbled forward. Shards of damaged cement and gravel bit into her palms. Maggie took a moment to catch her breath.

"Get up." The soldier kicked at her heels. "Or I'll make you get up."

Pressure at finding herself once again at someone else's mercy built until it cut off her air supply. Jones and his team were still working their way through the building. It'd take them minutes, maybe an hour before they found her, especially if they were forced to stand off with Hawkes's men. By then, it'd be too late. She had to do this herself. Because no amount of self-worth could really come from the people around her. She had to have it for herself first.

Maggie fisted a handful of the debris detaching from the structure every second. It wasn't much, but it could make all the difference. She arced her arm over her shoulder and twisted her upper body with everything she had. The debris shot straight into the soldier's face.

His growl echoed through the room a split second before a burst of gunfire exploded from his rifle.

She ducked and covered as she shoved herself to her feet.

Then ran like hell.

She'd never had the chance to map out this section of the compound when under Toledano's watch. Low punctures of gunshots registered as she turned right. Heading toward the action would give the senator the chance to finish what he'd started.

Staying alive until Socorro found her. That was all that mattered. Maggie headed in the opposite direction, away from the promise of safety, away from Jones. She skimmed her hand along one wall and bolted down the corridor.

Her left leg worked overtime as the steady thump of boots grew louder. She couldn't outrun the shooter. She couldn't fight him, but she sure as hell wouldn't give him the satisfaction of finishing his mission. Maggie ducked into the nearest room as another vibration rolled through the building. Seconds ticked off as she pressed her back to the wall, out of sight of the door into total darkness.

"It's nothing personal, Maggie," the soldier said. "We're all just following orders here."

Her breathing sounded overly loud. She tried to swallow the too-hard thud of her heartbeat in her throat. In vain. He was going to find her, and she'd have to fight back.

"I know you're in here." His voice sounded much closer now. Too close. "You're all alone. That team you think is going to save you? They ain't coming in time. I told you. Nothing stops me from following orders."

Maggie searched for something—anything—to use as a weapon without giving away her position. But this room seemed just as bare as the one she'd been held in.

"She's not alone." That familiar voice cut through the corridor and through the fear squeezing around her heart. Jones. Gotham's growl followed. "And neither am I."

THE MASKS HAD come off.

But that went both ways, didn't it?

The soldier responsible for making sure Maggie disappeared turned that rifle onto Jones. Lieutenant Jason Snow, six tours in Iraq and Afghanistan, two medals of valor, on the hook with the senator who'd sent him to take the fall.

Jones could practically feel the laser sight moving from his belly to his chest. It was okay. He had one on him, too. Gotham shook waiting for permission to lunge, despite not training for combat purposes. Turned out, the dog had gotten fond of having Maggie around this past week. They were in this together. Determined to get her out alive. And they weren't leaving without her. "My team already has Senator Hawkes in custody, lieutenant. The only way you get out of this unscathed is if you let her go."

"And break orders?" The voice wasn't as high and tight as it had been at the bonfire. More strangled and smoky. As though the son of a bitch had swallowed a lungful of mold and was choking on it granule by granule. Good. He deserved to suffer for what he'd put Maggie through. "Must come so easy for you at this point, Driscoll. What is this, the second—or third—time? Any good soldier knows his own hubris can get the people he cares about killed."

"The army only minded the one time. Lucky for me, I have a new unit now. One that would do the same thing for me. So I'll do what I have to today to ensure every single one of us makes it out of here alive." And he should've done it sooner. Maybe if he'd taken a stand with Ivy before Maggie had left headquarters, they wouldn't be here. Then again, it was because of her they now knew who'd signed Maggie's death warrant in the first place.

"No. You won't." The statement was punctuated by a pull of the trigger.

"No!" Maggie shot from the darkness, hiking the barrel of the soldier's rifle upward. Strobes of light lit up the corridor in millisecond increments and revealed her fight to get control of the weapon.

He couldn't take a shot. Not without putting her in his own cross hairs. "Stay," he commanded Gotham.

The gun ripped free of her hand. "You know. I said this wasn't personal, but now it is." Snow rocketed a fist into Maggie's face. She twisted and slammed into the wall behind her before slumping to the ground. Unconscious.

Jones launched forward, weapon up. One squeeze of the trigger bolted Snow's shoulder back. The groan of pain lasted a split second as Jones descended to get control of the rifle. A spray of gunfire exploded in a long line, missing Maggie by mere inches. "You're going to pay for that."

Jones slammed the end of the rifle into the wall where Maggie had made contact. An arm navigated around his neck and shoved him sideways. They struggled—bare strength versus strength. Jones ducked to relieve the pressure on his neck and maneuvered out of the hold. Only to put his back to his opponent. Rookie mistake.

Strong arms secured around his neck and squeezed.

Latching onto Snow's wrist, he tried wriggling free. To no avail.

Snow growled in his ear, out of breath and wheezing. "Accept it, Driscoll. You've gone soft since your discharge. All this—everyone you love, everything you care about, that team of yours—soldiers like me are the ones who made it possible. You never deserved any of it in the first place."

Leveraging his foot against the opposite wall, Jones launched them backward. He slammed Snow into the cinder block behind him, but it didn't have any effect on the bastard's hold. He fell to one side in an attempt to dislodge the stranglehold around his neck as pinpricks of white moved into his vision.

Only, a section of the floor fell away.

Gravity knotted in his gut a split second before pain exploded. They hit the level beneath as one. His entire body felt as though it was about to snap in half but somehow held together. Gotham's bark echoed down through the opening they'd created overhead. Jones could just make out the husky's outline through the floating debris.

Snow took the brunt of the impact but didn't seem to miss a beat as he locked his ankles around Jones's front and squeezed to push the air from Jones's chest. "Maggie's taken one too many hits to the head, Driscoll. What do you think the chances of her waking up after what I just did to her are?" The son of a bitch pressed his mouth to Jones's ear. "Mission complete, traitor."

No. She was alive. She had to be. Because if she wasn't... He'd never forgive himself. He'd have to live with another life ruined because of his unwillingness to move when certain situations asked him to bend, and he couldn't take that weight anymore. In the end, Kincaide had been a ghost of the brother who'd stood up for him that day after school. Maggie deserved better than that. She deserved everything he had to give and more. To be happy. He could make her happy. Dust created a veil of thickness around them, almost sparkling in the beam of their dueling flashlights. She was right there. Within reach. He just had to get to her.

He tried for his sidearm. Only he couldn't pull it free with Snow's leg pinning the weapon to his thigh. Jones locked his hand around his attacker's wrist and put everything he had into getting free. The soldier's arm broke its deadly grip. He rolled out of Snow's reach then launched himself onto the son of a bitch's back. Both arms cut off Snow's oxygen. Just as the lieutenant had done to him. He struggled to stay in place as Snow bucked underneath him, wild as a bull pissed as all hell about the cowboy trying to get him under control. Strangling sounds bounced off the walls around them, but Jones wouldn't let up. Not yet.

Snow kicked at the floor and managed to bring his upper body high enough to twist Jones back against the wall. The lieutenant clawed at his hands. His groans were getting weaker as oxygen burned in his lungs.

A few more seconds. That was all Jones needed.

The soldier's boots scuffed against the floor, carving out valleys in the piled layers of dust created over the past few minutes. It wouldn't do any good. It was Jones's turn to put his mouth to Snow's ear. "Some things in this world are more important than orders, Snow. One day you're going to figure that out. But if you come after us again, I'll kill you. I give you my word."

Snow didn't get a chance to answer as he went limp.

Shoving the soldier's body off of him, he checked the lieutenant's pulse. Weakened, but steady. The bastard would live. Though what kind of life waited for him up top, Jones couldn't say. He had a feeling Senator Hawkes wasn't going to go down alone. He'd drag everyone with him to take some of the heat off, including the very men and women he'd used to start a war.

Gotham's bark intensified as the husky pawed at the edges of the hole raining down dust on Jones. Agitated at being separated from his handler. Hell. The fight was over, but time was still running out. Jones jumped as high as his body weight would allow, but his fingers only brushed the edge of the cavity. He wasn't going to make it on his own. He swiped at the dust accumulating in the air. This room seemed to be separated from the entire compound. No way in or out. And Maggie needed him out. "Get Scarlett, Gotham. Go get Scarlett. Bring her here."

The dog disappeared from the opening, his collar echoing down the hall.

"Maggie!" There wasn't any answer, and Jones's entire body was all too aware of the fact Snow might be right. That she'd taken one too many hits and wouldn't have the capability of getting back up this time. And it'd be his fault. Jones dropped his chin to his chest as the heaviness of that possibility stabbed through him. "Maggie, if you can hear me. I'm sorry. I gave you my word that I would protect you until the end of this, and I failed. I backed out on you when you needed me the most. But the truth is, I was scared. Breaking orders is what got my brother captured in the first place, and I didn't want you to end up like him. Because I love you, Mags. I've been in love with you since the moment I pulled you out of this hellhole that first time, and I saw what you'd survived. You're strong. A hell of a lot stronger than me. I don't know how you do it, to be honest, but I want to be strong for you. Just give me another chance."

"Oh, that's sweet, Driscoll." Snow struggled to get one knee under him as he grappled with the rifle strapped around his chest. "Please, don't let the fact I'm about to kill you get in the way of telling her how you really feel."

Jones unholstered his Taser, took aim and fired it into Snow's inner thigh. The lieutenant fell back harder than expected, his entire body at the mercy of forty-thousand volts. "I wasn't talking to you."

A whimper escaped up Snow's throat, and Jones took pressure off the Taser's trigger.

"Please, Mags. Say something. Tell me you're okay. .

That after everything we've been through, I'm not the one who got you killed." He studied the opening in the ceiling. Only silence answered back. Then scraping. Something hesitant and steady. A hand clutched onto the crumbling shards of cement and rebar and pulled Maggie into sight.

Blood matted her blond hair and spread down one side of her face. But, hell, she was the most beautiful thing he'd ever seen. She dropped her hand, reaching for him. She wasn't strong enough to lift him out on her own, but that didn't stop him from locking his hand in hers. Her smile made him believe everything would be okay. That they could move past this, and he hadn't screwed everything up. That they could build a life—

"I love you, too, Jones. And thank you. For everything. For saving me in more ways than I can count. I owe you my life. But you did break your word, so I'll see you back at Socorro headquarters."

She slipped free of his hold and got to her feet, still unstable. He was prepared to catch her if she fell through, if needed. But Maggie simply backed away on her own strength.

"Wait. Are you joking?" He waited for an answer. However distant. For something to tell him she wasn't going to leave him down here as some kind of punishment until the team could get him and Snow out of this hole. "Maggie?"

"She ain't joking, man." Snow shook his head.

Jones pulled the Taser's trigger a second time and let the electric nodes do their job. "Still wasn't talking to you."

Chapter Fifteen

"Great. I'll look over the contract and get back to you tomorrow." Maggie disconnected the call, a smile tugging at one corner of her mouth as she reviewed her full email inbox. The offers hadn't stopped. There were contracts waiting for her review, pitches for articles to write. Voice mails from Bodhi begging her to call him back. The excitement hadn't let up since the moment she'd walked out of the *Sangre por Sangre* headquarters on her own two feet. Once the major news outlets had gotten hold of the piece she'd emailed, it seemed the entire world had opened up for her. She had her pick of assignments for a multitude of outlets if she wanted.

She was someone important now. A commodity everyone wanted.

The story hadn't stopped spreading. Senator Hawkes did exactly as she'd expected: run with his tail between his legs. The state police had picked him up just before he'd crossed into Mexico. The last she'd heard, his lawyer was going to earn every single penny of his retainer. Corruption charges waited on the horizon, along with a bunch of little ones the attorney general thought up along the way. Turned out the senator's constituents and fellow officials didn't so much agree with his attempt to undermine the Pentagon's choice in private military contractors or antagonize the cartel's kingpin by having the man's son murdered as much as he thought they would.

Maggie cut her attention to the news cycle across the room. And there he was. Being led by police out of a dark SUV and marched, in all his glory, in front of every camera in the state in cuffs. She rubbed at the cuts still stinging around her wrists. The wrinkles around those small pea-like eyes seemed deeper than the last time she'd seen him. Good. This was just a taste of the sleep he was going to lose over the next few months.

She hit the power button on the remote and turned off the TV.

As for the military unit at Hawkes's command, she hadn't been able to get much information. From what she understood, charges against Scarlett Beam had been dropped, but anything more than that had been deemed classified. It didn't really matter. This was one story she was happy to move on from. But the soldiers who'd sacrificed their lives on the senator's lie were still waiting for identification. Still had families in the dark. It would be a few more weeks before the crime lab in Albuquerque would have DNA results—if any had survived—but now that the truth was out there, she couldn't help but think this case had slipped to the top of the queue.

The dying plant on the back terrace swung with a gust of wind. Damn. She'd hoped to keep that one alive. Though having been abducted, then navigating the investigation was a good reason to forget to water. Shoving away from her desk, Maggie cut to the kitchen and pulled a small plastic cup from the cupboard. Her leg tingled as feeling returned in small increments every day. Most likely a benefit of slowing down and letting the inflammation in her back calm down instead of running from one threat to the next. She filled the cup with water from the filter in the refrigerator and wrenched the sliding glass door back on its track. Dry heat seared across her skin, and she was grateful for the sensation. Grateful to be feeling anything at all. "You're looking a little rough, my friend."

This plant was supposed to be a visual reminder to take care of herself. To not let her obsession to move forward and climb that worldly ladder get the best of her. A symbol of the new life she wanted for herself after the divorce. She pried dead leaves from the base of the plant and replaced them with a healthy serving of water. When she thought about it, humans were basically houseplants. They needed sunlight, water, love. Her heart constricted for a fraction of a second at the thought of leaving Jones down in that hole for his team to recover. She wouldn't have been able to pull him out herself. Not in her condition. But his plea—his attempt to fix things between them—followed her into her dreams every night since the final showdown. "Sunlight and water we're good on. But we're really sucking it up on the love part, aren't we?"

Because there hadn't been any contact between her and Socorro since Dr. Piel checked her over after the fight with Senator Hawkes and his gunmen. The laceration cutting across her temple was shallow enough to not need stitches. Just a whole lot of rest, considering how much she'd been knocked around. First by Toledano, the accident, then trying to escape the senator and his men. Seemed becoming Socorro's primary war correspondent had been taken off the table. She didn't blame Jones. She didn't blame any of them, really. But she couldn't ignore the void in her chest either. The one that hadn't hurt so much over the past couple weeks. While she'd been with Jones. Gotham, too. There was something about that oversize fuzz ball that'd settled her relentless drive for more.

A knock echoed from the front door.

Hope lodged in her throat as she turned back inside. Maybe she'd spoken too soon. Maggie crossed to the front door, ready for whatever waited on the other side.

Except for the man standing at her doorstep.

"What… What are you doing here?" The words lost their power at the mere sight of her ex, and Maggie couldn't help but hate the part of herself that feared him.

"Holy hell. It's true, isn't it? Everything they're saying on the news. That you were abducted and tortured by the cartel, that you uncovered that senator's plan to kill those soldiers. I can't believe it." Her ex-husband reached for the bandage at her temple, and she backed away. His hand froze, midair, as though reminded that he had no right to touch her. He retracted his closeness. Like a turtle ducking back into its shell. "Damn, Maggie. When I heard…"

She shook her head. She didn't need his pity. She didn't need him at all despite that little knot in her stomach telling her this was a familiar connection, that anything was better than nothing. Fortunately for her, Maggie recognized that healing wasn't a one-and-done kind of decision. It would take months, if not years, to unlearn those self-sabotaging behaviors. She just had to hold strong. "How did you find me?"

"My brother still works for the power company," he said.

"You had him look into me." Right. Not stalkerish at all. "What do you want?"

"I came here... You know what? I don't really know why I came here." Her ex shoved both hands into his slacks. The polo shirt straining around his upper body said he still spent way too much time working out rather than on things that actually mattered. "I tried reaching out, but you didn't return any of my calls. Guess I deserved that."

And a whole lot more. Maggie crossed her arms over her midsection, barring him from any idea he was invited inside. She could do this. Hell, she'd stood up to Toledano. She'd faced off with a US senator threatening her life. She'd even fought a soldier bent on burying her somewhere she'd never be found. "Well, I'm still recovering from what happened, and I have a lot of work to sort through over the next few days. If you don't mind, I need to get back to it."

She moved to close the door.

"Maggie, wait." His hand snapped against the wood. Too loud in the quiet hallway. The sound jarred her into fight-or-flight mode, and she instantly diverted her attention to the can of Mace attached to her keys on the entryway table. "I just wanted to explain why I said all those terrible things about you to your family. For the arrest. Looking back, I can see where it all went wrong. I got some bad advice from my business partner, to the point all I could see were dollar signs. Everything became about money, and because of that, I treated you like a threat. It won't happen again. I give you my word. Please, Mags. I want you to come home."

He was kidding. This had to be a joke.

"Your word. Somehow I don't believe you, seeing as how you couldn't even manage to squeeze an actual apology in there. You didn't come here to apologize. You came to justify what you did, and I deserve better than that. Unfortunately, I didn't realize that sooner in our marriage, but there's no way I'm coming back to you. Now get your hand off my door." Her fingers bit into the thin wood, ready to slam it into his nose if needed.

Apologetic husband disappeared from the surface of his expression. Replaced by that oh-so-familiar disappointment she was used to having directed at her. Her ex wedged his foot against the door to keep her from shutting it in his face, and she slowly reached for the Mace a few feet away without tipping him off. "Maggie, I'm trying—"

"I believe the lady told you to get your hand off the door." That voice. It filtered through the overwhelming chaos of the past few days and buried itself in the bruised parts of her body until she felt as though she could lift a truck with her own two hands.

"Who the hell are you?" Her ex physically took a

step back as all six-foot-something of Jones Driscoll stepped into her vision. No Kevlar, no sidearm, but just as prepared to take on another fight of hers if she let him.

"I'm the man who's going to watch her rip that arm from your body and shove it down your throat if you don't do what she says." Piercing gray eyes found her, and the world burst into a variety of color. "You good, Mags?"

"I'm good." Maggie fisted Jones's T-shirt and dragged him over the threshold, and he came all too willingly. His body heat swept through her at that mere contact between them. Not missing a beat since they'd last seen each other. She liked that. The little threads of electricity he seemed to charge inside of her. She turned her attention back to her ex. "Thanks for stopping by."

Then shut the door in his slack-jawed face.

"I'm never going to forget this moment or how good it feels." Maggie pressed her back against the door, trying to catch her breath. "That man has made me feel like less than the dirt under his feet so many times. It felt good to show him he doesn't affect me anymore."

"Glad I could be of assistance." Jones's half smile smoothed from his mouth as he closed the distance between them. "Now let's talk about how you left me to rot in that hole."

HER BREATH SHUDDERED through her. Unbalanced but confrontational. Not in the least threatened or intimidated by him. And, damn, it was good to get this close to her again, to see her on her feet and fighting for herself. "To be fair, I thought your team would know they needed to pull you out. It wasn't until I got to headquarters that I realized they'd taken their time."

"Six hours, to be precise." The feigned frustration was starting to slip. Though he'd lost count of how many times he'd had to tase Lieutenant Snow while they'd been stuck in that hole, he hadn't once let himself put the blame on her. He'd deserved to rot in that compound for backing out of his promise. "Seems Gotham isn't too good at following orders, either. Instead of bringing Scarlett back, he started wrestling with Hans and Gruber once the action had died down. Forgot all about me."

She tried to contain her laugh, shooting one hand to her mouth, but failed. "I'm sorry. I know it's not funny, but at the time, I was still dazed by what'd happened and you'd said all those things about being in love with me. I couldn't think straight. I just needed to step back, take a few days to get my head on straight. But look, you made it out. Call it even?"

The break in her composure loosened that tightness in his chest that'd formed while not hearing from her over the past few days. Maggie Caddel had finally put herself and her well-being first, and he couldn't fault her for that. "All right. I guess I can give you that, considering you're the reason I didn't get sprayed with a bunch of bullets."

"See? Compromise. That's how relationships are supposed to work," she said.

"Relationships?" The word pricked at the back of his neck. "Is that what this is? A relationship?"

Maggie set her palm against his chest, and an instant shot of ease tendrilled into his hands and under his rib cage. Stepping into him, she added to the hint of warmth churning from merely getting this close. "Did you forget about the part where you said you loved me, and I said I loved you, too?"

"I was in a hole for six hours. I had nothing else to think about. Well, other than arguing with Snow every time he wanted to kill me down there, but that's beside the point." His hands found her hips, holding her steady. "Maggie, I failed you. I did the one thing I swore to you I wouldn't do. I let you take on this battle with Hawkes alone, and I'm going to spend the rest of my life regretting not standing up for you sooner."

A heaviness pulled at his stomach. "I almost lost you down there. When you didn't answer me, I thought I had, and the feeling gutted me. I don't know how else to explain it, except that the thought of not having you in my life hurt more than losing my brother ever did. That's not to say I didn't love him or that I don't miss him. I do. I just love you more, and, after everything you've been through, I hated myself for being the one to hurt you. I'm sorry. I'm sorry that you had to be the brave one and save my ass in the end, and I will do whatever it takes to prove to you that you can rely on me from here on out. Anything you want. I'm here. As long as you'll have me."

"You didn't fail me, Jones." Maggie pressed her front to his, and something clicked. Like a piece of himself that'd been missing for a damn long time had finally been put back in its place. "And, you're right. For once

I had to be brave, and the weird thing is, even though I could've died, I'm grateful. Because I had to realize I've let the past control me all this time. I thought I'd left it behind once the divorce papers were signed and I started this new career, but I see now all the hurt, all the pain and the lies still had a grip. They were what drove me to obsess about being better and proving I didn't need anyone, and I don't want to live in spite, Jones. It's exhausting, and it's giving power to the wrong people. People I don't even like. And after I saw that soldier take aim at you—ready to kill you—in that corridor, I knew what I had to do. I couldn't let those things have a space inside me anymore. There just isn't room now that you're a part of my life, and I like the change. It makes everything I've been through worth it."

Hell, he loved her so damn much. They might've only kissed for the first time a week ago, but he'd fallen in love for what felt like a lot longer than that. "So where does that leave us?"

"I'm not sure." She shifted her weight between both legs, and the left seemed to support her a lot better than it had a few days ago. She was on the way to healing. In more ways than one, and he couldn't help but feed into that nodule of pride of her standing up to her ex as she'd done. "I have offers coming in every hour. Some from across the country. They all want to hire me, even the big guys. CNN, FOX, *The New York Times*. It's a lot to consider, but I didn't want to make a decision about any of them until I had a chance to talk to you."

"Maggie, you don't need my permission to take a

job, even if it is across the country," he said. "Whatever you choose, I'll support you."

"I know, and believe me, for the first time, I wasn't looking for anyone's permission but my own. But the past couple of weeks, even though they contain some of the most terrifying moments of my life, were a lot more manageable when you were around." She fisted her hand into his T-shirt. "I think that's something worth exploring. I meant what I said in that compound. I love you. I know it doesn't make a whole lot of sense considering what we survived together—or maybe it's because of what we survived together—but it's true. I'm not the same person you rescued that night. I'm stronger, I'm braver, I'm more willing to stand up for myself. Because of you. I wouldn't even be considering taking one of these jobs if you hadn't shown me who I really am and what I deserve for myself. And I think I want to keep you around."

She smiled then. Really smiled. That smile that only ever seemed to come out with him around. There was a spark she liked to keep buried and refused to show the world, but with him, Maggie lit up his whole damn insides with a mere glimpse of it.

"That is the most romantic thing anyone has ever said to me." He notched her chin higher and set his mouth against hers. He kissed her all the way through the kitchen and the living room, nearly ripping her clothes off her body on the way. Jones didn't get to take much of her bedroom in before he found himself flat on his back against the mattress and Maggie falling into bed with him. Her hair skimmed across his chest once

she finished tossing his shirt somewhere out of sight.
"I want to keep you around, too."

Maggie was someone he hadn't let himself want.
Not just because she'd been a client he'd sworn to protect, but because he couldn't put himself through another loss. But stripped down like this—physically,
emotionally—with her, Jones couldn't see any other
way of going on living. As though she should've been
at his side his entire life. One break in the seam of his
lips, and he was utterly devastated. By her. And damn,
he'd give anything to keep this feeling.

"I want to stay." Her words brushed against the underside of his jaw. "Here in New Mexico. Bodhi has
offered me my job back. Well, begged really, and I'm
going to take it as long as our deal still stands. You
being my source and me having exclusive access to
Socorro."

"Ivy's having the paperwork drawn up as we speak,"
he said.

She couldn't contain her smile. "Then I'm going to
stay, but I want to leave the city. I want to live slow and
enjoy this new chance I've been given instead of trying to survive one incident to the next. With you, Jones.
I know you have to stay on-site with Socorro as long
as you're contracted to work for them. So what would
you think of me moving to Alpine Valley to be closer
to you?"

A buzz of desire thudded hard under his skin as she
peeled away to look down at him. He understood what
she was asking, what she was willing to give up, but
Jones couldn't make the dots connect. She had every-

thing going for her right now, and she was willing to give it all up. For him. "Are you sure?"

"Yeah. I'm sure. I can submit pieces I'm working on to the other outlets on the side or take on freelance jobs as long as I have the room in my schedule. The cost of living is lower in Alpine Valley in case I decide to take a few vacation months here and there. That's the beauty of working from home. And you won't have to change anything. You can still go out there and protect the people who still need Socorro. *Sangre por Sangre* took a beating the past couple weeks, but I feel like something big is coming. And I want to be there. With you." She kissed him, deep and soft at the same time. "Besides, I'm pretty sure it's going to be hard to travel back and forth across the country with Gotham."

His growl drove him to flip her beneath him. The sad truth was the dog would leave with her in a heartbeat. That was the kind of effect she had on the people—and K9s—who cared about her. They were willing to give up their whole lives for the slightest chance she'd make them feel like this. Supported. Loved. Whole. "He's technically Socorro's property. You'd have to take up any custody disputes with Ivy."

"Does the same apply to you?" Trailing her fingers along his jaw, she seemed to memorize every inch of his face as though she'd never seen it before. "Am I going to have to fight for you again? Because I'm telling you, I'm feeling pretty good about my chances now that I've got experience."

"No, Mags. I'm yours." And he meant it in every way he hadn't thought possible before. Jones had convinced himself his heart had died in that cave with Kincaide's mind, unwilling to give up his armor. Only now it seemed the key had been surrendering to Maggie, and there was no going back. Not ever. "Forever."

"We have a new deal then." She kissed him again. "Forever."

* * * * *

The Red River Slayer

Katie Mettner

MILLS & BOON

Katie Mettner wears the title of "the only person to lose her leg after falling down the bunny hill" and loves decorating her prosthetic leg to fit the season. She lives in Northern Wisconsin with her own happily-ever-after and wishes for a dog now that her children are grown. Katie has an addiction to coffee and Twitter and a lessening aversion to Pinterest—now that she's quit trying to make the things she pins.

DEDICATION

For my three Es

Thank you for always supporting and encouraging my work, even when you have to admit to your friends that your mum writes romance novels. I couldn't have asked for kinder, more empathetic kids than you three, and I'm so proud to see you out making a positive impact on the world.

CAST OF CHARACTERS

Mack Holbock—Mack is a haunted man, and sees his time at Secure One as a way to right wrongs he couldn't in the army. Now, someone is hunting women like the one he's been protecting, and he's primed to take him down.

Charlotte—She's been at Secure One for six months, healing from the trauma of sex trafficking. Can she step up and help Mack end the Red River Slayer's reign of terror?

Eric Newman—Has he outgrown Secure One or has Secure One outgrown him? Eric doesn't know, but he's tired of playing third fiddle.

Selina—The responsibility of caring for traumatized women is starting to take its toll on Secure One's medic. The truth keeps hitting too close to home.

Senator Chet Dorian—The senator from Minnesota is known for making enemies. This time, he needs Secure One to find an unknown one.

Eleanor Dorian—The daughter of Chet Dorian, she lives a sheltered life away from the politics of Washington, or so she thinks.

The Red River Slayer—The FBI can't find him, and he thinks he's safe. Until one of his victims lands on Secure One's doorstep. Run, run, as fast as you can...

Chapter One

They shouldn't be here. Mack Holbock had had that thought since they were first briefed on the mission. The hair on the back of his neck stood up, and he swiveled, his gun at his shoulder. The area around the small village was silent, but Mack could feel their presence. Despite what his commander said, the insurgents were there and ready to take out any American at any time. The commander should have given them more time for recon. Instead, he executed a mission on the word of someone too far away to know how the burned-out buildings hid those seeking to add to their body count. Mack knew the insurgents in this area better than anyone. He'd killed more than his fair share of them. They didn't give up or give in. They'd put a bullet in their own head before letting you capture them. If you didn't get them, they'd get you. Survival of the fittest, or in this case, survival of their leader maintaining his grip on terrorized villages.

That said, the first thing you learn in the army is never to question authority. You follow orders—end of story. No one wants your opinion, even if you have intel they don't have. His team had no choice but to go in. Mack still didn't like it. He didn't join the army by choice. Well, unless you consider the choice was either the military or prison. He chose the army because if he had to go down, he would go down helping someone. In his opinion, that was better than being shivved in a prison shower.

The kid with a chip on his shoulder standing in the courtroom that day was long gone. The army had made him a man in body, mind and spirit. He'd learned to contain his temper and use his anger for good, like protecting innocent villagers being terrorized by men who wanted to control the country with violence. As long as Mack and his team sucked in this fetid air, they had another think coming.

"Secure one, Charlie," a voice said over the walkie attached to his vest. His team leader, Cal, was inside with their linguist, Hannah. They needed information that only Hannah could get.

"Secure two, Mike," he said after depressing the button.

"Secure three, Romeo," came another voice.

Roman Jacobs, Cal's foster brother, was standing guard on the opposite side of the building. So far, all was quiet, but Mack couldn't help but feel it wouldn't stay that way. They needed to get out before someone dropped something from the air they couldn't dodge. He shrugged his shoulders to keep the back of his shirt from sticking to him as the sun beat down with unrelenting heat. The one hundred degrees temp felt like an inferno when weighed down with all the equipment and the flak jacket.

"Come on, come on," he hummed, aiming high and swinging his rifle right, then left of the adjacent buildings. There were so many places for a sniper to hide. He checked his watch. It had been ten minutes since Cal checked in and thirty minutes since Hannah had gone *into the complex. She would have to sweet talk some of the older and wiser women in the community to cough up the bad guys' location. Sharing that information would be bad for their health, but so was not rooting the guys out and ending their reign of terror. If Hannah could ascertain a location, their team would ensure they never showed up around these parts again. There was far too much desert to search if they didn't have a place to start.*

"Charlie and Hotel on the move," Roman said. "Entering the complex veranda, headed to Mike."

"Ten-four," he answered before he backed up to the complex's entrance. With his rifle still at his shoulder, he swept the empty buildings in front of him, looking for movement.

A skitter of rocks. Mack's attention turned to a burned-out building on his right. A muzzle flashed, sending a bullet straight at the courtyard.

"Sniper! Get her down!" Mack yelled, bringing his rifle up just as another shot rang out. The "oof" from the complex hit him in the gut, but he aimed and fired, the macabre dance of the enemy as he collapsed in a heap of bones, satisfying to see.

"Charlie! Hotel!"

"Secure one, Charlie."

"Secure two, Romeo."

"Secure three, Echo."

"Mack!" Cal hissed his name, and it snapped him back to the present.

"Secure four, Mike," he said, using his call name for the team. His voice was shaky, and he hoped no one noticed. Not that they wouldn't understand. They'd all served to-

gether and they all came back from the war with memories
they didn't want but couldn't get rid of. Sometimes, when
the conditions were right, he couldn't stop them from in-
truding in the present.

At present, he was standing behind his boss, Cal Newfellow, dressed in fatigues and bulletproof vest. Was that
overkill for security at a sweet sixteen birthday party? Not
if the birthday girl's father was a sitting senator.

"Ya good, man?" Cal asked without turning.

"Ten-four," he said, even though his hands were still
shaking. It was hard to fight back those memories when
he had to stand behind Cal, the one who lost the most that
day. "Something doesn't feel right, boss."

"What do you see?"

"I don't see anything, but I can feel it. My hair is standing up on the back of my neck. My gut says run."

"We're the security force. We can't run." Cal's voice
was amused, but Mack noticed him bring his shoulders
up to his ears for a moment. "Keep your eyes open and
your head on a swivel. Treat it like any other job and stop
thinking about the past."

Mack wished it were that simple. Cal knew that not
thinking about the past was tricky when you'd seen the
things they had over there. War was ugly, whether foreign
or domestic, and Mack was glad to be done with that business. He liked the comforts of home, not to mention not
having to kill people daily.

He glanced at his boots, where the metal bars across
the toes reminded him that his losses over in that sandbox were his fault.

At least the loss that ended their army careers for good
was his fault. Mack had missed a car bomb tucked away in

the vehicle he was tasked with driving. He was carrying foreign dignitaries to a safe house that day, but nothing went as planned. In the end, Cal had lost most of his right hand, Eric had lost his hearing and Mack had suffered extensive nerve damage in his legs when the car bomb shot shrapnel across the sand. Now, the metal braces he wore around his legs and across his toes were the only thing that allowed him to walk and do his job. Something told him that tonight, he'd better concentrate on his job instead of worrying about the past.

"What are the weak points of the property?" Mack asked, fixing his hat to protect his ears better. It was early May, but that didn't mean it was warm in Minnesota. Especially at night in the rain. Sometimes working in damp clothes with temps hovering near forty-five was worse than working in ninety-degree heat.

Cal swept his arm out the length of the backyard. "The three hundred and fifty feet of shoreline. This cabin is remote, but anyone approaching from the road would be stopped by security. If someone wants to crash the party, it'll be via the water. We need to keep a tight leash on the shore."

A tight leash. That had been the story of Mack's life since he'd been four. His mother was the first to make helicopter parenting an Olympic sport. When his dad died in a car accident, and Mack survived, she became obsessed with keeping him safe. His mother would have kept him in a bubble were it possible, but she couldn't, so she kept the leash tight. Sports? Out of the question. He could get hurt, or worse, killed by a random baseball to the head! As much as Mack hated to say it, he was relieved when she'd passed of cancer when he was seventeen. She was more a keeper than a mother, and it had to be a terrible way to live. It wasn't until she was diagnosed with blood cancer when he was fourteen that she started living again. The sad truth was that she had to be dying to live. When she passed away after three years of making memories together, he was relieved not for himself but her. She was with her soulmate again, and he knew that was what she'd wanted since the day he'd passed. Mack was simply collateral damage.

When he was seventeen, he'd stood before a judge after breaking a guy's arm for talking trash about a female classmate. He was told there were better ways to defend people than with violence. If you asked him, the military personified using violence to defend people. He joined the army to find a brotherhood again. He'd found one in Cal, Roman, Eric and his other army brothers. They were Special Forces and went into battle willing to die to have their brothers' backs. Until the one time that he couldn't. It had taken Mack a long time to understand he shouldn't use the word *didn't* when it came to what happened that day when Cal's soulmate was taken before their eyes. It wasn't that he didn't. It was that he couldn't. His mind immediately slid down the rabbit hole toward the car full of people he didn't save. Mack shook his head to clear it. Going back there would result in losing sight of what they were doing here.

Mack eyed his friend of fifteen years and reminded himself that Hannah hadn't been Cal's soulmate. He used to think so, but then Cal met Marlise. Hannah had been a woman Cal loved in youth. Her death opened a path for Cal to start a successful security business and eventually find the woman who centered him. The moment Cal's and Marlise's eyes met while the bad guys bombarded them with bullets, time stood still. Cal used to think he started Secure One Security because of Hannah, but not anymore. They all believed Marlise was the reason. The tragedy that started years before was the catalyst to put Cal on that plane when Marlise needed him.

It had been three years now since they met. They were engaged one month and married the next, which hadn't surprised the team. Marlise had shown Cal that he could love again, but Mack never thought he'd see the day. Not after the scene that spread out before him in that court-yard. Then again, Cal never saw that scene. He never saw his girlfriend with a fatal shot to the head. He never had to drag his friend's body out of the square, stemming the blood oozing from his chest to keep him alive until help got there. Cal hadn't known any of that. It was Mack, Eric and Roman who lived that scene. They were left with the worst memories of a day when they could save one friend but not the other. Whether he liked it or not, Cal had been spared those images, and Mack was glad. There weren't many times you were spared the gruesome truth of war.

Not all wars are fought on foreign soil. The new team members of Secure One had taught him that three times over. Roman's wife and partner in the FBI had been under-cover in a house filled with women who had been sex traf-ficked and forced to work as escorts and drug mules. Mina had been injured to the point that she lost her leg and had come to work at Secure One when she married Roman. Their boss at the FBI, David Moore, was responsible for her injuries by putting her undercover in a house run by his wife, The Madame. Because of the deception, Roman and Mina could retire from the FBI with full benefits.

Marlise was one of The Madame's women in the house with Mina, and when she arrived at Secure One, she was broken and burned but determined. She wanted to help put The Madame behind bars. As she healed, Marlise worked her way up from kitchen manager to client coordinator, but not because she was Cal's girl. She had earned her position by observing, learning and caring about the people they were protecting.

His thoughts drifted to the other woman at Secure One who sought shelter there not long ago. About six months ago, Charlotte surrendered to Secure One under unusual circumstances. She was working for The Miss, the right-hand woman of The Madame in the same house Marlise and Mina had lived. The Miss had left Kansas and moved to Arizona to start her escort business, funded by drug trafficking. Charlotte was one of the women she took from Red Rye to help her. The Miss had made a mistake thinking Charlotte was devoted to her. She wasn't, and she wanted out. Last year, she'd helped them bring down The Miss by providing insider information they wouldn't have had any other way.

Charlotte took over the kitchen manager position when Marlise moved up to client coordinator and fit in well with the Secure One team. She had healed physically from the illness and injuries she'd suffered while living with The Miss, but her emotional and psychological injuries would take longer to scab over. She'd been homeless for years and then went to work for people who used and abused her without caring if she lived or died. There was a special kind of hell for people like that. Mack hoped The Miss had found her way there when he put a bullet in her chest.

Had he needed to kill her that night in the desert? Yes.

Her guards had had guns pointed at his team, and there was no way he would lose another friend to her evil. As it were, Marlise took a bullet trying to protect Cal. Thankfully, it had been a nonlethal shoulder wound.

On the other hand, the gaping chest wound he'd left The Miss with was quite lethal and well-deserved. Mack had learned to channel his temper in the army, but he couldn't pretend he wasn't angry at the atrocities that occurred in a country that was the home of the free to some, but not all. He would defend women like Charlotte until his final breath so they would have a voice.

Mack rolled his shoulders at the thought of the woman who currently sat in their mobile command center on the other side of the property. The mobile command center offered bunks, food and a hot shower to keep the men warm and fed when they were on jobs away from their home base of Secure One. A hot shower and warm food were on Mack's wish list at that moment.

The hot shower or seeing Charlotte again?

His groan echoed across the lake until it filtered back to his ears as a reminder that he didn't need to concern himself with the woman in the command center. He could protect her without falling for her. He noticed how his team raised a brow whenever he helped Char in the kitchen or took a walk with her. He didn't care what they thought. She needed practice in trusting someone again without worrying about being hurt. It was going to be a long hard road for her, so the way he saw it, he'd be the one to teach her that not all men were bad, evil or sick. Sure, he'd done some bad things, but it hadn't been out of evilness or demented pleasure. He had done bad things for good people in the name of justice or retribution, making the world a better place to live. She didn't need to know that, though.

His gaze traveled the lakeshore again, searching for oncoming lights and listening for outboard motors. It was silent other than the call of the loons. The hair on the back of his neck told him it wouldn't stay that way for long.

Chapter Two

"Charlotte?" Selina called from the front of the command center. "I need a break for a moment."

Charlotte stuck the pasta salad into the fridge and dried her hands before meeting Selina at the bank of computers in the front of the renovated RV. Cal had spared no expense when he'd gutted it to make it work for his business. Three bump-outs provided a large kitchen and bathroom, bunks in the back where six people could sleep at a time and a mobile command post to put the FBI to shame.

"What's up?" she asked the woman sitting at the computers.

"Hey," Selina said, motioning at the four screens in front of her. "Would you keep an eye on these for a few minutes? I need to use the restroom and get something to drink."

"Sure. I don't know what I'm looking for, but I'll hold down the chair."

Selina stood and patted her on the shoulder. "There's not much going on since the birthday girl is inside with her guests cutting the cake. Watch for anyone who isn't on the Secure One team or teenagers trying to sneak away." She pointed at a walkie-talkie on the table. "Radio someone if you see anything."

"Got it," she promised. "There's pasta salad in the fridge if you're hungry."

"I'm starving. I'll grab a bowl and bring it back up here. I know you don't like covering, but I gotta go," Selina said, hurrying to the bathroom while Charlotte chuckled.

The computers were intimidating, but Charlotte sat in the chair Selina had vacated and watched the screens, looking for interlopers as described. Selina was the nurse at Secure One, which meant she went on every mission as their med tech, but when she wasn't stitching wounds and handing out Advil, she was the team's eyes in the back of their heads. Selina had been trained as an operative when she joined Secure One and was as accurate with a 9mm as she was with an IV needle. Sometimes, Charlotte wondered if she covered for Wonder Woman when she needed a break because that's how pivotal Selina was to the team.

"Mike to mobile command." The walkie squawked with Mack's voice, and Charlotte nearly jumped out of her skin as she fumbled for it.

She had to take a deep breath before pushing the button to speak. Mack Holbock always had that effect on her. "This is Charlotte. Selina had to step away."

"Hey, Char, how's your evening?" Mack asked when she released the button. She wondered if he realized his voice softened whenever he addressed her. Probably not, and she shouldn't be taking notice either.

"Quiet as a church mouse in here. Did you need something?"

"Nope, it was just my check-in time. There's a clipboard to check off my nine p.m. call-in. Do you see it?"

Charlotte released the button and found the board he referred to, searching for his name and putting a check next to 9:00 p.m. "Done. It looks like you're due for a break in thirty."

"Negative. That's when the dance is going to pick up. I can't leave my post on the shoreline. I don't want guests wandering down and falling in the drink."

"Mack, you know how Cal feels about that stuff," Charlotte warned.

"What are you? My mother?" he asked, but she heard his lighthearted laughter that followed. "I'll clear it with Cal."

"Okay, be careful," she said, wishing her voice hadn't gone down to a whisper on the last two words.

"Ten-four, Char," he said, and the box fell silent.

Mack had been calling her Char since she'd arrived at Secure One last fall with her hat in her hand or rather her hands in the air. She had surrendered herself, hoping to gain immunity against The Miss the same way Marlise had when the Red Rye house burned. The night of the fire, she hadn't known Marlise wasn't going with them to the airport. Had she known that, Charlotte would have refused to go as well. Working for The Madame, and subsequently The Miss, had been demoralizing, scary and for some, downright deadly. When she saw Marlise escape their grasp, Charlotte had vowed to do the same if she ever got the chance.

That was the night she'd had her first interaction with Mack Holbock. It was the moment she realized she was safe, and they believed she hadn't been working for The Miss by choice. Exhaustion, fear and relief took over, and she had fallen apart right there in the little room where they'd been holding her. Mack had scooped her up and taken her to the med bay for treatment. She couldn't remember much about that time, but she remembered him. His presence, more than anything. He was smaller than Cal and Roman, but only in the height department. He was ripped, strong and capable regarding his work, but he was also kind, quiet and gentle when the occasion called for it.

When Cal, Marlise, Roman and Mina had left to find The Miss, Mack stayed behind for a few days to ensure everything ran smoothly. Initially, he was the only one who believed that she had no ulterior motive. She needed that unquestionable acceptance more than anyone understood.

"What did I miss?" Selina asked, carrying in a bowl of pasta salad with the fork halfway to her lips. Before Charlotte could answer, she was chewing, moaning and swallowing the first bite. "This is brilliant. Pepperoni and black olives?"

"And Italian dressing, to list a few." Charlotte laughed as she stood so Selina could sit.

"Seriously, you learned your lessons well from Marlise."

"I'm glad you enjoy it. To answer your question, Mack checked in for his nine p.m. but isn't going to take his break at nine thirty. The dance is about to start, and he doesn't want anyone wandering down to the water and falling in."

"That sounds like Mack," Selina agreed, setting the bowl down and jiggling the mouse. "Normally, Cal has a hardline about breaks, but this isn't a normal job, so I'm inclined to side with Mack."

"Same," Charlotte said, lounging on the back of the couch while she waited for one of the crew to come in looking for something to eat or drink. "It isn't every day that you're tasked with keeping one hundred teenagers safe when the birthday girl is a sitting senator's daughter."

"It's a little nerve-racking, not going to lie," Selina said before shoveling in more salad.

Charlotte kept her eyes on the screens in case she caught a glimpse of Mack. She liked watching him work, which might be weird, but it was true. When he was working, he moved with military precision, reminding her that he had fought his own battles in life. Some of those battles remained with him, she knew. He'd told her that in so many words one night as they worked together in the kitchen. She'd sensed that he didn't open up much about his time in the army, so she let him talk. While his stories weren't specific, his emotions were. He was struggling with the scars left from those battles as much as she was from hers. Maybe that was what made them immediate friends and easy companions. They understood each other on a level of unspoken atrocities and nightmare-riddled dreams.

Charlotte had only slept those first few nights at Secure One because Selina gave her medication to keep her calm. After that, she slept in fits and bursts. Her psyche struggled to know if the people surrounding her could be trusted, and it took her several months to feel comfortable enough to sleep through the night, at least as through the night as she could when plagued by nightmares of men's hands holding her down. Mack always seemed to materialize in the kitchen at 2:00 a.m. on those nights when she couldn't close her eyes again. He'd sit by the butcher-block counter and share cookies and milk with her rather than scold her about not going back to bed.

"You know it's okay if you want to date Mack," Selina said.

Charlotte's brain came to a full stop and nearly slung her backward off the couch. "Excuse me, what now?"

"I said it's okay if you—"

"I heard what you said, but what makes you think I want to date Mack?" Charlotte had forced the words through a too-dry throat, hoping it sounded genuine.

"Because you like each other, which is obvious. Everyone else tiptoes around you two like sleeping lions, but I'm all about calling it as I see it."

"Clearly," Charlotte said, tongue in cheek. "I don't want to date Mack, but I'm happy to know it would be okay if I did."

"If you say so," Selina answered in a singsong voice that was a bit juvenile as far as Charlotte was concerned.

"We're just friends, Selina. First of all, he's five years older than I am."

"Cal is five years older than Marlise."

Charlotte chose to ignore her. "Second of all, I'm not ready to date anyone. Since working for The Madame, I don't know how to date. I don't know how to be with a man who didn't pay for my company."

"Do you trust Mack?" Selina asked with her back to her now as she watched the screens.

"You know I do, with my life, but that's different."

"I understand what you're saying, Charlotte. You're scared. I get it. I know you don't know me or my past, but suffice it to say that I do understand being afraid to rock the boat. I just thought you should hear from someone on the team that moving on and living your life now that The Madame is in prison and The Miss is dead isn't rocking the boat. You earned your freedom, and you should enjoy it."

The woman who had nursed her back to health fell silent then, and Charlotte stared at the screens as she considered what Selina had said. She had earned her freedom from The Miss and had been pivotal in helping them find her and rescue the other women. She could leave Secure One whenever she was ready, Cal had told her, but he'd also said he wasn't putting an end date on her employment. As long as she wanted to be part of Secure One, the team would welcome her with open arms. They had, which was the reason she wouldn't rock the boat. If she had to leave Secure One and find work in a different city with a different company, she could end up back on the street. That was the very last place she wanted to be.

The man in question walked onto the screen, and Charlotte watched as he made his way down the bank and disappeared from view. She turned away and walked back to the kitchen. Secure One was her life, and while Mack might be part of it professionally, that was as far as it would go. For Charlotte, self-preservation would win out every time, even if that meant being alone for the rest of her life.

THE CABIN OF Senator Ron Dorian was well hidden among the trees until they parted for a view of the Mississippi River. The *cabin* was a six-bedroom, four-bath summer home with a grand staircase and wall-to-wall windows in the family room that looked out over the water. Mack wondered how ostentatious his DC house must be if he called this his *cabin*. Then again, that wasn't his job. His job was to keep a young girl and her friends safe while they were on the grounds celebrating a milestone. Secure One had been in charge of the security on this cabin for six years, and they'd run point on plenty of parties held here. His worry at tonight's party? The sun had set, and one hundred teenagers were ready to pour out onto a dance floor under a rented tent. There was a 100 percent chance a couple or six would sneak down to the river to make out. Having one of them fall in the drink and get swept downstream was not the reputation Secure One wanted.

He'd been patrolling the football field length of shoreline for the last three hours other than the ten-minute break he'd taken inside the command center to grab dry clothes, boots and a snack. He hoped the rest of the crew didn't eat all the pasta salad before he got back there. It was one of the best salads he'd ever had, and that was saying a lot, considering Marlise used to be the resident chef. When he'd tried to compliment Charlotte on it, she'd turned away and acted like she hadn't heard him. He knew she'd heard him when her lips tipped up a hair before she spun away. She'd been fine when he'd done his 9:00 p.m. check-in, so he couldn't help but wonder what had happened in the meantime.

Mack went over everything he'd said to her the last week and couldn't think of anything that would have upset her. Maybe she was just having a rough night. Security at these events required a lot of planning, and even tighter control, which put everyone on edge. She'd be fine once they returned to Secure One and were back in the swing of their usual duties. At least he hoped she would be. Mack didn't like the idea that someone had upset Charlotte, especially if it had been him. Before Charlotte arrived, he'd taken the time to listen to and observe Marlise during her two years at Secure One. He'd understood that women in their situation had a hard time trusting people and had limited, if any, self-esteem. That led to difficulty staying employed or in school, often leading them back to the streets. He didn't want that for Charlotte.

She reminded him a lot of Marlise though. Strong, determined and seeking a better life. Charlotte had been that way since they'd hauled her in off the shoreline the first night. She'd wanted to escape the woman holding her captive and was willing to risk getting shot. Unlike Marlise, Charlotte's scars weren't visible. They were buried deep in her mind and soul, and she rarely let them show. A few months ago, she'd been sketching on her pad when he walked into the kitchen for a snack. She was a skilled artist and had already helped Secure One clients by drafting plans to provide specific problem areas with better security. That night though, her drawing drew his eye immediately. She'd tried to hide it from him, but he hadn't allowed it. His eyes closed for a beat when he thought about it.

The drawing was of a naked woman with bleeding wounds, tears on her face and vulnerability in every pencil stroke. She told him it was a self-portrait of how she felt inside. The slashes across her body and blood pooling by her feet would rest in his mind for always—most especially the wound to her leg where The Miss had buried a tracker not meant for humans. Despite Selina's best efforts, Charlotte had gotten an infection and now had nerve damage in the leg. She'd sketched an intricate tattoo around the scar that spelled out *worthless,* and he'd assured her she was anything but that. Those were just words though, and Mack knew women like Charlotte didn't believe wo—

A scream pelted the air in a high-pitched frenzy that relayed fear in a way Mack had heard only a few times in his life. He started running toward the sound just a few hundred feet ahead. He stopped in front of two teenage girls, no longer screaming, just staring at the water with their mouths open in terror. One girl had her arm pointed out with her finger shaking as Mack followed it to the shore below.

"Secure two, Mike. I need help on the shore, stat!" He turned the girls away from the water just as Eric came running from the other direction.

"What's going on?" he huffed, and Mack flicked his eyes to the water. Eric's gaze followed, and his muffled curse told Mack he'd seen her too. "I'll take them to the command center while you call the cops. We'll need to keep these two separated from the rest of the group until then."

"After that, get the party shut down while I deal with this," Mack hissed, and with a nod, Eric led the two women toward the command center.

Mack walked down to the lakeshore, holding his gun doublehanded as he navigated the rocks and wet sand. What could first be mistaken for floating garbage, on a second glance, was a woman with her long blond hair floating over her red dress. When he stopped along the shore to stare down at her, the woman's eyes were wide open, and her mouth made an *O* as though whatever she saw in the last moments of her life were welcoming her into the new world.

"What do you have?" Cal asked as he came running up behind Mack.

"Young woman. No visible COD. We need to get her out before she floats downstream."

"Cops aren't going to want us to touch her," Cal said as Mack holstered his gun.

"They're going to like trying to find her again in the Mississippi much less." Mack snapped on a pair of gloves he'd pulled from his vest and then grabbed his telescoping gaff hook. Everyone had one on their belt when they worked on the water. You might have to pull a fellow team member out of the drink at any time.

"We need a tarp before you pull her out," Cal said quickly, stopping Mack's arm.

"You'd better get one then," Mack growled and shook his boss's arm loose. "I'm going to hook her dress just to hold her here. If I don't, she's going downstream."

Cal hit the button on his vest that connected him to command central. "Secure one, Charlie. I need a tarp or plastic on the shore directly below the dance tent."

"What size?" Mack heard Selina ask.

"Body size," Cal answered, and it ran a shiver down Mack's spine.

Now secured by his hook, the young woman wasn't going anywhere, but Mack couldn't take his eyes off her. She couldn't be twenty-five, and her long blond hair reminded him of Marlise and Charlotte. He prayed that someone was missing this woman, and she wasn't the victim of The Red River Slayer. His cynical side said the slayer was responsible for this woman's death, and he was only getting started.

Chapter Three

The muted light through the window told her the sun was setting. She knelt by the bed and scratched another line into the wood. It was the five hundred and fiftieth. She knew some were missing from the early days when fear kept her huddled on the bed for most of the day. That was before she realized he wouldn't kill her. Now she marked the end of each day rather than the beginning of a new one. She suspected her end would come at night.

Frustration filled the woman as she stood. She had to get out, but the room was a beautifully decorated and posh fortress. She had all the comforts of home except for a way to contact the outside world. She also didn't have a television or a radio. She'd been *his* captive for too long. Soon she'd be replaced with a new plaything. That was how it worked. What he did with his old playthings, she didn't know. Probably sold them or killed them.

The thought ran a shiver down her spine. She hoped he'd kill her. The last thing she wanted was to be sold to another man in another country. If she had a way to do it, she would kill herself just to steal his joy, but he made sure there were no weapons for her to use. Who was he? She had no idea, but he had money, and he must have power. You don't keep women locked away in the basement of your home for years without the ability to make people look the other way. Then again, she had no idea if anyone lived in this house other than her. Maybe he just came to visit her or lived alone upstairs. In the early days, she'd tried to ask questions but soon learned he wasn't interested in answering them. Her fingers played across the puckered scar on her cheek. The night she pushed him too far with her questions, he showed her rather than told her to stop.

Her gaze drifted to the window above her bed. She'd tried to break it until she realized it wasn't glass. It was layers of plexiglass that no amount of pounding would break. She paused. Were those footsteps?

She moved to the door quietly on practiced tiptoes to listen. He should be bringing her dinner soon. He would sit with her while she ate and engage her in conversation that would be considered mundane in a different time and place. He stayed to ensure she didn't try to hide the utensils or kill herself with them. When she finished eating, he'd want her to thank him for dinner if he were in the right mood. She learned early on to obey that order, or she'd spend a week drinking her food through a straw until the swelling in her face receded from his beating. Oh, sure, he'd always apologize for hurting her and bring her ice and medicine, but he wasn't sorry. He thrived on the power he held over her, and beating her turned him on.

The footsteps stopped at the door, and a key jingled. She was back on her bed as the door swung open, and her monster walked through with a tray balanced on his arm. He was wearing his full leather hood and his smoking jacket tonight. He always wore the mask, but the smoking jacket meant she'd have to thank him properly tonight. Initially, she had nightmares about the mask, but after a few months, she found a way to ignore it and imagine the man behind the mask. She came up with ways she would take him down if she ever escaped.

He set the tray down on the bed and ran a finger down her cheek. She forced herself not to recoil. "Good evening, my angel. Little Daddy brought you dinner. Are you hungry?"

"Yes, Little Daddy," she obediently said while trying hard not to roll her eyes. She stopped being scared of him months ago, but she'd learned if she didn't want a backhand, she'd best comply with his demented fantasies.

"This will be one of our last meals together, angel."

Her breath hitched in her chest. This was it. She had to act tonight.

"Soon, you'll go to your new home with your new daddy. He can't wait to meet you. I'll miss you, but you're ready for him now. Are you ready for a new daddy, angel?" he asked as he set up the food on the table.

She nodded but knew she was out of time. This was it. It was time to put her plan into action. She'd spent months earning his trust, and tonight, she'd thank him properly for all the things he'd given her, but more so for the things he'd taken away.

"How LONG UNTIL the cops get here?" Mack asked Cal as they stood in front of the body. They'd laid her on the shoreline on a tarp, but they didn't cover the body for fear of contaminating it more than it already was.

"At least another thirty minutes," Cal answered while he fielded questions from the rest of the team as they sent kids home with their parents.

Selina was caring for the two girls who had discovered the body. They would wait at mobile command until their parents arrived. The police would need to speak with them, but Mack had no doubt their parents would want to be present.

"Who are we kidding?" Mack muttered. "The tumble she took down the Mississippi left no evidence of her killer for us to find."

"Us?" Cal asked with a brow up in the air. "There is no us. This is for the cops to figure out."

"And they've done a smashing job with the other three bodies they've found in the last few months."

The authorities had pulled three women from three different rivers over the last six months. The first woman had been found in The Red River and was wearing a red dress, which was how this particular serial killer had earned his moniker.

"Not my monkey," Cal said again. "We can't get involved in this, Mack. We have enough on our plates at Secure One."

"We've been involved in this since the day you brought Marlise onto the compound," Mack reminded him. "If this is yet another nameless, background-less woman like Marlise or Charlotte, that means someone is buying and killing women from the street. How long are we going to brush it under the carpet before we *get involved*?"

Cal whirled around and stuck his finger in Mack's chest. "Don't."

"Don't what, Cal?" Mack knew challenging his boss was risky, but they were also brothers, and sometimes you had to call your own family on their crap.

"Don't accuse me of inviting this into our lives. That was not what I did when Marlise came to Secure One."

Mack held up his hands in defense. "That's not at all what I was saying, Cal. I simply meant that we're taking care of women just like this one," he said, motioning at the woman behind him, "while others are still dying. The cops are missing something. How long will we stand by without at least trying to prevent more deaths?"

Cal shook his head and planted a hand on his hip. "Mack, I wish there were a way to get involved in this case, but there isn't. The FBI is involved and—"

"The FBI can't find their way out of a paper bag!" Mack exclaimed.

"I don't disagree," Cal said with a smirk, "but we still can't go traipsing in like the *Mod Squad* and take over their investigation."

Mack snorted. "The *Mod Squad*. Okay, Grandpa, but I'm tired of women dying because of our inaction."

"Same," Cal said with a sigh. "In each victim, I see Marlise or Charlotte. It was just chance they made it out of The Miss's grasp alive. These poor women."

"All of them," Mack agreed.

As a man, he hated that some men thought they could use a woman and then throw her away like garbage. It enraged him to the point of violence, which didn't solve anything. The only way to stop it was for someone to figure out who was doing it. Unfortunately, Cal was right. With the feds involved, they couldn't be. Cal had been read the riot act after The Miss fiasco when he went rogue, and the woman ended up dead because of it. In the end, it was brushed under the carpet as a problem solved, but Secure One had to tread lightly whenever the feds were around. They didn't like their tiny toes stepped on.

"Secure two, Sierra."

"Secure one, Mike. Go ahead."

"Charlotte is on her way down," Selina said over the comm unit in his ear.

"What?"

"I said Charlotte is on her way down."

"No, don't let her leave the mobile center. She doesn't belong down here."

"Already tried that, Mack. You've met the woman, right?"

"I'll have Eric intercept her. Thanks for the heads-up."

Mack huffed as he grabbed his radio to call Eric. Of course, Charlotte would try to come down here. She felt responsible for these women as much as Marlise did. If Marlise weren't back at Secure One with Mina working the other client security, she'd be down here too. "Secure two, Mike," he said and waited for Eric to reply. Once he did, Mack explained the situation and signed off.

"You're not going to pass me off on someone else, Mack Holbock," a voice said from his left, and he spun in the dark without drawing his weapon. He knew it was her, even if he was frustrated by her inability to follow orders. He secretly loved that she still had some fight left in her. She didn't back down on something she believed in, regardless of what she'd been through in life, even if that personality trait made his job harder.

He stepped to the side enough to hide the woman on the ground, and Cal moved alongside him. "You shouldn't be here, Charlotte," Cal said firmly. "This is a crime scene."

She stopped and stood before them with her hand on her hip. Mack had to bite his tongue to keep from smiling. "I'm not contaminating your crime scene," she said, throwing around air quotes. "The Mississippi is contaminating your crime scene."

"What do you need, Char?" Mack asked, softening his voice as he took a step toward her. She needed to be on her way before she saw the body and realized she was a victim of the same nameless, faceless perp.

"I need to see the body."

"Not happening," Cal said, crossing his arms over his chest. "No one views the body without the police here."

"When the police get here, it will be too late. They'll bungle it the way they always do, and more women will die."

"More women will die? We don't know how this woman died," Mack reminded her.

Charlotte rolled her eyes so hard that Mack couldn't stop the smile from lifting his lips. "She's the fourth woman found dead in a river in six months. More women will die if we don't find the killer, Mack."

Mack turned and lifted a brow of *I told you so* at Cal before turning back to the woman in front of him. "Be that as it may, we must follow protocol, Charlotte. Protocol says we have to wait for the authorities."

"Are you going to tell them?" she asked, both hands on her hips.

"I won't put you through it. I know you want to help, but you can't."

"Don't tell me what I can and can't do, Mack," she hissed, standing chest to chest with him.

Cal's grunt was loud to Mack's ear, and he grimaced. His boss wasn't happy. Cal's flashlight snapped on, and he lifted it to Charlotte's chest. "It's not up to us, Charlotte—"

Her gasp was loud enough to stop him midsentence. His flashlight had illuminated the woman's head by accident, and Charlotte's eyes were pinned on her. Mack grasped her shoulder to turn her, but she fought him.

"I know her," she whispered, dropping to her knee on the muddy shore. "I know her, Mack."

Mack knelt on both knees, not caring that the cold mud soaked through his pants. He cared that someone on his team could identify this woman. "Char, how do you know her?" He could see shock kicking in, and he wanted the answer before she couldn't speak.

Cal switched the light off, and it went dark again just as Charlotte reached her hand out toward the body. "That's Layla."

"Layla who?" Cal asked as Mack put his arm around Charlotte. She was starting to shiver, whether from the cold or trauma, he couldn't say.

"I don't know," she whispered. "I met her in Arizona when I worked for The Miss. She was from one of the small towns around Tucson."

"Wait, she was with The Miss?" Cal asked from behind them to clarify.

Char nodded but dropped her gaze to the ground now that the body was in the shadows. "Layla wasn't there very long. She cried nonstop and cowered in the corner whenever The Miss came around. We woke up one morning, and she was gone. We figured she tried to run, and The Miss killed her. That or she got away."

"Would it be safe to say you met her two years ago?" Mack asked, trying to get some kind of timeline to help the police when they arrived.

Charlotte turned to him with wide eyes as she nodded.

"Something like that. Where has she been all this time, Mack?" She grabbed tightly to his coat when she asked, her face just inches from his now.

"I don't know, but now that we know who she is, maybe we can find out."

Charlotte shuddered, and Mack wrapped his arms around her as he glanced up at Cal and mouthed, "Don't tell the cops."

Cal tipped his head for a moment in confusion, but after a long stare, he cleared his throat. "Mack, please walk Charlotte back to the command center. I'll wait here for the police."

With a nod, he helped Charlotte up the grassy hill toward the lights shining in the distance. "I want you to listen to me, Char," he whispered, and she nodded. "Don't tell anyone outside of Secure One that you know the victim."

She tripped on her next step, and Mack steadied her as she lifted her gaze to his. "But, Mack, they have to find her killer!"

"Shh," he said, hushing her immediately. "First, the police will have to decide if she was murdered."

"You know she was!"

His finger against her lips muffled her exclamation. "We know she was, but the cops must *prove* she was. Does that make sense?" She nodded against his finger, and he lowered his hand and started walking with her again. "While they're busy proving she was murdered and searching for her identity, we'll be after her killer."

"But I already know who she is, Mack. If I don't tell them, I'll be in trouble when they find out I knew her."

He squeezed her to him to quiet her again. "You will

tell them as soon as they release her image to the press. That won't happen until they determine her cause of death. The same as they have with the other women found dead with no identity, though in this case, they may be able to get her identity if she wasn't washed like you and the women from The Madame's ring."

"That's true," she agreed with a nod. "She was a street girl but had a record, at least according to her."

"Good, good. Then the police will find out who she is without you telling them. When they do, you'll call to tell them you knew her for a few days and the dates she was with The Miss. That's as far as your responsibility goes with this case."

She stopped abruptly, and he caught himself from falling at the last second. "Wouldn't it save time if we could give them her identity tonight?"

"It would," Mack agreed, lowering his head closer to hers so no one overheard them, "but then we have no time to look into it at Secure One."

"But this sicko is out there hurting other women!" she exclaimed, and his finger returned to her lips.

"He's following a pattern. One woman every six weeks, at least that's been the frequency they've been finding the bodies. We can take a couple of days to try and track down the last knowns on this woman before we turn what we know over to the police. We're trying to prevent another woman from dying by helping the police, not working against them, okay?"

"Why do you think you can help now? Just because you have a name?"

He turned her and started walking toward the command center again. He wanted to get back before the cops showed up so he could hear what Cal told them. "This is the first time we've had the name of the victim, which means it's the first time we can put Mina on the task of following her trail before she disappeared. All we needed was one mistake from this guy, and he may have just made it."

"Killing a woman with an identity?"

"Killing a woman with an identity and leaving her where Secure One could find her. Our record speaks for itself regarding getting justice for women being held against their will."

A smile lifted Charlotte's lips, and he squeezed her shoulders one more time before reaching the steps to the command center. "It's safe to say Secure One has done better than the police, that's for sure," she agreed.

"Then trust us, just one more time, and we'll get justice for women like Layla too."

A shadow crossed her face, but it was gone before he could grasp its meaning. He had shadows of his own that he kept hidden, and he wouldn't judge her for hers. When she leaned in close to him, her scent of apple blossoms filled his senses, and he inhaled deeply. He reminded himself that he had no business liking this woman for any reason other than to keep her safe while on a job. At the mere thought, he laughed at himself. As if that were the only reason he liked Charlotte.

"Isn't it illegal to withhold information?" she whispered, so close to him that he could bury his nose in her neck and fill his head with her. He didn't, but it took every ounce of willpower not to.

"As far as the police know, only four people have seen the body, and only two up close—me and Cal. That's all they need to know. Right?"

She nodded once, zipped her lips and tossed away the key. Then she climbed the steps and disappeared inside the trailer. Mack couldn't keep the smile off his lips as he turned on his heel and walked back toward the shore in awe of the woman half his size with twice his strength.

Chapter Four

Charlotte approached the two girls who sat huddled together on the couch. Selina had covered them with a warm blanket and calmed them down so they could speak rather than just stutter words. Their names were Tia and Leticia, and they told Charlotte and Selina they were best friends.

She handed each girl a mug of hot cocoa and sat across from them on a chair. She'd seen a lot of horrible things on the street, and she remembered her reaction to the first dead body in a dark alley on the streets of Phoenix. Nothing prepared a person for that, and nothing could wipe the image away.

"Your parents are on their way to be with you until the police arrive," Selina said, hanging up her phone. "They're about ten minutes away."

"Okay, thank you," Leticia said before scooting closer to her friend. "What are the police going to ask us?"

"Basic questions," Selina assured them. "Your name and address, how long you've been friends with Eleanor Dorian, if you've ever been here before and what you were doing by the water tonight. It will be simple questions that you can answer easily. They know you didn't have anything to do with the woman's death. They just want to know if you remember anything that might be helpful to their investigation."

"Can we stay together?" Tia asked.

"That I don't know," Selina admitted. "It will be up to the police and how they decide to question you. You don't have anything to hide, so don't worry about it."

The girls glanced at each other again, and Charlotte noticed the fear that hid in their eyes. "What were you doing down by the water tonight?"

Another shared glance confirmed for Charlotte that they were hiding something they didn't want to come out.

"Girls, if you were drinking or smoking down there, the police will find out, so you may as well be honest," Selina said without judgment.

Tia shook her head and held her hands out to them. "No, no, we weren't. We'll do a test to prove it. We weren't doing that."

"Then you have nothing to worry about," Selina said again.

"Are you in a relationship together?" Charlotte asked, the truth evident.

"You can't tell our parents," Tia hissed, tears springing to her eyes. "Please."

Her protective arm around Leticia suddenly made more sense, especially when she pulled her closer. "We just wanted to dance together," Leticia whispered, "so we went down the hill where no one would see us. We aren't out because of my parents."

Selina knelt in front of them and rested her hands on their knees. "We aren't going to tell your parents. Let's take a minute to agree on what you'll tell the police if you're separated. You'll want your answers to match."

"You mean you'll help us hide the truth? Won't you get in trouble?" Tia's gaze flicked between the two women, and Charlotte took her other hand instinctively.

"There's nothing wrong with saying you went down the hill to escape the noise or see the river at night. Technically, that's what you did, right?" Charlotte asked, and they nodded.

"We danced and then walked out on the fancy lookout dock just as the moon came out from behind the clouds. The moonbeam on the water was magical and something you don't see living in the city, you know?" Tia asked, and both she and Selina nodded.

"Were there any boats on the water tonight?" Selina asked. It didn't surprise Charlotte that Selina would dig for more information when the opportunity presented itself. When she walked in the door earlier, Selina was already on the phone with Cal.

"No," Leticia said without hesitation. "All I heard was the rain falling on the water. I turned to kiss Tia, and that's when I saw the flash of red over her shoulder. When we focused on it, we realized it was a dress, and someone was still in it. She was floating down the river as though it were a sunny summer afternoon." They both shuddered again, and new tears sprang to Leticia's eyes.

"Okay," Selina said quickly, squeezing their knees. "Just tell the police that you were turning to go when you noticed the red dress." They both nodded robotically, and Selina glanced at Charlotte for a moment. "Did you see anyone else on the bank of the river? Anyone walking or running through the trees?"

"No, we didn't see anything, but it was so dark it would

have been hard. We wouldn't have heard footsteps with the music playing for the dance."

Selina patted their knees and then stood. "I just ran you through the questions the police will ask. Do you think you can handle it now?"

Both girls nodded, and smiles lifted their lips. "Yes, thank you," Tia whispered. "Thank you for understanding why we don't want to tell the police why we were down there."

"We understand you're in love, and that's a wonderful feeling," Charlotte said, leaning forward to talk to the girls. "Don't let what happened tonight steal that joy from you. Finish high school and then go to college where you can be together without worry. Life is hard, but love makes it worth it. Okay?" They nodded again, and Charlotte stood. "Want a refill?" She pointed at their empty mugs of cocoa and smiled as they handed them to her.

Charlotte disappeared into the kitchen to refill their mugs as her words flooded her head. *Being in love is a wonderful feeling.* She'd never been in love but hoped one day she'd find someone who understood her scars and loved her anyway. She ladled the sweet milk into the mugs and sighed. That was a tall order for anyone. Her mind's eye flicked to Mack tonight and the way he tried to protect her from the ugliness of life. She immediately shook it away. She wasn't here to fall in love with Mack Holbock. She was here to feed him and, if she had her way, heal him, so he could go out and find someone worthy of his love.

THE BRANCHES TUGGED at her skin, leaving red welts across her bare arms as she barreled through the dark, cold night.

She'd bested her *Little Daddy* and escaped the prison she'd been in for over eighteen months. She'd found an old pair of shoes by the door and a jacket, but with no phone and no money, she wasn't sure how she would find help. She was surprised how remote the house was when she tore out of the basement like the hounds of hell were on her heels.

She was tired but knew she had to keep going. How far was far enough? She didn't know. She'd been following the river, so she had to run into a town eventually, right? She had to find a car and get far, far away from wherever her current hell was.

Streetlights glowed in the distance, and she slowed to a walk. She had two choices: run past the town while it was still dark and keep going or stop and see what the town had to offer. Her first problem was a lack of money or identification. Her second problem was figuring out if The Miss was still in business without landing on some- one's radar who would call the cops. She glanced down at herself and sighed. Her cami and boy shorts would land her on someone's radar, and she couldn't risk the cops finding her or alerting The Miss.

Think, she told herself. *You're in a forest with trees and a river. That means you aren't in the desert anymore.* The thought lifted her head, and she saw the town with fresh eyes. She was a long way away from Arizona. If The Miss was still doing business, she'd need long tentacles to know she'd escaped.

The idea spurred her forward into the shadows. First things first—clothes and then transportation. Ahead was a service station. No lights were on, which meant it was closed or shut down. A glance up and down the dark as- phalt showed no cars, and she skittered across the road before sliding behind the brick building. She said a silent prayer as she dug in her coat pocket for the flashlight she'd found earlier. She'd been too afraid to use it before, but the risk was worth it now. Keeping it low to the ground, she searched the area behind the garage. A hulking metal body sat as a sentry next to the building. Focusing the weak beam of light on the license plate told her the first thing she needed to know.

Pennsylvania.

A long way from home, Toto, she thought. She didn't know the town's name, but it didn't matter. She wouldn't be there long. Sliding along the side of the truck, she noticed there was no logo on the side. That meant if she could get it started, it could be her salvation. A glance in the back of the rusty truck bed revealed old coveralls that she balled up under her arm for later. Hot-wiring a truck this old would be a piece of cake as long as the door was unlocked. She needed to get in fast if it was, especially if the dome light came on. With a steady breath, she pulled up on the truck's handle and prayed she'd caught her first big break.

It had been hours since Mack had pulled Layla onto shore, but the property was still buzzing with activity. The police were interviewing kids as their parents looked on in horror, and the ERT team was on the scene looking for any evidence they could pull in and analyze. It didn't take a genius to realize there wouldn't be much left on the body after being in the Mississippi. The medical examiner gave them a time of death between seventy-two and ninety-six hours ago. Whether it was three days or four didn't matter. Trace evidence would have been washed away in the

Mississippi within minutes. That was the way The Red River Slayer wanted it.

Mack suspected they wouldn't find any labels in her dress, which would match the MO of the other women they'd found. Even if they could track down the dress, it would likely be from a big box store and sold in every state. The Red River Slayer had repeatedly proven that he wasn't stupid or careless. Mack hoped killing Layla was the perp's first mistake.

When working with the feds—correction, when the feds are running a case—you had to be careful that you don't tamper with evidence. Mack knew that, but before they arrived, he'd felt it was essential to check for vitals, which was why with a gloved hand, he had palpated her neck. He couldn't help that while he was doing that, he noticed petechiae in her eyes and her swollen tongue. While there were no ligature marks on her neck, that didn't rule out strangulation. It was surprisingly easy to strangle someone to death without leaving a mark. Mack would know. The feds were selling the cause of death as drowning, but no one at Secure One was buying. The person killing these women wanted to be hands-on, even if it meant holding them under the water while they struggled. That said, neither Mack nor Cal believed that to be the case.

It was more likely the killer felt these women needed to be beautiful even after their death, which was why they were placed in the river wearing red gowns. The Red River Slayer was helping these women find a better afterlife, whether from their past lives or what they had to do while they were with him.

For the first time, Secure One may have finally got some solid information about the guy. Since Charlotte knew Layla disappeared around eighteen months ago, and the ME put her time of death around three days ago, the math told him the perp kept the women for a long time. To do that, he had to have a home or building to house them without raising suspicions. It was a huge risk to hold someone hostage that long, which meant wherever he was keeping them had to be isolated with no neighbors or regular deliveries. Then again, maybe he kept them bound and gagged when he wasn't home. The idea of it sent a shiver down Mack's spine.

He was itching to return to Secure One headquarters so they could plot all their information on Layla against the other victims of The Red River Slayer. They may not be actively involved in solving this case, but that was the very basis of the Secure One team in the army. They were a ghost team that went in and got the job done. It was starting to look like they would have to do the same this time if they were going to stop this guy.

"Who's in charge here?" The man's brusque tone put Mack on guard immediately. He stepped up next to Cal as the man, nearly fifty yards away, was yelling. "I demand to know what is going on here!"

"Ah, yes, we knew it was only a matter of time before Senator Dorian arrived," Cal said out of the corner of his mouth. "Should we pass him off to the cops or try to pacify him first?"

"Let's take him back to mobile command. We can keep him occupied by walking him through the entire party while the feds do their thing here. I'm sure the feds will want to talk to him, but since he wasn't here to celebrate his daughter's birthday, I might add, there isn't much information he can give them."

"Agreed," Cal said before stepping toward the man to head him off. Mack followed, breaking right of Cal so they could turn Dorian toward mobile command. "Senator Dorian."

"Cal Newfellow! What is this I hear about a dead woman on my property?"

The senator was shouting now, which was unnecessary with their proximity, so Cal took his shoulder and kept him walking toward the motor home. "Sir, let's go to our command center, and we can show you what occurred this evening. Everything was recorded."

"I want to see this woman!"

"Not possible," Mack said as he quickly texted Selina with one word, incoming, before he finished answering. "The ME has already removed the body. We should talk inside."

They'd managed to herd the senator and his protection detail to the command center quickly and efficiently without drawing too much attention to him. The door opened, and Selina stepped out, holding the door for their entourage to enter. Dorian motioned for his team to stay outside, so Selina closed the door behind them.

"Where's Charlotte?" Mack asked her under his breath. The last thing he wanted was for her to overhear them.

"She's overseeing the kids waiting for a ride at the house. I didn't want her here just in case."

Mack nodded, glad Selina had anticipated this situation and acted accordingly. Senator Dorian was difficult on a good day. Tonight, he was going to be impossible.

"What is going on?" Dorian asked, raising his voice again.

"Settle down, Senator," Cal said, motioning with his

hands. There were few people Dorian let order him around, but Cal was one of them.

"You'd better start talking, Newfellow. I pay you to keep my name out of the news, not plaster me across the front page!"

"Senator, we cannot control where a body floats to shore," Cal reminded him. "All we can do is control what happens if that situation arises, which is what we've done."

"It was him, wasn't it? The Red River Slayer?"

A shiver went through Mack when he said the name. He didn't know who the guy was, but he was ruthless, and too many women were paying the price.

"We don't know that, Senator. People drown in the Mississippi all the time. We can't jump to conclusions," Cal reminded him.

"Nice try, Newfellow. Do you have any idea how bad this is going to look for my reelection campaign? I can't host a party here now!"

"Why not?" Mack asked with his arms across his chest and feet spread. He wanted the senator to know they wouldn't back down to his demands.

"Why not? Do you think anyone will want to come here for a party when there's a killer on the loose?"

Dorian's voice was way too loud for the small space, and Mack took another step toward him. "If the woman was murdered, it didn't happen here. The ME put her time of death closer to three to four days ago. While it was unfortunate that she washed up on your shoreline, no one is at risk of being killed here. For any future campaign parties you may host, we'll be here with more staff to protect the property from the road, the woods and the shoreline as we always do. There's nothing to worry about, Senator."

The tension in the room was taut, and Mack steeled himself for the tongue-lashing from the man, but it never came. His shoulders slumped, and he wiped his hand across his forehead before he planted it on his hip. "I'm sorry. I was terrified something had happened to Eleanor, and then to find out another young woman had died riled me up. They have to stop this guy."

"We're all in agreement about that," Cal assured him, directing him to a chair in front of the computer monitors. "Let's go over the footage from tonight. Maybe you'll spot something we overlooked."

Cal started the camera replay and lifted a brow at Mack from behind the senator. Mack bit back his chuckle. They didn't miss anything, and he was confident they'd played the entire night by the book. None of that mattered unless the senator believed it as well. The last thing Secure One needed was Dorian bad-mouthing them all over the country. Cal would do anything to make sure that didn't happen.

Chapter Five

"When will my dad get here?" Eleanor asked in a huff.

"He's chatting with Cal and the team now, so I'm sure he will be here soon, Eleanor," Charlotte answered, trying to placate her.

"Chatting," she said with an eye roll. "More like yelling and throwing his name around."

Eric's snort from across the room drove Charlotte to glare at him.

"What? She clearly knows her father." He gave her the palms out, and this time it was Eleanor who giggle-snorted.

"I also know Cal doesn't let my dad push him around. I'm glad about that. You should always stand your ground with bullies."

"You're saying your father is a bully?" Charlotte asked.

"Just calling a spade a spade. My dad thinks he's president of the United States already. He hasn't even run yet."

"Is he planning to?" Eric asked, leaning forward.

"Last I heard," Eleanor said with boredom. "It's all he talks about right now. I'm sure that's what he's planning to reveal at the next party. He needs big bucks to throw his hat in the ring, which means he needs big donors to like him."

Charlotte didn't follow politics, much less Minnesota

politics, but she would do a deep dive once they got back to Secure One. Dorian was a long-time client of theirs, and she wanted to familiarize herself with him, his career and his family. Well, his family was easy. He was a single father to Eleanor and spent most of his time in Washington while his daughter lived in Minnesota with his mother. Her grandmother raised Eleanor while Dorian pursued his career. Eleanor's mother was killed in a car crash when she was a baby, and Dorian had never remarried. Eric shot Charlotte a look before he picked up the tablet and started typing. He was probably making notes since the team was busy with Dorian in the command center.

"Why can't I go to my room?" The girl was frustrated, and Charlotte couldn't blame her.

"I'm sorry, Eleanor. Cal wants you to stay here with us until they're done briefing your dad on what happened tonight. I'm sure it won't be much longer."

"Please, call me Ella. Eleanor makes me feel so…" She motioned her hand around in the air until Charlotte answered.

"Old?"

Ella pointed at her. "Ancient."

"I understand," Charlotte assured her with a chuckle. "I feel the same way about the name Charlotte."

"I don't think Charlotte is a bad name, but maybe a little old-fashioned. Do you have a nickname?"

"I used to," Charlotte said, pausing on the last word.

"Well, what is it?"

"I've only told one other person this before." She paused, and Ella cocked her head, fully engaged with her now. Charlotte didn't want to lose that connection, so she took a deep breath and spoke. "Hope. I was an artist in my former life."

"You're still an artist. A damn good one," Eric said without lifting his head from the tablet.

That made both Charlotte and Ella smile. "I'm still an artist, but I was a street artist back then. Do you know what that is?"

"Sure," Ella said with a shrug. "You tagged buildings. Graffiti."

"I guess some would call it graffiti, but I painted murals on buildings while everyone else slept. They were my way of bringing hope to the other kids on the streets."

"Your tag name was Hope?"

Charlotte nodded, trying to force a smile to her lips, but it didn't come. She noted Eric nodded his head once as though he respected her. No one had ever respected her before, but that was the feeling she got from him and Ella. She could change her name to what it was before The Madame washed her history, but doing that meant she'd have to face her past as Hope. After all, there was a reason she'd jumped on The Madame's offer to change her name and find a new life. She just hadn't expected that new life to be as an escort, drug mule and mercenary against her will.

"That's a cool story. You must be a fantastic artist if you painted murals on buildings."

"She is," Eric said, still without lifting his head. "Charlotte—Hope—should show you some of her work. She doesn't just draw a picture. She tells a story. She has natural talent, and that can't be learned."

"Would you show me?" Ella asked with excitement. "I do some drawing, but I'm not that good."

"Yet," Charlotte said with a wink. "We all get better with practice and time. I don't have my sketchbook here, but I promise to bring it to the next party. We can hang out in mobile command and draw."

"That would be great," Ella said with excitement, but Charlotte also noted a hint of relief in her voice. "I hate his parties. He makes me show my face for a little bit, but then I always find a place to hide to avoid all those people."

"I feel your pain," Eric said, lowering the tablet. "There's nothing worse than a bunch of snobby adults jockeying for the top spot as richest in the room."

Ella laughed while she pointed at Eric. "I like you. Not many people get what it's like to deal with politicians and their donors. It's exhausting. That's why I live in St. Paul with my grandma. I want to go to school and live a normal life. Well, as normal as possible. Yes, I have to go to private school, but I could never live in Washington, DC, year-round. I go in the summer, and that's enough for me."

"I'm ex-army," Eric said. "I know what it's like to deal with the government and politicians. I don't blame you for wanting time away from that three-ring circus."

Eric's phone rang, and he held up his finger, then answered it, stepping into the corner of the room to talk to the caller.

Ella glanced at him and then leaned in closer to Charlotte. "I'm not kidding here when I say I need to go to the bathroom in my room or I'm going to ruin this gown."

"Understood," Charlotte said with a nod. "Let me get Eric."

"He's busy. Besides, I don't want him ushering me to my room to get pads. Please."

Charlotte could see Ella was embarrassed, but she bit

her lip with nervousness. They weren't supposed to leave the room on Cal's orders. Then again, he didn't put them in a room with a bathroom either, so she had to assume he knew they'd have to leave for that.

"Okay. This place is crawling with cops. It won't be a big deal to run up there, but I need to tell Eric, and I'm going with you. To your room and back. No other stops."

Ella held up her hands in agreement, so Charlotte walked over to Eric and leaned in to whisper. "She needs the restroom. It's an emergency. I'll take her there and bring her right back. Will Cal object?"

Eric put his hand over the receiver, glanced at Ella and back to her. "Not much we can do other than be careful. There are cops everywhere but stay alert. I'm not expecting any other problems tonight though."

Charlotte nodded and tucked her required Secure One Taser into the holster on her belt. While she was trained on handling a gun, she rarely carried one. Too many innocent people had died from a bullet meant for someone else, and she couldn't live with herself if she were the cause of an innocent person's death.

She motioned for Eleanor to follow her to the door. This was her chance to prove to Cal that she was part of the team, whether she was cooking for them or doing unexpected bodyguard duty on a US senator's daughter. Cal had trained her for this, and when she'd asked him why, his answer was simple: *You never know when you will have to keep yourself or someone else safe in this business. If you work here, you're part of the team, and everyone on the team does this training.* She always thought she'd never need it, but tonight, she was ready to prove she'd learned her lessons well.

CHARLOTTE STOOD OUTSIDE the bathroom door and waited for Ella. She had agreed to let her change clothes before they went back to where Eric was waiting. She was right, it didn't make sense to parade around in a ball gown, but Charlotte also didn't want to be gone too long.

"Hey, Hope," Ella called from inside the bathroom. Charlotte didn't cringe at the name, and that surprised her. "Did you happen to see Tia and Leticia before they left?"

"I did," Charlotte said, reminding herself not to spill their secret. "They left with their parents after they talked to the cops."

"Were they okay?" she called back through the door, and Charlotte heard rustling on the other side as though she were hanging up the gown.

"They were fine. Why?"

"They found a dead woman in the river. I figured they'd be shaken."

The door opened, and Ella stepped out wearing a pair of pajama pants and a long T-shirt. She was ready for bed, and honestly, so was Charlotte, but she dragged a smile to her face and nodded. "They were shaken up, but by the time they left, they'd calmed down."

"I felt so bad when I found out they were the ones who found her," Ella said, following Charlotte to the door.

"Why?" A look left and then right had Charlotte stepping out into the hallway with Ella.

"They go through enough already. It's hard being in the closet. Then, when you finally get some time alone, that happens."

"Wait. You know?" Charlotte asked.

"Everyone knows," Ella said with an eye roll. "We go

to a Catholic school, so we all pretend we don't know just to protect them."

"Wow, I wasn't expecting that."

"Why? Because I'm a snobby rich kid who doesn't care about anyone else?"

Charlotte stopped and spun on her heel to face her. "I would never think that, Ella. I've known you barely an hour and know you're nothing like your father. You care about getting to know people. I wasn't expecting you to say that because the girls told us no one else knew."

Ella's shrug was simple. "That's what they need to believe, so as a class, we decided we would let them believe it. We protect them whenever someone starts asking too many questions and always make sure we have parties where there's a place for them to escape together. Did you see them together?" Charlotte nodded but didn't say anything. "Then you know that they've already found their soulmate at sixteen."

Charlotte turned and started back down the hallway, keeping Ella on the inside of her against the wall. "Do you believe in soulmates?"

"I do. I think that's why my dad has never remarried. My mom was his, and when she died, a piece of him did too. He never dated again after she died. Women try, trust me, but he's not interested. I wish he would though."

"Why?"

"It might chill him out a little. He's always wound so tightly that I'm afraid he'll have a heart attack one day."

"I agree with you. Your dad strikes me as an all-work-and-no-play kind of guy."

"He so is, but this summer, when I'm in Washington, I'm going to do something about it."

Charlotte had already messaged Eric to let him know they were on their way back, and as they started down the stairs, she noticed that the house had cleared out and was much quieter.

"What are you going to do about it? Set him up?"

"That's exactly what I'm going to do!" Ella said, laughter filling the stairwell as they stepped onto the lavish parquet flooring. Calling this house a "cabin" insulted the artists who'd poured their souls into it. The view during the day must be breathtaking from the large bay windows that faced the back of it, and the chef's kitchen and extensive library weren't something you saw in most "cabins" in Minnesota. Charlotte hadn't lived in Minnesota long, but she did know that much.

"I'm sure that'll go over well," Charlotte said with a chuckle just as a man dressed in black stepped out of a hallway and grasped Ella's elbow.

"I'll take Miss Dorian to her father now. Thank you for your help," he said, tugging Ella's arm to follow him.

Charlotte instinctively grabbed Ella's other arm and held tight. "I need to see ID, and I'll have to call my boss before I can relinquish Miss Dorian into your care." She sounded calm, but she wasn't. She was panicking, so she forced the sensation back and focused on her training. *If you ever feel like something is off, hit your all-call button, and we'll come running.*

Mack's words ran through her head, but she hesitated, taking stock of the man again. He wore a black suit and coat, a black hat and had an earpiece running from his jacket to his ear. The tall man kept his head bent low, ensuring that Charlotte couldn't get a good look at him.

"I said, I need to see your ID."

"I'm protection detail for Senator Dorian," he repeated. "I don't have to show you anything."

"Then you can't take Miss Dorian. We'll wait for her father in the designated area. Come on, Ella."

Charlotte tugged on Ella's arm, but the man didn't release her. The girl looked terrified, which told Charlotte that she had never seen this man before. Without hesitation, Charlotte hit the button on her vest and then took hold of Ella with both hands. "You should leave now unless you have ID."

She unhooked the button on her holster, but she never got to pull the Taser before a fist flew at her from her right. She dodged it but not before it glanced off her jaw and tossed her head to the side. She didn't let go of Ella, who was now screaming for someone to help them. Charlotte couldn't worry about help arriving. She had to concentrate on protecting Ella. She was afraid he would punch Ella next, so she yanked the girl to the left and then kicked out with her right leg, landing a hit in the guy's solar plexus. He let out a huff, but it wasn't enough to stop him from hitting her dead in the eye with a sharp jab.

Ella had fallen to the floor and was crab-walking backward as the man went for her. Gathering her wits, Charlotte struck him in the back with her elbow and then hit him behind the knees with a back kick that sent him to the floor. Commotion and shouting filled the house as men came running from all doors, but the man in black wasn't giving up. He turned and swept Charlotte's feet out from under her, and she fell, hitting the floor with her head. Dazed, she knew she had to fight him off long enough for Mack or Eric to get to them. All she could think to do was lift her feet and kick up. A smile lifted her lips when the resounding crack told her she'd made contact with her target. He bellowed and pinwheeled backward, right into Eric's waiting arms, who quickly subdued him.

Charlotte didn't get up off the floor. She just stared at the cathedral ceiling, the colors swirling and spinning in the atmosphere around her. She had to catch her breath before she could move again. The fight had taken everything out of her.

"Hope!" Ella said, her face swimming in her line of sight. "Are you okay?"

Charlotte wanted to answer her, but all she could do was watch the swirling colors above her head.

"Hope, I mean, Charlotte needs help!" Ella yelled. Charlotte could hear the frantic tone of her voice and reached for her, trying to reassure her, but her hand missed its target and fell back to the hardwood floor. "Someone, please, help her!"

A voice broke through the din in the room, and she begged her mind to focus on the sound. It was her name on Mack's lips as he scooped her up, wrapped her in his protective arms and started running.

"I need a medic!" Charlotte found his bellowing voice more soothing than scary. "I'm going to get you help, Charlotte," he promised, and it was only then that she closed her eyes.

MACK PACED ACROSS the floor of mobile command, where the team had met up after the attempted kidnapping of Dorian's daughter. They'd have lost Ella tonight if it hadn't been for Charlotte. What had Eric been thinking letting them go alone? He would never say it to the man, he felt bad enough, but Charlotte had paid a heavy price.

"I'm fine, Mack," she said from the corner chair where she sat with an ice pack on her face. Not only did she have a concussion from hitting her head on the floor, but the jerk had given her a black eye and swollen jaw.

"You're a warrior, Charlotte, but I can't stop thinking about how close we came to a kidnapping on our watch."

"Me neither," she said, wincing when she held the ice to her eye. "Did anyone get anything out of the guy?"

All eyes were on Cal and Eric. They'd taken the guy aside and had a "chat" with him before the police arrived. "Not much," Cal said with a shake of his head. "I have to hand it to you. You broke the guy's jaw with that last kick. He was twice your size and strength."

"He wasn't taking Ella on my watch. When she looked at me with terror, I knew she didn't know the guy, which meant he wasn't part of the senator's detail. I had to stop him long enough for you guys to wade in and help me."

"I'm proud of you, Charlotte. Hand-to-hand isn't easy for anyone, especially when you're outsized the way you were. That was Secure One protection at its finest."

Mack noticed her chest puff up and her shoulders straighten at Cal's words.

"He's right, Charlotte. You saved Ella, and all of us here know it." Mack glanced at Eric, who was glaring at them with his arms crossed over his chest. Whether he was ticked at them or himself, Mack couldn't say.

"I'm glad she's safe, but we have to find out who this guy is."

"The cops will know that quickly, but so will we," Cal said, holding up a glass slide. "I accidentally got the guy to touch this." He gave her a wink. "I'll get Mina working on it back at Secure One. In the meantime, we have to assume that it's either tied to Dorian's reelection campaign or the body they found tonight."

"I'm leaning toward his reelection campaign," Mack said. "He's got enemies, and what better way to get you to back off something than to leverage the one person you love the most."

"Agreed," Cal said. "I think it was coincidence, or else the person behind the kidnapping got wind of the chaotic events tonight and decided he'd take advantage of it. It was smart to send someone in when there were already so many people in a tight space. You could get away without being noticed."

"Wait," Charlotte said, leaning forward. "The guy we got isn't the person behind the kidnapping?"

"Not according to him," Eric said, finally engaging with the team. "He told me he was hired to get the girl and bring her to a secure location where he'd hand her off for a big payday."

"More likely, he'd trade her for a bullet to the head," Cal muttered, and Eric pointed at him.

"So he was doing someone's dirty work. What does Senator Dorian think?" Selina asked while checking Charlotte's blood pressure.

Mack kept his gaze trained on the readout and was relieved when her blood pressure was normal.

"He thinks it has something to do with his future bid for the presidency," Eric said. "Mack's right. He's made enemies. There aren't many politicians who don't, but Dorian seems especially good at it. Someone saw an opportunity and took it tonight. I shouldn't have let you go alone to her room."

Charlotte brushed her free hand at him and sighed. "I

thought nothing of it either," she said, trying to reassure him. "When I took her up there, cops were everywhere. There was no way to know this guy would appear out of nowhere and attempt a kidnapping amid that much law enforcement."

"It was brazen," Cal said. "No doubt about it, but there's nothing we can do until Mina gets me a name and we can look into his past."

"I doubt it will lead us anywhere. I would bet my month's salary that he's got a laundry list of previous convictions and multiple addresses where he's lived," Eric said. It was easy to hear the frustration in his tone, which was mirrored in everyone's body language. It was after 3:00 a.m., and they'd been going for over eighteen hours. Everyone needed rest and food. Good thing their cook turned bodyguard had stocked the kitchen with easy-to-grab meals.

"Most likely," Cal agreed, "but you know Mina. All she needs is one tiny hint of a path, and she will find where it leads. We trust our team at home until we can get there, which won't be until tomorrow. Right now, we all need sleep." Heads nodded, and shoulders slumped at the idea of finally closing their eyes.

"Selina, let's keep Charlotte—"

A knock on the door interrupted Cal. "I want to talk to you, Newfellow!"

Mack heard Eric swear from the corner, giving him a mental fist bump. Dorian was the last person they needed to deal with right now.

"Let me do the talking," Cal said, and heads nodded as he opened the door to the senator and his entourage.

Dorian climbed the stairs and stood with his hands on

his hips in front of the team. "How in the hell did that happen?" he demanded, pointing behind him. "I pay you exorbitant amounts of money to keep the security tight on this place!"

Cal held up his hand and nodded. "You do, Senator. What happened tonight was unforgivable. I completely understand if you want to cancel your contract with Secure One. We let you down tonight."

Mack glanced at his boss with surprise and wasn't entirely sure that Cal didn't want exactly that to happen. Cal had grown tired of the senator's dramatics long before tonight. The man was fussy, ornery, demanding and never took the time to understand why or how something did or didn't work before he flew off the handle.

Ron Dorian's shoulders dropped an inch when he shook his head before he spoke. "I don't want to cancel my contract. I realize there were extenuating circumstances tonight that you had no control over. Though, I do want to know how that little thing in the corner was the only one around to save my daughter from a kidnapper!"

He gestured at Charlotte while he glared at the rest of the men in the room. Eric stood and walked toward the man. He wasn't going to follow Cal's no-talking order. "She was with your daughter because you put us in a room without access to necessary facilities. Ella is a sixteen-year-old girl who needed a restroom for reasons I don't think I should go into here. I sent the trained Secure One operative your daughter felt comfortable with and stayed in contact with them the entire time they were gone. I had all the exits covered, meaning no one was getting out of the house without an ID check." Eric held up his hand to the man who was ready to speak. "And before you ask, we don't know how he got inside. He may have snuck in when parents were coming and going with their kids. We will search our camera footage for that. When our operative indicated she needed help, I was there in less than twenty seconds to offer her assistance, though I'm sure it felt much longer to her and Ella. You can be unhappy with what happened here tonight, but our team did what we're trained to do regardless of the situation. So, yes, our trained operative in the corner currently nursing a concussion saved your daughter tonight, as any of us would have."

Eric faced off with the man for a moment and then stepped back and sat in the chair again. If a pin had dropped, everyone would have heard it. Mack couldn't remember the last time Eric had stepped up and taken the lead role. He wasn't sure he picked the right time to do it, but that was between him and Cal.

Dorian turned to Cal. "My daughter wants her," he said, pointing at Charlotte, "as her bodyguard until this guy is caught."

"Charlotte is not a bodyguard," Cal said.

"I don't care what you call her, but she will be by my daughter's side until this guy is behind bars."

"Sir—"

"Don't sir me," Dorian said. "Just listen. I want the girl, Mack, and the mouthy one," he pointed at Eric, "in my house in twenty minutes."

"I'll arrange it, sir," Cal said rather than continue to argue with him. "But Charlotte will need rest tonight. She can't take charge of your daughter until she is no longer concussed."

"That's what he is for," he said, pointing at Eric again.

"We both know she's in no shape to protect my daughter now, but Eleanor doesn't, so we'll let her continue to think Charlotte is her bodyguard while he provides the muscle. I want Mack there because I trust him to keep the perimeter safe."

"Eleanor is staying at the cabin and not returning to St. Paul?" Mack asked to clarify.

"I don't want my mother involved in this, so I'm keeping Ella here until they have the guy behind the kidnapping in handcuffs. She's on spring break this coming week, and if it takes longer than that to find the guy, she will do school online for the duration."

"I don't know how long I can be without two of my head men," Cal said, and Mack could hear in his voice that he was dead serious. Leaving Mack and Eric here meant a heavier workload at Secure One for the rest of the team. At least they wouldn't have to worry about Dorian's place, but that still spread them thin.

"Then you better find more guys or tell the police to hurry up. I have to fly to Washington for a vote. I will return to Minnesota once that is completed to prepare for my reelection campaign party. Understood?"

"Understood. I'll need to brief the team staying here and set them up with equipment in the morning. That means our mobile command will remain here until then."

"I'll need to assess Charlotte before we can leave as well," Selina added.

Mack bit back a smile. Everyone was tired of Dorian pushing them around, it appeared. He noticed that Charlotte had remained silent through the entire exchange. He glanced at her and noticed she was sagging in the chair. She needed rest.

"Dorian, I need a room for Charlotte immediately. She needs rest if she's going to hang out with Eleanor tomorrow," Mack said, taking a step forward.

"My staff has already readied a room. I'll see you there shortly."

Before anyone could respond, he turned and left the command center, his entourage closing in behind him and following him back to the house. When Mack turned back to the team, they were all awaiting Cal's orders.

"You heard the man. Mack, carry Charlotte to the house and get her settled."

"I can walk," she said, but Mack didn't like how soft her voice sounded. He glanced at Selina, who gave him a headshake. He'd be carrying her.

"Eric will follow you with bags for the night. Tomorrow, we'll regroup and figure this out. Nothing we can do until we've had some sleep."

Mack walked over to Charlotte and scooped her into his arms, her cry of surprise weak enough that everyone made way for them as he left the RV. Mack glanced down into the battered face of the woman in his arms and smiled.

"I know you feel like you went ten rounds with Mike Tyson, but remember, you were the hero we needed tonight. I'm so proud of you for not backing down and protecting Ella when she needed it."

"I've been Ella, and no one was there for me, Mack," she said as she rested her head against his chest. "I righted more than one wrong with a few of those kicks."

She fell quiet, and soon, her soft even breathing reached his ears. He wanted to rage against the world that she'd had to go through those things, but they had made her the strong determined woman who refused to shrink away from the flame. She had been burned so many times, but she proved to him tonight that she wasn't afraid to walk right back into the fire when it mattered most.

Her past made her a soldier.

What she'd done tonight made her a hero.

Chapter Six

The bus rumbled beneath her as she settled back into her seat and pulled a blanket up to her neck. The darkness surrounding the bus relaxed her. She was one step closer to safety. It had been sheer luck when she clicked on the radio in the truck and heard that news bulletin. Another woman had been found in the river, and she'd bet anything she'd once been in the same house in Pennsylvania. Her first piece of luck came when they mentioned a company, Secure One, had found her while working for a party at Senator Dorian's house outside of St. Paul.

When the sun came up, she ditched the truck and walked into a Salvation Army. They had bought her story that she was trying to return home to Minnesota but lost all her belongings and wallet when she accepted a ride with the wrong person. She had fought hard not to roll her eyes when she said it. She hadn't been given a choice when she took that ride, but she wasn't about to tell them that. They'd fed her, clothed her and bought her a bus ticket to St. Paul. Now all she had to do was figure out how to contact this Secure One place when she got there. She hoped they'd listen to her story and try to help her figure out this mess. Now that she knew The Miss was dead and The Madame was behind bars, she had to take the chance that Secure One could help her. If she didn't, she might as well have died in that room.

MACK TOOK IN the space around him. He was satisfied with the equipment Cal had given him to stay in touch with the team at Secure One. They'd be connected in real-time, and whenever they needed answers, someone would be there to give them. He didn't think Cal would stay gone long, but he did need to get back to Secure One and help Roman sort out their priorities before he returned to St. Paul. Mack was confident that he and Eric could handle any situation that arose. While they were in a holding pattern, he'd look for answers about the river deaths.

Before they left this morning, Selina checked Charlotte over one more time and gave her a list of things she should and shouldn't do with a concussion. Mack and Eric had plenty of experience taking care of head injuries and wouldn't let her do anything she shouldn't for a few days. When Charlotte woke this morning, she was chipper and not in much pain, so Selina was sure the bruises would stick around longer than the concussion. She was in the kitchen with Ella, making cookies and discussing art, which seemed to make Ella incredibly happy.

He hit the button on their quick connect link and waited while the system rang through to the Secure One control room.

"Secure one, Whiskey," a voice said.

"Secure two, Mike," he answered, and Mina's face popped up on the screen.

"Miss me already?" she asked with a chuckle.

"I didn't want you to think I didn't care." His wink made her smile. "I had a free minute and wanted to ask a favor."

"I'll do what I can."

"I know you have a database where you're keeping track of what rivers the women were found in, correct?"

"I cannot confirm nor deny that information."

Mack couldn't help but grin. She had been an FBI agent for years, and old habits died hard. The fact remained that she wasn't supposed to have that information and didn't get it through the proper channels at the FBI.

"Should you have that information, would you be able to highlight the rivers on a map for me? It would help me to see it laid out that way."

"If I have that information, I can send it through our secure channels in about an hour."

Mack pointed and winked. "Thanks, Min, you're the best."

"Are you hitting on my wife, sir?" Roman asked, sticking his face into the camera from behind Mina.

"Wouldn't dream of it," Mack answered with laughter. "I'm afraid of her husband."

"Someone should be since she's not. Are you guys managing okay over there? That was a hell of a night you had."

"We're good. It was a rough night, but it could have turned out worse than it did, so we'll take it as a win."

"How is our young scrappy one?" Mina asked. "I was terrified and proud all at the same time when Cal told us what she did."

Mack knew the feeling well. "I'm not sure if terrified even begins to cover it. I've been in combat situations that scared me less than the events of last night."

"It's okay, Mack," Roman said, leaning on the desk now. "It's okay to feel both of those things and admit you have a connection to her."

A brisk cross of his arms had Roman smirking before Mack even said a word. "A connection of commonality, maybe. Otherwise, that's a negative."

Roman and Mina had to bite back a snort, but Mina recovered first. "I'll prioritize that info and get it to you in a few minutes. Okay to tell Cal?"

"Of course," Mack agreed, straightening his back and letting go of the tension in his shoulders from their razzing. "I'm looking for a pattern, so if any of you find one, shout it out. We have to start somewhere."

Mina pointed at the camera. "Couldn't agree more. Whiskey, out."

The screen went blank, and Mack sighed as he lowered himself to a chair. They were right, there was a connection between him and Charlotte, but it was one he had to force himself not to think about or consider. They both had ghosts, but he wore his every day as a reminder that he had been weak when he should have been strong. He couldn't forgive himself for how those ghosts died, so there was no way she would ever look at him twice once she knew the truth. Being trapped here with her wasn't making it easier to distance himself, especially when he'd been the one to wake her every two hours last night.

The exhaustion wasn't helping him look at this case with a clear lens either. He forced his mind to look at the information analytically. What did they know about this guy? He pulled a pad of paper closer to him and grabbed a pen. In the beginning, he was impulsive but slowly, over time, perfected his presentation of his victims and his timeline. *Why didn't they find any victims for two years?* Mack underlined that question several times. Maybe he was in jail or out of the country? His last victim was found shortly before The Madame was arrested, and his next victim wasn't found until The Miss was in Arizona. *Coincidence?* Mack underlined that word several times too.

As far as they knew, the guy had to have connections to get the women and hold them somewhere. That is, assuming he'd held onto Layla for the whole of the eighteen months she'd been gone. Maybe he hadn't. Maybe he got her from someone else. Either way, he had to have connections and be cunning enough not to get caught. He would also need money and a vehicle. If he were using the same river repeatedly, it would be easy to pinpoint his location within the river's course, but he never used the same river twice.

He sat up immediately. That had been hiding in the back of his mind somewhere. He'd double-check when Mina sent him the map, but as far as he remembered, the women were never in the same river. Why was their perp driving around the country? Just to throw the feds off his tail? Was he getting the women from the same states, or was he transporting them already dead? Or was he transporting them alive and then killing them near the river?

Drawing a new column, he wrote the traits they knew the perp to have just by what his crimes revealed. He was connected, cunning, well-off, likely narcissistic, controlling and got off on having power over others. Mack paused with his pen on the pad. Maybe they were looking for this guy in all the wrong places. He dropped the pen and grabbed a laptop, then opened an incognito window. Narcissists like to talk about themselves. They yearned for accolades, even when they couldn't come right out and talk about their crimes.

Narcissists were everywhere, but Mack knew one place

a lot of them assembled to swap war stories, so to speak. There was a forum for everything, but some forums held darker content than others, and Mack intended to start his search there.

Chapter Seven

Mack stood in the makeshift office and stared at the map projected on the wall. Something was bugging him about this case, but he couldn't put his finger on it.

"Mack?" a voice asked from the doorway, and he turned to see Charlotte peeking in the door. "Everything okay? It's late."

"Everything's fine," he said. "It is late. Why are you still up?"

Her smile brightened his day no matter when she hit him with it, and tonight was no different. Her black eye and bruised chin didn't detract from her beauty. In fact, in his eyes, those bruises reminded him that behind her beauty was an irrefutable strength few people had.

She stepped into the room and walked past the large wooden desk the senator used when he was home. Now it held Secure One computers and link-ups to headquarters. They had a dead body and attempted kidnapping on their watch, and he wasn't any happier about it than Cal. While it was beyond their control, it also put their name back in the media. Cal had tried to minimize publicity about their security service since The Miss was killed, but it appeared the universe was not cooperating with him.

"That or this is still tied to The Madame," Mack muttered.

"What now?" Charlotte asked, her back stiffening at the utterance of her former boss's name.

"I'm sorry." He grimaced at himself. "I didn't mean to say that aloud. I was thinking about how we can't keep Secure One out of the news no matter how hard we try. Cal is frustrated that The Madame and The Miss have kept us on the public's radar."

"And you think all of this," she motioned around the map, "is tied to The Madame?"

"I don't know, but according to Roman and Mina, several women were found in rivers while The Madame was operating." His head swung back and forth in frustration as he tried to see a pattern that wasn't there.

"What is this?" Charlotte pointed at the map of the United States. "Rivers?"

"Yeah," he said, his hand going through his short brown hair in frustration. Unlike Cal, he'd gotten rid of the high and tight hairstyle the moment he left the field on a stretcher. His boss liked to tease him that he looked like an FBI agent now, just like Roman. He'd shake his head in disdain but be laughing while he did it. "Each highlighted river represents a place where at least one body was found since they started finding women. The most recent women were wearing red gowns."

"So, the bodies found in the rivers while The Madame was in operation weren't in red?" she asked.

"Not according to Mina. It was only when the recent bodies were discovered that they were wearing red gowns. A news reporter dubbed him The Red River Slayer, and it stuck." The moniker might be accurate, but something about it set his teeth on edge.

"If you think about it, I could have been one of those women."

Mack sucked in air through his nose. "I try not to think about that, okay?"

"I think about it all the time." She stared at the wall rather than make eye contact with him. "When they found the first woman, I was new to the Red Rye House. When other women I lived with started disappearing, I thought they left of their own free will. But I was naive enough back then to believe we could leave."

"But you didn't know if the women who disappeared were the women they found."

Her shrug gave him the answer. "How could I? It wasn't like we were allowed to watch or listen to the news. We were very sheltered in Red Rye."

"Nothing?" Mack asked in surprise with a lifted brow.

"Nothing. We had no cable or news channels on the television, and all we could do was stream movies. We also didn't have a radio. I heard about them finding the women on the radio when I was on a *date*," which she put in quotation marks, "but they said they hadn't identified them yet. Not that they *couldn't* identify them. I didn't find that out until I left The Miss and came here."

"And now we've found another woman from The Miss."

"Layla." She said the name with reverence. As though saying it that way gave her an identity. "When she disappeared, I figured The Miss sold or killed her. She wasn't bringing any money in, and The Miss didn't put up with that for long."

"And she disappeared eighteen months ago?" Mack asked again.

"I thought about it, and the timeline is correct within a few months. I've already been at Secure One for six months, and she disappeared about a year before I surrendered."

"This is the first time we've had a timeline. You're the reason we have it, even if you did disobey orders. We'll have to talk about your propensity to do that."

"Last time I checked, Cal's my boss, not you." She looked him up and down in a way that brought a smile to his lips.

"Noted, but when you're here with me, I'm the boss regarding quick decisions as the situation warrants."

"Accepted, but I will protect Ella no matter the cost. You may as well know that."

"I do," he promised, tracing his thumb over her jaw, the bump smaller after a night of rest and ice. "But I don't have to like it. Have you always been this brave, Char?"

Her blue eyes held his, and he watched her wrap her arms around herself in a hug. "No. I used to live in fear every second of the day. I was afraid of my foster parents and siblings when I was a kid. When I hit the streets, I was afraid of the dark and the things it held, so I painted at night. It was safer to be awake and see them coming. When I started working for The Madame, I was afraid of the men she made me date. When I started working for The Miss, I was afraid of everything."

"What changed?"

"Me." Her answer was simple, but he knew the explanation was far more complicated. "When I looked back on my life, fear was the common thread running through it. I could keep being afraid and keep being taken advantage of, or I could snip the thread of fear and see what happened."

Mack nodded, the explanation making sense to him. "I understand." Her snort was sarcastic and pithy. He turned her chin to meet his gaze. "I know you don't think so, but I do. My dad and I were in a car accident when I was a toddler. I lived. He didn't. My mother struggled the rest of her life with the fear of losing me. She didn't let me do anything out of fear that I'd get hurt and die too. I grew up thinking every new experience was scary and should be avoided. Our experiences were different, there is no doubt, but I understand what you mean by a thread of fear. I had to cut mine too."

"When you went into the service?"

"No, when my mother got cancer when I was a teenager, I realized she wasn't going to make it. Suddenly, I had to figure out how to live unafraid."

"I'm still afraid a lot of the time, but I tell myself that when I do something even while I'm afraid, the next thing I have to do will be a little easier."

A smile lifted his lips, and he nodded. "You're right, and it's working. I remember the woman who surrendered to us six months ago, and she's not the same woman standing before me today."

This time, it was her smile that beamed back at him. "I'm glad someone noticed. I've worked hard in therapy to accept that a lot of what's happened to me was done to me and not something I did to myself."

"That's important to remember," Mack agreed. It was true for her, but not for him. What happened to him was something he had done to himself. He only had to look at his boots to be reminded of that.

"I argued that I did make a lot of bad choices, and the therapist agreed, but she also pointed out that I never had any good choices to start with."

"She makes a point."

Charlotte tipped her head in agreement and crossed her arms over her chest. "After I thought about it, I decided that I could continue to make bad choices or start from scratch and make better ones. Go to therapy. Work a job. Be part of a team instead of going it alone."

"The changes you've made the last six months haven't been overlooked. I hope you know that. We're all incredibly proud of you."

Mack noted the pink creep up her cheeks at his compliment. That was something else she needed to learn how to accept—how integral she was to the team.

"Thank you," she said, glancing down at the floor.

He tipped her chin up again and held her gaze. "Hold your head high, Charlotte. You've got grit and proved it, including when you fought off someone twice your size to protect a young girl. That takes guts. How is your head?"

"Okay," she said with a shy smile. "I'm being careful and following Selina's orders so I don't make anything worse. It's been fun hanging out and being with Ella today, but I'm ready to work now."

"Eric is here to protect Ella."

"Understood, but I can help in other ways. Let me help you figure this out." She motioned at the map and took a step closer. "Some of these rivers run through more than one state. How do we know what location he put them in the river?"

"We don't," Mack answered with frustration. "That's part of the problem. Obviously, everything floats downstream, and some rivers run through several states. For instance, the Mississippi flows through seven states. It's nearly impossible to know where the body was dumped."

"Which means he gets away with it longer because these rivers run all over the country. Well, except for Layla."

Mack's attention shifted from the map to the woman who always, despite her ordeal, had a ready smile. Her long blond hair was wavy, and she wore it tied behind her head with a band. Her blue eyes were luminous in the light from the projector, even with a black eye, and her lips were pursed as she finished the last word.

"Except for Layla?"

"Think about it, Mack," she said, stepping in front of him to point at the map. Her body slid across his in a whisper of material that sent a burning need straight through him. "She was found outside St. Paul, right?" He nodded, and she raised her hand to point at the top of the map. "And we know the Mississippi originates at Lake Itasca. That's what, about three hours north of where she was found?"

How had he not thought of that? She was right. The Mississippi headwaters were only an hour from Secure One, the way the crow flies.

"We should have thought of that," he said, snapping the projector off and leaving the lights low. "Thank you for pointing it out. I can't believe we missed something so obvious."

Her tiny hand waved his words away. "The difference is that you have too much information about all the other women. Since I don't know anything about those cases, my mind tracked the possibilities for just Layla. Do you think that means the killer is from Minnesota?"

Mack didn't cut himself any slack despite her insistence. He should have been concentrating on one woman's journey at a time instead of as a group. That was exactly what he would do tomorrow. He'd focus solely on each woman and see if a pattern developed rather than as a whole, where the pattern seemed willy-nilly.

"There's no way to know that, but my gut says no. The women have been found in rivers all over the country. In the beginning, the bodies were found randomly, then we had a period of inactivity, and now, they're finding a woman every six weeks."

"Which means we only have about five weeks until another woman like Layla is found," Charlotte said, and Mack noticed a shiver go up her spine.

He didn't stop himself from reaching over to tenderly rub the base of her back. "I'm sorry. You shouldn't have to keep witnessing women you know dying in this way."

"Those women didn't do anything to deserve this. They were looking for a better life than one on the streets, just like I was, so as long as I'm still breathing, I'll fight for them."

"I know," Mack assured her, pulling her into him and wrapping his arm around her shoulder. "We know the women were innocent victims. The FBI has known that for years, but when the perp was killing women with no identities, they had nothing to go on."

"They never convinced The Madame or her husband to tell them who the women were?"

Mack wished he could hide his anger when he shook his head, but he knew she could see the way his jaw pulsed at the idea of how badly the FBI had botched the investigation. "Of course not. If they admitted they knew who the women were, it would implicate them in their murders. I'm sure their lawyers told them to remain silent."

"True," she agreed. "Do you have a list of the victims along with when and where they were found?"

"Yes."

"Good, then we take it one step further and mark the exact location where a body was found on the map."

"That still doesn't tell us where the body was dumped."

He felt her shrug under his hand before she spoke. "Just trying to help."

Mack swore internally for shooting her down. "I'm sorry," he said, turning her to face him. "I'm frustrated with this case. It's hard when I know that every time the sun comes up, another woman is one day closer to death. I may no longer be in the army, but I'll always be someone who wades into battle to save the innocents. This," he said with frustration as he flicked his hand at the projector, "has to stop."

Char braced her delicate hand on his chest, and her warmth spread through him like wildfire. It calmed and centered him. She made such a difference in his life just by being in it, and she grounded him when he was ready to pop off into the atmosphere from frustration. She was also the calming touch he needed when he wanted to rage against the world, and he wasn't sure how he felt about that. He could never be with this woman, so having that kind of reaction to her was problematic.

"If anyone can find this guy, Secure One can. You work together to save the people you care about, and that's what makes the team successful. Maybe a pattern will naturally develop if you plot out the places where the women were found."

Mack ran a hand down his face as he stared at the map. "You're right. I'll have Mina do it tomorrow since she has the kind of mind that will see the pattern developing as she goes."

"She'll also be rested, and you're not, Mack. You need to sleep, or you won't be any good to anyone."

He shut off the computer and walked with her to the door. "I'll try to sleep, but I'll end up staring at the ceiling until the sun comes up."

Her laughter was genuine when it reached his ears. "Some nights, I'd rather stare at the ceiling than deal with the nightmares."

"Those are the nights I find you in the kitchen," Mack pointed out as he shut the lights off.

"There's something comforting about a quiet kitchen at two a.m. with the scent of bread baking in the oven. I'd rather be tired and busy than tired and idle."

"It leaves too much time to think," they said in unison.

She glanced at him for a moment with a look of consideration, sympathy and understanding in her blue eyes before she waved and turned away from him. He stood rooted in place until she disappeared. As he walked to his room, the memories of his time with Char filled him. She was far more intuitive than she understood, which made him wonder why she was the way she was. Life on the street hardened a person, but something happened to her before she found herself on the street. What was it? That was the question. Mack was sure the answer would be no more forthcoming than his answer to the question she'd asked one night in the kitchen.

What happened out there in that giant sandbox no one wants to play in, Mack?

There were things he wouldn't discuss with anyone, and that included Charlotte. One of those things was the sandbox that held nothing but pain and regret. Charlotte had enough of those two things in her short life.

Chapter Eight

Charlotte didn't want to wait for Mina to plot the rivers that once held women in their watery grip. She didn't work well with computer-generated models, so she'd drawn her own map of the United States and marked the rivers in their full routes through each state, including their tributaries. Now all she needed were the locations of the bodies. That was easy enough to find. She brought up Google and typed in *The Red River Slayer victims*; within three seconds, she had the list she needed. She plotted the city or town closest to where the victim was brought ashore. That would only help them if they needed information from local authorities.

There was a knock on the office door, and Charlotte glanced up, expecting Mack or Eric, but Ella stood there instead. "Hey," she said to the girl. "Did you need something?"

"Not really. I'm bored, and Eric is hovering. He can go grab some food if I'm in here with you."

Charlotte motioned her in and then closed the office door and locked it. Eric and Mack had a key, but no one else did. "I can't say I'm not boring, but you're welcome to hang out here."

"What are you working on?" Ella asked, taking in the

map. "This is huge. How did you find paper big enough for a map?"

"It's parchment paper from the kitchen."

"Really?" She was surprised when she ran her hand over it and realized it was true. "I never thought about drawing on it."

"I like it for certain projects, especially when heavy markers are involved because it doesn't bleed through the back."

Ella's finger followed the rivers on the map with her head cocked. "Rivers? What are the numbers and the towns?" Charlotte didn't have a chance to say anything before Ella let out a shocked breath. "The women from The Red River Slayer?"

"You shouldn't see this," Charlotte said, starting to roll it up, but Ella slapped her hand down on it.

"Please, I'm practically an adult, and it's not like any of this is a huge secret. The last woman was found just steps outside this door."

"I just don't want to get in trouble with the senator. I'm supposed to guard you, not get you involved in a murder case."

Ella brushed her words away with her hand. "He's not here, and trust me when I say he has no idea what I'm doing most of the time." She fell silent and tapped her chin, repeatedly pointing at the rivers as though she were counting. She opened her phone, grabbed the blue marker, and made lines in several states. After more pecking on her phone, she grabbed a red one and made similar lines in others.

"What are you doing?"

"He's hit the Mississippi, Kansas, Arkansas, Red, Rio Grande, Chattahoochee, Missouri, Platte, Snake, Colorado, Canadian and Tennessee rivers, which run through both predominately blue and red states."

"You're talking about politics?" Charlotte asked, and Ella nodded. "I don't follow politics."

"I was thinking about it when they found the woman here. My dad is running for reelection, so I wondered if politics were the reason for the murders. If you look at the map, the blue or red line means a senator from that party is running for reelection this year. The color of the line indicates a democrat or republican."

"Seriously?"

"I mean, yeah, I know this stuff because of my dad."

"Are these all the senators running for reelection?"

"Oh, no, there are more. We'd have to make the map a little more detailed, but then I could tell you who was running in what state."

Charlotte grabbed the black marker and finished drawing the state lines until she had a complete map of the forty-eight states. She stepped aside and let Ella finish marking the map with senators running for reelection. When they finished, they stared at the map while Charlotte did some fast math in her head. "There are a lot of states that still haven't been touched."

"For sure," Ella agreed. "Every two years, a third of the Senate is up for reelection. This year there are thirty-three."

Charlotte tipped her head to the side. "But wait. Some of these murders occurred more than two years ago." She put an *X* next to the ones found when the murders started. There were six of those women.

Ella shrugged as though she'd grown bored with the whole thing. "I'm probably wrong, but at least you have the information on the map now." Her phone rang, and she looked at the caller ID before she hit the decline button. "That was my grandma. I'm going to go up to my room and call her back. She wants to FaceTime to prove I'm still alive." Her eye roll was heavy, as was her sigh.

Charlotte grabbed a walkie off the table. "Secure two, Charlotte."

"Secure one, Echo," Eric replied, which he wouldn't do if he were being forced, and then the key slid into the lock and the door opened.

"Ella is ready to return to her room," Charlotte said, patting her shoulder. "Thanks, Eric."

"No problem. The place is quiet. I'll take her up and stay with her. Mack is grabbing a bite, and then he'll be in."

Charlotte nodded and waved as Ella left. Her mind should be on the case, but instead, she was busy picturing the dark brown eyes of the man in the kitchen. The man who starred in her dreams, both day and night. It was becoming a problem, and she didn't know how to fix it.

WHEN MACK WALKED into the office, Charlotte was pacing and muttering to herself. He stood by the door and watched her for longer than he should, but he was taken by her strength and determination to be part of this team. She could do her job and go back to her room, but she didn't do that. She jumped in with both feet and worked the problem with them until it was resolved. Usually, her role was to bring them dinner in the boardroom or command center because they couldn't leave the monitors, but she always stayed. She stayed and offered suggestions from a different perspective they didn't have. That of a woman who had been attacked more times than Mack cared to think about and as a woman kept as property somewhere that looked completely normal. Charlotte always added to the conversation, which was why he wasn't surprised she was trying to work the problem now.

"Charlotte?" he asked from the doorway, and she jumped, spinning to stare at him with her hand on her chest.

"You scared me."

"Sorry," he said, pushing off the door and walking to her. He rubbed her arms gently and waited for her to settle again. "You were so lost in thought you didn't notice me come in. What has you so worked up?" Her gaze darted to the side, and that was when he noticed the map on the table.

His hands fell from her arms, and he walked over to the table to take in the map. "What's this?"

"It's nothing," she said quickly, attempting to roll it up. Mack held it down.

"It's obviously something. These are rivers in the United States. What are the other symbols?"

Charlotte brought him up to speed on the plotted areas and the colored markings. His mouth was hanging open by the time she finished. She must have noticed because she held up her hand to him as though he shouldn't speak.

"I can't make it work either. There was a two-year pause on the murders, but his original victims were before this election cycle."

That break from the murders would haunt them and keep them from solving this case. Mack was sure of it.

Two years.

"Senators run for reelection every two years," Mack said, thinking out loud.

"Yes," Charlotte agreed. "Ella said that every two years, a third of the Senate is up for reelection."

"Okay, so six women died three years ago, which would have been during the previous reelection cycle. You might be onto something here," Mack said in disbelief. "I need to call Mina." He sat and fired up their connection to Secure One. Once they were hooked up, he pulled the tablet from its moorings and walked around the table. He wanted to show Mina the extensive map Charlotte had drawn.

"Secure two, Whiskey." Mina's voice was heard over the tablet, but there was no video.

"Secure one, Mike," Mack answered, and Mina's face popped up on the screen.

"Miss me already?"

Mack noted the smile on Charlotte's face from the corner of his eye before speaking. "I always miss you, Mina, but this time I have a question."

"What do you mean, this time? You always have a question."

Charlotte snorted while trying to hold in her laughter, and Mack chuckled. "Fair point. This one is about our perp. First, I want you to check out this map."

Mack held the tablet out and scanned the extensive map while he filled her in on their theory that the killings may be politically driven.

"That's an interesting theory," Mina said, her head tipped. "What is your question?"

"You were around when the original women were found, correct?"

"Yes," she answered immediately. "Well, for some of them. Others were found while I was on the run, but since it made national news, I was aware of them."

"Then my question is do the early murders mirror our current ones?"

Mina blinked several times before she spoke. "Do you mean in their cause of death?"

"Cause of death and the way they're dressed. That kind of thing."

"Oh, no," she said immediately.

"The new murders differ from the original murders two years ago?" Charlotte asked with surprise.

"Well, the cause of death has been consistent. Always strangulation. From what I read in the FBI documents, the first six women had obvious strangulation marks on their necks. Those were the bodies found during The Madame's time in Red Rye."

"The new victims do not," Mack pointed out immediately.

"No, they don't, but they had broken hyoid bones, which only happens when someone is strangulated."

"What's a hyoid bone?" Charlotte asked.

Mack glanced at her and noted her deep concentration. She wanted to understand, so he nodded at Mina to answer.

"Your hyoid bone looks like a horseshoe, and it's under your chin here," Mina said, lifting her head to point at the spot at the top of her trachea. "Essentially, it connects the tongue and voice box and supports the airway. When it breaks—"

"The airway collapses, and you can't breathe," Charlotte finished.

Mina pointed at her. "Smart girl, and that's correct. Of course, if the bone is fractured in a different setting, the person often survives after seeking treatment. However, in strangulation cases, normally, the bone isn't just fractured but obliterated. Therefore, the victim dies from lack of airway."

Charlotte ran her hand under her chin near her neck. "Isn't strangulation usually lower though? Like here?" She motioned at her mid-trachea while Mina nodded.

"That is where the six original women had strangulation marks."

"What about the presentation of the victims?"

"Negative," Mina replied. "The first six women were dumped. Some were naked. Others were just in their underclothes."

"Are we dealing with two different perps?" Mack asked with frustration.

"Not necessarily. It's not uncommon for serial killers to perfect their game. At the FBI, we called it developing a method. They often start killing helter-skelter—"

"Coined by another serial killer," Mack said grimly.

"The difference is Charles Manson was a psychopath who never killed anyone. He convinced other people to do it for him. That's not the case with our perp."

"You're saying that maybe during the period he wasn't killing women, he was learning and improving his technique?"

"We can't say he didn't kill women during that time. We just didn't find any."

"Fair point," Mack agreed. "Assuming it's the same guy, he's figured out how to strangle without leaving marks and decides to present the women rather than just toss them?"

"Strangulation is generally a crime of passion. Where

the hyoid bone sits, the victim would have to be lying down for him to break it without leaving ligature marks."

"Like during sex."

"That's exactly right. Or, at the very least, he must be the one with leverage and power."

Mack briefly slid his eyes to Charlotte and then back to the tablet. "That was helpful, thanks. Should we proceed with the assumption that this is the same guy?"

"That or it's a copycat with better techniques."

"What is your gut telling you, Mina?" Mack asked her point-blank because he needed to know if he should pivot on this investigation.

"My gut says it's the same guy. He craves power. He may have a job where he has no power or he may have a job where he has all the power. That's not exactly helpful, unless you consider that he keeps these women for long periods and drives around the country to dump them in different rivers."

"That would lead a person to believe he has a job with power and money," Charlotte said from behind him.

Mina pointed at her from the camera. "Exactly. Our perp likely has a powerful job but one that doesn't fulfill him the way controlling a woman does. Having power over a woman he can force to bend to his every whim turns him on. Strangulation is always a crime of passion in this kind of setting. It's possible he has certain kinks that lend themselves to strangulation or he could kill them accidentally when he loses control. I suspect the first few times that was the case. He killed them by accident, so he dumped the bodies just to get rid of them. The next few times were intentional, but he still hadn't perfected his technique. What happened over the next two years,

I don't know, but I still believe it's the same person killing these women now. I'm not sold on it being politically driven though."

"It's just a working theory," Charlotte jumped in. "I thought it was a good train of thought to follow for now."

"Agreed—"

The walkie-talkie buzzed to life, and Charlotte grabbed it. "Secure One? This is the estate security guard at the gate. I need assistance."

Charlotte pushed the button so Mack could speak. "Assistance? Is there a threat?"

"I don't think she's a threat, but she's demanding to talk to someone from Secure One. The person who killed The Miss is what she said."

"The Miss?" Charlotte asked, her gaze traveling to Mina's, who sat frozen on the screen while she listened to the exchange.

She released the button, and another voice filled the room. "Charlotte! Oh, my God, Charlotte, is that you?"

Within one second, Mack noticed Mina's and Charlotte's eyes widen when they heard the voice. Charlotte did nothing but hold the walkie with her mouth hanging open, so Mack grabbed it and depressed the button. "We'll be right down."

"I know that voice, so I'll inform the team that the game just changed," Mina said, her voice tight. "Call me back as soon as you have a handle on this."

"Ten-four. Mike, out."

Chapter Nine

"Charlotte." Mack was in front of her, taking hold of her shaking hands. "Charlotte, you need to breathe. Breathe in and then out," he said, demonstrating until she did the same thing. His warm hand grasped her chin. "You look like you've seen a ghost."

"I heard one," she whispered, shaking her head to clear it. "I think that was Bethany."

"Bethany?"

Her exaggerated nod continued until he gently grasped her chin to stop it. "She was one of the women who disappeared when she challenged The Miss."

The light came on in his eyes, and he took a small breath. "Bethany and Emelia."

"It's been almost two years. I thought for sure they were dead."

He grabbed her hand and started pulling her behind him. "Let's head to the gate and check this out. I need to let Eric know to stay put."

He brought the walkie to his lips to contact Eric, but Charlotte's mind was on the woman at the gate. If she had been alive all this time, where had she been? Why didn't she come back when she learned The Miss was dead? Was she alone, or was Emelia with her? Lost in thought, she didn't notice Mack stop until she ran up against him, her body plastered against the length of his back. He was hot in every way a man could be, and her skin tingled from the contact she worked so hard to avoid.

She was still daydreaming about how warm he was when he held her out by the shoulder. "Charlotte, where's your head?"

"My head?"

"We can't go out there if your head is not in the game. This could be a trick. They could be trying to lure us out to leave Eric vulnerable or take us out. I want you to stay behind me at all times."

"But Bethany," she whispered, her voice breaking on the name.

"If Bethany is out there and alone, we'll make a new plan. We have to proceed with caution until we know otherwise. Okay?"

After taking a breath in and letting it out, Charlotte nodded. "I'm good. It threw me to hear her voice again, but you're right, it could be a trick." She patted the gun at the small of her back. The one they insisted she carry after the last kidnapping attempt on Ella. "I still have my gun from when I was alone with Ella earlier."

"Good, be ready to use it. Just make sure none of us are in the line of fire."

They had a short walk to the front door, but the walk to the front gate was a couple of hundred feet. The cabin was gated, but that didn't mean someone couldn't approach by water and sneak onto the property from the river with no one the wiser. They both pulled their guns, and started their walk, their heads on a swivel. They made it to the gate without difficulty. The night guardsman stood inside the booth while a blond woman sat on a stool across from him.

"Oh, my God, it's her," she whispered to Mack. They waited until the guard opened the gate for them to approach the booth. "Bethany?"

The woman glanced up, and instantly, her face crumpled. "Charlotte! It is you. I heard your voice, but I couldn't believe it." She never said another word, just cried silent tears, her body spasming from the emotion.

"Is she alone?" Mack asked Lucas, the guard.

"As far as I can tell."

"Is this a trick, Bethany?" Charlotte asked the woman. She had lost weight and was paler than anyone she'd ever seen before.

"No, not a trick," the woman answered. "I need help. I heard on the news that another woman was found by the people who killed The Miss. I didn't know where else to go. I'm—I'm in danger." Her last sentence was whispered with so much fear that Charlotte's gut clenched from reflex. She knew that kind of fear.

Charlotte glanced at Mack and waited for him to make a decision. He lifted a brow and then tipped his head before he spoke. "We'll take her from here, Lucas," he told the guard. "Be on high alert just in case this is an attack we don't see coming."

"It's not," Bethany said in a choked whisper. "I've been on a bus and came straight here. I haven't spoken to anyone and no one knows who I am. I swear."

Mack made a hand signal that Charlotte recognized as the two and one formation. She was to walk with Bethany into the house while he brought up the rear. It was her job to police their approach. Her hand was shaking when she switched her gun to her right hand and motioned Bethany out of the security hut. The woman ran to her and threw her arms around Charlotte, nearly knocking them both to the ground if it hadn't been for Mack grabbing her belt loop at the back of her pants. His warmth there helped ground her as the woman in her arms sobbed incoherently.

"We have to move," Mack said in her ear, sending a shiver down her spine both from desire and fear.

After a nod, she convinced Bethany to walk to the house, but she couldn't help but think Mina was correct and the game had changed. Her biggest fear was that The Miss hadn't stayed buried after all.

WHEN MACK WALKED back into the office, Charlotte was hunched over her pad, the swish of her charcoal pencil the only sound in the room. He wasn't sure if she was breathing as she concentrated on the pad.

"Is Bethany settled?"

The jolt of her body told him she hadn't known he was there. Her pencil fell to the desk, and she quickly closed the sketch pad and rested her elbow on it.

"Sorry, I didn't hear you come in. She's resting in the room next to Ella. I helped her shower, and she had something to eat. Now we wait."

"Do you think she needs more medical care than Selina can provide?"

Cal, Selina, Roman and Mina were in the chopper, and they'd arrive within the hour. Charlotte was glad because they needed more help than they had, but understandably, Cal didn't want to involve the police just yet.

"She's thin, but overall, physically healthy. I think she will need a lot of mental health care after what happened.

I don't even know where she's been the last two years, but it was nowhere good."

"I agree, which is why I'm glad Cal is coming in. We need to ask the right questions, and Mina is excellent at that. Once Bethany can give us some answers, we'll let Selina decide what kind of care she needs and where."

"I want to know where Emelia is, Mack. Those two were inseparable."

"She may not know, so don't get too hung up on the need for one answer, Char. This could be as simple as she was hiding from The Miss and didn't know she was dead until now."

Charlotte raised her brow at him slowly. "If she had been hiding out, she would have heard The Miss was dead, Mack. I suspect wherever she was living, it wasn't by choice. My guess would be she's been a captive woman the last two years."

Mack's jaw set and pulsed once as an answer. "The tentacles of those two women always seem to work themselves back into our lives. One's in prison, and one's dead, but we still aren't free of them."

"And never will be, Mack," she whispered, staring at her feet. "Ever."

He pulled her into his arms just as a shudder went through her. He cursed himself for not thinking before he spoke. "I'm sorry, that was insensitive," he whispered. "I'm frustrated, but I often forget those women ruined your life, not mine."

"Not true," she countered, stepping out of his arms. "You carry the burden of killing The Miss."

"I carry no burden about her death, Char. Sometimes

the right choice is to take a life if it prevents them from hurting others. I learned that first hand in the army."

He walked toward her. Her blue globes filled with fear, and he paused, holding his next step. Was she afraid of him? "You don't need to be afraid of me, Charlotte."

"I—I'm not," she stuttered before she pushed the pad behind her from where she rested on the edge of the desk.

"I see the look in your eyes when I move toward you too quickly. I try to give you your space because I know that feeling inside your chest when terror grips your heart," he whispered, holding his hand near his chest. "It's all you can do to stop yourself from running."

"I'm not afraid of you, Mack. I just know it's smart to keep you at arm's length. I don't trust easily, but I trust you. That scares me more than anything."

Mack cocked his head. "Because trusting me means I could hurt you?" Her head barely tipped in acknowledgment. "I wouldn't do that, Charlotte. I've been where you're at." He held up his hand to stem her words. "I mean that I've been traumatized, hurt and let down by the people who were supposed to look out for me. The feeling of betrayal is so powerful you can taste it. That's when you realize the only person you can trust is yourself. Am I close?"

"Spot on," she agreed in a whispered tone. "Looking back, I can see that has been true since day one. It took me too long to see it, and the one time I tried to take care of myself, I ended up a pawn in someone else's game. I don't want to be that again."

"You aren't." Mack took another step until he was right in front of her, staring down into her tired blue eyes. He expected her to cower at an entire foot taller than her, but she didn't. She held her ground and lifted her chin. "At Secure One, you're an equal team member."

"I'm the cook. I don't think that's equal to anyone, Mack. That's the hired help."

He laid his finger against her lips. "Wrong. That's not how Cal runs Secure One, and you know it. Everyone contributes to the success of the business. As the cook, you're one of the most important people on the team. We're a group of big guys with healthy appetites, but we can't tell a saucepan from a broiler. You fuel us, which is one less thing we have to worry about when we're busy. It may feel like you're in the background, but you're not. Never doubt that."

Her nod was quick as his gaze traveled to the pad behind her. "You've also contributed to the team with your art. Cal took your suggestions to the client and secured the job as their security company because of your work. He'll square up with you for your contributions. Talent is talent, Charlotte, regardless of our pasts, abilities or disabilities. We aren't one-dimensional."

"I know," she said, sliding her hand up his chest to rest there.

It was as though she knew the secrets that he held but couldn't say.

He allowed himself the pleasure of grasping her tiny hand in his for a moment before he pulled her into a hug when her eyes said yes. With one arm, he held her, and with the other, he flipped the lid open on her sketch pad. When she hid what she was working on, he knew it was important to her. He took in the image on the pad and froze. The next breath wouldn't come as he stared at himself dressed in army fatigues. He was looking over his shoulder with sheer terror on his face. His gaze traveled down the pad to see his pants in tattered, jagged edges at the knees. He wore no boots or socks but had open wounds and blood pooling around his feet that congealed into a broken heart. It was the blood falling from the wounds on the left that broke him.

Has been. Useless. Inadequate. Failure.

The right leg told a different story.

Hope. Victory. Skill. Knowledge. New life.

When his lungs finally released a breath, it sounded like a grunt of pain. He stumbled backward until he hit the wall. "How did you know?"

Charlotte glanced at him in confusion and then at the pad. Her grimace was noticeable when she turned back to him. "I didn't want you to see that."

"Then why did you draw it?"

"I draw what I see, Mack. I'm an artist. It's how I express emotion."

"I don't understand how you knew about my legs."

"I see more than you think," she answered. "I noticed when you were changing your boots and socks that night in the mobile command unit, but I also saw the metal bars across your boots and how your gait is slightly different than the other guys. I asked Roman about it, and all he would say was you were injured in a mission gone wrong. He said the injury was the reason why you left the army."

A mission gone wrong. More like a mission that blew up in his face. Literally.

Chapter Ten

Mack rubbed his hands over his face while he paced the room. She was silent, but he worried it was in judgment rather than patience. "I don't talk about this with anyone, Charlotte."

"I'm not asking you to, Mack. My drawings are for me. They help me process the emotions that are too big to hold inside. I don't know how you were hurt or why. Chances are, what I drew is all wrong, but that's what I see."

The nod of his head was barely there, and she fell silent, staring at her hands rather than meeting his gaze. "We were moving a diplomat and his family to a safe house."

"You don't have to tell me, Mack," she said, halting his words. "That's not why I drew it."

He lifted his chin to hold her gaze. Her blue eyes didn't hold pity as he'd expected. They were open and clear, their depths holding some of the same pain and experiences in his. They'd both fought battles that hadn't ended up in the win column.

"Maybe I don't have to tell you," he said, not breaking eye contact, "but that drawing…" He shook his head and dropped his gaze to the floor. "It brought everything back. Without knowing it, you captured my emotions, from my expression to the words that bled from my soul. Maybe I have to tell someone, so I can finally be free of the shame."

"You have nothing to be ashamed of, Mack."

"You don't know that," he whispered. "The truth is I ran the wrong way. I protected the wrong team."

"I don't believe that." Her refusal was punctuated with her arms crossing over her chest in defiance.

"My job was to protect the diplomat, and I failed to do that, Charlotte. The caravan made it to the safe house without attracting any attention from the insurgents. I was driving the diplomat and his family while my team sandwiched us. The front half of the team was securing the area for me. I told the diplomat, his family and the traveling security team to wait while I reconned with Cal. I climbed from the car and walked toward him when I heard the back door of the car squeak open. That was the last sound I heard before an explosion rocked the air. I glanced behind me to see the fireball from the diplomat's car. I didn't run back, Charlotte. I ran toward Cal and the team like a coward!"

"Mack, no," she said, her tone soft and nonjudgmental. "What made you run for the team?"

He tossed his hand up, the smell of fire and fuel stuck in his head as he relived those moments. "The car was nothing more than a burning shell instantly, but we're trained to render aid, and I didn't."

"If nothing was left but a burning shell, is it safe to say that you knew with just one look that everyone in that car was already gone?"

"Without a doubt." The breath he let out was heavy and filled with disappointment. Disappointment in himself.

"I still should have gone back. Instead, I ran toward my team, worried they'd been hit by flying debris."

"When the truth was, you had been."

His nod was immediate and short. "I was screaming for them to get down and find cover, but they ran toward me. Cal and Roman caught me as I fell, dragged me into a vehicle and took off. I don't remember anything else until I woke up in the hospital."

"And what did you learn when you woke up?"

He stood and paced to the window, pulling the curtain back a hair to stare into the darkness. "They think the bomb was set to detonate when the back door opened. I'm sure whoever rigged it never thought we'd get past loading them into the vehicle. It was just chance that we loaded the family through the opposite door."

"No one had inspected the car for a bomb?"

"They did. That doesn't mean anything in the game of warfare though. For all we know, someone on the security team could have planted it after the inspection. It was a typical device to blow up the gas tank and cause an inferno. The bomb wasn't complicated and didn't require much explosive to get the job done."

"What else did you learn at the hospital, Mack?" she asked as she swiveled her body to face him again.

The curtain fell to obscure the moon, and he leaned against the wall. "I learned that I wasn't the only one hurt. Cal and Eric were also in the hospital. Both of my lower legs were damaged by shrapnel. The nerves in my legs that control my feet were severed or damaged. It took too long to get me into surgery and the ischemia set in. They tried transferring the nerve, but it was too scarred down and didn't take. My time in the army was over."

"I still can't figure out what part of that makes you a coward, Mack. You did your job and paid a high price for something someone else did."

"I didn't go back for them, Charlotte. Right or wrong, I should have gone back."

"You should have gone back to a burning car to do what? Watch the fire? Get burned? What could you do when one glance told you they were dead?"

"They weren't just dead. The fire was so hot they had evaporated. I knew it. I'd seen it before. I still should have gone back."

"Here's the thing, Mack," she whispered, planting her hands on her hips. "Could have. Should have. Would have. Those are dangerous statements. They're all past tense. There's no rewind and replay in life. There's only did and did not."

"I did not do my job. There's your truth."

"Wrong. You did not die. That's the real truth here, Mack. Those people did, and you did not. This isn't about the decisions you made after the explosion. As humans, when we're faced with situations like those, trained or untrained, we can't predict what we will do. In a split second, you knew those people were gone, but your team was in danger. You didn't even know you were hurt in those first few seconds, did you?" He shook his head but kept his lips pursed, so he didn't argue with her about how wrong she was. "Adrenaline and fear are highly motivating to the human mind, Mack. Toss in the shock of a sudden injury, and the rule book goes out the window. Let me ask you a question?" He nodded, and she stood, walking over to him and standing directly in front of him. "What did the rest of your team do?"

"I told you. My team grabbed me and dragged me out of there. Eric picked us up in his truck and raced us to a waiting chopper."

"Did any of them run toward the burning car, Mack?"

He paused, holding her gaze as his mind returned to the heat and the noise that day. "Cal and Roman were in the front vehicle alone. They were out of their truck and securing the area. Eric and a second team were in a vehicle behind us when the explosion happened. I remember Eric drove around the car and picked us all up."

"Then, from what I'm hearing, you had a full team in two different vehicles, but none of them approached the car either?"

"Not that I remember. In the report, Eric said the fire was so hot they could feel the heat inside their truck as they passed it."

"Did the report say if Eric stopped to check on the occupants?"

"He didn't. He followed Cal's directive to abandon the mission."

"So why, in light of all that, do you feel like a coward? Were you the mission leader?" He shook his head, his jaw pulsing with anger and fear. The terror from that day filled him again, and he clenched his hands into fists to stop them from trembling. "Have you ever considered that no matter what choices you made that day, you couldn't have saved those people? Have you ever considered that it was beyond your pay grade and your control? Has anyone told you that it wasn't your fault? I'm telling you now. It wasn't your fault, Mack. You did your job, and the scars you carry are proof of that. You can't control the way that day changed your body or your mind. I understand that more than anyone, but the guilt is too heavy when it's not yours to carry."

Mack sucked air in through his nostrils and stared her down. "I guess I could say the same to you, Charlotte, but I suspect you'd tell me our situations were different, and you can't compare them. You'd be right. No one died because you didn't do your job. People died because I didn't do mine."

Before she could say anything, he pushed past her and walked out the door. He'd do well to remember that before Charlotte joined Secure One, his singular focus had been to help people in bad situations or protect them from bad people. He'd lost sight of that momentarily when Charlotte came into his life, but it was time he focused on that again. Doing anything else made him think he had a chance at a different life. He knew the truth. Being alone was his path in life. He had to make her understand that before she too became a casualty of his war.

MACK STARED OUT the cabin's window at the tumultuous water of the Mississippi, hoping it would help him sort out the noise in his head. What did Charlotte know about war? Nothing. She knew nothing. At least nothing about the kind of war he fought, right?

Mack walked over to Eric, who had been watching him pace. "Hey," he said, but Eric held his fingers in front of him, wagged them for a second, then punched around on his phone.

That was the sign for *hang on*, which Eric used when his hearing aids weren't connected properly. His hearing had been damaged in the same botched transport that injured Mack's legs. Without his hearing aids, he was legally deaf. Thankfully, he had the best of the best in aids to help him hear.

"Sorry, I had to disconnect the phone's Bluetooth from my hearing aids. What's up?"

"Checking in. Who were you talking to?"

"Cal," he said, holding up the phone before he pocketed it. "They're landing soon."

"Good, with any luck, we can try to make sense of this newest development. How is she?" Mack motioned at the door where Bethany slept.

"Charlotte stayed with her until she fell asleep. I'm supposed to tell her if Bethany wakes up, but she's out."

Mack grunted, frustration evident in the sound. Something had to break soon, or another woman was going to die. Frustration was all he felt tonight, both with the case and Charlotte.

"What crawled up your pants leg?" Eric asked, turning to him.

"Nothing. I'm frustrated with how nothing makes sense in this case."

"No, you're frustrated with how long it's taking to move on it."

"I'd like to figure it out before another woman dies, Eric."

"So would I, but in the end, we have one hand tied trying to work around the authorities. It will take more time when we don't have access to all the evidence."

Swiping his hand through his hair, Mack buried his fingers and left them there, his elbow swinging in the air. "I know, but I don't have to like it."

"Can't say that I do either."

"What do you remember about that day that ended our

service career?" Mack asked out of the blue, his trained eye noticing Eric's shoulders stiffen.

"You're asking what haunts me about it, right?" Eric asked, and Mack gave half a nod. "I vividly remember the back door cracking open and a little leg coming out right before the car exploded."

Mack glanced at him sharply. "You could see who opened the door?"

"I don't know if the boy opened it, but he would be the first one out. He probably was the one to open it. He was enamored with you, remember? He may not have understood the stay-in-the-car order."

"I never knew that," Mack said with a shudder. "I don't think it makes me feel better about it either."

"I didn't think it would, which is why I never told you. I also remember seeing you walk toward Cal, and then you just disappeared. I thought you dropped when the car exploded."

"I did, just not by choice."

"It wasn't until I got the truck around the burning car that I realized you were hurt."

"So were you."

"I didn't know that at the time. Getting you to a helo was our priority."

Mack shook his head with frustration. "Cal, me, you, all injured for nothing. I failed to do my job, and people were maimed and killed. Such a waste."

"You didn't fail to do your job."

Mack's snort was loud and sarcastic. "You and Charlotte."

"Charlotte doesn't know the first thing about war."

"Civilized warfare is still warfare, and the streets aren't

always civilized, Eric." Mack's tone was defensive, and Eric noticed.

"You're saying she knows a lot about war, just not your war."

With a finger pointed at his friend, Mack nodded. "When she was on the streets, she was an army of one. She was the only one who needed to walk away alive and unhurt. I had an entire team I let down when that mission went sideways."

"I never could figure out why you took that blame when there was never any blame to be had. You followed protocol by exiting the vehicle and taking your position before security inside the car led the family from the vehicle. We'd done it a dozen times the same way. It was unfortunate circumstances that weren't your fault. You didn't put that bomb in the car."

His chest was heavy when he let out a breath. Unfortunate circumstances that weren't his fault. Maybe that was true. Even if he couldn't control them, he still carried the scars from them.

"Listen, Mack, none of us escaped that mission without guilt. I think about that little foot sticking out every night when I go to bed. I have to remind myself that they were never getting out alive regardless of what we did. More of us would be dead if you opened that door at the airport rather than the other side. Stop feeling guilty. Nothing you did would have saved that family, but you did save many other people from dying. I know it will never fade away, just like all the other carnage we saw and participated in, but it's been too many years for you to let it control your life. I know that's easier said than done, but it's time to try."

"I've tried for years, Eric. I'm exhausted from trying."

Eric turned and crossed his arms over his chest, facing Mack with determination in his stance. "No, you haven't. You find it easier to deal with your disability by pretending it's your fault, but it's not. It's time you try to find some happiness in life, Mack. You don't even have to look for it. Happiness is waiting downstairs, but you're too dense to see it. It might be easier to let your past fade if you had someone to share your future with."

"Charlotte?" Eric's head tipped to the left slightly. "It's not like that, man. I'm part of her life to teach her how to trust again. That's it. That's all it can be."

"What a shame," Eric said, dropping his arms to his sides. "She smooths out your rough edges. I'll go prepare the rest of the security team for Cal's arrival. You're on bodyguard duty until I get back."

The treads of his boots made a hiss on the wood floor as he walked away, leaving Mack to stare at the wall. Eric's words echoed in his ears.

She smooths out your rough edges.

She absolutely did, but he'd never ask a woman like Charlotte to tie herself to a guy like him. His demons took up too much space and left no room for love.

Chapter Eleven

"Charlotte?"

Surprised by the intrusion, she spun around to see Mina standing in the doorway. She wore her Secure One uniform with a gun on her hip and her running blade prosthesis strapped inside a tennis shoe. Mina had several prostheses, but when working a job, she always wore the one that made her the fastest.

"Mina!" Before she could say another word, she was wrapped in a warm hug from her friend. "I'm so glad you're here."

"I was the first one on the helicopter. I heard Bethany's voice, and it sent a shiver down my spine. How is she?"

"She's sleeping after she had something to eat. Eric and Mack are taking turns on guard duty. Bethany is beyond exhausted. She'll need a lot of help if she's going to have a life after what she's been through."

"There are resources out there for women like her. We'll get the information we need from her and then, depending on what she tells us, protect her or find her someplace with the services she needs. Until I hear her story, I won't know which one comes first."

Charlotte nodded after ending the hug. "The only thing she told me before she fell asleep was that she escaped someone who had been holding her hostage. She ran, stole a truck and rode a bus to get here."

"But how did she know about here?" Cal asked, walking through the open door with Roman.

"Hey, guys," Charlotte said, her gaze flicking to Mina for a moment, who nodded for her to answer. "She escaped the night we found Layla on the shore. She had the radio on and heard them talking about Secure One finding the body. They also mentioned we'd been involved in the death of The Miss. Since she had no other choice, she made her way here by bus and on foot, hoping she could find us."

"She sounds like a real spitfire," Cal said, bouncing up on his toes. "I know a couple of other women like her too. I can't wait to meet her."

"She's precarious, Cal," Charlotte warned him.

"Meaning?"

"Meaning she's been through hell, and we need to ask questions that don't push her over the razor-thin edge she's on."

"We understand that," Roman said. "Selina and Marlise are upstairs with her right now. Selina is going to check her over in case she needs a hospital. Marlise is there as a familiar face."

"I could have gone up. You didn't need to drag Marlise here," Charlotte said defensively.

Cal held out his hand to hush her. "I need you here to walk me through what we have before they bring Bethany down. You're in the thick of this case, and I need your insight."

Mack strode into the room then and didn't stop until he stood behind her. His hands went to her shoulders as though he noticed her tension. "Everything okay?"

"Fine," Cal assured him. "We were just talking about Bethany and the case. Charlotte is upset, which is completely understandable. This case gets more and more disturbing every day."

Mack rubbed her shoulders up and down as he spoke. "Agreed, and we don't even know if Bethany's situation is tied to The Red River Slayer."

"That's why we're here," Mina said, setting her bag up on the desk. "We can work remotely, and we will, but first, I wanted to talk to everyone in person. That way, I can start a more focused dive into our evidence when I get back to Secure One."

"You mean so you can hack the right agency to get more information," Mack said, tongue in cheek.

"You say potato," Mina answered with a grin.

She unloaded her pack and set up her computer while Cal and Roman taped Charlotte's map to the office wall.

Mack leaned into her ear and whispered, "We'll talk later about earlier."

His breath blew across her skin and raised goose bumps along her neck that she couldn't hide or deny. Why did his simple words and actions raise such a response in her? She was trying hard not to like him, but he wasn't making it easy. What he was doing was making it easy to fall into his arms and let him protect her. She couldn't let that happen though. If she was going to take back her life and find success, it would be because she worked hard. If she let someone else save her every time, that didn't teach her how to take care of herself.

What if he doesn't want to save you as much as he wants to love you?

Absolutely not. Charlotte shut that voice down without

hesitation. There was no way she was falling for Mack. Her gaze flicked to Cal at the board, and she wondered how he made it work with Marlise. They lived and worked together all day, every day, but their relationship felt seamless. Her wayward gaze drifted to Mack, who had stepped back to the door to guard it as everyone prepared for the meeting. He was a giant. As much in kindness, empathy and understanding as he was in size. An unfamiliar heat flickered through her. She suspected it was the flame she would carry for this man forever. She'd never been with a man who didn't want something from her. Every man she'd encountered had an ulterior motive behind taking care of her, being with her, dating her or taking advantage of her. There had never been anyone in her life like Mack.

Safe.

Part of her believed that word, but the rest knew he wasn't safe. At least to her heart. He made it feel things it shouldn't, and that made him dangerous. Her therapist told her it was okay to want that kind of life, but she wasn't sure she deserved it. She had done things— illegal things—that harmed others. The drugs she ferried for The Madame probably killed people. She was the kind of person Mack actively worked to put behind bars. Maybe she hadn't done those things willingly, but she'd still done them.

"This is a mess," Cal said where he stood by the map. "The case, I mean. It's not even our case, but we're still in the middle of it."

Eric walked in at that moment and stood at the back by Mack. Charlotte could see that he was tired, they all were, but until this case was solved, no one was getting much sleep.

"All we can do is work the evidence, Cal," Mina said from behind her computer. "That's the only way out of this mess."

"We keep saying that, but it never happens," Roman pointed out, leaning on the desk next to his wife. "It feels like that game *Whac-A-Mole*. We knock one bad girl down, and another one pops up."

"Or, in this case, a bad boy," Mack said from the doorway while motioning at the map on the wall.

"Could still be a bad girl," Roman said with a shrug.

"You think this is tied to Red Rye?" Eric asked. Charlotte could hear the skepticism in his voice, but she had none in her mind.

"I don't know if it's tied directly to Red Rye, but it could be tied to the business The Madame had going at the time."

"The first bodies were found while you were all at Red Rye." Cal pointed at the six rivers where the original women were found. "That's a little suspect if you ask me."

"Especially when you consider what SAC Moore told me the night he kidnapped me," Mina said, glancing at Roman.

"What did he tell you?" Cal asked.

"That Liam Albrecht had some serious kinks, and The Miss had to do cleanup on more than one occasion."

Cal took a step toward the desk. "You could have mentioned that sooner."

Mina shrugged. "It just crossed my mind again when you said the first bodies were all from Red Rye. Maybe The Miss cleaned those women up by passing them off to someone else to do the deed rather than do it herself. We know it wasn't Liam killing the women because he's dead, and we're still finding them."

"But, of the recent women found, only one didn't have an identity, and that was the last one," Mack said, walking to the front of the room.

"Layla," Charlotte said through gritted teeth. "Her name was Layla, and she was just a scared young woman who didn't deserve to die that way."

Mina held up her hand. "The FBI knows her identity. They just haven't released her name yet."

Mack kept his hand on the small of her back to calm her. "Okay, so now we know all the women from this killing spree were identified."

"Which makes sense," Cal said. "There aren't many washed women left from The Madame's empire."

"No, but he's still taking throwaway women," Mina said from behind her computer. "Our perp chooses victims from the street because homeless people always move around. Even if she had friends on the street, they wouldn't think anything of her going missing."

"And even if they did, the police aren't going to spend time looking for her," Charlotte added. Her voice was thin, tired and exhausted from life, which made her appreciate Mack's strong but caring touch on her back even more. "We know he's not impulsive. He's taking the time to pick the right women and not just grabbing random ones."

"He might even get off on the hunt," Eric said as he walked to the front of the room to sit. "He probably watched each victim for days. Learned their routine. Decided if anyone would notice that her things were there, but she wasn't. He may even watch her long enough to know what things are important to her and makes sure he grabs her when she has those items. That makes it look to her friends like she just took off."

"Or he just grabs the first street woman he sees. We have twelve bodies, but that doesn't mean that all the victims have been found," Cal reminded everyone. "There could be more victims who never floated to shore."

"All true," Mina agreed, typing away on her computer. "I've had my ear to the ground for bodies of drowning victims found anywhere during the two years between Red Rye and now."

"Nothing, right?" Eric asked, but Mina stuck her head around the computer and shook it.

"Actually, no. Two more women were found, but they didn't fare well in the water. A gator probably attacked one, and one was caught in a dam for some time. No ability to run facial recognition and no recognizable marks to tell a family if it was their missing child. The police couldn't say it was The Red River Slayer, so they didn't."

"They weren't strangled?" Mack asked from next to her. A shiver ran through Charlotte, and he rubbed it away with his hand on her back.

"No way to know. Their heads were either gone or damaged in a way that could have caused the trauma. DNA identification will take a significant amount of time."

"Do you know what rivers?" Cal asked, walking to the giant map Charlotte had drawn.

Mina held up a finger and typed more on the computer before answering. "The Savannah River, which explains the gator attack, and the Colorado River."

"We have a victim in the Colorado already," Cal said, putting his finger on the *X* Charlotte had made on the map.

"We do," Charlotte agreed, moving to the front of the room. She took the marker from Cal, "but that doesn't mean anything. The Colorado runs through like, what?"

She paused and counted on the map. "Seven states. The first victim in that river was found in the state of Colorado. Mina, what state was this woman found in?"

"Arizona," she answered. "They think she was caught in the Glen Canyon Dam."

"That's not too far from where we found The Miss," Mack pointed out.

"And we're back to whether this is tied to The Madame," Cal said with frustration.

"I can say it's always in the back of my mind," Mack said. "It's possible someone was killing The Madame's women, and that was why bodies were being found during that time. Then The Madame was on trial, and rather than draw unwanted attention to himself, he stuck a pin in the business until things quieted down."

"The only tie we have is that some of the women killed worked for her. That could be a coincidence."

"Could be," Cal agreed, "but it's not. The Red River Slayer could have started as a client or a fan of what The Madame was doing, but he quickly became a psychopathic serial killer. Regardless of whether he or she was mixed up with the Red Rye fiasco, we need to move that to the back burner while we try to find him."

"Agreed," Eric said from his seat, "but we don't know how to find him."

"Or why someone tried to kidnap Ella the other night," Charlotte added.

"The more I think about it, the more I don't think it's connected," Mack said. "I think the kidnapping had more to do with who her father is, and the attempted kidnapper thought the chaos of that night was a good way to grab the girl without notice."

"And do what with her?" Charlotte asked. "Hold her hostage?"

"Ransom," Mina said from the computer. "Dorian would pay anything to get his daughter back."

"Which brings us back to whether the river slayings are politically driven. I'll need to plot the other bodies in what state and town they were found. Based on Ella's theory that killings have to do with senators seeking re-election, we have to ask ourselves two questions. First, did the killer take a break during those two years because the elections were over? Second, did he take a break for a different reason?"

"Or if he was practicing his technique and we just haven't found the bodies. He may have been preparing for when this election cycle came around." Mina stood and motioned at the map. "A sixteen-year-old girl came up with it as soon as it was laid out on paper. We should have."

"We're not in the business of politics or solving murders, Mina. Ella is immersed in politics, so to her, it was obvious. *If* that's the motivating factor," Cal reminded her.

"When will the police release Layla's sketch to the public?" Charlotte asked. "It's been radio silence for days."

"They're not going to," Cal answered. "They know who she is already, and their theory is every time they release information about the river slayings, they're giving the killer airtime, which is what he wants."

"But she deserves justice!" Charlotte exclaimed in anger.

Mina peeked around the computer again. "Layla didn't have a family, right?" Charlotte shook her head. "The police aren't hurting anything by keeping this under their hat then. From the perspective of a law enforcement agent, I understand what they're doing. As a woman, it angers me that they're stealing her justice."

"My fear is, not giving the guy airtime will result in another woman dying," Cal said with a sigh.

"We can't let that happen," Eric said, standing and grabbing a marker. "List off the senators up for reelection. I'm going to write them in their corresponding state."

Charlotte hadn't turned away from Mack. She was lost in the way his gaze calmed her pounding heart. She wanted to run from the room and the nightmare of this investigation, but he wouldn't let her. He would help her face her past to move on to a better future. That was all she wanted, but it couldn't be with him. Not to be cliché, but he deserved better, and she knew it. Her entire life went against his code of ethics. She was what he was trying to stop by fighting for this country.

"Ron Dorian, Minnesota. Pete Fuller, South Carolina. Greg Weiss, Maine," Roman was reading off the computer when Mina stood up with a gasp.

"Greg Weiss?" She lowered herself to the chair again and looked at the other computer that Roman was on.

"Do you know him?" Mack asked.

She stood but shook her head with confusion. "He was friends with the two guys The Madame killed in the warehouse the night she kidnapped me. I found his name several times tied to Red Rye. I assumed he knew Liam Albrecht, the city manager for Red Rye, because they were all involved in politics."

"Was there evidence that he was involved with any women in the Red Rye house?"

"None," Mina said. "He knew Albrecht, but that doesn't mean anything in the world of politics. It's all a game. He could have been working them for money for his campaign, or they were friends through an organization. I was never able to sort out their exact relationship."

"Another point in the Red Rye column," Mack said. "Is that all of them, Roman?"

"Yes, for the current cycle. A third of the senate is re-elected every two years—this year, there are thirty-three. If we remove the eight women found, including the two who they aren't sure about, from the last election cycle, only six of the thirty-three states have a dead body." Eric put a check next to the senators from each state that already had a victim. "I'm afraid many more women will be killed if this is politically motivated."

Selina walked in the door at that moment, and everyone turned to her. "Sorry to interrupt, but I can't put Bethany through anything more tonight with good conscience. Her body and mind aren't even working together anymore since she's so exhausted. I can barely rouse her long enough to do her vitals."

Everyone looked at each other and waited for Cal to speak. When he did, it was no surprise what he said. "Then we give her until morning. It's already midnight, so a few more hours won't break the bank. We're rested and will take over security duty so Eric, Mack and Charlotte can get some rest. Selina, you and Marlise stay with Bethany. Roman, you and I will pull guard duty. Mina, can you keep working on this?"

He got a thumbs-up from behind her computer, but she barely broke stride in her typing long enough to give it.

"We'll reconvene here at seven a.m. unless something arises beforehand. We will have to talk to Bethany at that point," Cal said to Selina. "When most of the team is here, the rest of the team at Secure One is in a bind."

"Understood," Selina said. "I think a good stretch of sleep will be enough to help her mind put everything in order. This poor woman was held hostage for nearly two years. Everyone needs to understand that she may or may not have answers, but once we're done talking to her, I have to check her into a facility that can take care of her mental and emotional wounds besides her physical ones."

"That is heard and understood," Cal said. "She came to us, which means she wanted to tell us something. That's the only reason I'm staying here other than to give the team a break. Honestly, I need more help than I have right now. We're stretched too thin."

"I know a guy," Mina said, popping up.

"You know a guy?" Mack asked with a chuckle. "Is he trustworthy?"

"He's an amp friend. He did a tour for the army in the sandbox and lost his left leg but earned a purple heart and a medal of honor for saving two guys even as he was bleeding out. Rehabbed and returned for a tour in the mountains, this time as private security since the government said no to a second tour."

"Private security meaning mercenary," Mack muttered.

"Call him whatever you want. He won't care. He's stateside now and working private security as a bodyguard."

"A bodyguard who's an amp?" Eric asked with a raised brow.

"He can do more on one leg than you can do with both of your own. He can overtake you in seconds when he puts on his running blade. He runs marathons for fun on the weekend. I wouldn't hesitate to let him protect me."

"Does he have a name?" Cal asked, his tone holding interest.

"Efren."

"Sounds like he'd fit in well here. Give him a call. See if he's available. Run our standard background on him. I know you know him, but he has to align with our clearances for our clients."

"On it," she said, sitting again.

"The rest of you find an empty room and get some sleep. It might be your only chance for a few more days."

Charlotte feared he was right, so she headed to the room where she'd left her bag. She was going to grab a shower and some shut-eye. She made sure not to make eye contact with Mack when she left the room. He may want to talk about what happened earlier, but she did not. She planned to be asleep before he ever found her.

Chapter Twelve

Mack's hand rested on the doorknob, and he took a deep breath. It was time to clear the air with Charlotte. He turned the knob and pushed the door open just a crack. He put his lips to the opening to speak. "Char, it's Mack. I'm coming in."

He stood by the door and waited for a response that didn't come. Charlotte was fooling herself if she thought he'd go away if she pretended to be asleep. He stepped into the room and turned the light on next to the bed, expecting to see her there. She wasn't. Fear lanced his chest. Where was she? Had someone gotten to her?

A sound came from the bathroom, and he let out a sigh. His heart was pounding as he lowered himself to the bed and braced his hands on his knees. This case was getting to him, and so was this woman. He was about to do something he'd never done before, and the mere idea of being that open with someone scared him.

The bathroom door opened, and he lifted his head to come face-to-face with Char wrapped in a towel and nothing else. Her long hair was damp around the edges but hung free without a tie.

"Mack? Wha—what are you doing in here?" He noticed

her hands pull the towel a little tighter around herself, but it was too late. He was already imagining her without it.

"We need to talk, Char."

"Not tonight, Mack. We're both tired, and Cal is giving us a chance to get some sleep."

"This won't take long," he promised, standing and taking the robe off the bathroom door. He held it out for Charlotte to slip her arms in, and she stared him down for a solid minute before she turned her back and slid one arm into the robe. She grasped the towel with that hand and slipped her other one in, tying it around her before letting the towel fall.

She may be good at keeping herself hidden, but he saw her and liked all of her. She was wrong if she thought he didn't notice her beautiful skin that glowed in the light of the lamp or the swell of her breasts from under the towel. He noticed all of her, the good and what she thought was bad, but he knew he wanted all of her. He was positive convincing Char of that would be more difficult than it should be.

He hung the towel on the bathroom doorknob and motioned for her to sit on the bed. "What do you want, Mack?" she asked, her fingers toying with the bathrobe's belt.

"I want to talk. You said could have, should have and would have are dangerous because they're past tense."

Char lifted her gaze to his. "So?"

"I talked to Eric, and he said some things that surprised me about the mission that day."

"Things like it wasn't your fault, and you did nothing wrong?"

"That and how others could have died, including me,

had I opened the other door to load the family for the transport."

"I suppose he's not wrong," she agreed. "I hadn't thought of that."

"Surprisingly, during all these years, neither had I. There were so many situations in that sandbox that should have killed me. Do you know about Hannah?"

"Cal's girlfriend in the army?" she asked, and he nodded. "Marlise told me she was killed, and Cal was shot."

"I was there. I killed the insurgent who was firing those bullets at my friends. Cal recovered and returned to the team, but he was never the same. Then the transport happened, and we all left for good."

"And started Secure One. There were worse things you could have done, Mack."

"Cal started Secure One," he clarified. "First, he worked as a mercenary and weapons expert for a few years while I wallowed."

"You wallowed?"

"In self-pity," he said, leaning down and loosening the laces on his boots. He lifted his pant leg, loosened the Velcro strap around his calf, and pulled his foot out. Immediately, his toes pointed to the floor while he pulled the sock off. He did the same on the other side until both feet were sock free and resting on the floor. "I went from running miles daily to barely walking to the bathroom with a walker, Char. The self-pity was strong, but the self-hatred was stronger. It was Cal and Eric who finally forced me to face the truth. This was my life now." He motioned at his feet, then lifted them up again. They hung down, his big toes touching the floor. "No amount of working out will make my feet move again. No matter how long

I stare at them, I'll never be able to raise my toes off the floor the way you do. Willpower won't make the muscles, nerves and tendons all work together again. I had to face the truth, accept it and move forward with the hand I'd been dealt. Or in this case, foot."

She turned to face him. "You're trying to say I need to accept my past so I can find a new life."

"No, not at all," he said with a shake of his head. "I'm trying to say it's okay to want a new life. For the longest time, I thought these scars held me back from life. Then I turned the scars around and used them for good."

"They reminded you that there are bad people in the world who need to be stopped." He nodded, and she couldn't hide her grimace. "That's the problem, Mack. I'm one of those bad people you've worked to stop."

He tipped her chin up with his finger until she was forced to hold his gaze. "That's not true, Char. You're not a bad person."

"I've done a lot of bad things. Things that go against who you are and what you believe, Mack. I've run drugs, been an escort and even had to, you know."

Her gaze hit the floor again, and he rested his forehead against hers. "I do know, but the difference is you didn't do any of those things because you wanted to. You did those things because you had to. I understand the difference, Char. The fact that you're here tonight tells me that you're inherently a good person. You want to help others and rid the world of people like The Madame who prey on innocent people."

"I do, but I still did those other things, Mack. Being with someone like me goes against everything you believe in."

He was silent, simply gazing into her eyes from where he rested against her forehead. "Did you want to do those things?"

"Of course not!" she exclaimed, jumping up and falling into the bathroom door. Mack steadied her, but she ripped her elbow from his grip to walk to the chair in the corner. "I did what I had to do to survive."

He moved his boots aside and stood, readying himself for something he'd never done before. He was about to be vulnerable with someone he only wanted to be strong for. He took an exaggerated step, lifting his thigh high to clear the floor of his toes that hung down. His foot made a "thwap" as it landed back on the hardwood floor. The same happened with the other leg, back and forth, until he stood before her.

"That's all any of us can do, Char. I don't believe in killing people, but I still had to do it in the army. I'm technically a murderer. Does that mean I'm a bad person?"

"No," she whispered, staring at her lap. "You were protecting innocent people and us at home, Mack. Nothing you did in the service can be considered bad if you followed orders."

"Then I say we level the playing field when it comes to you and me." He sat on the ottoman in front of her and took her hands.

"How?" she asked, lifting her head to gaze into his eyes. He got so lost in the depths of her blue ones that he fought to answer her.

"We consider ourselves equals."

"But we're not!" she exclaimed. "You're so much more than I am, Mack. You deserve so much more than I can offer you in this life. You need to leave, please."

She hung her head again, but he didn't leave. He leaned forward and did what he'd wanted to do since he first laid eyes on her. He kissed her. Her lips were soft, and she tasted of stolen innocence. She went stock still the moment their lips connected. He waited, his lips on hers, to see if she would find a way past her fear to enjoy the kiss. He worried she would force herself to kiss him because that was what she thought she had to do. He wanted the first, but if the second happened, he'd stop the kiss until she learned the difference.

Instead, she pulled away and brought her hands to her lips. "What are you doing?"

"Kissing you," he answered. The truth was simple. It was the acceptance that was hard.

"Why?"

"I want to, Char. I've wanted to kiss you since the day I met you."

"You're just saying that to get me to kiss you back."

His sigh was heavy when he shook his head. "No, I'm not, but I understand why you feel that way. It's hard to be vulnerable." He held up his pants legs to show her the scars, pitting and missing flesh from his calves. "But being vulnerable also requires bravery and courage. I didn't want to take my boots off and show you these scars. I'm as vulnerable as I can get when my legs are bare. It's hard to trust someone with the parts of you that you're ashamed of, but sometimes, the right person teaches you how to accept them and lose the shame."

He stood and walked to the bed, his high steppage gait leaving a slapping sound on the floor with every footfall. He bent, picked up his boots in one hand and grabbed the bedpost to steady himself.

"Where are you going?"

"To my room to get some sleep, you should too."

Mack took two steps and stopped when she moved in front of the door. "You aren't going to try to kiss me again?"

"No, Char. The next time I kiss you, it will be because you asked me to."

She was silent, and they faced off. Mack could see the turmoil in her eyes. For a moment, he felt terrible for putting it there. Then that emotion disappeared, and a new one replaced it. Pride. He had given her something to think about—she could change her life if she found a way to be vulnerable again. It wouldn't be easy for her after what she'd been through, but she would be better because of it.

"Aren't you going to put your boots on? You never let anyone see you without them."

Mack glanced down at the boots and then back to her. "No. I'm no longer ashamed of my legs, Char. Your drawing was the reason I could be vulnerable here tonight. When I saw the expression you'd drawn, it was how I feel inside every day. That's the fear I have of someone thinking I'm less because of these. The words you wrote about my legs were validation about something I couldn't change. If I couldn't change it, I shouldn't feel ashamed." He walked to the door and turned the knob when she stepped out of the way. "Thank you for giving me that little piece of myself back. I'd love to have the drawing when and if you're ready to part with it. Get some sleep, Char. Tomorrow will be another long day."

He bent down and kissed her cheek before he left her room and walked down the hallway, waiting to hear her shut the door. She never did.

Chapter Thirteen

Sleep wouldn't come no matter what. Charlotte had been in bed for almost two hours but kept falling into short dreams about Mack, where all his pain and life experiences hung from him like appendages. It was disturbing, and she finally sat up and tossed her feet over the bed. She needed to walk off some nervous energy, or she'd never sleep. It was almost 3:00 a.m., so the grounds would be quiet. Maybe she'd walk down to the river and breathe the fresh air to clear her head.

After dressing, she slipped down the darkened hallways to avoid the guards stationed at the doorways. She didn't want anyone tagging along with her outside. She wanted to stand by the water and decide if Mack was right. Did vulnerability do the opposite of what you expected it to do?

She stepped outside and walked across the lawn toward the river, wishing it were true, but in her case, there was no way to vanquish the shame she carried. It filled every gaping hole in her soul and filtered into every crack and crevice. No, vulnerability could not take her shame away. That was something she would have to live with forever.

She stepped onto the dock and walked to the end, looking out over the dark flowing water. A tear fell down her cheek as she pictured Mack taking his boots off and walking toward her. It wasn't pity making her cry, but instead that he put himself out there, and she pushed him away. Her fingers brushed her lips where he'd kissed her. For a split second, she was terrified, but then a different sensation took over. After Mack left her room, it took her a long time to understand that his kiss showed her how much he cared. Mack wasn't there for a quick roll in the hay. He was there because he cared deeply about her.

Charlotte thought back over her life but couldn't think of another man who had made her feel that way. For the most part, men were indifferent to her unless they thought they could somehow use her to better their position. That was certainly true during her time with The Madame. The expression on Mack's face as he told her that her drawing gave him the courage to be vulnerable held nothing but honesty. That wasn't lip service. He meant it. He'd shown it by holding his head high as he left the room, no longer hiding his disability.

"Secure two, Whiskey," came a voice from behind her, and Charlotte jumped, spinning around to face Mina as she walked down the dock.

"Mina, you scared me."

"Imagine if I'd been someone out to do you harm. You wouldn't have seen them coming."

"How did you find me out here?" Charlotte discreetly wiped her eyes while she waited for an answer. Mina was right. She hadn't been paying attention, and that could have been deadly. *Damn you, Mack Holbock, and your ridiculously soft lips.*

"Cameras cover this entire property. Or did you forget?"

A groan left Charlotte's lips as her chin fell to her chest. "I just wanted to be alone. I forgot about the cameras."

"That's why I gave you some time. There aren't many reasons for a single woman to be out here at this time of night unless she needs to be alone. Mack?"

She gave her friend a shoulder shrug as she leaned on the deck railing.

"Listen, let me give you a little piece of advice. It's time to take your power back, Charlotte. If you don't, you'll find yourself standing in this same place year after year, wondering why life isn't working out for you."

"How do I take my power back when I never had any to begin with?" Charlotte was angry, and she balled her hands into fists at her sides.

"You're wrong. You are the only one with the power when it comes to yourself. That's the first thing you do to take power back. You stop blaming everyone else for where you are in life."

"But it's their fault!"

Mina held up her hand to calm her. "I know it's their fault. Everyone in your life did you wrong. There's no question. But blame is like poison. The longer you swallow it, the more toxic it becomes and the weaker you get. Letting go of the blame and starting fresh from where you are today gives you back all the power they took from you."

Charlotte stared at Mina for a long moment and then tipped her head. "I guess that kind of makes sense."

"It makes a lot of sense and will be easier to say than do. I get that. You have to trust yourself. Just the way you did the other night when you didn't hesitate to defend Ella. Confidence in who you are as a person helps you let the blame go."

"I don't have a lot of confidence. I never have."

"That's the whole idea of reclaiming your power, Char-

lotte. You picture yourself as the beautiful, strong, coura-
geous and brave woman we all see rather than what all the
toxic people in your life said you were. Once you do that
consistently, you have all the control again. Do the things
that make you feel powerful, even if that means you take
those things back from the toxic people too."

"Like art?" Charlotte leaned against the railing and
wiped her face one more time of a wayward tear that refused to stay behind her lid.

"Yes, like art. I'm not going to tell you to go out and
start tagging buildings again," Mina said with a lip tilt
that made Charlotte laugh. "But you can use your art to
do good the same as you have been with Secure One. The
map you drew for Mack to help him visualize the rivers across the country was so intricate and defined that
it blew my computer-based model out of the water. See
what I did there?"

A smile tilted Charlotte's lips up, and she nodded. "Well
done. I'm glad I can use my only talent to help others."

"Wrong," Mina said instantly. "You have so many more
talents than art. You just made my point. You're listening
to the toxic people from your past rather than trusting in
what you know about yourself."

After sharing a moment of silence, Charlotte could see
her point. "You're right. Why do I do that? I'm free now.
I should be celebrating that and moving forward rather
than keeping myself locked in that past." Mina nodded and
gave her a playful punch on the arm. Charlotte groaned
and let her head fall backward. "I screwed up tonight."

"With Mack?"

"How did you know?"

"Woman's intuition," she answered with a wink. Then

she hooked Charlotte's arm in hers, and they walked back toward the house. "You can fix it."

"You don't know what happened."

"I don't need to know," she promised, her head swiveling as they walked across the grass toward the house. "I can see the emotion that flows between you when you're together. There will be fits and starts to any relationship, especially with your complicated past, but if you're honest with him, things will smooth out."

Mina held the door open, and Charlotte walked back to her room in a daze. Did she want a relationship with Mack? When she picked up her drawing pad and opened it, the truth was there in black and white.

AFTER A SHOWER and coffee, Mack was still tired. Try as he might, sleep hadn't come easily. He knew he'd done the right thing with Charlotte, even if it hadn't been the easy thing. Now he had to get his head in the game and work this case before another woman died—a woman just like Charlotte.

Wrong. A woman like Charlotte used to be.

The voice was right. Charlotte wasn't a helpless woman caught in dire circumstances anymore. She was an essential part of the team and didn't hesitate to jump into the fray for the good of others. He had to remember that. She didn't need to be saved.

"Everything quiet?" Mack asked Eric as he walked by Ella's room.

"There was a bit of a disturbance, but Mina took care of it." Mack cocked his head, and Eric's gaze drifted to the windows for a moment. "Charlotte went for a walk without telling anyone. Mina saw her on the cameras and pulled her back in."

A curse word fell from Mack's lips. "She knows better than to go out alone."

Eric held up his hands. "Take it up with her. They're in command central. Selina is preparing Bethany to bring her down."

"Are you coming down too?"

A shake of his head said that was a negative. "No one to put on Ella. We're too short-staffed."

"Bring her down."

"To command central?"

Mack shrugged. "Why not? Let's face it. She's already knee-deep in this sludge. Maybe listening to us will spark something she remembers about her dad and his campaign. If nothing else, she can be there for Bethany. We need you down there so you know what's going on."

"Ten-four. I'll prepare her and be down shortly."

Mack gave him a salute and jogged down the stairs toward the office. They needed a break on this case soon. He already knew what the police were doing, and the answer to that was nothing. Every day they wasted was another day closer to a woman's death. He doubted Bethany had anything to add as far as the river killings went, but she may be able to tie up The Madame's loose strings, including where the other three Misses had gone when they escaped the raids.

Voices drifted out of the control room, and Mack stopped next to the door and leaned on the frame, watching Charlotte at the whiteboard. She had a marker and was making lists next to her paper map. One was in blue, and one was in red. Mack recognized a few of the names on each list. They were the senators up for reelection.

"Good morning," Mack said, walking in the door as though he hadn't been standing there, watching her. "Everything quiet?"

"For now," Mina answered, her gaze flicking to Charlotte. "Just waiting on the rest of the team."

"I told Eric to bring Ella down with him. He needs to be in the loop, and she's up to her waist in this disaster anyway."

Mina stood and stretched. "I agree. Dorian may not, but we just won't tell him." Mack and Charlotte both laughed, but Mack let his die off just to hear Charlotte's. When she laughed, it felt like hope to him. "I'm going to get some coffee. Do you guys want anything?"

"I'd have a cup," Charlotte said. "Let me come with you."

Mina brushed her away with her hand and walked to the door. "I can handle two cups of coffee. I'll be back before everyone gets here."

The room was silent as Mack walked up to the board where Charlotte stood. "How did you sleep?" He brushed a piece of hair off her face and behind her ear.

"I didn't. How about you?"

"Equally as well. I heard you took a walk. You shouldn't do that right now."

To his surprise, she didn't drop her gaze or look away. She held him in her atmosphere as her spine stiffened, and she lifted her chin a hair. "I decide what I do, not you. I was perfectly safe, considering this place is a fortress."

Mack lifted a brow but bit back the need to point out that while they were there, Cal was in charge and gave the orders. He didn't say it because he liked her spunk.

She was holding onto the power she'd found within herself here, and he wasn't going to be the one to clip her wings.

Rather than say anything more, he motioned at the boards. "What's this?"

Charlotte smiled as though she were thankful for the subject change. "I was making a list of the senators running for reelection listed by the party. It's hard when they're all over the map. I thought it might help us recognize patterns or common denominators."

"Has it?"

"Not yet, but I just finished the list." She was laughing, and Mack ate up the sound. She didn't laugh freely that often, so when she did, he wanted to be there to hear it. "About last night," she whispered, staring over his shoulder. "I'm sorry for treating you the way I did. I was scared and didn't know how to react."

"I understood that," Mack promised, giving her a gentle hug. "Never apologize for standing up for yourself. You weren't ready, and you let me know that. I wasn't upset. I respect your boundaries, Char."

She sank into him as though those were the exact words she needed to hear.

Chapter Fourteen

"Charlotte?"

Mack and Charlotte jumped apart to see Bethany in the doorway with Marlise on one side and Selina on the other.

"Bethany." Charlotte walked to her and took her hand. "How are you doing?"

"I'm okay," she said with a smile. "Selina and Marlise have been taking good care of me. I'm sorry to scare you the way I did. I didn't know what else to do."

"Don't apologize," Charlotte said, giving her a gentle squeeze. "I wasn't scared as much as I was in shock that you were here. I worried so much about you and Emelia. To hear your voice was a shock."

"You worried about us? Even after what we did?"

Marlise and Selina led Bethany to a chair where she sat. Charlotte sat next to her and offered her a smile.

"You did what you thought you had to do to be free. I would never judge you for that, even if you saw overthrowing The Miss as your only option."

"That wasn't what we wanted to do!" she exclaimed. "We wanted to overthrow her, so we could let all the women go!"

"It's okay," Charlotte said, trying to calm her. "I believe you. There was no way for you to know that her father was running drugs into the states and funding her operation. Take a deep breath and try to stay calm. We want to hear your story, but we want everyone here, so let's wait for Cal and the rest of the team to arrive."

"Her father was supplying the drugs we had to move?"

"Yes," Charlotte said, squeezing her hand gently. "You never had a chance of overthrowing her. Her death was the only way to be free."

"And she's dead?" she asked, glancing between everyone, but Mack answered.

"She is. Unfortunately, I had to protect my team, and she was the casualty."

"Nothing unfortunate about that woman being dead." Her tone was firm and left no question regarding how she felt about the matter. "The Madame is in jail?"

"For a good long time," Charlotte assured her. "We don't have to worry about her anymore."

Mina walked in with a carafe of coffee while Cal and the rest of the team filtered in. After Mina handed out cups of coffee, everyone sat comfortably in a semicircle to hear what Bethany had to say. The discussion was being recorded in case there was information for the police. Mack was sure that would be their next step, but they'd listen to what she had to say since Bethany came to them first.

"Tell us what you remember about the last time you saw The Miss," Charlotte said. Cal had asked her to take the lead on questioning because the last thing they wanted to do was scare Bethany or make things harder for her. She had a story to tell. That was why she was here, but allowing her to tell it would be the trickiest part.

"After we talked to The Miss about our plan, it was late. She told us she'd think about making us more pivotal members of the team. Satisfied, we went to bed in our pod. When I woke up, I was in a basement bedroom. That's all I remember. I don't know how many days I was out or how I got there. I know it was a basement because the window was at the top of the room and I could see the ground at the window level. Before I had time to figure out what had happened, he walked in."

"He?" Charlotte asked. "Did he have a name?"

Bethany nodded but then shook her head. She finally shrugged as though she didn't know the answer. "He told me my new name was Angel and forced me to call him Little Daddy."

"Little Daddy? That's different. Usually, they just want to be called daddy," Charlotte said, taking Bethany's hand.

"Right?" she asked, trying to lighten the mood with girl banter, but it didn't hit the same way when you'd been held hostage for years by someone using the name Little Daddy. "But the thing is, there's a Big Daddy somewhere," she whispered, her words falling on each other out of fear. "When Little Daddy thinks you're ready, he sends you to Big Daddy."

"Did you ever meet Big Daddy?" Charlotte asked, and Bethany immediately began shaking her head.

She leaned in to whisper to Charlotte. "The night I escaped, Little Daddy told me I was ready for Big Daddy. That's when I knew I had to run."

"Running was the right thing to do, Bethany. Were you the only woman there? What happened to Emelia?"

"I don't know," she said as her voice broke. "When I woke up in the basement, she wasn't with me."

Mina glanced at Mack, and he knew what she was thinking. Was Emelia one of those unidentified women from two years ago? At this point, he'd believe anything was possible.

"You woke up almost eighteen months ago and were alone in the house?" Charlotte asked to clarify.

"In the beginning, another woman was there with me, but she didn't last very long before he took her to Big Daddy. He never brought another woman home that I heard after that. There could have been more that I couldn't hear if they were upstairs or in a different room. I didn't stop to check when I locked him in my room that night. I should have checked! What if I left Emelia behind?"

"Shh," Selina said, glancing over her head at Cal for a moment. "You did the right thing getting out of there. Do you remember where the house was located?"

Mack knew Selina was trying to redirect Bethany before she had a meltdown and couldn't answer more questions. He'd seen it happen with Marlise and Charlotte and didn't want to see it again. The fear was paralyzing for these women after they escaped. Fear that they'd done something wrong. Fear someone was coming after them. Fear that they didn't do enough. That was the hardest part for him to swallow. Watching them so filled with fear that they couldn't even move.

"It was in the woods. Deep in the woods. I ran along the river, and when I came out of the woods, I found a little gas station. I managed to hot-wire an old truck, and on my way out of town, I passed a sign that said Sugarville, Pennsylvania. I made it to a bigger city before I ran out of gas, so I asked The Salvation Army for help. They got me a bus ticket to here."

"Because you heard that Secure One had killed The

Miss?" Charlotte asked, and Bethany nodded her head immediately.

"I heard that Secure One was here when another body was found. I didn't know if you'd still be here, but I didn't know how else to find you."

"That was quick thinking," Mack encouraged the woman. "Why did you want to find us specifically?"

Bethany turned to look at him, and he saw all the fear in her eyes. There was so much that he worried she would drown in it before she finished her story. "If you killed The Miss, then you had to be good people. I needed help and knew I couldn't go to the police."

"Why not?" Charlotte asked with her head tipped in confusion. "The Miss was already dead and The Madame in prison. There was no one left to hurt you."

"But the police might not believe me when I told them my story. I left Little Daddy in that room, and I don't know if he's dead." A shiver ran through her. "If he's not dead, he might find me. If he is dead, the police might be looking for me."

"I can understand that thinking," Charlotte agreed. "How did you get the better of Little Daddy that night?"

"I don't want to talk about that," she whispered so low that Mack almost didn't make out what she said.

"That's okay," Charlotte promised. "You don't have to talk about it, but I need to know if you escaped the same night the body was found here?"

"I think so," Bethany answered. "I ran the first night, was on the bus the second night and here last night."

Bethany was sinking fast, but there was still so much to ask her. Mack was about to ask a question when Charlotte did. "Bethany, you said you were in Pennsylvania when you found the truck, right?"

"Yes, that's what the license plate said. I hope he finds the truck. I don't want to get into trouble for stealing it, but I was so tired and had to get away."

"You won't get in trouble," Cal assured her. "They were extenuating circumstances that the police will understand. Besides, you left it for them to find."

"Do you know how long you ran on foot?" Charlotte asked to complete her question.

"Maybe two hours? I know it was after ten when I left the room and way after midnight when I found the truck."

Mack was making notes on the whiteboard, so he added that to the list. Maybe Mina could do some calculations and get close to the town where Bethany was held hostage.

"You were there a long time, Bethany. I'm impressed that you were strong enough to run that far."

Bethany straightened as though Charlotte's words sparked her determination. "I knew from the beginning that he was going to move me. I spent a couple of months in a stupor but then decided if I was going to try to run when I had the chance, I needed to be strong. He brought me healthy food, and I did a lot of exercise in my room to stay in shape. That was how I overtook him that night. He thought I was asleep, so he dozed off and I took advantage of it."

Cal leaned forward and clasped his hands together casually. "Did you talk to the other women in the house, Bethany?"

"I shared one wall of my bedroom with another room. When I first got there, a woman named Andrea was in that room. Then she left and was replaced by another woman shortly after that. That woman mostly just cried the whole time she was there."

Mack glanced at Charlotte, whose eyes were wide when she looked up at him. He nodded and motioned with his eyes to ask Bethany the next question.

"Did she tell you her name or where she was from?"

"Andrea went to Big Daddy before me. I think I was supposed to be next, and Layla was supposed to be training to go after me."

"Wait, did you say Layla?" Charlotte asked, leaning forward on her chair.

"I think that's what she said her name was, but it was hard to understand because she was always crying, and we had to talk through the wall. I was surprised when Little Daddy said he would take her to Big Daddy before me. He said only he could train her to do what had to be done."

"What had to be done?" Mack asked, shelving the information about Layla for a moment.

"We were being trained to take care of Big Daddy. We had to be ready to do anything he needed from writing a letter to, you know, in bed."

"They had you perform sexual favors? Did you ever see his face?" Cal asked, but Bethany shook her head.

"No. Little Daddy wore a leather mask over his face. I never saw more than his lips and his eyes."

"Do you think you could describe him for me, and I could draw him?" Charlotte asked the woman, whose eyes widened. "If you can't, we all understand."

"I can try," she whispered. "I feel like I failed by running. I didn't get the right information to help you."

"No," Cal said before she finished her sentence. "You didn't fail. You got out alive, and that's miraculous after being there for that long. You survived, Bethany. That's all that matters. Any information you can give us will help, but you did the right thing by running and not looking back."

Bethany nodded as she stared at her hands. "I wish I could have helped the other women, but once you went to Big Daddy, you never came back."

"You've been a huge help to us this morning," Charlotte said, squeezing her hand. "I'm so proud of you for getting out and finding us. We're going to help you now, okay?"

Bethany's face crumpled as she nodded. "I need help. Just like you and Marlise did."

"And we'll get it for you," Selina promised, helping her stand and putting an arm around her.

"We'll take her back to rest," Marlise said to Cal, who nodded. "Then we'll figure out where to go from there for her."

They led the trembling woman from the room, and Mack knew life would never go back to the way it was ten minutes ago.

"Layla was with Big Daddy. Big Daddy has to be The Red River Slayer." Mack heard the fear in Charlotte's voice when she spoke.

"It appears so," said Cal, who sat leaning forward with his hands propped under his chin. "But if Layla had only been dead for three days before we found her, that means Big Daddy kept her for a long time. It's hard to hide a human being for that long."

"Unless they're kept in plain sight," Mack said, lowering the tablet. "Bethany said they had to learn to do everything, including writing a letter. Maybe they're his assistant," he said using quotations, "and they're brainwashed enough not to say otherwise."

"You mean he tells them that they're safe and he will take care of them and give them a job?" Charlotte asked, and Mack nodded. "He had to have convinced Layla she was safe."

"Or that he was on the up and up," Roman agreed.

"You're forgetting that he expects sexual favors," Mina said. "How do you convince someone that is part of an assistant's job?"

Charlotte shrugged and glanced down at her hands. "You give them everything they never had," she whispered. "You buy them nice things, let them get their hair and nails done, tell them you love them. When a woman has never had those things, it's effortless to ply her with them."

Mina started to nod as she spoke and then pointed at her. "She's right. I bet that's how he's doing it. Bethany said they took care of her and brought her healthy food. They wanted the women to be functional when they got to Big Daddy."

"We're still missing a piece of the puzzle," Roman said. He was frustrated by the partial information that didn't make a whole.

"We're missing a lot of the puzzle, Roman," Mack said, his head shaking.

"But wait." Charlotte stood up and grabbed a marker by the whiteboard. She wrote Andrea, Bethany and Layla. "We'll assume, since we don't know, that one of the last five women was Andrea, right?"

Everyone nodded, but Mina spoke. "I'm searching now to see if I can find that name in the databases, but she could have been one of the two that weren't identified, or she hasn't been found yet."

"All of the what-ifs aside," Charlotte said, putting a red *X* through Andrea's name. "We have a pattern developing. Bethany was supposed to go to Big Daddy before Layla, but Little Daddy couldn't train Layla, so she jumped ahead in the queue." She made an arrow over Bethany's name and then put a red *X* through Layla, rewriting Bethany's name on the other side of Layla. "That explains why Bethany was held for so long and why she was being moved to Big Daddy right after we found Layla. However, look what happens when we take Bethany away." She scrubbed out her name with her hand.

"She broke the cycle," Mack said immediately.

Charlotte pointed at him with excitement. "Yes! The woman he was planning to move to the coveted position is gone. So now what? Where does he get his next victim if he has no other women with Little Daddy?"

"And if the cycle is broken, will he stick to his schedule of a death every six weeks, or will he become unpredictable because his perfect order has been broken?" Mack was standing next to Charlotte now by the whiteboard. "Does anyone have an opinion?"

The rest of the team sat open-mouthed as they stared at them. Charlotte was right, the cycle had been broken, and now Mack feared that their perp would react by killing more women.

"He might go underground and try to regroup. Especially if Little Daddy is dead," Roman said. "Or he might have women in other houses that we don't know about yet."

"That I doubt." Mina stood and walked to her computer. "He has to maintain the house where the women are kept with Little Daddy as well as his own living quarters. Unless he's a millionaire, it would be difficult to run three households."

"Then we need to find the guy before he kills another innocent woman," Cal said, his voice tight. "But how? How do we find a guy so good at hiding in plain sight?"

"Do we have a body in the Susquehanna River yet?" Roman asked Charlotte, who stood by the board.

The Susquehanna River was the main river in Pennsylvania and Charlotte knew what he was thinking immediately. "No, but we already know he's transporting these women a long way to leave them in a river, so we can't assume that's the next river."

"We can if the guy's chain of women was broken," Mack said. "It would be safe to assume that he'll act rashly now. Either he's going to kill a random woman, or he's going to go underground, and it will be another two years before we hear from him again. We don't want that."

"We need to go to Pennsylvania," Roman said.

Cal shook his head. "Impossible. I don't have the staffing for that. We're already stretched too thin."

"I have Efren coming on, but he can't be here until tomorrow," Mina piped up from behind her computer. "Then we have the party security to worry about next."

Mack met Charlotte's gaze across the board and knew what she was thinking. She was going to figure out a way to get to Pennsylvania and offer herself up for The Red River Slayer to grab. He wasn't going to let that happen.

Chapter Fifteen

Marlise and Selina arrived to fill them in on Bethany's condition. "She needs medical care," Selina said, "but I can't convince her to leave yet. I keep telling her she needs to talk to the police, but she's afraid to do that too. She has been held in captivity for years. She needs a psychiatrist and a therapist to help her."

"We agree," Cal said. "But we can give her one more day before we force anything on her."

Charlotte was trying to follow the conversation and sort out the information in her head and on the board. Thirty-three senators were running for reelection, but so far, only six, possibly eight, bodies had been found.

"There's no way," Charlotte muttered as she stared at the board. "There's just no way."

Mack walked up to her and took her shoulder. "There's no way for what, sweetheart?"

"For this guy to kill the number of women necessary to equal the thirty-three senators running for reelection. Now that we know he keeps them for an extended period, if Bethany's captor is The Red River Slayer, there isn't enough time." Charlotte looked over at Mina. "Did they do autopsies on all the women?" Mina nodded immediately. "Did they get a time of death on all of them?"

"No," Mina said, standing and walking around the computer. "Layla's was the first autopsy that was within that tight of a window. It was impossible to know with the other women."

"You're saying they could have been dead much longer?" Mack asked.

"Whether they took that long to float to shore or he held them after death, there's no way to know. It could be pure coincidence that the women were found at that time interval."

"My science teacher said that rivers don't freeze over like lakes," Ella said from the back of the room. Charlotte had forgotten she was there since she'd had her earphones in and was watching a movie. "But shallow parts of rivers can freeze. If a body floated under the ice and got trapped, it wouldn't move again until spring arrived. He also said that the streamflow of rivers changes by seasons."

"Following that train of thought," Mina said, standing up. "If spring hits and there's more snowmelt in one area of the river, that pushes a big deluge of water through the river at a high rate of speed."

"Which could easily upend a body trapped in sludge," Mack finished.

"If he's trying to make a point, wouldn't he want the bodies to be found immediately? He's taking a chance they won't be found where he wanted them to be or at all."

"Serial killers don't think the same as we do, Mack," Mina said, and Charlotte smiled. Mina was going to school him about the psychology of psychopaths, and she couldn't wait. "They do things that aren't logical to us, but to them, it's completely logical. Sometimes, they don't care if and when their victims are found."

"That would explain the longer period with no bodies," Roman added.

"You're saying we got lucky finding Layla just three days after her death." Mack waited for someone to answer.

"Highly probable," Mina confirmed. "This is spring, and the river is high and swift. He may have misjudged how long it would take her to come ashore this time."

Charlotte glanced over at Ella, who was staring at the list of names on the whiteboard. "Did I forget one?" she asked the teen, who shook her head.

"No. The names are all there. Your comment about there being no way for him to kill that many women started me thinking." She took a marker from the board and put checkmarks next to nine names.

"What do the checkmarks mean?" Charlotte asked.

"Those nine senators are committee members on fisheries, wildlife and water. I know because my dad is on the committee."

Charlotte noticed the surprise on Mack's face even before he spoke. "Would this committee deal with rivers?"

Ella shrugged. "Well, sure. I know there's a big fight about dams and the damage they do to the waterways. Or something like that anyway. My dad talks about it all the time."

Mack grabbed a marker and underlined the nine senators' names on their states. There were three senators' states that had rivers where bodies were found, which included Senator Dorian. "If I'm following this correctly, the three bodies recently found match up to a state with a senator on this list."

"And that means instead of twenty-seven more women, there could be six more before this is over," Charlotte said, her voice filled with fury and fear. "We can't let that happen."

Mack walked over to Mina and leaned on her desk. "Can you see if the previous reelection cycle river deaths match the states of any previous committee members?"

"I'm on it," she said, putting her hands on the keyboard. "Give me thirty minutes."

"If this is some nut trying to bring attention to a cause by killing women, we need to stop him now," Mack said, walking back to Charlotte and putting a protective hand on her back.

Cal stood. "I couldn't agree more. Charlotte, take Ella back to her room, please. Eric, Roman and Mack, you're with me. We'll reconvene here in thirty."

Charlotte put her arm around Ella and walked with her to the kitchen. "Forget going to your room. We're going to have breakfast, and then you'll be there to hear what Mina discovered."

"I don't know if Cal will like that," Ella said, nervously chewing on her lip.

"Too bad. If it weren't for you picking up on that pattern, we'd still be stuck in neutral. A good friend recently told me we must control our power if we want respect. This is us demanding respect."

She winked at the young girl and then led her through the kitchen door for pancakes and juice.

HE LISTENED TO the incessant ringing in his ear as he sat at his desk, the low drone of voices outside his office door reminding him to play it cool. The call went to voice mail again, and he angrily slammed the phone down on his blotter. So much for playing it cool.

"Where the hell is he?" His growl scared the cat, who darted back under the leather sofa against one wall. It was his ex-wife's cat, but she'd decided she hadn't wanted it when she moved to the Bahamas to live with her new boyfriend. He often wondered if they were enjoying their extended time under the blue-green waters.

A smile lifted his lips at the thought. That memory didn't solve his problem though. He had no idea where his guy was or why he wasn't answering his phone. Maybe he was just busy, but even he couldn't swallow that excuse anymore. If that were the case, he would have called him back after the first ten voice mails, each one increasingly angrier.

He glanced at the clock and sighed. He was going to have to mix business with pleasure. He already regretted what was to come, but his guy had left him no choice. He walked to a side door of his office and opened it. "Miss Andrea, I'd like to see you for a moment."

He waited while the young blond woman joined him in the office. Today she was wearing a pencil skirt that accentuated her bottom and a silk blouse that made her look professional and sex kitten at the same time. He motioned for her to close the door, and she couldn't hide the apprehension on her face as she turned to do it. His desire stirred. She knew what was to come and would obey him no matter what he asked her.

When she turned back, her face changed to that of a contented woman ready to please her protector. "How can I help?"

She asked the question that made his beast roar to life, but he forced it down. This was not the time or the place.

"Have you enjoyed your time with me, Miss Andrea?"

He propped his elbows on his sizeable executive desk and steepled his fingers against his lips.

"Very much so," she agreed. She sat in the chair he motioned to and crossed her legs. "I'm quite happy working for you."

His mouth watered at the sight of her tanned skin just waiting for his touch, but he didn't. Touch, that is. "And I'm happy to hear you say that, Andrea. I need a favor, and I can't ask anyone else. No one can know about this."

"I wouldn't tell a soul." She batted her lashes at him the way he demanded of her, but he wasn't looking to score today…at least not yet.

"Good. Be ready to leave in thirty minutes."

"We're taking a trip? Is it for work or pleasure?"

"A little of both, Miss Andrea. A little of both," he said, allowing his inner beast to come through in the smile he offered her. "Work first with pleasure to follow."

She stood and left his office, his gaze savoring the moment. It would be the last time he'd see that bottom walking out his door.

Chapter Sixteen

"A macabre scene played out on the bank of the Susque-hanna River this morning," the newscaster began, and Charlotte swiveled toward the television in the corner of the room. "There were two bodies discovered by a fish-erman in a weed-filled slough this morning. Initially, the police suspected The Red River Slayer had killed again until they discovered the bodies were locked in a lovers' embrace. The man and woman were taken to the local medical examiner's office to await identification. If you think you may have information about this couple, please call—"

Charlotte didn't hear another word as she was already out the door and running to command central. Eric was alone in the room, staring at the whiteboard when she arrived.

"Eric," she said, out of breath enough that she needed to pause before saying anything more. "Two bodies were found in Pennsylvania this morning along the river."

He whirled around before she finished speaking. "Women?"

"That's the weird part," she said, walking into the room. "They said it was a man and a woman locked in a lovers' embrace."

"Did they give any other information?" he asked, grabbing a walkie from the table.

"They were taken to the local medical examiner for identification."

"Secure two, Echo," he said into the black box.

"Secure one, Whiskey," came Mina's voice.

"Mina, can you come to the office? I need some help on the computer."

"Be there in two," she answered, and then the box went silent.

"It has to be a coincidence." Eric was addressing Charlotte this time. "Other than the river, it's too far off the norm for our perp. There would be no reason for him to kill a man."

"Unless it was Little Daddy."

"How does the woman come into play then?"

"I don't know, okay! I'm just telling you what the news report said." Frustrated, Charlotte plopped down in a chair and rubbed her face with her hands. She needed sleep, but she suspected that wasn't happening soon.

Mina jogged into the room, and Eric explained what he needed. She started searching for the early copies of the story to see if one had more information than the other. While she did that, Charlotte paced. She had too much nervous energy. Eric might not believe her, but she had a gut feeling about this guy, and her gut never lied. How the woman came into play, she didn't know yet, but if anyone could figure it out, Mina could. They'd have to tell Cal what they discovered when he landed back at Secure One. He'd taken Roman and Marlise back with him, so the team at headquarters wasn't shorthanded. Mina stayed behind to help with anything computer-based since she could work remotely for Secure One simultaneously. Charlotte was suddenly glad she'd stayed.

"From what I can gather, a fisherman found the couple early this morning. The police reported that it was difficult to disengage the pair, but once they did, they realized the couple had died together."

"Rigor mortis?" Eric asked.

"Seems like it," Mina said from behind the computer.

"If rigor was set, then they had to have died recently. Full rigor only lasts for twenty-four hours after death. If the water was cold though, rigor could last much longer." Eric put his hand on his hip. "Anything else?"

"No, they don't have much to go on right now. The police asked the public to come forward with any information."

"Where did they find the bodies?" Charlotte asked. "Near a town?"

"Every station reported it, so I can't use that as the first identifier. I might have to go through some back doors to find that information."

"They worked hard to keep the location from the news report," Eric said, pacing toward the door. "They didn't say where the bodies were found or what ME has them."

"Let me look into this," Mina said as she typed. "If I can come up with the ME who has the bodies, or a report entered by a police station, I'll know within a few miles where they were found."

Charlotte grabbed a walkie and held it up. "Call me when you know something. I'm going to offer breaks."

Eric waved her off, and she headed for the stairs where Mack was standing guard over the women. Selina had stayed back to take care of Bethany until she could transfer her to a facility, and Ella was doing schoolwork in her room. Charlotte knew Mack didn't need a break, but she wanted to update him.

You want to see him.

With an eye roll, Charlotte shut that voice down. There was no sense even considering a life with Mack. He might want her at the moment, but there was a lifetime of things he didn't know about her.

And he doesn't care.

The grunt she gave that voice was loud and clear as she stomped up the stairs.

Do the things that make you feel powerful, even if that means you have to take those things back from the toxic people too.

Mina's words ran through her mind as she hit the landing and headed toward the bedrooms. What made her feel powerful? That was the question she had to answer.

STANDING AROUND DOING nothing was making Mack antsy. He needed to move, but there was nowhere to go. His gut told him something was about to go down, and he widened his stance a bit in acknowledgment. When Cal returned to Secure One, he would immediately send in the extra help he'd hired for the campaign party rather than wait. Once Mina's new guy arrived, Mack would hand over the bodyguard duties with gratitude. There was nothing Mack hated more than standing around idle.

He ran a hand over his face and closed his eyes for a moment. Exhaustion hung on him after the night he'd had, but he could only blame himself. Instead of dreaming about Charlotte, he should have reminded himself that he couldn't get involved with her. That reminder had nothing to do with who she was and everything to do with what she'd been through in life. She didn't need his ugly baggage to carry when she had enough of her own—

"Kiss me."

Mack looked down at the woman standing in his path with confusion. "What?"

"I said, kiss me."

"I heard what you said," he whispered, leaning closer. "I'm confused why you said it."

"You said you wouldn't kiss me again until I asked you to. I just asked. Now kiss me."

Mack lifted a brow. He liked her spunk, but this felt like a test he could fail no matter his choice. "I would love to, but there are cameras everywhere. We should save that for a time when we're—"

Finishing the sentence wasn't an option when she grabbed him and planted her lips on his. Hers were warm and tasted of sweet strawberries. His head swam at the sensations she evoked in him until he was left little choice but to grasp her waist and pull her to him. He shouldn't be kissing her, but none of him cared. If Charlotte was initiating a kiss, he would enjoy every moment of it, in case it was the only one he ever got.

Tilting his head, he dug in deeper, still letting her control it, but pushing back enough for her to know he was all in no matter where she took it. He wouldn't force it further than she was comfortable with, but he would need the strength of a god to let her go when she ended it. The little moan that escaped the back of her throat fanned his desire until he was sure their closeness revealed his true feelings for her. Again, not one part of him cared. It wasn't a secret that he desired her, and this kiss made it known that she felt the same, even if the whole situation was complicated beyond measure.

Her tongue traced the closed split in his lips until he parted them and let her roam his mouth, his tongue tangling with hers until neither one could breathe, and they had to fall apart just to suck in air. She stood before him, her chest heaving as she lowered her forehead to his chest.

"I shouldn't have done that. I'm sorry."

Mack tipped her chin up until they made eye contact. "Do. Not. Apologize. In case you didn't notice, I loved every second of it, so no apology is needed."

"But the cameras—"

"Will show them what they already know," he said with a wink. "I am curious to hear what changed between last night and today."

"Mina told me to do what makes me feel powerful, even if I have to take those things back from my toxic past."

"That's good advice," he agreed, tucking a piece of hair behind her ear as she rested her forehead on his chest. "Being the one to initiate the kiss took back your power from the men who always said they owned you, right?" Her head nodded against his sweater, but she still didn't look up. Rather than push her away and force eye contact that would make her uncomfortable, Mack wrapped his arms around her and squeezed. "I'm proud of you. It's not easy to leave our bad experiences in the past and live in the moment. Thank you for letting me be the one to help you do that."

"I didn't use you, Mack. I wanted to kiss you." She finally lifted her face to his and smiled.

"I know you didn't use me, Char. That wasn't what I was implying. I was genuinely thanking you for trusting me enough to know you could. For the record, I wanted to kiss you too. I think I proved that last night."

Her head bob was enough to tell him he'd gotten through to her, and she understood. Slowly, he loosened his arms so she could step back and collect herself. He figured Mina was in command central doing a fist pump if she'd seen them on camera, and he couldn't stop the smirk that filled his face. Until he remembered Eric was down there too.

Mack wasn't sure what was up with Eric, but something was. He was constantly defensive and pushing back on any order Mack or Cal gave. They'd been friends for a dozen years, so he hoped if Eric had a real problem, he'd come to them and talk openly about it, but so far, that hadn't happened. Mack made a mental note to talk to Cal about it once he was back at Secure One and had a moment to think.

"I also have an update to give you," Charlotte said after straightening her hair. Mack listened while she filled him in on the two bodies found in Pennsylvania.

"That's odd, but not necessarily tied to The Red River Slayer."

Charlotte shrugged when she nodded. "I know, but they were found in the same river as the one Bethany was near when she ran." She held her hand out at the door on his right. "She did say she wasn't sure if she killed the guy."

Mack considered this but then shook his head. "It still doesn't make sense. If she killed him, he wouldn't end up in the river. He would have decayed in the house."

"You're ignoring the obvious, Mack. Big Daddy."

"You think Big Daddy found Little Daddy and threw him in the river? Who's the woman?"

A text alert came in, and Mack grabbed his phone. There

was a text from Mina, and all it said was get a room. He couldn't hide the smirk on his face, and Charlotte noticed.

"What? Is it Cal?"

He turned the phone for her to read. Her lips tipped up, and she bit the inside of her cheek to keep from laughing. "I'm not great at stealth mode yet."

Mack's laughter filled the hallway, and he put his arm around her shoulders and brushed his lips across her ear. "I'm not complaining."

Her huff was easy to decipher and only made his smirk grow into a full-blown grin. Char had no idea how special she was to him. "Back to the case," she said in the perfunctory tone of an experienced teacher. "The woman."

"Oh, yes, the woman. It doesn't fit, Char."

Her finger came up into his chest. "Maybe not, but you were the one who said removing Bethany from the chain may make him do something rash or unexpected."

"Fair point," he agreed. "I did say that, and this would be rash and unexpected. Hopefully, Mina has something for us by the time Cal gets back to Secure One. Then we can set up a conference call with him to discuss it."

"We need to go to Pennsylvania, Mack."

Her statement was so decisive that he paused on his next thought. "We? Whatever for?"

"I don't know, but my gut tells me we'll find pieces of the puzzle out there."

Mack grasped her shoulders and held her gaze. "This isn't our puzzle to solve. If the feds got wind that we were sticking our nose into this case again, they might lock Cal down, and I don't want that to happen."

"Neither do I, but they aren't doing their job!" she exclaimed in frustration. "They should have solved this case already!"

Mack didn't react to her frustration except to squeeze her shoulder as a reminder that he was there. Once she settled, he spoke gently to her. "I understand you're angry about this case, and you've come by that right naturally. I can separate myself from the case more because I didn't live that kind of life. Then I think about you, and I know in my heart that it could have been you if you'd played the wrong card at the wrong time. The feds may not devote time to this case because the victims are women without families. They don't feel as compelled to solve it quickly since no one is prodding them to keep after it."

"Yes," she said, her shoulders loosening in his grasp. "No one understands that part of it. It could have been me, and I don't want it to be another woman I know. I can't let that happen, Mack."

He nodded with her just to give her a moment to own those feelings of fear and determination. "Okay, let's see what Mina finds, and then we'll talk to Cal about letting us do more boots-on-the-ground work in Pennsylvania. Our turnaround will be quick though, since the party is in ten days, and it all rests on Efren getting here to help out."

"Understood," she agreed with a nod.

Mack couldn't help but wonder if her intuition was correct. If their perp found Little Daddy dead and Bethany gone, would he kill a random woman just to make a point? If Mina's answer to that question was yes, then he wouldn't ask Cal if they could go to Pennsylvania—he'd tell him they were going.

Chapter Seventeen

The two-hour ride was made light by the occasional country road he'd pull over on to be assisted by his assistant. It was a perk none of his colleagues had, but none of them were nearly as brilliant as they thought they were. No one suspected a thing, but he wasn't surprised by that. As someone who studied the human mind, he'd learned that a simple explanation was enough for 99 percent of the population. Thankfully, his interactions with the 1 percent of the population that asked too many questions were few and far between. When he ran across one, he usually had to remove them from the population rather unexpectedly.

He put the car in Park and stared straight ahead. He hated what he was about to do, but there was no choice. It had been four days since he'd had contact with his wingman, and he was worried. Dead was okay. Arrested was not.

"Where are we? There's like, no one out here."

He opened his door and walked around the car to open her door and help her out. He was a gentleman after all. "This is a friend's house," he lied. "I haven't been able to reach him, and I thought someone should check on him."

"The police are closer than a two-hour drive," she pointed out. "They could have done a welfare check."

Shame, he thought. She had been in the 99 percent,

but she just landed herself in the 1 percent. Honestly, he was surprised. He had her pegged for the typical bimbo. After all, she'd been doing his bidding without question for months. Today, she decided to question him. It didn't matter, she wasn't coming home with him anyway, but it was a reminder that he would have to make it clearer to his next assistant never to question him.

He unlocked the door and motioned her through before him. "Wow, you have a key to his house. Are you that close to him?"

"You should ask fewer questions," he said as he walked through the empty house.

"Is he moving? There's no furniture in here."

The man's sigh echoed through the cavernous space. Suddenly, she was *Chatty Cathy*. He rolled his eyes and flipped on the light to the basement, waiting for her to meet him there. When she did, he motioned for her to go down the stairs, but a flash of self-preservation struck. If his guy was down there, and she saw him, she might try to run. He couldn't be chasing her through the woods if he had a job to clean up here. Without a second thought, he shoved her from behind, and she sailed through the air and landed with a thud at the bottom.

He strolled down the stairs and smiled down at her. "Don't go anywhere. I'll be right back."

He stepped over her twisted body and noticed the door at the end of the hall was closed. That was either a good thing or a very bad thing. He dug out the key and stuck it in the lock with a sigh. He had a bad feeling about this, but he pushed the door in and flipped on the light. What he saw was too much to comprehend, and his beast broke free and took over. All he could do was stand there and watch.

CHARLOTTE WAS FIXING Mack and Selina lunch when Mina walked into the kitchen. The man she had with her held himself in a manner that said messing with him was bad for your health.

"Everyone, meet Efren Brenna."

Efren shook hands with everyone while wearing an easy smile. "Thanks for the welcome. I know these are unusual circumstances, but Mina and I go way back. You can trust me to get the job done."

"I could have guarded the women," Selina muttered around the last of her sandwich, and Charlotte lifted a brow but didn't say anything.

"You could have, but we need you to care for Bethany, not worry about her and Ella."

"I have a lot of experience guarding VIPs. I'll take care of the senator's daughter," Efren said, offering Selina a calm smile, but stiffness to his shoulders told Charlotte he was on the defense.

"Aren't we lucky then?" Selina said with an even tighter smile. "I better head back up and do vitals on Bethany. Physically, she's fine, but emotionally and mentally, she needs a facility. When will I be able to transfer her and get the hell out of here?"

Charlotte glanced at Mina, who had also picked up on Selina's catty attitude. Something was up because Selina was never contrary, and you could always depend on her.

"Once Efren is upstairs to replace Eric, I have some updates to share with the team. We may have a question or two to ask her, but it will be safe to find her the help she needs after that."

"Any questions go through me," Selina said, poking herself in the chest while she eyed Efren up and down with disdain. "Call me on the walkie, and I'll ask her. I'm not putting her through another Q and A like this morning."

"That would be fine." Mina's tone of voice was calm and accepting, but Charlotte knew she too was wondering what was going on with their friend. Maybe it was just this place. Everyone was walking on eggshells, wondering when the next body would show up.

Selina glared at Efren before she left the room, and they all looked at each other for a few moments before anyone spoke. "What's wrong with her?" Mack asked. "I don't think I've ever heard her speak to anyone that way."

"Same," Mina said, still staring after their friend. "Maybe this case is getting to her. She's the one who keeps patching these women up." Mina turned to Charlotte. "No offense meant."

"None taken, you're correct. It's got to be hard on Selina. We need this to end. Do you have updates on the last two bodies found?"

"Yes!" Mina said, clapping her hands together. "Let me take Efren up to meet Eric and take over guarding Ella. Then we can all meet to discuss the new information."

"We'll meet you in the office in five minutes," Mack said, carrying his plate to the sink. "Glad to have you on the team, Efren, despite the lack of welcome from some of our members."

"No offense taken," Efren assured them. "I know what it's like to walk into an established team. You have to find your place on it and then earn your stripes. I've done it before, and I can do it again if this assignment is long-term. For now, I'll take care of Ella and help with the party."

He shook Mack's hand again and then left the kitchen behind Mina. Charlotte was about to start cleaning up the dishes, but Mack grasped her elbow to stop her. "Leave them. We have a few minutes, and we need to discuss something."

"Mack, I won't demand that you kiss me again if that's what you're worrie—"

Before she could finish, his lips crashed down on hers and stole her breath away. She could feel the tremble of desire go through him when she opened her mouth and let him in. She planted her hands on his chest to push him away, but with his strong muscles rippling under her hands and his tongue in her mouth, she didn't want to push him away. The thought made her body tingle with heat and desire in a way it never had before. The therapist had tried to help her understand that there was a difference between being with a man she wanted to be with versus being with a man she was forced to be with, but she struggled to understand it until this very moment. Suddenly, she understood that a man who cared would kiss her differently than a man who wanted to take advantage of her.

Charlotte leaned into his chest and sighed. She felt safe with Mack. After all the men she'd had to deal with working for The Madame and The Miss, she never thought she'd feel safe with a man. Especially a man the size and strength of Mack Holbock, but somehow, he had worked himself around her defenses to show her the difference. With the other men, her heart pounded with fear and dread. With Mack, it pounded with want and maybe a little hope that she wasn't too damaged to love someone else.

The kiss ended, but Mack returned twice more for a quick kiss of her lips before he released her for good. "To be clear," he said, with his breath heavy in his chest. "You never have to demand anything from me. I give it to you freely. Understood?"

"You're as clear as water," she whispered, her fingers going to her lips to check if they were still there. The man could kiss, and the heat kicked up fast and furious when he took over her lips. "If that wasn't what you wanted to talk about, what was it?"

Mack motioned for her to sit and leaned in close to her ear. "Are we a team, Char?" Her nod was immediate. "Are you ready to prove it?" He gazed at her with a brow up and waited for her answer. She nodded once, and he grinned as he took her hand. "Then let's go prove it."

AFTER THEY MET with Mina and the rest of the team at lunch, they'd immediately hopped on a flight from Minneapolis to Chicago and from there to Harrisburg, Pennsylvania. Charlotte hadn't asked how Mina managed to get them on flights so quickly because she suspected it wasn't the same way others did. Once they landed in Harrisburg, she had a rental car waiting for them too. Mina was good at her job, but now they had to step up and do the rest.

Mack put the rental car into Park and pulled out his phone. "Mina got us the only room she could find this far out in the sticks. As she put it," he added, glancing at her. They'd been traveling for well over six hours, and she was ready to stretch her legs.

"As long as there's a shower, I don't even care if it's the Bates Motel," she said, bringing a smile to his face.

He chuckled and motioned for her to wait while he grabbed their bags from the back seat and helped her out of the car. They walked toward the small motel to check in, and Charlotte couldn't help but hesitate.

"Everything's okay," Mack promised, putting a protective arm around her waist. "No one is going to hurt you."

"It's not that. It's just the last time I was at one of these motels, it was rent-by-the-hour." She paused and then shook her head. "Never mind."

Mack cocked his head, but before he could say anything, they were at the small check-in area of the motel. There was an empty chair but a light in the room behind it. "Hello? Anyone around?"

A man popped his head out and held up his finger. When he finally came out, he was wearing nothing but a pair of shorts and a tank top. "Sorry about that. You woke me from my beauty sleep. What can I do for you?"

"I'm Mack Holbock. There should be a reservation for us."

"Oh, yes, I only have one room left though. The woman who called didn't think you'd mind."

"No problem at all. We won't be here long."

Charlotte bit her lip to keep from groaning at his choice of words. As though things weren't awkward enough between them, now the man thought she and Mack were getting a room for their secret tryst.

After they had the keys and found the room, Mack opened the door and motioned her in. When he flipped on the light, she was glad he couldn't see the grimace on her face. There was one queen bed in the middle of the room and nothing else. Mack would fill most of that bed by himself. She couldn't imagine having to be that close to him all night and not touch him.

"I'll take the chair. You can have the bed," Mack whispered as he moved around her to set their bags down.

She eyed the chair, and there was no way he would fit

in it, much less sleep in it. "We're adults, Mack. We can share the bed."

"Fine with me if it's fine with you," he said so casually that it felt wrong. "Do you want to shower first, or should I?"

"I'll go." She grabbed her bag and disappeared behind the bathroom door to escape the awkward situation. The shower was hot, but she finished quickly so there was enough hot water left for him. After dressing in her pants and T-shirt, she left the bathroom. "Next."

He gave her a tight smile as he walked around her and disappeared behind the door. She set her bag down on the floor and eyed the small desk he'd already covered with technical equipment from Secure One. She hoped he didn't plan to have another virtual meeting with the team tonight. She wasn't sure she would stay awake for it.

When they'd all met in the office after lunch, Mina had a plethora of information. The couple was found on the riverbank near Southwood, Pennsylvania. When they put that into their map and asked for directions to Sugarville, the town Bethany had stopped at, it was less than an hour's drive away. It made sense that Bethany was probably held somewhere in the same area where the bodies were found. It was sloppy on the part of the killer if that were the case, but if he had bodies to clean up, he might not have had a choice.

It wasn't until they discovered that Senator Tanner from Pennsylvania was not only up for reelection but also on the subcommittee that Cal agreed they needed boots on the ground. If this was The Red River Slayer, he was coming unglued, and the possibility of finding another body in the area was high. He still hadn't hit five other committee members' home states, but they were all on the East Coast. However, Cal didn't think he would stick with his original plan. If the killer felt threatened, he'd go underground just like he had last time. He'd have had to get rid of the two bodies, assuming the man was Little Daddy, but he would likely be highly cautious for some time now.

All they needed was a little time and a break to lead them to the house where Bethany was kept. Charlotte didn't know for sure, but her gut told her the man found in the river today was Little Daddy. They didn't know the identities of either person, but Mina was going to keep them abreast of any updates as they came in. In the meantime, she and Mack would use a grid-like search of the area to find the house. It was a long shot, and they didn't have much time, but they couldn't sit around and do nothing.

Cal was afraid Bethany wouldn't be safe until The Red River Slayer was found. It was a thought that hadn't entered her mind, but he was right. Since they didn't know who he was, they couldn't protect her if she wasn't with them. Selina wasn't happy about the delay in transferring her care and made it known, which was highly unusual. It was a rare occasion when someone questioned Cal's authority, but Selina kept pushing the yard line until he agreed to bring a therapist in to meet with Bethany. Selina still left the meeting with a huff, and Charlotte was worried there was something more going on with her.

For right now though, she didn't have time to worry about anything but locating The Red River Slayer. Women everywhere were in danger and weren't even aware of it. They could be snatched off the street by this sicko and never be seen again until they floated to shore. Charlotte wouldn't let that happen. She was here with Mack not only to prove herself to Cal and the team but to herself. Cal wanted to send Eric instead of her, but Mack insisted he needed a woman with him to soften their questioning. When Cal finally agreed, she was sure Eric gave her a death glare. Something was up with the Secure One team, and she hoped they'd be able to pull off the senator's campaign party without showing dissent in the ranks. If anything happened at that party to endanger a sitting senator or their family, there would be hell to pay, and it would be Cal's head on the chopping block. She and Mack were needed in Minnesota, so time was of the essence. She just hoped when they returned to the state, it wasn't in a body bag.

Chapter Eighteen

The shifting of the woman on top of him was torture. Mack had to figure out a way to slide her back down onto the bed and off his chest before she woke up from the hard rod poking her in the belly. He'd seen the look on her face when she saw the one bed in the room, and it was easy to imagine what she was thinking. He never wanted Char to feel like he didn't respect her or her body. He did, and he'd bend over backward to prove it, even if that meant standing in the corner to sleep. At least the corner gave him better odds of getting shut-eye than being in bed with her on top of him. Her soft, sweet body warmed his skin, and he wanted to let his hands roam over her back and waist to cup her tight backside. He'd dreamed about touching her that way for months, but he wouldn't. She wasn't ready for that kind of relationship yet.

She's not ready, or you're not ready?

Mack tried not to groan at the voice just as she murmured his name.

"Why are you sleeping with a gun?"

He grunted with unabashed amusement. "Sweetheart, that's not my gun. I'm just happy to see you."

The warmth he'd cherished disappeared when she sat up in bed to rub her face.

"In my defense, you were on top of me when I woke up. I wanted to move you but didn't want to wake you."

"What time is it?"

"Only three a.m. Go back to sleep."

"As though that's going to happen," she muttered. She scooted closer to the edge of the bed. "I'm sorry for," she waved her hand over his groin, "that. It wasn't intentional."

"I know," he promised. He patiently rubbed Char's back while she gathered her thoughts. "You were scared and needed someone, which is why I climbed into bed and didn't sleep in the chair."

"I'm not scared of you, Mack," she said, crossing her arms over her chest, but he noticed she didn't ask him to remove his hand.

"I didn't say of me, but I saw the look on your face when we approached the building tonight. You were scared."

"The last time I was in a place like this, I was forced to do things to *earn my keep*, as The Miss used to say. Those men saw me as nothing more than a way to scratch an itch or to have control over someone smaller than them."

He paused. "I bet Mina didn't think about it when she booked the room. I'm sorry. We should have been more considerate."

Her blond hair swayed across her back when she shook her head and it brushed over his already hyperaware skin. "Don't worry about it. There wasn't much choice if we wanted to sleep for the night. Not that we're getting much sleep."

"Hey," Mack said, sitting up and wrapping his arm around her side to pull her into him. "Take a moment to feel your feelings, okay? I know you're trying to take your power back, but sometimes you have to acknowledge the past and how it shaped you. Some experiences in life leave scars on our minds. When that happens, we'll always struggle in that situation. It's understandable, and I accept you no matter what, Char."

Slowly, her head lowered to his shoulder, and she sighed. "You're talking about PTSD."

"I suppose I am. I don't know many who have fought battles in war who don't have it in one form or another."

"Maybe for soldiers, but I wasn't a soldier."

"Oh, darling, you absolutely were," he whispered, resting his cheek on her head. "You lived through those battles, but just like mine, they left scars. My battles were more straightforward. I knew my enemy, and I had a lethal weapon to defend myself. You had neither of those things. All you had were your wits and a prayer."

"My wits kept me alive, but the prayers didn't work," she murmured, burrowing her head into his chest.

"You'll never have to use your wits with me. I'll never tell you to let it go or get over it. I'm a safe zone for you to feel what you need to feel, Char."

When she laughed, there was no humor behind it. "But you aren't safe, Mack," she whispered. "When we're together, the things I feel are confusing. When you kiss me, there's so much emotion in my chest that I don't know what to do with it."

"Confusing good or confusing bad?"

"Good, but also bad. I like how you make me feel, and I like being with you, but I also know you deserve someone who hasn't fought battles while unarmed and outmanned."

Mack kissed the top of her head. He wanted to connect with her again, if only briefly. "Life doesn't work that way, Char. I will live with my disability for the rest of my life.

What if I said you deserve better than being with someone who can't walk without strapping on braces every morning? Would you agree and walk away?"

"Of course not." Her eyes sparked with anger as she sat up to glare at him. "The scars on your legs don't make you less than anyone else. They're just part of you."

"More proof that life doesn't work that way. When we connect with another soul, that's all that matters."

Char was silent for so long he thought she'd fallen asleep as he rubbed her back. "Do you think our souls have connected?" she whispered. "Like, do you think soulmates exist?"

"Do soulmates exist? Yes. I only have to look at Cal and Marlise. Did our souls connect?" he asked, running a finger down her cheek. "The moment I took you in my arms."

"Mack, will you show me what you mean? I learn better that way."

When he gazed into her eyes, the truth was obvious. She wanted him to show her the connection. He scooted backward on the bed until he could lean against the headboard and then pulled her onto his lap to straddle him. "If you get uncomfortable or scared, tell me to stop."

Her only response was to capture his lips and press herself against his chest. She wrapped her arms around his neck and buried her fingers in his hair. He held her around the waist, her warmth a balm to his injured soul while he searched for a foothold on this slippery slope. He was afraid he'd fall over the edge and do something he shouldn't. But her kisses and caresses made him want more. They made him want to be more for her even when she didn't ask. He still wanted to give her everything.

The need for air overtook his desire to keep caress-

ing her tongue. He let his lips fall away from hers to trail
down her neck to her collarbone. He suckled gently, raising goose bumps on her flesh as he made love to her with
his lips. He tugged her T-shirt lower to kiss the tender skin
at the base of her neck. Her pulse raced beneath his lips
because of him. For him. With him.

"Mack," she moaned, the sound of his name airy on
her lips. "I want more." To make her point, she rubbed
her hips against his desire, dragging a moan from him.

He didn't want to hurt her. He also didn't know if he
could make love to her and walk away when the inevitable
happened. The old saying about it better to have loved and
lost came back to him, and he suckled hard on her chest,
leaving his mark where only she would see.

While she was lost in the sensation of his lips, he slid
his hand under her shirt. His fingertips skirted across her
ribs to the edge of her breast. She stilled, so he did too,
waiting for her to decide what she wanted.

"I want you, Mack, but I don't know if I can do it. I
want to, but I can't promise—"

With his finger to her lips, he hushed her. "I understand, sweetheart. You don't have to do anything. That's
not why we're here tonight. I'm safe. I won't take more
than you can give. You're in control of everything."

It was as though she needed to hear him validate her
fears and desire in a way that put her in control. He saw the
shift in her when she remembered that she could trust him
to stop if she said stop. And he would, even if it killed him
to hold her until she fell asleep and nothing else. He would.
He would protect her, whether on the job or in his bed.

Before he could clear his head of the thoughts running
through it, Charlotte lowered her lips again and drank

from his, her desire no longer capped by fear but fanned by trust.

Trust.

The word hit him in the gut as she leaned back and stripped her T-shirt off, revealing her perfectly taut nipples waiting for his attention. He took a few moments to appreciate her beauty and learn her curves, picturing the path his tongue would take from her nipple to her navel and then if she was ready, lower still. "You are gorgeous," he whispered, his finger trailing down her ribs. "I want all of you, Char."

"Even the broken parts?" she asked in a whisper that made his chest clench from an emotion he didn't want to acknowledge.

"Especially the broken parts."

Then her lips were back on his, and he knew, given enough time and trust, they'd heal each other.

"SECURE TWO, WHISKEY." Mina's voice filled the room, and Mack scrambled to answer before she hung up.

"Secure one, Mike."

The tablet came to life, and Mina's face filled the screen. "Good morning, early birds," she said, her trained eye taking in Charlotte on the bed as she tied on her shoes. It was the reason she insisted on making the bed rather than leaving the bedclothes rumpled.

"Good morning, Mina. Do you have an update?" Mack asked. "We were just making a plan of attack."

"Glad I caught you then," she said, typing on her computer as she spoke. Charlotte was always in awe of how she could do both and not lose track of either. "I have an identity on the man found in the river yesterday."

"Seriously?" Charlotte stood up and walked closer to the tablet. "That was fast."

"Fast, but not helpful. His name is Chip Winston."

"Did you run specs on him?" Mack asked, strapping on his gun belt and vest.

"I did, but lo and behold, he doesn't exist except on paper."

"Washed?" Charlotte asked with surprise. "How is that possible?"

"I don't know, but I'm still digging. Someone washed him, but I don't believe he was CIA or FBI. I can't say for sure though."

"What about the woman?"

"Police haven't had any hits on her, and I'm still waiting to pilfer the autopsy photos so I can run facial recognition. But if Winston is washed, I don't have high hopes."

"None of this makes sense," Mack said, his fist bouncing against his leg as he paced. "I don't buy that it's unrelated, but he's never dumped a male body before."

"He's never dumped two locked together before either," Mina pointed out. "It makes me wonder if he had to get rid of the body and wanted to throw the cops off so they wouldn't link the two victims to him."

"Possible," Mack said with a head tilt and then paused in his pacing.

"Likely if the man is Little Daddy," Charlotte said, still incredibly aware of Mack's maleness every time he got near her. "If he came up with no past, I'm inclined to believe it's him."

"Me too," Mina agreed. "I'm trying to get an autopsy photo of him to show to Bethany."

"Is that smart?" Mack asked before Charlotte could say anything. "She said she never saw his face."

"The eyes don't lie," Charlotte whispered, and Mina pointed at her through the camera.

"The eyes don't lie. A woman will always recognize the eyes of the person who hurt her."

Mack glanced at Charlotte. She knew what he was thinking, so she smiled. He hadn't hurt her last night. If anything, he healed another little piece of her.

"In the meantime, I found six properties within twenty miles of where the bodies were found that are owned by holding companies. I will send the addresses to your GPS unit."

"Are they rented or empty?" Charlotte asked, grabbing her gun belt from the bed and strapping it on. Mack was insistent that they both be armed, so she had no choice but to wear it today. She still didn't like carrying a gun, but she'd come to realize that sometimes they were necessary to protect those you cared about—and she cared about Mack.

"I'm still trying to get a bead on all of that. For now, approach with caution."

"Affirmative," Mack said, holstering his gun.

"You're not going to approach the houses dressed like that, are you?" Mina asked, her head shaking. "You'll get shot."

"If that's the case, at least we'll know we found the right house." Mack's statement was tongue-in-cheek but didn't make Charlotte feel better. He glanced between the two women and rolled his eyes. "I was kidding. When people see someone dressed in all black with a flak jacket, security logo and a gun, they automatically see you as an authority figure. It might help us get information from neighbors who surround these places."

"Sounds like you have your work cut out for you. I'll stay in touch via your phone. If I call, answer it, no matter what. It could mean life or death depending on what comes through in the next few hours."

"Ten-four. Mike out."

Mina gave a beauty queen wave, and then the screen went black, plunging them into silence. They had to get going if they were going to check out all six houses today. Charlotte grabbed her things and followed Mack to their rental.

"Ready?" Mack asked, straightening her vest. "Remember, head on a swivel and stay behind me until we know the house is empty."

"I got it, Mack," she promised, offering him a smile. Less than two hours ago, they were exploring each other's bodies. He'd been a gentle and patient lover, but she still couldn't give him what he wanted, what he needed. Not in a seedy motel. Her time in places like this one had left scars too deep to overcome last night. She'd helped him reach a satisfying conclusion, but she knew it wasn't how he'd hoped.

"Stop," he whispered, leaning into her ear to kiss it. "What did we talk about this morning?"

"That you have no expectations, and I have the control over any relationship we have."

"And do you believe that, or are you just repeating it back to me?"

She paused for a minute to gaze into his chocolate eyes. "I believe it." He raised a brow. "I believe it." The words were firm and loud. "I believe in you, Mack, and I trust you."

He pulled her to him by her vest and took her lips in a too-short kiss. "Now I believe you. We're in this together, Char. Let's find this killer and return to our lives at Secure One."

"Ten-four, Char out," she said with a wink as she climbed into the car and prepared for battle.

Chapter Nineteen

The first three houses had been a waste of time. There were two without basements, and the third one was rented by a lovely family who was scared to see the "police" arrive. Charlotte had quickly assured them they had done nothing wrong, but after chatting with them, it was easy to see they knew nothing. Mack was frustrated but determined to find the rest of the properties even if it was a waste of time. They'd managed to avoid the actual police, and he was glad the place wasn't crawling with FBI agents. If he had to guess, he'd say the police hadn't tied the two victims to The Red River Slayer, so they hadn't called in the feds. He was starting to think this was a wild goose chase.

A glance at the passenger seat reminded him to trust his gut. Char was, so he'd follow her lead. The couple had gone into the river relatively close to where they were found, considering the time of death. Earlier, they'd parked off the beaten path and used high-powered binoculars to scope out the crime scene. Mack noticed a reedy area that could have trapped the bodies if he'd dumped them in just a little farther upstream. He hoped Mina would get them more information before they had to return for Dorian's party. They had one more night here, two at best, before they'd have to leave for Minnesota.

He slid his gaze to Char for a moment before focusing back on the road. Last night had been special. In his mind, they had made love. Maybe not in the traditional sense, but she had learned to trust him with her body. He always knew baby steps would be required when teaching her about intimacy, and he was okay with that. They were a team, no matter what.

He couldn't help but think how gorgeous she was in the light of the noon sun, but he knew he could never be with her once she healed. Despite the things he told her about healing and hope, none of it applied to him. He would live the rest of his life knowing what he did, but he couldn't ask someone else to live it too. He didn't deserve a family. Not when one died because of his mistakes.

Mack waited for his gut to clench at the thought of that day as it usually did. He waited for another mile but still nothing. He tried to drag the memory up front and center, but all he could see was her curves in the moonlight, and all he could hear was the sound of her moans in his ear.

"You broke the rules." His voice was harsh and needy inside the car, and he cleared his throat. "I told you to stay behind me."

Char rolled her eyes, but he pretended not to notice. "We were approaching a house with a woman and two little kids outside. I didn't want her calling the cops before we could talk to them. Sometimes, you have to know when to lead and when to follow, Mack."

Her sentence was pointed, and then she fell silent. Maybe she could sense the anxiety rolling off him about the case and what happened last night. Would last night change their working relationship once they returned to Secure One? He'd like to say no, but he knew better. He could pretend it didn't affect him, but every time he saw her, he'd know he could never have her. He slammed his palm down on the steering wheel with disgust.

"Everything okay?" Her question was meek and worried, so he forced himself to relax. He didn't want to scare her.

"I'm just frustrated," he said with resignation. "This guy is out there killing people, and we're running all over creation on a wild goose chase."

"We don't know that it's a wild goose chase, and besides, at least we're doing something. That's more than we can say for the authorities. Did they ever get anything out of the guy who tried to kidnap Ella?"

Before he could stop himself, his thumb came up to trace the bruise across the bottom of her chin. The bruising on her face had turned to a sickly yellow as it started to fade, but it never detracted from her beauty.

"No. The guy took his right to remain silent and has done so, but Mina is looking into his background. She has to be careful since Secure One is also wrapped up in that situation."

"Secure One is wrapped up in many situations, it seems."

"We're a security company," he said with a shrug. "It's bound to happen when you have high-profile clients. This won't be the last tangle we have with law enforcement, but we earn our stripes with them by cooperating and working together."

"I thought the feds didn't want us involved in this."

"I'm not talking about the feds. They're entirely different animals as far as cooperation and working together. They don't and won't."

Mack noticed the smirk on Char's face before she spoke.

"I wonder if they know one of their former agents is the one who gets us the information."

"I'm sure they often look the other way regarding what Mina does. Roman figures that they don't come down on her because they can't prove she's hacking their system."

"Mina thinks they feel guilty for what happened with her boss and The Madame."

"That could be too," Mack said on a shrug. "They owe that woman more than they can ever repay her. Besides, they know if anyone can figure out what's going on, it's Mina Jacobs."

"True story," Char said with a smile. "Are we almost to the next place?"

"About two miles out. We have two on this side of Sugarville and one a few miles outside of town. After we stop at these two, we'll look around Sugarville for something to eat and a little information."

"Lunch with a side of snooping. I'm in," she said, throwing him a wink that sank low in his belly and reminded him just how empty his life would be without her.

CHARLOTTE CLIMBED FROM the car and stretched. She'd taken the flak jacket and gun belt off after the last house was nothing more than rubble. She'd put it back on after lunch, but if they wanted to blend in and get information about Bethany or the people in the river, they couldn't look like cops. She eyed Mack as he pumped gas. That was going to be harder for him than for her. Maybe she should take the lead and do the talking.

When they'd pulled into Sugarville, Mack had pointed out the service station as the one Bethany had used the night she ran away. He'd even smiled for the first time all day when he saw the truck parked next to the station. He said Bethany would be pleased to know they got it back. Bethany would be pleased, but Charlotte wasn't. Since they'd climbed out of bed this morning, Mack had been distant and gruff. She tried to tell herself he was just frustrated by the case, but part of her knew that was a lie. Before the sun rose, he had already pulled away from her and climbed back inside his armor.

A warmth slid through her at the thought of their night together. She never intended to fall into bed with him, but their connection was too strong to ignore when they were alone. How he touched, kissed and cared about her spoke volumes about him. Mack wanted to pretend he was hardened by war and unwilling or unable to care about someone now, but that was all it was. Pretending. She knew the war had changed him. Shaped him. Hurt him. But all of that made him more empathetic and in touch with people's emotions. He'd have to come to that realization by himself though.

They walked into the tiny gas station to pay for their fuel. With any luck, they'd learn a bit of information from the attendant as well. A man turned from the back counter when they walked in.

"Welcome to Sugarville Service Center. Find everything you need, folks?"

"Sure did," Mack said with an easy smile. Charlotte noticed he did that whenever they wanted information. She could picture soldier Mack doing the same thing. She'd tell him anything he wanted to know if he flashed that smile at her. "I noticed the old truck by the station. Is that a '61 Ford?"

A grin lit the man's face as he took Mack's money to

cash him out. "Sure is. It's been a workhorse all these years. It was stolen, and I nearly cried when I discovered it was gone. I was never more surprised than when the sheriff from two towns over drove it back to me. It wasn't even damaged."

"Sounds like some kids took it for a joyride."

"Could be. The police said people near where it was abandoned saw a woman get out of it and take off on foot. I tell myself she was in trouble, and the truck got her to safety. That way, I don't get too mad about her stealing it."

Mack dipped his head in agreement, but his gaze slid to Charlotte's for a moment. "I'm glad you got it back." He took his change from the man and motioned outside. "We're looking at some property and heard there was a house for sale up the way here. I'm having difficulty finding it on my GPS though."

The man shook his head for a moment before he spoke. "No houses for sale that I know of unless they're selling the old Hennessy place. Last I heard, it was in probation. No, what's the word?"

"Probate?"

He pointed at Mack. "That's it. Probate. Old man Hennessy died years ago, and nothing has happened with it since. Maybe it is for sale now, but I'm usually the first to know if a place goes up. I wouldn't buy it though."

"Bad water or foundation?" Mack asked, stepping closer as though he were ready for some hot tea to spill.

"Bad juju," he said, looking over Mack's shoulder to the door. "We call it the murder house around here. Someone should have torn it down long ago. Nothing good is going to come from that place. Years ago, a young couple rented the place. Their lives ended in a murder-suicide with a young baby in the house. By the time they found the couple way out there in the woods, the youngster was nearly dead from lack of food and water. It was an ugly scene, but the landlord, old man Hennessy, wouldn't part with the place. He kept saying one day he'd clean it up and sell it. He may have cleaned it up, but he never sold it. He just let it sit empty. I'm still hoping they tear it down. Nothing good comes from land tainted with that kind of violence."

A shiver ran through Charlotte. *Nothing good comes from land tainted with that kind of violence.* Something told her he was right.

THE ALLURE OF a hot meal lured them into the small café. Mack's stomach grumbled from hunger, and he was ready to dive into a plate of whatever the server set in front of him. He wasn't picky. The army had cured him of that. MREs were no joke, and you learned quickly that the hot sauce was there for a reason. Besides, when you're hungry and hunkered down, trying not to get shot, you don't care what you put in your mouth as long as it keeps you alive long enough to escape.

"What did Mina say?" Charlotte asked when they slid into a booth.

"She's looking into it. She said the house is now owned by a holding company, which contradicts what the service station guy said."

"I didn't get too far in school, so I don't know what a holding company does."

The look on her face told him she was embarrassed to admit that, but he was proud of her for asking questions rather than wondering what things meant.

Stop it. You cannot be proud of this woman. She is not yours.

After a firm reminder to himself, he answered her. "A holding company is a business that owns, holds, sells or leases real estate. They get paid multiple different ways depending on the property. If a holding company owns the property in question, there were likely no heirs to leave it to, or the heirs didn't want to deal with the property, so they sold it to a holding company."

"Is it a way to hide properties you don't want people to know you own?"

Mack made the so-so hand. "It takes longer to find the owner, but the information is still there. On the surface, yes, if you don't dig any deeper."

"But Mina will dig to the bottom."

He tossed her a wink as the server approached them to take their order. After ordering a burger and fries with a cold pop, they waited for the server to return with their drinks. Mack had his phone on the bench, awaiting Mina's call or text. He had a bad feeling about this place, and the last thing he wanted was to put Char in the middle of an ambush. He forced his mind to slow and remember that the house was probably crumbling like all the others.

The server brought their drinks and set them down. "Can I get you anything else?"

Mack promptly picked up his glass and took a long swallow, giving Char the chance to jump in. "Actually," she said, holding up her finger. "Do you know anything about the murder house?"

Mack cringed, but rather than shut her down or try to smooth it over, he decided to wait her out. Sometimes shock value was the best value.

"You shouldn't be asking after that place now," the server said in an accent that made Mack smile. "Nothing good gonna come by talking about it."

Charlotte smiled the smile he'd seen before when she was summoning patience from within herself. "We are here to represent the property owners and just wanted to get a feel from the locals before we went out there."

This time Mack opened his mouth to jump in because the last thing he wanted was to have the actual holding company find out someone was impersonating them. He snapped his jaw shut when the server started to speak. After all, they wouldn't be here long enough for anyone to know who they were anyway.

"Oh, I see, ya," she said, putting her hands on her hips. "Well, that place has been empty so long that it should be torn down. Who'd want to live there anyway? Devil worship and rituals, sex rings and murders. I'm glad it's hidden in the woods, so we don't have to look at it."

Mack raised a brow at Charlotte as if to say, *Next question.* She didn't disappoint him.

"Devil worship and sex rings? We knew about the deaths and the poor baby inside the house, but devil worship? You don't say?"

"The seventies were wild times," she said with a shake of her head. "The locals say the pentagram is still on the wooden floor in the living room. Before the owner put up a gate, kids used to go out there huntin' ghosts. The new generation doesn't bother it now, but the stories will be campfire legends forever."

"I see," Charlotte said with a smile. "Thank you for your candidness."

"No problem. Your food will be up in a few minutes."

The waitress turned away, and Mack waited until she had disappeared behind the counter before he leaned in and spoke to Char. "Excellent interrogation. Just be careful about misrepresenting us. We don't want that to roll back on Secure One."

She sipped from her pop, her perfectly pink lips wrapped around the straw, and his groin tightened at the thought of them being wrapped around him. Working with her but not having her was going to be the greatest torture he'd ever been through, and he knew torture.

"We won't be here long enough for anyone to know the truth," she said with a shrug. "A little white lie was warranted. I took a chance."

Mack leaned back in the booth but couldn't wipe the smirk off his face. He was so damn proud of this woman, and no matter how much he told himself not to be, he couldn't help it.

"So now we know there's a gate," she said, pulling him from his thoughts. "How do we plan to get around that?"

"Go in from the backside." His answer was simple, but the execution would be more difficult. "I'm not pulling a rental car up the driveway and hopping a fence. We don't know if they have cameras on the place or a security system. It won't be an easy walk through the woods, but it will give us the advantage of checking out the property before we step foot on it."

"I'm ready," she assured him. "Or I will be after I down that burger and fries. Breakfast left me unsatisfied, but I guess that was my fault. I'll make sure you get a raincheck." She threw in a wink that said she was serious.

Mack groaned, partly at the memory of her body under his hands and partly because he wanted that raincheck more than anything else in this world. He was already on a slippery slope, and making love to her would have him tumbling right into love with her. That couldn't happen.

Chapter Twenty

Charlotte followed Mack through the woods, and the sun filtered down through the heavy overhang of leaves this time of year. Under her feet, the earth was spongy, and with every step, she sank deeper and deeper into the history of this house. If even some of the stories about this house were true, it should be torn down. No one should live in a place with that kind of violence. She stumbled, nearly face-planting on a fallen tree, until Mack grabbed her vest and stopped her fall.

"Careful, sweetheart," he whispered, his voice husky instead of gruff. "I don't want to carry you out of here on a stretcher."

She looked up at him and smiled with a nod before they started moving again. According to his GPS, they should be getting close to the property line. Charlotte could see nothing but trees, leaves and shadows of light and dark. She couldn't deny that she was creeped out being encased in the woods on their way to a murder house. Who wouldn't be?

Mack held up his hand, so she held her position, waiting for him to tell her what to do. He pointed to his right and then motioned to a fallen log. They walked to it and sat, using the log as back support. He pulled out his phone and flipped open the top. It might look like an old-fashioned flip phone, but it was as high-tech as they came. It was text, call and GPS sensors and trackers.

"Has Mina sent more information yet?"

"That's why I stopped. The property is just through those trees, but before we approach, I want to know if there's a security fence."

He opened the text app and read silently for a moment, a heavy sigh escaping as he hit two buttons and then snapped the phone shut.

"Bad news?" she asked, his posture now soldier-straight.

"More like Mina was able to confirm what the waitress said. All of it. The house has been abandoned, and the holding company plans to take it down and sell the land. The couple who lived there were known to be devil worshippers, and the townspeople weren't happy about it. Especially when they found out the couple held rituals on the land and near the river. The police suspect the murder-suicide was staged, but they could never prove it."

"Staged? As in someone else killed them both?"

"Exactly," he said, grasping his lower lip as a shiver went down her spine. "The townsfolk may have had enough and taken them out, shifting the blame to the guy as the shooter."

"It wouldn't be hard to do that, I suppose," Charlotte said. "Disgusting and wrong, but not hard."

"And with a baby in the house," he said, his teeth clenched. He had seen atrocities done to families and children while in the service. Sometimes, the human race angered him beyond words.

"They may not have known the baby was there if it

was sleeping," she mused. "Regardless of all of that, what about a security system?"

"None that Mina could find. There's the gate to stop interlopers and a fence that fell years ago, but no one bothered to repair it. We'll approach with our eyes open and look for signs of recent use before we go in. If I say fall back, you do it. Do not question it. Agreed?"

"Agreed," she said as they stood and stepped over the log, heading for the small knoll that would let them look down on the property before they tried to walk in.

Driving in and parking the car in the driveway would be much simpler but too obvious. Secure One preferred ghost status. If they could get in and out with the information for the team without leaving a trace, it would be worth the long walk through the woods. When they got to the knoll, they rested on their bellies while Mack surveyed the property with his binoculars. They couldn't see a car, but the property was too overrun with vines and leaves to look for tracks from this far away.

"Hey," Charlotte said when he put away the binoculars. "What happened to the kid?"

"Mina hit a dead end with that one. The baby was taken to the hospital, nursed back to health and then adopted. The adoption was closed due to the crime and stigma, so no one knows where the baby ended up." Mack reached for his pants at that moment. "Just got a text." He pulled out the phone and checked it, his brow going up this time while he read. "They identified the woman. Her name is May Rosenburg. She's from Philly. She lived on the streets and had a sheet for minors like theft and prostitution. She was reported missing by a friend about two years ago, but no one has seen her since."

"That means he held her about the same amount of time as Bethany," Charlotte said, her heart in her throat. "Maybe she was the woman who went to Big Daddy when Bethany first arrived. She may have been told by Little Daddy to use a different name, just like Bethany."

"Feels like it. Bethany never saw her face, so it won't help to ask her. The problem is the couple's cause of death."

"They weren't strangled?" she asked, and Mack shook his head.

"No. May had a broken neck and what looked like recent trauma to her body. Chip died of cerebral edema and a head wound."

"If it is The Red River Slayer, something happened that threw him off, and he just had to get rid of the bodies."

"Little Daddy," Mack said with conviction. "I bet he found Little Daddy locked in the room where Bethany left him. Why May would have a broken neck, I can't say."

"If this is him, he's coming apart at the seams, that's why," Charlotte muttered. "Can we go check this place out so we can leave? I don't like the air here."

"Me either." He helped her up so they could start down the hill. "It reminds me of this one time in the sandbox when we were guarding a village. There was a rumor among the locals that a witch put a spell on the town that required bloodshed every twelve and a half days. You felt the blood on the ground under your feet and tasted the copper on your tongue. The evil seeped into your soul. That's what this place reminds me of."

As they approached the house from behind, a cold shiver of dread worked its way down her spine. The place may be empty of souls, but the evil remained. He motioned for her to follow him to the back of the house, where he plastered himself along the door. After looking through the window, he stepped around her, and she followed as he walked to the edge of the house.

"I've seen no cameras, and the kitchen was empty," he whispered as they walked around the side. He paused to peer in every window and ran a hand across his neck before he went to the next one. At the edge of the building, he searched for cameras on the eaves or near the front door. "No cameras on the front of the house. No tire tracks. There's a concrete walkway, so there is no way to check for footprints. Stay tight to the house, and we'll check windows."

She nodded, and they slid around the corner. Mack ducked his head around the edge of the first window and gave her another hand gesture. He pointed for her to stop by the concrete steps leading to the front door. He climbed them quietly and looked through the sheer curtain that hung over the window. He gave her a headshake and a gesture to come around the steps and meet him on the other side. She followed him around the house as he looked in the windows until they got to the back of the house again.

"The house is old and empty. There's a basement, but didn't Bethany say she went out a door in the basement and ran?"

"That's what she said. Is there an old-fashioned cellar door in the yard?" she whispered, afraid to speak at full volume in case they weren't alone.

"I didn't see one, but that doesn't mean it isn't there. We're here. I say we go in."

"Is that smart without backup?" Charlotte asked, her stomach tossing the hamburger and fries around like a blender. Her nerves were taut, and she didn't like the feel of the place.

"No one is around, and Mina is monitoring us on the GPS link. We'll take a quick peek and then head that direction to the river." He pointed straight ahead through the trees from the back of the house. "It can't be far."

"I don't hear the water though."

"It's a slough, so you wouldn't." He pulled out a kit from his vest, but she stopped his hand before he could pick open the door.

"Shouldn't one of us stand guard?"

"In and out. I'll check the basement while you aim your gun at the top of the stairs. Shoot anyone who shows their face because it will be no one good. Got it?"

"Understood," she said and waited while he picked open the door. She understood it, but she didn't like it.

THEY SHOULDN'T BE HERE. The hair on the back of Mack's neck stood up as they crept through the house. It was empty, of that he had no doubt, but the evil permeated the air like a black fog. Mack held up until Charlotte bumped into him. They were walking back-to-back, keeping both exits covered, just in case.

"We're running on the assumption that the basement is clear, but you know what they say about assuming. Can you walk down backward, or do you want me to?"

"I can," she whispered, and he noticed her avert her eyes from the faded pentagram on the floor.

He twisted the knob on the basement and swung his gun down the stairs, the filtered lights from the windows illuminating the floor below. It was finished with worn '70s carpet and smelled of mildew and pine cleaner. It appeared empty. His mind's eye was still stuck on that pentagram as he started the slow and careful trek down the stairs. He swung his gun in both directions of the open stairway, being slow and cautious to ensure Char could keep up with him.

You shouldn't be here.

The warning was louder in his mind this time, and he shook his head, forcing his heart to slow and stop pounding so loudly he couldn't hear his own thoughts. His boots hit the carpet, and he paused, waiting for Char to take her position with her gun aimed at the stairs. He looked right and left, noticing a utility room with a washer, dryer, hot plate and old fridge in avocado-green. It had been new fifty years ago. His trained eye took in the washer and dryer, and he swallowed around the nervousness in his chest. The doors hung open on the machines, and a bottle of laundry soap sat atop one. They had been used recently.

He motioned to Char that he was going down the hallway to the right, and she nodded her agreement but kept her concentration on the stairs. They hadn't found a second set of stairs or a door to the outside, which meant this probably wasn't the house Bethany had been held hostage in, but he wasn't taking any chances until he knew that for sure.

His gun braced on his flashlight, he turned the beam on and aimed it waist height, swinging it left and right to glance in the open doors as he walked down the hallway. The first door was a small room with a bed and nothing else. The carpet was newer, but the bedding was brand new.

He walked to the next room and swung his flashlight inside. It was a bathroom. There was a toilet, shower and vanity. The floral print shower curtain hung open, and he could smell the fancy soaps from the door. He ducked into the room and took a deep breath before he opened the sink cabinet. Feminine supplies were stacked on the bottom, and a nearly silent grunt left his lips. The garbage can was empty, and the shower was dry. No one had been here recently.

Mack swung out the door, and the flashlight beam flashed off a doorknob at the end of the hallway. It wasn't open like the rest of the doors in the basement, which meant it could be a closet or a door leading out of the basement. There was a doormat on the carpet below the door. Not a closet. With his gun pointed ahead, he glanced backward at Char, still braced to shoot with total concentration. Once he checked the last room, he'd see if the other door led to a set of stairs. If it did, he'd grab Char, and they'd follow them to see where they went.

The third room in the hallway was bigger. Mack stepped in and swept his light in an arc. The room was in shambles. Shattered dishes were strewn across the floor, a broken table and a bed with sheets and blankets sliding onto the floor. He could see that the bedding and dishes were modern, which meant they'd been bought long after the appliances.

It's time to leave.

The voice was right, but not before he got solid proof that this house was where Bethany had been held. He walked to the bed and lifted the bedsheets to see lines of four scratches slashed out by a fifth, repeating across the wood in a macabre pattern of desperation. He stood and lowered his flashlight to the floor long enough to get his phone. He'd take a picture, and then they were heading straight to the authorities with what they knew.

He checked the door and then knelt to take the picture, the low light making it difficult, so he set his gun down on the bed and picked up his flashlight. Something tickled his nose, and he sniffed. There was a soft swish of fabric, and he turned, expecting Char. Instead, a crack of pain was followed by encroaching blackness around his head. He fell to the floor and slumped over as the door to the room slammed shut and the lock engaged.

I told you we shouldn't be here.

THE GASOLINE MADE a satisfying sound as it spilled onto the ground around the house. It was time to burn this place down the way it should have been years ago. Was he taking a chance that the rest of the town would go up with it? Sure, but that'd be fine too. Let everyone in this town burn for the sins of their parents. Things were getting a little hot for him here anyway. He chuckled at his joke as he stood in the middle of the yard with the can. He'd allow himself the joy of staging a dramatic scene for the towns-people first. *This would be the most fitting tribute of all though*, he thought as he poured the gasoline, following the lines in his mind to draw the pentagram. It always came back to the blackness in his soul. He couldn't get rid of it. He'd been born with it, and no matter how hard his parents tried, they couldn't cast it out of him. And they'd tried so many times. He had flashbacks to the priest toss-ing the holy water on him repeatedly until he was drip-ping wet. He was never saved because he was owned by the darkness, and he would remain there until he died.

He proved that when he killed his parents in broad day-light and tossed them in the river the day he turned eigh-teen. They were never found, which didn't surprise him, considering where he'd dumped them. The hardest part had been playing the woeful son who didn't know why his parents hadn't returned from vacation. They'd never found their car, and after thirty years, they never would.

The match flared to life, and he tossed it into the middle of the design, the beast inside roaring as the design came to life in flames of beauty. The heat seared his skin, and he took several steps back, watching as it licked and burned until it ran out of fuel to stay alive. He took the can back to the garage and slipped inside, stowing it in the front of the garage where it would only add to the inferno once he touched a match to this piece of his history. People thought him to be so normal and morally upstanding, but they had never seen the beast that lived within him. They had, but they didn't know those women in the river were offerings from the beast himself.

One final walk down these steps, and he'd say goodbye to the piece of his childhood that had shaped him as a man. This house had nearly killed him, but in the end, it had offered him so much life. He would miss it, but he had to go underground for a bit until he knew where that woman ended up. A shame. He had just gotten into a rhythm too.

A beam of light flashed under the door, and he froze on the third stair from the bottom. It flicked across the door two more times before it disappeared. He wasn't alone. The game had just changed, but no matter who waited on the other side, they'd perish in a fire hotter than the bowels of hell.

CHARLOTTE CONCENTRATED ON the stairs, but it wasn't without difficulty. Mack had disappeared down the hallway what felt like an eternity ago. It probably hadn't been more than a few minutes, but she slid a glance to her right without moving her gun. She caught his vest as he disappeared into the final room at the end of the hall. They had to get out of here. She could feel it in her bones. The scent of laundry detergent and cleaner filled her head, telling her someone had been here recently.

A door slammed, and she swung her arm in an arc toward the sound. "Mack?"

The response was a guttural roar as a figure ran at her from the end of the hallway. It wasn't Mack. The man's face was twisted into a mask of horror, his hands out, ready to grasp her neck and take her down. The gun went off, the bullet striking him in the shoulder, but it barely slowed him down. Three more shots rang out in the basement, the sound echoing around the cement until she was sure she would never hear anything again. The man stumbled and then fell to his knees at her feet.

Charlotte gasped when he gazed up at her. With the mask gone, she knew the man sitting before her. He was a United States senator. He fell to his side, one hand gripping his chest as blood poured from his wounds.

She kept her gun aimed at him while she screamed Mack's name. When she got no response, she gazed at the man before her. "What did you do to him?"

He gasped, and blood bubbled up around his lips. "Help me," he muttered, gripping his belly where more blood oozed over his fingers.

Charlotte grabbed her cuffs and attached one of his ankles to the stair railing. He wasn't going anywhere in his condition, and she had to help Mack. She jumped over his writhing body and ran to the room at the end of the hallway, but the door was locked when she tried to turn the knob. "Mack!" she screamed, throwing her shoulder into the door without it budging. She ran back to the man on the floor. "Where's the key?"

Greg Weiss smiled at her, his teeth stained pink from the blood bubbling out of his lips. He spat at her. "Go to hell."

"I've already been there because of men like you," she growled, placing her foot on his gut and pressing until he howled in pain the way her soul had wanted to for years. She dug in his pockets until she found a key ring and gave him one solid kick to remember her by before she ran back to the closed door, her boot leaving a blood print on the carpet every other step.

Her fingers weren't cooperating, and she fumbled with the keys while Weiss howled. The sound had changed. It was no longer pain. It was anger and the fading light of a man who had taken souls that were now driving him down into hell where he belonged. The key went into the lock, and she flipped it, the door opening to reveal the man she loved. The thought nearly sent her to her knees, but she couldn't take the time to stop. She had to help him.

"Mack!" she screamed again, running to him and sliding to a stop next to where he lay crumpled on the carpet. "Mack," she cried, checking for a pulse. It was strong and steady, but that gave her only a modicum of relief. He was alive but unconscious, and they needed to get out of the house. Charlotte lifted his head onto her lap and noticed a spot on his head that was matted and bloody. "Come on, Mack," she cried, slapping his face gently to wake him.

The man in the other room had quieted other than an occasional moan and stream of cuss words sent her way. Charlotte hoped he lived so everyone could see the monster he was.

"Mack," she whispered, kissing his soft warm lips. "Please, Mack, wake up. I need your help. I don't know what to do." She begged him to wake up, kissing him over and over until she left her lips on his, and tears ran down her cheeks. "I love you, Mack Holbock. You can't do this to me." Her tears fell silently until a hand came up to hold her waist. She started but realized it was Mack's warm hand holding her hip.

"Char," he whispered until she met his pained gaze. "Slayer."

Weiss took that moment to cuss her out again, and Mack's lips tipped up in a smile. "He's been neutralized," she promised, rubbing his cheek.

"Who is it?" he managed to ask, putting his hand to the side of his head by the wet spot.

"You won't believe me, but it's Senator Greg Weiss."

"Call Mina. Now."

Charlotte grinned and lifted the phone from his pants pocket. "No need to rush. He's got four of my bullets in him, and they all had a woman's name on them. He's not going anywhere other than hell."

She flipped the phone open and hit the call button while Mack grinned. "Sweetheart, I love you too."

His eyelid went down in a wink as she heard, "Secure two, Whiskey."

That was when she knew they were finally safe.

Epilogue

Charlotte closed the sketchbook with a sigh. It had been a week since they had unknowingly ended the reign of terror The Red River Slayer had had over the country. When the news broke that Senator Greg Weiss was fighting for his life in surgery as the suspected slayer, the media converged on the little town of Sugarville like the vultures they were. Charlotte didn't care. She was already in Cal's plane after Mack was treated and released from a hospital for his head laceration.

Weiss had used a weapon of convenience and hit Mack with a piece of the broken table he had killed Little Daddy with just a few days before. According to his confession, Weiss had pushed May down the stairs, which resulted in a broken neck and her death. To throw the authorities off, he wrapped May in Little Daddy's arms and tossed them in the river as a red herring. If the authorities were busy concentrating on a new twist to the case, he had time to disappear.

First, Weiss had to destroy the evidence. He planned to burn down the old house, but Char and Mack had beat him to the property. Had they been thirty minutes later, the house and the evidence would have been gone.

As it turned out, Little Daddy was one of the senator's

"staffers." The only thing he staffed was the senator's deranged house of horrors. He trained the women to be the senator's "assistant."

The fact that no one on Capitol Hill questioned his turnover of assistants or his story of where the last one went was concerning, but that was above her pay grade. It was good that Bethany had never been transferred up as his assistant because she wouldn't have kept his secret the way the other women had. They believed that he would take care of them forever and be their sugar daddy if they did his bidding. Bethany knew better.

Greg survived his surgery, but one of her bullets had hit his spine, and he would never walk another day in his life. When the police deposed him with a list of his suspected crimes and the threat of life in prison without parole looming over his head, he asked for a deal. He knew he would never survive in the general population in a wheelchair, so there was little choice. He sang like a canary, documenting his killings on a timeline that shocked even the seasoned FBI agents. It started, he said, when he found out that his birth parents had been killed by Christian conservatives in their house and left him there to die. He swore that he sold his soul to the devil for the chance to avenge their deaths. Adopted by a loving family in Maine, he had a charmed life on the surface, but underneath simmered a monster so evil that Charlotte wasn't convinced anyone was safe until he was dead, no matter how many doors they locked him behind.

And then he died.

The nurses walked in one morning to find him dead in bed. An autopsy revealed he threw a clot, and it went to his heart. Good riddance was Charlotte's first thought.

Her second thought was she was the one to bring closure and justice to the families of his victims. Sure, some of his victims had no family, but that didn't mean they didn't deserve justice. Before he died, he'd signed the confession and accepted the title of The Red River Slayer.

A shudder went through her, and warm hands came up to grasp her shoulders. "Hey, you okay?" Mack asked from near her ear.

"Fine," she promised, shaking off the evil of a man who no longer walked the earth. "I was just finishing a sketch. How are things in the control room? I know I caused Cal a huge headache."

"No, you saved my life and the lives of countless other people by killing that monster. A little time and money are nothing in the scheme of things. You can always make more money but you can't bring people back to life."

Her sigh was heavy, and she nodded, not making eye contact with him. They hadn't discussed their adrenaline-driven declaration of love since it happened, and she wasn't sure they ever would. She promised herself she would wait for him to bring it up again, but so far, he'd remained mum. "Do you have a minute? I was wondering if I could give you something."

Mack walked around the table and perched on a stool. "Sure, what's up?"

With her heart pounding, she opened her sketch pad and pulled out the loose sheet waiting there. She slid it across the table and waited while he gazed at it.

"The real-me sketch," he whispered, running his finger across her signature at the bottom. "That's what I call it in my head," he explained, lifting his gaze to make eye contact with her.

"You said you'd like to have it when and if I was ready to give it to you. Is that still the case?"

"Absolutely," he said, drawing it nearer as though she may take it back. "I love that you signed it Hope."

"That's what you've given me, Mack. You gave me hope back that first night I was here, and you've continued to offer it over and over until I was strong enough to believe that I deserve it."

"You do deserve it, Char. You became my hope the moment you walked onto this property."

"Do I deserve your heart too, or is that not on the table?" she asked, fear making the words shake. "I'm sorry for asking, but I have to know—"

His finger stopped her words, and he stood in front of her, his forehead touching hers. "My heart is yours if you think you can also accept my ghosts."

"I'll carry yours if you carry mine. Sharing will make them lighter."

He didn't wait. He kissed her with the love of a man who finally had what he needed in life. "I'm so thankful for you, Char," he whispered when the kiss ended. "I didn't know how to come to you and ask, so I prayed you'd come to me. Mina called me a chicken and a coward. In fairness, I agreed with her."

Her laughter was soft, but there were tears of pain, fear, acceptance and hope in the sound. "Mina is never afraid to call it as she sees it."

"And I always will," Mina said from behind them. "I'm glad you two finally figured yourselves out before we formed a Secure One intervention."

Mack grabbed Charlotte when she tried to pull away and kissed her neck. "You're ruining our moment, Whiskey."

"Sorry, but you'll have to save that moment for later when you're alone. We've been summoned to the conference room. There are updates to the case."

Charlotte had to admit that she was curious, so she followed Mack to the conference room where the team had gathered. Cal was at the front and motioned for Charlotte and Mack to sit in the empty seats. Eric, Selina, Roman and Efren had rounded out the table.

"Efren," Charlotte said with a smile. "Good to see you again."

"You'll be seeing more of him," Cal said. "He's agreed to sign on as another security member for Secure One. We're growing, and we need the help." Selina rolled her eyes with a huff but said nothing else. Cal handed Efren a security badge. "Everyone, welcome Tango to the team."

"Tango. Because I have two left feet?" he asked with a raised brow.

"The way I hear it, you have at least four, but you have to admit, it's the perfect call sign for you," Mina said with a wink.

"I'll accept it, as long as dancing isn't required."

"I can't promise that," Cal said. "As a bodyguard, you may have to take one for the team if your subject has to attend a ball, but we'll try to keep it to a minimum."

The team offered him some good-natured ribbing, minus Selina, who sat mute, her arms crossed over her chest. The moment she'd heard that The Red River Slayer had been taken down, Selina transferred Bethany to a hospital. She was undergoing treatment for her physical conditions as well as her mental health. Bethany had a long road ahead of her, but Charlotte had every intention of being there to help her. Maybe Cal would offer to let her finish her recovery at Secure One when she was released from the treatment facility. Something about the land and the people here healed broken hearts and minds.

After a few moments, Cal brought the room to attention. "As you know," he began, "Weiss confessed before his death, and I was able to obtain a copy of the confession." He glanced at Mina, who was smirking but said nothing. "Mina, would you like to take over?"

She stood and leaned on the table as she stared down Marlise and Charlotte. "Before The Madame set up shop in Red Rye, Greg was killing people sporadically and weighing them down in lakes and rivers where the chance they'd be found again was slim. He killed his adoptive parents and anyone else who got in his way. Then his childhood summer camp friend, Liam Albrecht, called him from Red Rye to tell him about a new escort service in town. Since Liam was on the *special practice date committee*—" which she put in quotation marks "—he funneled women that The Miss wasn't happy with to Weiss. He kept them in the house and used them, but that was when he came up with the idea of dropping them in rivers to make it look like the serial killer was targeting politicians. What he was doing was satisfying his sick fantasies."

"The early women were from The Madame's house in Red Rye?" Marlise asked, and Mina nodded.

"Hard to confirm, but since their identities were washed, we know they were women from within The Madame's empire, no matter what house they lived in."

"And he went underground when The Madame was arrested?" Charlotte asked.

"He never stopped killing. He just didn't showcase the

bodies. We know now that the woman in Arizona stuck in the dam was Emilia. According to the confession, he joined the committee for the waterways in order to throw the cops off his tracks by making the killings look political. That's why he made sure the bodies of those he killed during the two-year break weren't found immediately."

"So he purposely drove to other states with women to dump them in rivers?" Mack asked.

"According to his confession, he transported the women to the river, killed them while they were underwater to make the police think they drowned and then dressed them before their final journey downstream. He claimed in the confession that Layla was a sacrificial lamb, his words," she said, holding her hands up. "May, the woman found with Little Daddy, was a good assistant, and since Layla was untrainable, he killed her specifically to coincide with Ella's party. He was a sick, sick man, and the twenty-page typed confession will take a long time to get through. The point is there was no doubt he was the man behind the slayings."

A shiver settled down Charlotte's spine at the thought, and it was as though Mack knew because his warm hand rubbed it away. "I'm sorry for the trouble my part in this caused you, Cal."

"No," Cal said firmly. "You were the hero that day, Charlotte. Scum like that should eat the bullet of a person they wronged, in my opinion. He may not have held you hostage, but he was responsible for the deaths of so many women in your same situation."

"We couldn't agree more," a voice said from the back of the room. Everyone turned, and Senator Dorian and Ella stood in the doorway.

"Ella!" Charlotte exclaimed, grabbing the young woman as she ran to her for a hug. "I'm sorry I didn't get back to the house after everything."

"I missed you, but I'm so glad you're okay," Ella said, hugging her tightly.

They'd had to postpone the senator's reelection party when he was called back to Washington to deal with the fallout from Weiss's arrest. The party had been rescheduled for next weekend, and Charlotte was looking forward to spending more time with Ella.

She joined her father at the side of the table and squeezed Charlotte's hand. "I just wanted to thank the woman who saved my daughter from a murderer. When Weiss died, the man in custody admitted that Weiss had hired him to kidnap my daughter and take her to the murder house. If you hadn't been there to stop him that night…" He waved his hand around in the air. "I don't even allow myself to think about it. I just know I owe you a debt of gratitude."

"I'm glad she's safe," Charlotte said, embarrassed by the attention. She preferred to stay in the background. "I still intend to give you those drawing lessons, Ella."

"Maybe you can get a few in later this year when you fly to DC to accept an award for your exemplary bravery and service to your country," Dorian said, putting his arm around his daughter.

"What now?" Charlotte asked as everyone else around the table smirked. "DC? Award? Not necessary."

"I will pass your opinion on to the president, but I'm certain he will not feel the same."

"The—the president?" Charlotte stuttered, and Ella was the one to laugh.

"He's the guy who sits in that oval room and runs the country."

Charlotte snorted and put her hand on her hip. "Please, no. That's… No. I was doing my job."

"Technically, you weren't," Cal said from the front of the room. "Your job is to cook, but you were a soldier that day. You didn't hesitate to protect your fellow soldier, even if that protection was driven by love rather than brotherhood."

Charlotte's face heated as Cal handed her a box. She lifted the lid off, and inside was a badge like the one she wore in the Secure One control room. This one didn't say Charlotte though. It said *Public Liaison, Secure One, Hotel*. She glanced up at Cal. "No. I can't take Hotel. My name starts with *C*." Mack rested his hand on her shoulder, which calmed her instantly.

"You can, and you will," Cal said with a smile. "I'm Charlie, so we had to pick a different call name for you. Mack told me that you went by Hope on the streets. In my opinion, Hotel is fitting, and I know Hannah would approve. I hold wonderful memories of her in my heart, but I'm with my soulmate now," he said, winking at Marlise. "Hannah would be proud to share her call name with a woman of your caliber."

Charlotte nodded, tears pricking her eyes as she looped the badge around her neck. "I'll wear the name proudly then. I don't know anything about being a public liaison though. Also, you guys realize I was terrified, and my knees shook the whole time I was in that basement. I think you might be taking things a bit far."

Mack chuckled from behind her as Cal shook his head. "I've never gone into battle and not been terrified with my knees shaking. I don't think anyone around this table has either." Heads shook to the negative until Cal spoke again. "Regardless, you did what had to be done. That's what makes you a soldier and a hero. As for the new job title, we'll talk about that tomorrow."

"Now," Dorian said, motioning toward the door. "There's a whole host of goodies waiting for us in the dining room, and I'm starving!"

Everyone offered congratulations, hugs and laughter before slowly working their way out of the conference room. Charlotte was at the door when an arm looped around her waist and held her back.

"Hold up, Hotel," Mack whispered in her ear. "I need a moment."

Charlotte swung around and draped her arms around his neck. "You can have a moment anytime, Mike."

"Good, because I'm low on hope and need a refill."

"I'm not sure I know how to refill your hope," she quipped, her brow dipping. "Maybe you better give me directions."

"Now that I can do," he promised before he dropped his lips to hers.

* * * * *

INTRIGUE

Seek thrills. Solve crimes. Justice served.

Available Next Month

Conard County: Murderous Intent Rachel Lee
Peril In Piney Woods Debra Webb

....

Smoky Mountains Graveyard Lena Diaz
K-9 Missing Person Cassie Miles

....

Innocent Witness Julie Anne Lindsey
Shadow Survivors Julie Miller

Larger Print

6 brand new stories each month
INTRIGUE
Seek thrills. Solve crimes. Justice served.
MILLS & BOON

Keep reading for an excerpt of a new title
from the Romantic Suspense series,
CLOSE RANGE CATTLEMAN
by Amber Leigh Williams

Chapter 1

"Hell's bells," Everett Eaton groaned as he crouched in the sagebrush.

Over his shoulder, his newest ranch hand, Lucas, bounced on the heels of his roughed-up Ariats and cursed vividly. "Jesus, boss," he hissed. "Jesus Christ."

"Calm your britches," Everett said as he examined the blood trail in the red dirt of his high desert country homeland. Among the signs of struggle, he saw the telltale teardrop-shaped prints with no discernible claw marks. He lifted his fingers, tilted his head and squinted, following the drag lines in the soil. "He went off thataway."

"Taking Number 23's calf with him," Javier Rivera, Everett's lead wrangler, added.

Everett swapped the wad of gum from one side of his mouth to the other. Standing, he shifted his feet and placed his hands on his hips. The trail disappeared over the next ridge, into the thicket of trees that surrounded Wapusa River, the lifeblood of his family's fourteen-hundred-acre cattle ranch, Eaton Edge and the sandstone cliffs that served as its natural border to the north. He nodded toward the mountain that straddled the river. "I reckon 23 dropped the calf during the night and the damn thing was lying in wait."

"Or smelled the afterbirth and came running," Javier guessed.

"He could have been out stalking and got lucky," Everett weighed. "Either way, he took it up Ol' Whalebones, ate what he wanted and covered up the rest."

"How do you know he's up there?" Lucas asked. His bronze cheeks contrasted with the paleness around the area of his mouth. His head swiveled in all directions as he tried looking everywhere at once. "He could be anywhere."

Everett eyed the back side of the mountain. It curved toward the bright blue sky. "You can hear him in winter. He's most active then. He doesn't go into torpor, like the bear. When Ellis and I rode out to check fences once the snow cleared after Christmas, we could hear his screams echoing off everything and nothing."

"Ah, hell," Lucas moaned. He gave an involuntary shudder.

Javier clapped him on the back. "You stay sharp."

"Watch your mount when you're up in these parts," Everett told him. "And make sure you're strapped. Got it?"

Lucas nodded jerkily. "Geez. Shouldn't the bastard have died like five, ten years ago or something? Ellis figures Tombs is eighteen. Mountain lions aren't supposed to live that long. Are they?"

"Not in the wild," Javier considered. He swapped his rifle from his left hand to his right, following the river with dark eyes. "Twelve years is a long life for a cougar. Could be another cat, moving into Tombstone's territory. Right, boss?"

"Maybe." Everett scanned the sagebrush, the canyons and the sandstone and couldn't chase the eerie sensation creeping along his spine.

Someone…or something was watching. "Mount up. I told the sheriff we'd meet near the falls."

Lucas sighed as they approached the three horses knotted together near the river's edge. "Sure wish we were riding in the other direction."

Everett laid his hand on his red mare's flank. Crazy Alice had been restless approaching Ol' Whalebones, tossing her head and the reins. She'd sensed that something was off long before he had. He patted her, then seated his rifle into the sleeve on the saddle and swung up into position with the ease of someone who'd spent a lifetime there. As he waited for the others to do the same, he knuckled his ten-gallon hat up an inch on his brow to get a better look at the canyon.

Tombstone was a legend and had been for as long as he could remember. Everett had first seen the mountain lion while camping with his brother, Ellis. Tombstone had watched them around their fire for the better part of the night. No one had slept. Everett remembered how the cat's eyes had tossed the firelight back at them. It was then he'd first seen what distinguished Tombstone from other cats— a missing eye.

His behavior, too, set him apart. Mountain lions shied away from human activity. It was why so little was known about them. In the last hundred years, only twenty-seven fatal cougar attacks had been reported. It was the rattlesnake they had to worry about most on the high desert plain.

But Everett had known that night what it was to be prey. He hadn't cared for it.

He'd seen Tombstone again off and on through the years. Males were territorial and Tombs ruled Eaton Edge's northern quarter and the surrounding hunting grounds.

Everett didn't believe in omens, but even he had to admit that it was strange how every time he or Ellis or their father, Hammond, had spotted Tombs high in the hills, trouble had followed. Hammond's first heart attack, the deaths of Everett's mother, Josephine Coldero, and his half sister, Angel, his sister Eveline's car accident…

Over the last year, Everett had convinced himself the animal was dead…until his father's death over the summer and a ride into the high country where he had seen Tombs take down a small elk.

Everett may be chief of operations at Eaton Edge, but it was Tombs who was king in these parts—and Everett reluctantly gave him his due.

He clicked his tongue at Crazy Alice, urging her to walk on.

"What's the sheriff and deputies think they're going to find up here?" Lucas asked as his neck mimicked a barred owl, rotating at an impressive angle so he could scan the shadows cast by boulders.

"Hiker," Everett grunted.

"Just one?" Javier asked.

"Yep. Kid thought he'd livestream his ascent," Everett said.

"He didn't make it?" Lucas asked. "Seems easy enough."

"The climb's intermediate," Javier noted.

"The broadcast cut off before he reached the top," Everett said. "No one's seen or heard from him in three days. Parents in San Gabriel are worried."

"How old?" Javier asked.

"Sixteen," Everett noted.

Javier made a pitying noise. "Same age as my Armand."

"Shouldn't he be in school?" Lucas asked.

Everett raised a brow. "Shouldn't you?"

"I got kicked out," Lucas informed him. "Didn't my mom tell you?"

Everett pursed his lips. "Your mama told me you were too much to handle and thought I could do something about it."

"How's that coming, *amigo*?" Javier asked, with a sly grin under the shade of his hat.

Everett shook his head. "I have a habit of inheriting problems of monumental proportions."

"Sure wish you had your dogs with you," Lucas told Everett as they crossed a stream. "They'd be able to smell a lion. They'd warn us, wouldn't they?"

Everett scowled, thinking of the three cattle dogs he'd raised from pups. "I'm not keen on putting any of them on Tombs' menu."

"He wouldn't attack them. Any animal would run from their baying. Even a predator."

Everett couldn't predict what Tombs would do, but he had trained the dogs for protection as much as herding. If they scented danger, they'd go looking for it. Everett couldn't think of any circumstance where Bones, Boomer and Boaz meeting Tombs wouldn't end in at least one of them maimed or killed.

"You've got a hot date tonight," Lucas recalled.

"What do you know about it?" Everett barked.

Lucas scrambled. "I heard it."

"From?"

"Mateo. Spencer told him. Spencer heard it from the house. Nobody knows who you're going out with."

Lucas was baiting him, and Everett wasn't willing to share any of his plans for the evening. He gnawed at the wad of gum in his mouth. "What've my plans got to do with anything?"

"We won't make it back to headquarters by sundown,"

Lucas considered. "I figure you'd have sent Ellis in your place to find the guy."

"Kid went missing," Everett reminded him. "If he's camped out somewhere on the Edge, I aim to find him."

The horses climbed to the mouth of a natural arch where the river sluiced and gurgled busily from the mouth of a cave. Water flowed freely now that the snow had melted in the Sangre de Cristo Mountains.

This was the lifeblood of Eaton Edge. The river fed the grass that made cattle ranching in the high desert of New Mexico possible.

As they neared the falls, Everett tugged on Crazy Alice's reins. A smile transformed the grim set of his mouth. The loss of 23's calf had unsettled him. But the sight ahead made the trouble slink back to the corners of his mind. "Howdy, Sheriff," he called. He took off his hat.

The Jicarilla-Apache Native American woman was five feet three inches at the crest of her uniformed hat. Under the two-toned, neutral threads that suited her position, she was built solid. Everett couldn't help but let his gaze travel over the hips under her weapons belt or the swell of her breast underneath her gold badge and name plate.

Sheriff Kaya Altaha's black-lensed aviators hid eyes as dark as unexplored canyons. If she'd take them off, he'd see the usual assemblage of amusement and exasperation that greeted him under most circumstances. She addressed him. "You're late, cattle baron."

"We set out at dawn, like I promised," he assured her, dismounting. He flicked the reins over Alice's ears and led the horse the rest of the way. "Ran into a snag a quarter of a mile south of here."

Her frown quickened. "Trouble?"

"Heifer dropped a calf before dawn," he said, fitting the hat back to his crown. "Something carried it off."

Kaya's frown deepened. "Did you find any remains?"

"Other than a blood trail…" He shook his head. "Cat took off in this direction."

"You think it was lion."

"I know it was. Normally, we don't keep the heifers this far north when the mountain's waking up for spring, especially not during calving season. 23's a wily one—makes a habit of slipping through fences. The big cats are more likely to carry off pronghorn, small deer, rabbit…" He wished she'd take her hair down for once. She kept it knotted in a thick braid at the nape of her neck.

Everett would love to see it free. He'd bet money it was as dense as plateau nights and as soft as the Wapusa between his fingers when it ran down from the mountain.

Something tugged just beneath his navel—a long, low pull that snagged his breath for a second or two.

That wasn't new, either.

Everett had had to come to terms with the fact that he had the hots for the new sheriff of Fuego County. He'd been wallowing in that understanding for some time—since the shoot-out at Eaton Edge over Christmas that had led to her being shot in the leg and, after some recovery, promoted to the high office she held now.

Everett knew what he wanted, always, and he chased it relentlessly. But the last eight months of his life had changed him. He'd been shot, too, in a standoff between a cutthroat backwoodsman and his family. He'd nearly died. Recovery had been a long mental process with PTSD playing cat and mouse with him. He'd found himself in therapy at the behest of Ellis and their housekeeper turned adoptive mother, Paloma Coldero. He'd set aside his chief of operations duties until doctors had given him the go-ahead to continue.

He had hated the hiatus. He'd worked since he was a boy—to the bone. He'd quit high school his senior year to help his father manage the Edge. Everett had never *not* worked.

After Hammond had died in July, work had felt vital. If he wasn't working, he was thinking about the state of his family and the grief he still hardly knew how to handle, even after all his months sitting across from a head doctor in San Gabriel.

Kaya Altaha had been a bright spot. The then-deputy had saved his life in the box canyon last July. Not only that—she'd checked in on him regularly. She'd worked to clear the name of Ellis's soon-to-be wife, Luella Decker.

The first time he'd smiled during his recovery, it'd been with her.

He hadn't known there were feelings attached...until Christmastime, when he'd seen her blood in the hay of his barn. He'd smelled it over the stench of cattle and gunpowder. To say he'd been worried was a damned lie—he'd gone over the flippin' edge.

She tucked her full lower lip underneath the white edge of her teeth, nibbling as she looked beyond him into the hills that tumbled off south. "Anyone get a look at the predator?" she asked.

He had to school himself to keep from rubbing his lips together. "Happened before dawn, as I said. Blood was dry."

"I'm sorry to hear about the calf," she said sincerely.

He could feel her eyes through the shades. He felt them from tip to tail. "I'm not looking forward to telling my nieces. They love the little ones come spring."

She studied him a moment before the professional line of her mouth fell away and a slow smile took over.

He darted a look at the two deputies roving around the space between the falls and the arch walls before he brought himself a touch closer, the toes of his thick-skinned boots nearly overlapping hers. He lowered his voice. "You can't be doing that."

"What am I doing?" Her jaw flared wide from its stubborn point when she smiled.

He'd thought about kissing that point…and a good many things south of it. "Flashing secret smiles at me and pretending I'm not going to do anything about it."

"I don't play games."

"You know what that mess does to me," he said, "and you're betting on me not doing anything about it."

"You wouldn't," she said.

"Why d'you figure that, Sheriff Sweetheart?" he asked with a laugh.

The smile turned smug. "Because I know the only things Everett Eaton fears in this life are bullets and bars. Not the honky-tonk kind—the ones that hem him in and keep him away from…all this." She gestured widely. "Despite how much we both know you like a challenge." She tossed him back a step with the brunt of her hand and raised her voice to be heard by the others. "Hiker's name is Miller Higgins. He's sixteen years of age. Five-eight. Roughly one hundred and fifty pounds. His last known contact was three days ago at approximately 10:23 a.m. The family reported him missing yesterday when they couldn't get in touch with him via cell."

"Cell service is low here," Javier noted. "How good was the quality of the livestream video?"

"Not great, but good enough to establish where he was

and what he was doing," Kaya replied. "If he fell during the hike and injured himself, he might have lost his cell phone or damaged it. That's the working theory. He left his car on the access road to the northeast. Deputy Root will fly the surveillance drone once we get to the top. I plan on combing every inch of this mountain and the surrounding area until we find Higgins. If we need to bring in more search and rescue people, we'll do so."

"Nobody knows Ol' Whalebones as well as me and Ellis," Everett explained. "He'll join us tomorrow, if need be. We'll find Higgins. I'd like Lucas to wait here with the horses since there've been signs of predators about."

She inclined her head. "Fine. Let's split into groups and hit the trail."

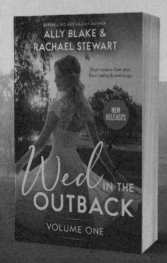

Subscribe and fall in love with a Mills & Boon series today!

You'll be among the first to read stories delivered to your door monthly and enjoy great savings.

WE SIMPLY LOVE ROMANCE